ANDIA-TA-ROC-TE

BEHIND THE MASK OF WILDERNESS

DOMENICK GASPARRO

Instagram: gaspardx81

this book is humbly dedicated

to

ernest miller hemingway

CONTENTS

Epigraph   VII

                                      VIII

1. Chapter 1   1

2. Chapter 2   18

3. Chapter 3   29

4. Chapter 4   44

5. Chapter 5   56

6. Chapter 6   68

7. Chapter 7   81

8. Chapter 8   93

9. Chapter 9   103

10. Chapter 10   111

11. Chapter 11   124

12. Chapter 12   137

13. Chapter 13   151

14. Chapter 14   161

15.	Chapter 15	175
16.	Chapter 16	186
17.	Chapter 17	197
18.	Chapter 18	205
19.	Chapter 19	221
20.	Chapter 20	232
21.	Chapter 21	246
22.	Chapter 22	260
23.	Chapter 23	270
24.	Chapter 24	276
25.	Chapter 25	288
26.	Chapter 26	310

'Go back to your home and people,
    Live among them, toil among them,
    Cleanse the earth from all that harms it,
    Clear the fishing-grounds and rivers,
    Slay all monsters and magicians,
    All the Wendigoes, the giants,
    All the serpents, the Kenabeeks,
    As I slew the Mishe-Mokwa,
    Slew the Great Bear of the mountains.
    'And at last when Death draws near you,
    When the awful eyes of Pauguk
    Glare upon you in the darkness,I will share my kingdom with you,
    Ruler shall you be thenceforward...'

Henry Wadsworth Longfellow, '*The Song of Hiawatha*', Book IV (Lines 219-232)

A Word.

Windigo (Algonquin, Chippewas, Ojibwa People, North America):

There are multiple spellings of this word, which can be presented as Wendigo, Weendigo, Wehtiko, Whitiko, Witigo. They are a race of giant cannibal who hunt humans in the winter when food is scarce.

There is only one way to destroy a Wendigo. It involves fire.

Stories of the Windigo, or *Wendigo* as is used in this work, have been told and retold for centuries. The precise mythology is never quite the same depending on which authorities you've tapped. In this retelling you'll find yet another wrinkle. I have taken no pains to adhere to one specific set of rules or mythology for this creature. I've taken some aspects from various incarnations and made the creature my own. Please heed and take notice before starting this tale.

Thank you.

D.G

Chapter One

The first time I met Sabrina we were both drunk.

She leaned her back against one of those shiny black wrought iron lampposts that dotted the lake's southern shoreline. Her hands held the sides of her head and her fingers were immediately lost among the tight coiled ribbons of her hair. She looked as if she were caught in the throes of exasperation. The string of lamps punctuated individual white bursts of light in the darkness and made it appear that the southern rim of the lake had donned a diamond necklace for the evening. It was quite the formal look for a small town in upstate New York. Sabrina was wearing a beige raincoat even though the weather didn't call for it. That detail always hung on my memory like a crooked picture. Then again, everything about her has relentlessly paced my thoughts like one of those Saratoga thoroughbreds ever since our paths crossed that night. There was a heavy mist clinging to the air that night and it hung over the docks with the slipperiness of old woman's silk shawl. It was one of those April evenings that reminded you that the chill of March wasn't that far removed and that the fibs of warm days couldn't be completely trusted.

The light thrown from the streetlamp lit her like a theater spotlight; a round, warm orb of illumination singling her out for an audience of one. She appeared poised to recite a few lines from '*Penelope*' or one of those other Greek tragedies. For all I knew she could've been a walking tragedy herself. Her face was half hidden in shadow and the rest of her was obscured behind twisted waves of hair. When I walked over to her that night my initial intent, and this is the God's honest truth, no lie, was to lend her a hand.

She was alone. There wasn't another soul on the promenade that night. Just her, leaning against that post with her hands at her temples looking poised to tear her hair out of her scalp. She wobbled but never fell. I'd seen my fair share of banged-up broads around pubs on both sides of the Atlantic and this one didn't seem much different. These types of women typically ended up leaving a deposit of vomit on my loafers before taking a few stumbling steps, mumbling incoherently, while I tried to help them regain their balance and some sense of pride. Within moments of my heroism they'd usually be whisked away by a girlfriend or gal-pal with a quick hand wave and a 'thank you very much'. "*Oh don't worry about Millie or Sarah Jane or Helene,*" they'd say. "*She gets like this sometimes*". Sure. They all get like *this* sometimes. They weren't the ones you'd strategically place in a fantasy of a white picket fence and beefy roasted aromatics wafted from the kitchen. Oh no. These were the types that left your mouth and memories saturated in that musky aftertaste of brine and stale beer. Not exactly familial types.

But, Sabrina. I truly wanted to help her, which was funny because I could've used a hand myself. I stumbled a few steps and the world took on that strange focus that only drunks can know. It seemed that objects that were far away were in crystal clear focus and things next to me were composed of opaque colors and shapes like a kaleidoscope.

As I drew closer my movements became skittish like a nervous cat investigating a wounded bird. Her face began to emerge from the shadows. Her hair was mahogany and done up in rolled ribbons that danced playfully through the light breeze that swooped down through the valley and across the lake. She stood up straight and remained that way for an extended moment. She turned and looked at me stone-faced like someone possessed. "Excuse me," she asked. "You don't smoke, do you?"

"Only when I'm on fire," I retorted. Not my best work.

In her drunken stupor she either didn't get the joke, or she didn't care to entertain it. This was not the first time I was on the wrong side of such an interaction. She looked at me with her eyes looking like panes of glass from an abandoned church and her movements as mechanical as a farm rig that desperately needed oil. She once again asked, this time in staccato, "Do. You. Smoke?"

I reached into my corduroy pockets and produced a Lucky Strike that had seen better days from my crushed pack. The first clear look I got of her face was in the light given off of the dancing flame from my stainless steel, and highly scuffed, lighter. I'd kept that thing with me since before I got drafted and it had served me well in occasions both serious and romantic. I'd carved my name and rank on the bottom using the edge of a paper clip in case something had happened to me. You just never knew what was going to happen over there. In slashed, uneven markings was etched: Phelps, PFC.

Her skin was flawless and smooth like golden olive oil, and she wore only the tiniest bit of lipstick on the center ridges of her thin mouth. Her eyes were crushing, deep, and solemn. The high ridges of her cheekbones were so sharp and clearly defined, they appeared able to cut glass. As I snapped the lighter shut, she tipped her head towards me to say thank you.

I leaned my back on the opposite side of the post facing away from her and looked out towards the blackness and the nodding boats. I thought I might try my luck at a little small talk.

"Are you from around here," I asked.

"I'm from over there," she said, exhaling two perfectly symmetrical streams of smoke from her nostrils. "I'm from over there," she repeated.

"Hadley," I asked. "Hague? Bolton?" I didn't see where she was pointing.

"Over there," she said once again.

The previously mellow wind that blew in off the water suddenly stiffened to a cool breeze. The rush of cold air across my sweating brow allowed me a momentary reprieve, but it quickly gave way to a woozy unsteadiness. My head began to spin. My eyes rolled back a bit and a strange sensation came over the sides of my mouth. The sides of my gums filled with saliva, and I felt a familiar contraction in my upper stomach. *Not now*, I sternly told my stomach. *You are not going to heave all over the ground in front of a woman. A stranger, no less. There are plenty of other places you can make that deposit. For the love of God, don't do it here!* I leaned against the lamppost too, on the opposite side, and tried my best to keep the contents of my stomach right where they were. I had no intention of going back into the Lookout Bar with vomit all over myself. If I did, there was a good chance Jasper would cut me off. I had no intention of that happening. After all, it was still early.

"Where are *you* from," she asked, sounding surprisingly sober for the moment.

"Me," I asked inquisitively as if I didn't understand the question. "Why, I'm from here." I stretched my arm out as if to hug the small village to our left.

"Here," she asked. "Caldwell? Queensbury? Warrensburg?"

"Here," I repeated, following her lead as if we were dancing. And I suppose in a way we were. We didn't know it, and I suppose no one ever does, but we had begun the ritual dance that has gone on for eternity. I knew this much; I was rapidly losing interest in returning to the smoky, depressed dungeon that was the Lookout Bar. *Maybe in a little while,* I thought to myself. Even in my drunken haze, I was enjoying the beginnings of this one-on-one interaction, even if its genesis was marinated in the burnt aftertaste of scotch whiskey.

"So, what's your story," I remember her asking me. She put it in those words. Blunt. Short.

"My story? That's a dangerous question to ask a writer," I quipped. I launched myself off the lamppost and turned to face her. "We could be here for hours." I collected my thoughts and realized that what I had said was probably going to be taken as pompous. However, at that moment, I didn't have the neurological wherewithal to do anything about it. If she was going to think I was a jackass, there was little I could do at that point to deter it.

"You write," she asked, somewhere between confused and interested. "What do you write about?"

"I work for *The Mirror*. I'm a reporter." I might've been piss-poor at keeping things brief in print, but when talking to a beautiful woman, I was my own best editor.

She squashed the remainder of the cigarette under her shoe and shimmied a little dance maneuver with the tip of her foot to make sure it was stamped out. I couldn't help but wonder how many hearts had met that same fate.

"A reporter? What the hell is there to report about around here," she asked, with the beginnings of a snicker forming in her belly. Her laugh started low and gradually got louder. "Oh, there's a new tree growing in the forest! A guy bagged a ten-pointer!"

I tried to make myself feel better by faux-laughing along with her. I faked a smile as best as I could and let out a few low chortles. I tried to convince myself that she was laughing *with* me, but anyone could see that wasn't the case. My smile was pure plastic. She was having a hearty laugh at my expense. All that was missing was her index finger pointed at my face and a few knee slaps for good measure.

When she finally stopped laughing her face dropped into a pout of earnestness. She peered over her shoulders suspiciously and licked her lips. She leaned in close and grabbed my shirt between the two buttons above my navel. The taut shirt fabric balled in her clenched fist gave me a thrill in the depths of my lower stomach. "You know what you should do? You should write about what goes on over there," she whispered, pointing towards the darkened eastern side of the lake. "Lots of stuff happens over there." She was so close her plosives made me wince.

"Like what," I asked.

"Things you wouldn't even begin to understand." She released my shirt and turned to cross the street. Unfortunately, this was an all too familiar scene that had played itself out time and time again in my life. Another brief encounter. Another quick conversation.

"Wait," I called out. "That's how you're going to leave? You're just going to up and walk away like that? I didn't even get your name."

"Gertrude," she said. "But my friends call me Trudy."

"It's a pleasure to make your acquaintance, Trudy," I yelled to her as she walked across the street. "Maybe we could walk in together. You don't seem like you have an escort tonight."

She reached into the pocket of her raincoat and pulled out a handkerchief. She wiped a few dabs of saliva from the sides of her mouth and placed the hankie back in her pocket. "No, I don't have an escort," she admitted, almost depressed. "But I'm sure there are plenty of Joes in there that would like to be my escort."

The fact that I wasn't immediately at the head of that list made my insides feel hollow like I'd drank acid. The simmering machismo inside of me wanted to spit on her and let her get fondled and fingered by the big-time losers who were bellied up to the bar. I'd stomp away to my car and go home and have that be the end of it. I'm sure this 'Gertrude' character would meet a less than desirable end when she waltzed back in there and Jasper and I would settle up tomorrow night and everything would turn out just fine. No skin off my nose.

Unfortunately, I was unable to unleash that furious fervor. The anger was there, plenty of it. A barrel of it, you could say. But I couldn't tap it. I just couldn't bring myself to release the torrent, the blanket of ill will I wanted her to feel. I had spent a lifetime spreading and tilling sorrow, so it shouldn't have been any trouble for me to open the spigot. I couldn't do it. All I could do was wallow in my hurt feelings on the Steel Peer and pathetically ask her if maybe I could be considered her accompaniment for the remainder of the evening.

"Well, what about me, Trudy," I asked pathetically. Some soldier.

She snickered again, this time more subtly. "What about you?" Her face told everything. That smirk was worth a thousand words. "Do you want to be my date for the rest of the evening?" She placed her hand to her hip and pretended to think about it. "Well, I don't know," she said. "Are you going to be a gentleman or are you going to be a bad boy?"

"Gertrude…Trudy, sorry. I will do my best to keep your drinks full and a laugh in your heart. Sound good?"

She ignored me. She gave me a long once-over, flipped her hair over her shoulder, and started towards the bar as she had originally intended.

I should have let her go. I should have let her walk back through that red door and leave me forever. There's a good probability I would have never seen her again. But then again, things have a way of coming around.

The Lookout Bar was one of the only non-touristy places in Caldwell at the time. Unlike its saloon brethren that lined Route 9 on the western bank of the lake, its appeal was not a summertime getaway haven. There were no fake lobsters on the walls. There were no fishing nets or painted murals, either. There was no homely decor designed to attract vacationers who arrived yearly to indulge in their leisure time. Large sedans with trunks strapped to the roof and freckled children barking out the windows were not welcome here. This place was not for them. This was most definitely a townie bar.

It stood alone like a last tollbooth on the way out of town on the newly named

'Steel Pier' at the southernmost part of the lake. It was a typical shanty, not much to it on the inside save a few exposed beams in the rafters that had ceiling fans lazily spinning. In the small porthole windows there were tiny neon signs advertising Schlitz beer and Camel cigarettes.

Occasionally, and thankfully it wasn't often, a vacationer would wander in, perhaps not knowing they'd trespassed. Mr. Clean Linen Shirt and his pomade-slicked hair would come in, usually drunk. They'd order some sort of drink that Jasper had no idea about. They'd sometimes slap their hands against the bar in rapid succession. The local flies would look at the bozo, maybe get some entertainment out of his embarrassment, and try not to pop him one in the mouth. The night usually ended with the guy getting put in a cab and getting airmailed back to whatever motel he was haunting for the week. But those one-offs were the exception. Tourists had their places, and we had ours. And there was an unwritten rule about townies comingling with outsiders. It just wasn't done. The Lookout was for us. Everyone who frequented the joint knew everyone else.

I followed her back inside where loose clouds and sharp, direct streams of gray cigarette and cigar smoke hovered above half-filled yellow pint glasses and someone was playing '*Beg Your Pardon*' by Francis Craig on the bubbling orange Wurlitzer jukebox that emanated its glow from the rear of the bar like some sort of musical demigod. Upon hearing the music, she began to dance. She carelessly threw her raincoat over an empty barstool and began to thrust her hips back and forth and threw her arms up and down. She obviously loved the song. Those few scoundrels who were whetting their whistles briefly paused to give her a once over as this seemingly possessed girl gyrated before them. I shook my head in amazement at the way she moved her hips.

My group of pals was huddled around a game of 5 Card Stud in the rear corner booth, with the tops of their (mostly balding) heads illuminated by a dull lamp. They were back there, cordoned away from everyone else, in hushed concentration, on a lonely hermetic frontier where only Jasper would dare venture. They were doing serious work, you see, and couldn't be bothered by any distraction. I noticed that my spot at the table had been considered vacated, as they had tilted my chair forward as if I had died. They didn't seem overly concerned about my whereabouts, and I wasn't about to waste any time worrying about them, either.

Ron Beauchamps was chomping on his Romeo Y Julieta, with his thick-faced snarl lording over the table. Sammy Watkins with his long face and wrinkles at every crevasse looked nervous; his wife was a bit of a hen pecker and he tended to pull his watch out approximately once every three minutes to look at the time. Davey D'Agostino looked happier than a pig in shit; he always had the lousiest poker face.

My alcoholic haze was beginning to lift the way fog gets burned off in summer sunlight. I needed to do something about that, and fast. The bar's lighting was somewhere between dawn's first light and the waking moments after a night full of dreams; ethereal, low, almost eerie. It was as if there was a perpetual mist in the place. I could see each of the small lamps clearly defined, and not as the kaleidoscopic plumes of light that I saw while pie-eyed. My newly found girl-pal twirled herself around to the bar and I ran over immediately. I was determined not to let anyone come within six feet of her. I resolved that no other person in that bar was going to buy her a drink. No one.

Jasper Delacroix, the aforementioned 'Jasper' was bartending that night. He was the prototype bartender. Look it up in Webster's. Round face. Beer gut hunched over his pants. Apron. He waddled over and began to chat up the girl. "Sabrina," he said. "What can I get you for your next round?"

"Sabrina?" She had said her name was Gertrude. Trudy for short.

"I don't remember getting your name," she asked me coyly, ignoring my shock.

"Why did you tell me that your name was Gertrude?"

"Some people know me as Sabrina and some people know me as Gertrude." She quickly turned to Jasper and made a wheeling motion with her index finger. Whatever she was drinking, she wanted another.

Her face looked as satisfied as an overstuffed cat. While she was occupying herself with trying to flirt with me, Jasper fixed her a brown drink with a maraschino cherry garnish and slid it to her hand. Not the typical drink of hearty Adirondack stock, to be sure.

"How much," she asked him, her eyes still locked onto me.

"Don't worry about it," the old barkeep said.

She sipped her drink and left a rather large lipstick print on the rim of the glass. For someone who looked like she used her makeup sparingly, she'd left quite an impression. She brought the glass once again to her mouth and this time took a heftier swig. Her face winced at the taste of the alcohol, and it went down her gullet. I knew that face. She was drinking with a purpose.

"So, you're not going to tell me where you're from," I asked, once again trying to prod her into a conversation. It felt like I was attempting to light a fire with wood that had been left out in the rain. I looked down into my own rocks glass of scotch, which Jasper had been nice enough to refill. I brought it to my lips and welcomed back that lovely burn.

"I told you," she said. "Over there."

"The eastern side of the lake?"

She said nothing and raised her eyebrows. "Why are you so interested in where I come from?"

I didn't have an answer, which irked me. "It's called small talk. I don't see you doing anything here except laughing at me at every given opportunity. Frankly, I'm two seconds from leaving you here, toots." My back was flat against a wall of annoyance and any bit of patience I did have was dwindling rapidly. With my change of tone, I realized that perhaps my anger had started to manifest. Perhaps she would realize that I was getting a little frustrated with this cat-and-mouse game she was playing. That wasn't what happened.

She started to laugh at me again, quietly at first. Her laughter gradually rose louder and louder as if someone was slowly increasing the volume knob on a radio, and she eventually began to slam her closed fist against the bar making the peanuts dance in their wicker baskets. This laughing fit eventually spread like a fire and took over her entire body. She moved away from the bar, threw herself onto the floor, and flailed her arms and legs against the filthy grimy, slimy wooden slats. She didn't care. She rolled back and forth in her euphoric laughing ecstasy. Her mouth came within inches of tiny, crushed cigarette butts, bottle caps, and heaps of clumped sawdust.

Jasper stood back and slowly dried a pint glass with the bottom of his apron. He peered over the bar at what was going on and peeked a raised eyebrow. The boys playing 5 Card in the corner momentarily lifted their attention from the game to take in the show. The other barflies that were nursing warm brews briefly paused their loathing for one moment to see what was going on.

Jasper slithered backward so that his back was almost flush with the rear of the bar. He crept over to me sideways, like a crab. He motioned with his index finger for me to come in close as if he had some secret to tell me.

"You better get her out of here, Frank," he said. "Or I'll grab her by the scruff and do it myself."

I watched her laughing on the floor, with her face nearly buried in the piles of grime, coming within inches of the soles of the barfly's feet. I wondered if she'd ever been this low, or if I'd ever been like that. Her blue and white polka dot dress had hiked up when she rolled around and more of her naked legs were exposed, beyond her girdle. After a few more moments her laughter spasms had ceased, and she was now simply a pitiable wreck on the floor of a bar with a pulse. Nothing more to it than that.

This dummy isn't my problem, I thought to myself. She was a quaking, shaking mess. I didn't know where she lived. I wasn't sure I even knew her actual name. I knew nothing. By all accounts, I should've pulled an Irish goodbye and slipped off into the night.

Like a newborn calf, she steadied herself on one of the stools and like a winch pulled her body straight up to the bar. She attempted to grab her drink, but Jasper's catlike reflexes were a step ahead of her.

When he pulled the glass from her she slammed her fist against the bar once again.

Jasper looked at me, his thick no-nonsense brow in full crinkle, and said loudly, "Now!"

"Hey, you," I yelled to her. "Whatever your name is, hey!"

Her eyes were bloodshot, and a few strands of hair stuck to the sweat on her forehead. She had tears in her eyes. Whatever grime and sawdust that had been on the floor were caked to her dress in splotches and the stench smelled somewhere between urine and stale beer. She was sweating like she'd run miles for days.

"Come on," I said, sticking my hand out. "Let's go, it's time to leave."

She grabbed my hand with her clammy digits, and we made our way back out to the street, with the blue-gray tint of moonlight casting a pall on the whole town.

My watch read twenty after two in the morning. On a Wednesday. I shuffled her over to the Steel Pier once again, like an artist walking an oversized easel, and we sat down on one of the benches that faced the dark water of the lake. In the darkness, you could hear the gentle slapping of the waves against the concrete bulkhead. For all the lake's calm, there was still some restlessness in the darkness.

Her head was slung backward towards the sky. I sat there, guarded concern abounding, unsure of what to do next. I supposed I could take her to my house. Or the hospital. Or maybe she would stop being a floozy and tell me where she lived so I could drop her off. She brought her head forward slowly and faced the solemn, dark, rippled lake.

"Do you know about the lake," she asked me in slurred words that sounded like a snake was speaking.

"I know a little. Father Jogues. Last of the Mohegans." I thought it was a little strange to have a history lesson at that time. "Maybe it's better if you don't talk right now. Just close your eyes."

"Lake's got secrets," she said. She extended the word secrets so she hissed. *Secretsssssss.* "Lots of them. Buried under the water," She made a motion of rippling water with her hand. "People think it's this beautiful place and on the surface it is. But..." She stopped speaking. Wind and waves were the only sounds to fill the silence.

She opened her mouth to speak again but clammed it shut the way people do when they realize they've spoken too much or are in the process of choosing their words carefully. Like a musician trying to strike the correct note, sliding their fingers over the keys, searching for the correct sound she started and stopped a few times. I didn't interrupt, although I desperately wanted to. She looked over my shoulder, into the darkness where the Eastern Woods lay dormant in the late evening gloom.

"There's stuff going on up in those eastern mountains that no one around here knows about." Once again, she leaned in close to me, and I prepared my lips prematurely. She whispered into my ear, giving me the tickles. "We tell our secrets to the mountain and wash our sins in the water. Once in the water, it's washed and buried."

My mouth was like sandpaper from the alcohol and my breath smelled like stale whiskey. I kept trying to conjure up saliva to swallow, but my tongue felt like an unpaved road. The beginnings of a hangover were in full force. My temples started to throb, and I just wanted water. I wanted water, that giver of life and cooler of flames.

"You want a story, newspaperman? I'll give you a story. I'll tell you..."

"SABRINA," a voice shouted from behind us, interrupting her. "Sabrina, what are you doing here?"

The voice belonged to a man who stood on a dock near one of the moored boats. He donned a full-length black raincoat; like the one Sabrina was wearing and round black sunglasses. A black Stetson Cowboy hat capped his head, and his hands were planted in the pockets. He stood away from us, so his voice had to be somewhat forceful, but he took no steps closer. Among the rocking boats, he stood motionless; the coat's flared bottom was the sole part of him that moved even a bit.

His sheer presence bothered me. I wondered who he was and how long he had been standing there watching us. The first impression I got was: husband. This guy had husband written all over him. And small-town jealous husbands usually carry guns. Second was pimp, which didn't make much sense up here. Down in Albany, maybe. But either way, I was uncomfortable.

"I'm sorry, I have to go." She stood up and did all she could to jog over to him, nearly falling over her legs in the process. She eventually navigated the boards of the dock despite her impaired senses and made it to him in one piece. They were far enough out of earshot that I couldn't hear what was being said, but I did get one hell of a pantomime show. Their arms flailed like garden hoses that had been left on. At the end of it, I watched him grab her elbow and shake it a few times and she recoiled it back. I took a step toward them and then halted.

They eventually began to walk together and disappeared down the Steel Pier and slipped into the darkness. Just like that, she was gone. There was a part of me that felt relief. Another part of me felt a little upset. I turned around and looked back at The Lookout. From deep within its bowels, I heard laughter and music belch out as if a carnival had set up shop. I didn't want to go back in. I didn't necessarily want to head for home, but I didn't want to go back in there either.

I walked back towards Canada Street and mentally counted my steps as I gradually ascended the slight hill that connected the Steel Pier with Route 9. My car was parked around the corner on Montcalm and Ottawa and at this time of night, there would be no one to impede my progress. I mention that because during the day it could get quite congested at that intersection, even in the off-season. But at this hour of the morning, I knew nothing would get in my path. My feet began to ache from my shoes being tied a little too tight and my steps became deliberate. My five-minute walk was rapidly becoming more of a slow, painful march. Sweat was beading up and sliding down my flushed cheeks.

The touristy pubs were all closed now. Their neon lights were turned off and were simply dead glass tubes in the windows. There was no music. No hustle or bustle. No husbands and wives carrying nothing but their smiles. They were the lifeblood of our community and while I knew we needed them to support our very existence, there was a feeling of being spied on and gawked at that made us all uncomfortable. They just show up, enjoy, and leave.

Rexall's Drug Store on the corner next to Shepard's Park was a place I had frequented many times. I stood outside the store, peeking through the large front window at the perfectly lined apothecary bottles and magazine racks. The floor, which was composed of uneven wooden slats, creaked when you walked inside. You had to be extra careful not to get your shoe hung up on one of the staggered planks. On more than one occasion a tyke had been overzealous about getting to the comic book rack and took a face-first dive into the floor. I had bought many penny candies out of the old, stout barrels that lined the wall. I had gone into the store a week prior and picked up some cough syrup because I couldn't afford a bottle of gin. The space on the counter where my bottle once sat was still vacant. 'I guess they haven't restocked it yet,' I thought, silently.

I walked over to Shepard Park, which was next to the drugstore. The park had a natural amphitheater built into its sloping hill and the lake as its backdrop. There was a band shell at the bottom of the hill, which was now dark and quiet. I tried to flood my thoughts with other things like sentimental memories and lines from famous plays but there was no escaping it; my mind continued to revert to Sabrina and that horrible man that took her away. I walked down to the empty band shell and hopped onto the stage, peering out at the slate slabs that were used as bleachers when there was a performance. The band shell had no rear wall, so you could see directly out onto the lake, and further, across to the eastern bank.

The lake's water swayed in the late-night air, gently rippled to the beach, and created a hush that eased my head. I looked across the water, to the eastern shore and muted outline of the tall mountains. "What the hell is going on over there," I said aloud, not caring if I sounded crazy. "What secrets are you keeping?"

CHAPTER TWO

The following morning, I jerked into my usual parking spot at *The Mirror* with a knot the size of a softball performing contortion acts in my stomach. I felt like I was about to give birth to an ulcer. It was twenty after ten when I slid the shifter into place; I was an hour and twenty minutes late. I'd seriously considered staying home with my face planted in my pillow and having an old-fashioned day of writhing in bed because I knew Herlihy was going to give me a hard time. Well, a hard time would be putting it extremely lightly. He was going to break my balls into about sixteen million tiny pieces and take extreme enjoyment while doing it. And his wrath wasn't without warrant. I'd been late a lot. I'd been behind deadline. I still didn't want to hear it.

Before stepping out of my car I paused for a moment and reflected on what my day *could* have been. I could have stayed home. I could have broken the seal on a new bottle of Dewar's and just daydreamed the afternoon away. I *could* have done that. But I didn't. Like a good soldier, I grabbed myself by the metaphorical scruff of the neck and pulled myself into the bathroom, where I shit, showered, shaved, and made it into my car no worse for the wear.

I parked my car awkwardly, not caring one way or the other, slammed the door behind me, straightened my tie, and secured my

Houndstooth fedora on top of my still-drying hair. I instantly regretted leaving my sunglasses at home. The sunlight was cutting my eyes like razor blades. But it was too late to abort. I was going in.

While we weren't churning out the hard-hitting above-folds of *The Times*, the office of *The Lake George Mirror* was about as bustling as one could expect from a small-town newspaper. The paper was based out of Bolton, the next town sequentially north of Caldwell. Our offices were housed in a converted animal barn that still had the red cow's blood paint on the sides and accented with freshly painted white trim. It even had a weathercock perched on a cupola. Neither the weathervane nor the cupola was functional, but they gave the building a pastoral look that seamlessly blended with the rural aesthetic that the tourists loved. On summer days when the weather got particularly warm and just humid enough, you could still pick up ancient wafts of musty hay and cow shit among the secretary's perfume and burned coffee.

I walked up the first stairway that led to what I referred to as 'the killing floor;' an open area of desks where editors and advertising salesmen sat and typed away creating a relentless hum that sounded like chattering teeth. Above them, a storm cloud of smoke hovered, collected from hours of burned Camels and Luckies. A few secretaries walked past me, and the spicy smell of heliotrope and mimosa wafted up my nose, which in turn made my ulcer kick a bit. *The Mirror's* writing staff were mostly guys around my age, some of them vets like me, with horrible comb-overs and neckties that were tied much too short. I might've been their contemporary in terms of age, but when it came to style and grace, I had them all beat by at least a half-mile. Most of them had silver on their ring fingers and a few extra mouths to feed to exacerbate their problems. Some of them were okay, although their faces were blank most of the time. They looked like mannequins in a store window. Herlihy's office was in the far-right corner. My desk was in the far-left corner, directly across the floor. I thought, *if I could manage to slip by him and get to my desk, everything would be fine.*

I bobbed and weaved through the labyrinth of desks, all the while picking up bits and pieces of conversations as I went. Derek LaFountain was talking on the phone and asking someone "what they thought of certain ideas to develop more lakefront property." Hank Jessup was barking out a box score for the prior night's Yankees game into a telephone receiver he held away from his mouth as he always did. They were entrenched enough in their own work to not make a fuss that I had finally arrived, like coal miners with picks in the mines. I was able to careen and veer through this gauntlet of the mundane with my small briefcase swinging at my side and didn't knock into anyone or anything.

When I reached my desk, I popped the briefcase on the small portion of unclaimed real estate and breathed a sigh of relief. '*Beat the man one more time,*' I thought. '*You're getting pretty good at this. Maybe next week you should try to show up after 12 and see if anyone says anything.*' I was pleased as punch with myself. I would have toasted, but all the good stuff I had was at home. I made it a rule not to leave any valuable beverages in my desk due to the scavengers that would lurk around the office after hours.

As I turned around and sat down, I was able to take one comfortable breath before I felt the unmistakable, crushing, stone-like hands of Martin Herlihy on my shoulders. "Welcome," his baritone voice said. "So nice of you to join us this morning." I have no idea where he came from. For a hulking brute of a man, he'd been as stealthy as Batman. And I knew this; his condescending attitude indicated he meant business. His thick fingers burrowed down into my shoulders and from my peripheral vision, I could see the sprouts of brown tangled hair on his knuckles. I wanted to turn around and just start swinging, but constrained myself. I turned on the meek and left it there.

"Marty, please," I pleaded. "You're going to break my shoulder if you keep that up." His squeeze hit a fever pitch before he released me. I rotated my arms, trying to make that pinching feeling subside.

"You were drunk again last night, weren't you," he asked me while giving me the once-over. "Too damn hung over to get out of bed. Was that the issue today?"

"Actually, I got caught behind a carnival on Route 9 this morning. Looks like the circus is in town."

His rotund build made his suspenders look like they were going to pop at any moment. From where I stood, I imagined all the anger he had towards me had manifested inside in his gut and was ready to explode at any moment. He was 65 years old, a hard brute of a man. When he walked, he sort of waddled due to his brute physique. He wore his white hair cropped as if he was ready at any moment to drop everything and join the Marine Corps. Marty was a true son of the area. One of his grandfathers was a lumberjack and full-blooded Lenape. He was a boat builder in Diamond Point for years. Marty had been the first person in his family to go to college, attending Skidmore.

Although Marty worked in what was considered an 'office environment' he retained the physique and hands of his outdoorsman ancestors. And if we're being completely truthful, he wasn't a bad guy. He knew his job and did it well. Before he took over as Editor-in-Chief the paper was on the verge of collapse. Within three years, he was able to double subscriptions and add advertising revenue. He fired most of the old writing staff. He had hired all new secretaries. Under his watch, the legitimacy of the paper had become something real. He was firm with all of us, barking requests, rarely saying thank you or anything like that. But there was never any real malice to him. There is a rather large part of me that feels bad that I put the guy through so many episodes of grief.

"Don't give me any of that shit, will you please," he demanded. I could see the agitation slowly creep out of him. That was typical; when angry, Marty would come in like a shitstorm and then it would slowly fade. He leaned against a beam and crossed his arms, waiting. "What are you working on now, anyway?"

I plopped back down into my chair and began to rummage through the myriad of manila folders that were stacked high on my desk. I never considered myself an organized person, and that has come back to bite me in the ass on quite a few occasions. I tend to just *know* where things are. It didn't take me too long to rifle through some papers, remove some paperclips, and hand Marty the first draft of a piece I was working on for a Sunday expanded edition. "It's a piece on the effects of chopping down large swaths of trees and not replacing them. The bottom line is, Marty, for every one they chop down over there, they should be planting two in its place. That's what they've been telling me." I had done two months' worth of research for that story, interviewed over thirty people, and dedicated many nights to compiling quotes and composing paragraphs. It was a movement that hadn't caught on yet, but I felt the embers beginning to take. In my estimation, the more people knew about what was going on, the quicker they'd take action to ensure that there would be trees and precious scenery for future generations. One way or another, the trees were the bread and butter of the area. Whether it was for the mills or the tourists that would come up every summer to gawk at the lush terrain, it all centered on the damned trees.

"And do you honestly think these people are going to give a rat's ass and read about something like that," he asked, snickering.

I was left holding my work out towards him and his arms remained folded, unflinching, concrete. He never once budged to merely take a look at my research or consider, even momentarily, what I'd written. "Tell you what," he interrupted himself. "You are going to take this story," he finally acknowledged my hard work by vaguely pointing at it, "and put it on the back burner. You, my friend, going to work on an assignment for me, okay?"

That pain in the pit of my stomach flared up once again. It felt like a kid was kicking around inside of me. I hadn't been handed an assignment since I was a junior reporter for the *Queensbury Dispatch*. I quickly switched to recovery and anticipation mode in an attempt to brace for what was going to be dished out. I knew he was going to wallop me with a dreadful assignment and make sure my life would be nothing short of a living hell for the foreseeable future. Marty was just as creative as the rest of us, and he knew how to frost a cake, so to speak. I figured it would be something akin to '*a rare chickadee has been spotted in Tupper Lake- go follow it*' or '*John Branson has been making buckskin jackets for well over fifty years, visit his shop in Warrensburg and do a bio-piece.*' I would no doubt sound like some sort of nonsense essay puff piece that no one would take pleasure in writing.

All I could do was take this medicine like a man. Harkening back to my military experience, I stood up so that our faces were close. His face reeked of pleasure, a snide, sly grin crimping the side of his mouth. If I had any fear, trepidation, or concern, I used every ounce of will that I could to mask it. I slapped my hands against my thighs and said, "OK then. Lay it on me."

He waited for a few young interns to pass us by with their Victory roll hairdos and hot cups of coffee clutched with two hands. Once the coast was clear, he invited me to sit down at my own desk; a motion that I always felt was incredibly disrespectful. Where I come from you don't invite people to sit down at their desks. I followed his order and sat down, awaiting my punishment. "You are going to go up into the mountains with an Adirondack guide as your companion and chronicle your exploits. You will have little to no modern conveniences, except the clothes on your back. I took the liberty of making a list of things you'll need to bring along with you, so you'll be as prepared as possible." He produced a folded yellow sheet of paper from his back pocket and tossed it onto my desk. "We're going to use this piece to drum up interest for the upcoming season. We've got a few smaller papers downstate that are going to run it too, so our exposure should be off the charts."

I leaned back in my seat and let the '*list he'd took the liberty of making*' sit on my desk as if it were riddled with smallpox. My face felt hot, and my lower jaw began to tremble a bit. I fought it back, though. I wasn't about to throw a fit right then and there, but I had seen this movie once before. I knew when I was being used. I was being used as a god damned promotional tool. He might as well have slapped a sandwich board over my head and had me stand in the middle of Route 9 with my hands waving at passing cars.

I wasn't exactly the 'outdoorsy' type. The last time I'd attempted anything like that was during my time in the service and that was a time I preferred to forget. We had to forage a few times, pitched tents, cooked over open fires, but that was out of necessity. If I was hearing him right, we'd be hitting the top ten: No shelter. Sleeping outside. No modern conveniences. And who the hell was this Adirondack guide? Did those things even still exist? I wasn't sure what any of this was supposed to mean. A bit of indignance snuck out of me. "And what if I refuse to go?"

His fat cheeks crinkled from his smile. "Oh, you don't have to if you don't want to. But, if that is indeed the case, I would hop my no-good carcass down into Albany and start handing out resumes to the *Post Star* and *Times Union*, if you know what I mean."

I quickly stood up and our stomachs nearly touched. "You son of a bitch!" I was dizzy from anger and from standing too fast.

"Easy, easy," he said. "No need for vulgarity."

I morphed into a five-year-old who had been warned multiple times about his behavior and then had his ball taken away. Herlihy knew precisely what he was doing and knew it was burrowing under my skin like maggots. At that point my, life wasn't the greatest, but it was even keel. It was a serene stretch of water in a lifetime of white thrashing rapids. I made sure the lights stayed on. I had enough money to put to good use. I was beholden to no one. All things considered; I still needed a goddamn job.

"Besides," he said. "You might like it." He waddled away from me, oozing satisfaction. He looked like a walrus who had just finished off an entire school of mackerel.

I leaned back in my chair, looked up to the tin roof of the barn, and closed my eyes. I breathed deeply a few times, replaying what had just gone on over and over, as if that would somehow mystically change the outcome. The longer I sat and considered what had happened the worse I felt. With each revolution of the same scene, a small amount of guilt crept into my thoughts. What was happening was a truth coming out in the wash. There had been a rash of my actions that required accountability for which I had gleefully escaped the hangman's noose. Multiple assignments had been turned in late. Grammar had been sloppy. I hadn't proofread my work. Herlihy probably could have dished out much, much worse. He could've fired me right there on the spot if he wanted. So, I deserved his wrath, all of it. But I felt there was still something wrong with the satisfaction he got. There is a line between satisfaction and deviance. Martin Herlihy straddled that line that morning.

After I had calmed myself by taking a short stroll to the water fountain, I returned to my desk. Placed on top of the papers I had shuffled earlier was an envelope I hadn't noticed before. Across the front was written, WRITER, LAKE GEORGE MIRROR. I blindly asked those who were scurrying around the killing floor, "Does anyone know who dropped this on my desk or what it may be in reference to?" Most of them ignored me. I got a few pity laughs from some of the guys who thought I was joking. I'm sure a few of the women pretended to not hear me.

Everyone continued filing, writing, and shuffling of papers. Like I said, some days the ticking of the typewriters would make my head almost feel numb. This was one of those days. I slid a finger under the glued flap and opened the envelope.

Eastern woods.

I sat down at my desk deliberately slowly and looked over both shoulders the way spies do in espionage films. I studied the small scrap of yellowing lined paper and folded it in half. I tucked it in my shirt pocket and began to rifle through my paperwork. I needed to get something in my vision, something that wasn't so ominous or cryptic. I had endured quite enough of those things over the past twelve hours. I flipped through papers, opened folders, shuffled old notes, opened every one of my desk drawers, refilled my stapler, pulled out my Rolodex, and studied some pencils.

My shirt pocket began to throb like the heart under the floorboards in Poe's story. I took the paper out again. 'Eastern woods.' It didn't take a genius to figure out who had left it. But I wondered why. Was there trouble? 'There was always trouble with women,' I reminded myself. More dramatics than in Ancient Greece. Did it have anything to do with that man that was roughing her up? Or was there no problem at all and this was just another one of her stupid games to make me crazy.?

I slid the paper back into my pocket as I saw Herlihy walking towards me again with a thin stack of papers in his paws. His walk was with a purpose; he made a beeline right for me.

"Hey," he said. "Here's the information for your guide. I set up an appointment for you to meet him later tonight at the bar at the *Surfside on the Lake Hotel*. Make sure you're on time. From what I hear he can be a pretty nasty firecracker if you know what I mean."

My mouth must've looked like a bass that had just been pulled from the water. "You're kidding," I asked. "I have to meet this guy after hours? Tonight?"

"Yes. And yes," he said, beaming. "Eight o'clock. Surfside Bar."

I took the paperwork without breaking eye contact. If this guy was going to make my life a living hell, then I wasn't going to make it easy for him. I was going to grill him so bad that his cheeks would have singe lines on them. Steam was practically shooting out of my ears by that point.

He added, "I'm sure it won't be too much of a chore for you to pony up to the bar and knock a few back." He bounced away from me once again.

I took the short stack of papers and made it like I was going to tear them in half. My temper had got me into trouble before and I wasn't about to give it the green light on this occasion. I calmly placed the papers back down on the desk, where they took their spot among all the other work I had been compiling. Just like everything else that I touched; I added it to the pile.

As I sat back in my chair, I tried with all my brainpower to come up with a way to get out of this. I didn't like the story. I had no faith in the story. I had zero interest in meeting this guy (whoever he was) and I had no interest in sleeping on the forest floor or any of that stuff. I wasn't about to use a pinecone to wipe my ass, either.

Through the fog of my disappointment there seemed to be a small flicker of hope. Maybe Herilhy was right about one thing; at least I'd get a drink out of it.

CHAPTER THREE

Surfside on the Lake was one of the newer hotel/ motel combinations that nestled against the western shoreline of Lake George. Its booming red and orange neon sign sat practically on Canada Street, beckoning weary travelers to take a respite from the road and unload for a few hours. During the busy season, armies of pastel-colored Fords and Chevys with luggage precariously roped to their roofs would fill the motel parking lots, each car brimming with tired men and their patient wives and misbehaved children. Most of the motels that lined the strip had similar beckoning neon lights, which made a view of the nighttime strip look like a child's crayon drawing on black construction paper. *Surfside* was set up perpendicular to the water, as most of the motels and hotels were, with a small marina and beach at the very bottom of the parking lot. A small patch of gravely sand and some graying docks with moored mahogany day liners were all visitors would find down there. It wasn't Palm Springs, but it was nice.

At this time of year, the motels weren't fully open for business; most of the establishments didn't crack open fresh ledgers until Memorial Day and hung their shingles until Labor Day. There were a few of them that stayed open until just after Thanksgiving to cater to the hunters, but they were few and far between, and most of those were located further inland. There wasn't much good hunting close to the lake anyway. Tupper Lake, maybe. North Creek. Thurman. But not many hunters would want to make the trek from Caldwell all the way inland. Each fall the motels would slip into their winter cocoons and those bright neon signs would stand dark. The windows would be hidden behind thin sheets of balsa wood that were screwed into the window frames. Jesus, it looked like the damn buildings were asleep. When they reopened for the spring, the smells of cleaning products and stale mothballs would welcome the motel and innkeepers. White sheets on clotheslines would get tossed in the breeze behind the buildings to signal that the rampage of outsiders was shortly on the way. There would be the obligatory once-over for dead critters, too. Verne Blair once claimed to have removed 16 deceased woodchucks from his place in Warrensburg; to the best of my knowledge, an Adirondack record.

I walked into the lobby of *Surfside* and onto the blue carpet that covered every square inch of the floor. My nose was greeted with the stinging pungent smell of cleaning fluids and paint; telltale signs that a new season was just around the corner. I walked past the check-in station, which was in a room outfitted with wood paneling and stylized posters of canoes, and continued through a light blue waterfall of hanging beads that acted as the door to the bar. Above the door was a small cardboard sign, which read, *ALOHA*. It was ambiance at its finest. I had been in there once or twice before and it was a decent spot.

In the offseason, it was okay for locals to imbibe at such a place since the out-of-towners hadn't arrived yet. There were three woodworkers saddled at the bar when I walked in; evident by their dress and the way they sat. They were all seated in the same manner; slouched shoulders, heads cocked down, elbows on the bar. During the season, you'd never catch three characters like that in a place like Surfside. I was pretty damn surprised to see them all there so close to opening weekend. I figured they must've picked this place because it was on their way home.

I walked in and Eddy Arnold was singing about what a *'fool he was to ever let you go'*. Besides the three lumberjacks, who I'm quite sure were all brothers, I might add, there was not another soul in the place. I can't remember their names, but I knew their lumberyard was past Warrensburg on the way up to Blue Mountain Lake off Route 28. I surmised that they were probably in town for a fix-up job of some kind and wanted to whet the whistle a little before heading back home. In the center of, what I supposed was, the dance floor was a large, illuminated fish tank with various koi fish swimming around. Some were Halloween orange, with black stripes. Others were yellow with purple markings. The fish tank looked out of place in the center of the room, but I guessed it was put there to give the illusion of everyone in the room being underwater.

I walked over to the bar and as I stepped my shoes clicked on the parquet floor. I looked over to the lumberjacks and none of them were speaking. They wore variations of the same red and black buffalo flannel with the sleeves rolled up to the elbow, and faces full of scraggly beard. They sat in a row; the same desolate look on their faces, with empty mugs in front of them. If I had been a traveler or stranger, I would've made a quick about-face and left immediately. Their overalls were covered in a thin layer of sawdust, and they reeked of a musty smell of oil and freshly cut timber. I shuffled away from them to the other end of the long bar.

The bartender, whom I surprisingly didn't know, was on the op-posite side of the bar, counting dollar bills from out of an empty repurposed pickle jar. Unlike Jasper at the Lookout, this barkeep was dressed splendidly, in a white shirt and black vest with black pants. He had no apron, no stains, and no character. I waved my hands like a madman trying to get his attention, but nothing was doing. He was in the midst of an old-fashioned tip count and there was nothing that was going to break that spell. "Hey," I yelled, slamming my palm against the mahogany bar. "Hey, can I get a drink down here, please?" The fact that I said please was an afterthought.

He walked over, youngish face, didn't look a day over twenty-five. Hair combed over and slicked down to the scalp. "What," he asked.

"Jack and Coke," I ordered. "Mostly Jack."

I looked around and shook my head. I had gone into overdrive trying to convince myself this wasn't as bad as it seemed. But the truth was I had an entire book of places I could've been. I could've been home, listening to the Yanks on the radio (we finally got broadcasts from downstate two years prior). Although I was a tried-and-true Dodgers fan, they didn't broadcast that far north. But I loved baseball, the game itself, so the Yankees would have to do. Besides, I got as much joy listening to the Yankees lose as I did hearing news that the Dodgers won. I could have been at home, lying down, looking at my ceiling, thinking about Ingrid Bergman. I could've been over at *The Lookout*, keeping a watchful eye to see if Sabrina or Gertrude would make an appearance. Or I could just sit myself down on a rock and drive myself up the wall.

Eastern woods. That note had been at the end of my nose all day and showed no signs of leaving any time soon. I looked down at the trampled lumbermen and thought, '*Nah, this isn't so bad at all. Not bad at all.*' It could have been worse, after all. I could have been one of them.

Whiskey has an initial burn that guys like me crave all the time. It hurts a little at first, but once it gets down into your throat it soothes the soul. That's how it felt when I slid back the first sips of my drink that evening. It was antiseptic. It burned all the nonsense and garbage away and paved a road that led to feeling good. I was on my way and no man or beast was going to stop me. I put the glass to my lips and guzzled the drink as easily as if I were drinking plain old water out of the tap. I slammed the glass down indignantly and spun around in my barstool.

Through the fish tank, I was able to make out a figure through the shimmering water. The most prominent feature was its beard, which looked to be grisly, thick, and brownish gray, although it was hard to tell because of the lighting. He wore a tattered brown leather coat that hit just above the knee, with boots that matched. It was hard to discern any real detail because I was viewing this scene through water. He could have been another lumberjack for all I knew. But he wasn't. Even from across the room and through a 60-gallon tank of water I knew who he was. I regretted only sinking one Jack and Coke before his arrival.

He walked uncomfortably around the bar, scanning all the while as if the world might've been plotting against him. His movements were quick and suspicious. He looked about as comfortable as a gorilla in a baby carriage. He finicked with his hat, which looked like a cross between a pith helmet and a straw sombrero, and finally waltzed over to where I was sitting. His forehead was large and pronounced with bushy salt and pepper eyebrows.

"You have got to be the guide," I said with my whiskey breath sliding toward him.

"And you're the acquainted which is a'comin'?" His voice didn't fit his appearance or apparent demeanor. It was surprisingly high-pitched and clear for someone who looked like they had just eaten a porcupine. He fidgeted in place for a while and finally pulled up one of the swiveling stools next to me. I said nothing but took him all in. "You gonna fill some clarity with spirits, young man," he asked.

I chuckled. "What do you drink, my friend?"

"White lightnin' if they got it."

"I don't think so," I answered. "How about some bourbon? Might be the next best thing."

"Whatever. Shit rots you from the guts to the skin anyways. I'm only taking part to be nice."

My inner voice commented on how something ceased to be nice once you've vocally pointed out that you were only doing it to be nice. Herlihy had said he was a firecracker, but I felt like he was more of a jumping jack. I ordered him a Jim Beam neat, and it came quickly enough from the pre-pubescent barkeep. The guide steadied it up to his mouth and sipped at it slowly like he was trying to drink gasoline. I couldn't help but chuckle at the situation. Watching this grizzled old guide, who had probably killed grizzlies with his bare hands and castrated a bull moose with a piece of piano wire, cringe back at the taste of alcohol was pure comedy. Maybe this wasn't going to be so bad after all. It then hit me that I could turn this little endeavor to my advantage. I figured the best way to get back at Herlihy would involve me having a good time with this old mongrel. I was determined to try and put my best foot forward and see where the river took me. He said it himself, 'you might like it.' Well, maybe I *would* like it. And maybe I would tell him under no uncertain terms to go to hell in the morning.

"So, you've lived in these mountains your entire life," I asked, trying to pace myself on my second drink.

"Nah, my mom shit me out in Albany and I walked," he said. "Of course I been here my whole life! I'll be seventy plus two in August, and you'd better believe I'll be here next August too."

It had been only a few minutes, probably under ten if my memory is where it should be, but I already knew that I was going to take a liking to this guy. He had the look of a hobo and the voice and diction of a vagabond poet. He used phrasing in his speech that I'd never heard before. His verbiage seemed rehearsed and crisp, with a grizzled edge to it. It was both beautiful and painful.

"You know the troub is with all these parkassers around here? They come here to bask in the old-fashioned glory of the skies. But they turn themselves around and sleep on white pillows. Now I ask you, how'n the name o'lordies son are you gonna appreesh anythin' when you act like that?"

Parkassers? Lordies son? I could have probably written an entire article on the way this guy spoke, let alone a tour of the mountains. I had to keep on my toes when listening to him speak. If my mind decided to wander a bit, I would be lost in no time and have no idea what he was talking about.

"I never got your name, friend," I said.

"Shep Gooley," he said. "Born Sheppard." He took another sip of his Jim Beam and slid it back onto the bar. "And you," he asked me.

"Franklin Phelps," I said. "People call me Frank, though."

"Got two like me, do ya?"

"I guess so. Are you a friend of Mr. Herlihy?"

He furrowed his brow and put a hand to his ear as if he'd misheard what I'd said. "'Fraid that book ain't in the collection," he said, tapping the side of his head.

"The man from the paper," I said. "My boss. The one who told you to meet me here."

He snapped his fingers and began to shake his head in affirmation. "Course! The old suity soot. First shook the 5 in '34! Good!"

I decided to cut to the chase and see if he could offer any insight as to what I was going to be in store for. "Why don't you tell me about what trail we're going to take when we go on our trip?" I knew Warren County pretty well and wondered if we were venturing someplace I had been before. Meanwhile in the back of my thoughts, like a ghoul peeking out from a darkened corner, Sabrina still lurked. I desperately wanted to ask if visiting the Eastern Woods was a possibility. But needed to get the gumption to ask.

"Figger we'd get the jump over on the side of Black Mount an' make it up."

I had downed a whiskey and a half by that point. My cheeks had begun to flush a bit and the onset of the numbness that I craved had started. Maybe the booze was starting to play its magic flute. Or maybe, I was simply *supposed* to ask him. Either way, I closed my eyes the way children do before asking their parents for something they knew they might not get and fired my question at him. "Say, friend, is there any chance of us going up into the Eastern Woods?"

His eyebrows raised. He began to rub his knees and nervously drummed his thick digits on the tops of his kneecaps with such ferocity that they made a chunky thudding sound. He slowly shook his head. It was almost as if I had triggered an allergic reaction. It was like he was in a trance. "No. I don' put no foot on that dirt. None of it. Bad stuff up on that side."

My blood chilled. The tip of my nose ran ice cold and I slugged another mouthful of whiskey, which was mostly mingled with melted ice water. It was the only way I could make anything on my body feel warm again. He chilled me to my core with that response. "What kind of bad stuff."

He shook his head rapidly. "Bad stuff. Secret bad stuff. Kind of stuff you wouldn't wanna eat on."

Worry gripped my throat, and I couldn't breathe.

We tell our secrets to the mountain and wash our sins in the water. Once it's in the water, it's washed and buried.

That nonsensical line. At the time Sabrina had first said it, my mind had been impaired so I couldn't quite decipher her point. Sitting there with Shep, it wasn't making much sense, either. However, I would have bet three months' salary that old Shep would have some ideas. He could probably tell me more about Sabrina too. Sabrina, whom I'd only met the night before, had been tugging at my psyche from the second I made her acquaintance.

And the note I found at my desk. What was that all about? Who had been at my desk and why? Why me? I could feel the world begin to blur around me like an out-of-focus camera. My cheeks turned from flushed to red fire and small sweat beads started to pool around the corners of my eyes. I got to my destination rather quickly that night, which was good for my wallet, but not for my soul. The soft yellow and orange glow of the Wurlitzer jukebox in the corner swayed in my veiled vision and it looked like a giant beacon. '*Come over here where the music's hot, Frankie boy. The light will guide you home. Come to the light.*'

While we were chatting, some other patrons had entered the bar and were seated at the small tables with chairs with braided wicker backs that were situated around the perimeter of the room. They were all locals and even through my haze, I was able to pick out a few of them. In a few weeks, they wouldn't be caught dead in here, comingling with the invaders that came to roost once a year. I placed my drink to my lips, polishing off my third whiskey, this one straight. The cubes in the glass swirled around, the only remainders. I was no longer in a straight mind.

It was in this first stage of drunkenness that my attention began to drift away from Shep, like a boat that had become unmoored from a dock. My focus shifted beyond Shep's shoulder and picked up bits of the bantering small talk that went on around the bar. Although I was well on the way to pie-eyed, I was able to hear as sharply as a bat.

"So, what do you think about this Marshall plan," someone asked.

"Why the hell should we help rebuild what we just destroyed," another chimed in.

"Isn't' nothing but a goddamned waste of money. My money."

"All they're going to do is stab you in the back once they're rebuilt."

In remembering all of this, I have to look back on it with a lens that I didn't have back then. There wasn't a Rhoades scholar among them, and that was okay. I can say that now. In my drunken stupor back then, I wasn't so quick to rationalize.

As I listened to them, I began to get progressively angrier. I was able to halfheartedly divide my attention between Shep, the lumberjacks, and the other patrons. Enough of it was focused on the loudmouths to cause my blood pressure to rise to a boiling point. One of them that was especially getting under my skin was wearing a red flannel shirt. His views were not the same as mine and I didn't like it. He kept calling Truman a 'pussy' and said that we shouldn't 'help another damn soul on the planet'. His attitude began to piss me off. He used his hands a lot and seemed to have a mouth full of saliva, which was evident by his slurred speech. I didn't like him. I dare say at that moment I hated him. It pushed me over the edge far enough that I felt I needed to take action.

I abruptly stood up, and nearly knocked the stool I was sitting on backward. Shep sat there, his head cocked sideways and looking like a rather confused dog. Surely nothing he had said could have possibly pulled such a reaction from me.

I stupidly walked to the table where the man I hated sat, and I shoved his shoulder with two fingers, hard. He was in the middle of taking a sip of his drink, and quite a bit of it ended up on the table in front of him. Some of it seeped into his shirt and gave the appearance of a dark red splotch like he'd been shot. The look on his face was pure shock. His beard was grizzly and straggly. The exposed skin above his beard and below his eyes was red and raw. He looked about as sober as I did. I tapped him on the shoulder again. He dropped his glass on the table, never saying a word, and stood. Our faces met. The look on mine must've been pure stupidity.

After another second or two of staring, the man's identity finally entered my brain. The man I shoved was Kenny Fistle. I had gone to school with Kenny. I sat in front of him in Ms. Williamson's class. We had eaten sardine sandwiches in the school cafeteria together. I fantasized about walloping him something good with my right fist. As I cocked my balled right hand to slug him in the face, fate intervened.

Shep decided to interject in this moment of drunken idiocy by placing his arm between Kenny and me. "That'll dot it! That'll dot it," Shep said in his lyrical, lilting whine. "Not an inch closer to the ledge!"

Kenny's face looked more disappointed than anything by the time I had stopped my little Jake LaMotta impression. The world spun around me and there were no straight lines that I could see on anything. Everything looked like a Van Gogh painting with only clusters of color in bunches to make shapes. I grabbed onto one of the small tables, dumbly unaware that I had attracted a crowd of onlookers. Even Shep stood before me with his head cocked to one side. I hadn't felt that embarrassed in years. Naturally, I did what was customary for people like me to do; I flipped a round table over and stormed out like an agitated bull.

When I stepped outside onto Canada Street the cool lake breeze washed over my tomato-red face. I was trying like hell to catch my breath to not look winded or upset. I turned around and Shep was standing there in front of the door. He walked over to where I was hunched over and said, "Why don't we put a few feet together that ways?" He pointed down towards the water.

As we descended the parking lot, I felt my stomach begin to tighten up and my salivary glands were going off like lawn sprinklers. I tried to swallow the spit back, but it was no use. I let loose what whiskey I had drank all over the pavement and got some on the corner of my loafer for good measure. I had never thrown up after three drinks. This was the first time anything like that had ever happened.

"Bet'cher as good as a goose now, eh," Shep asked.

We stood before the great lake, and I stared across to the eastern shore. The water had made its nightly transition into a murmuring void. The eastern shore and the mountains that grew beyond it were indistinguishable. No denoting marks. Nothing. Just blackness. "Sabrina," I called out to the darkness. "Sabrina."

Shep put his hand on my shoulder and began to rub it. "Issues with a slit, do ya?"

I dropped to one knee, right where the small beach touched the parking lot. I sat with my legs crossed and Shep followed. "It's been a long time since I've had issues with slits, Shep. I just don't venture down that road too often. You getting what I'm saying?"

He tightened his lips back and said, "I got the drift."

I thought of how stupid it was to bring up Sabrina at that point. I felt immature and impetuous. I was never one to stand in front of my locker in high school and profess my love for the unattainable damsel who'd walk by with her hair all neat and her face done up. That wasn't me. But in that moment, the intrigue and the sheer impact she had on me culminated in me taking the steps to verbalize what I was feeling. "There was one girl I met. Only last night. I only knew her for an hour or so." That's when the ridiculous nature of the situation slapped me across the face. Infatuation was typically a dish cooked in a Dutch oven. My situation had barely popped out of the toaster. I didn't like it. It embarrassed me. I added, "I think she might be in trouble or something."

"Trouble," he said, acting as if we should take action on this immediately.

"Trouble?" He stood up next to me. "Well, if that's the printed word, let's get the cart going and see what be what!"

"Sit down, Shep. There's no need to rush. I'm not even sure where she is right now." That was a lie. I once again cast my glance to the dark eastern wilderness that sprawled before us on the other side of the lake. His eagerness to help the situation made me hopeful.

"Why dilly-dally? Reasons are piling up! For when we stay is a time's delay!"

I had to hold my smirk back at my good fortune. I didn't know my way around the wilderness. But I had someone who was now chomping at the bit to get involved. There would be some convincing, though. He did seem very apprehensive when I brought up going to the woods beyond the eastern shore. Maybe everything was made to fall together this way. Maybe it was the crazed face of fortune rearing its image once again. Or maybe, just maybe, I was drinking too much and this was all a hallucination. It had come to that.

"When I told you I didn't know where she was, I was lying," I said.

Shep looked perplexed. "You sold me a fudge of the truth?"

I nodded. "Yeah. I know she's in trouble and I know where she is."

"Well," he asked. "You gonna parlay the deets or what?"

"She's somewhere in the Eastern Woods."

The color ran from his face until the small patches of skin above his beard looked like a plucked chicken. He inhaled a deep breath and looked to the sky. "Eastern woods," he said. "Haven't tread on those rocks in a book of calendars." He sat down next to me and pointed across the lake with a weathered, crooked finger. "In the young hours o'my manhood, I plodded those woods. I plotted and tramped wit' a gang o'scamps. It was life's mid-mornin' as I recall. And I recall what we came jaw to jaw to. It was...it was and still lives. Rotten, putrid souls. Doin' the work of old Scratch. Our pupils tried to forget. But as the vine ripened our cheeks we had visitors in the upstairs noggin for years. I bibled it that I'd never go again. But occasions change the wind and the wind breathes into the sail. We're on the skiff and headed for shore. I reckon you need a rope. I'm good enough to have one to give. My one star-ask is that my bones are galvy enough to withstand the blow."

"What did you see up there," I asked.

He put his head down. "A query," he said. "You have a-tent on grabbin' this girl?"

I nodded.

"In that case, my mouth is closed. Should it be opened by wry or by pry you'll run th'other way. You'll gaze when it's set to gaze."

"When will we go?"

"Next time the sun shines. Rundeevoo on the dock. 8."

Shep stood up, brushed some dirt from his pants and extended his hand, and helped me stand up. I felt a sense of relief that someone else was going to be with me to help solve whatever issue was going on in the Eastern Woods. There was, of course, a part of me that felt a shred of remorse for getting him mixed up in something he had no business getting involved in. Shep was only supposed to guide me up a mountain and I was technically using him. I shook my head like a dog after a bath to breeze those thoughts away. I couldn't afford a conscience at that moment.

He saluted me as an army officer would and turned and walked north on Route 9.

"See you tomorrow," I said. "See you tomorrow."

Chapter Four

My eyes were closed.

There was a stinging around the sides of the sockets, and I was fearful to try opening my eyelids for fear of exacerbating the pain. It felt like I had gotten soap in them. After I'd mustered enough courage to slowly crack my eyes open, the confines of my bedroom began to slowly focus and the shafts of light that were streaming through my curtains singed my pupils as if they'd been waiting for me. The curtains on my bedroom windows were lacy and yellowing and did little to dull the light. They had been sparkling white when I moved in, left by the previous owner of the apartment, and after a few years of sun staining they'd turned a sour milk yellow. I simply hadn't had the inspiration to climb up on a chair and take them down.

I closed my eyes, which left photographic negative imprints lingering in my vision. I returned to the safety of blindness; away from that burning sun. I raised my balled fists and massaged the images away. By the time the sun had fully risen my head was sore, my eyes hurt, and I realized that I'd slept in my clothes. I had that awful feeling of regret that one has when waking in the clothes they were wearing the night before. The feeling stuck to me like tar.

My bedroom was a tiny mouse hole where I stored away clothes in various corners the way squirrels compile acorns for the winter. My apartment had a large living room, with a slick-looking red leather couch that I'd purchased in Troy soon after I got out of the Army. I bought the couch before I had an apartment to put it in. Those were the days when I was still living with my sister Jane and her husband Bruce down in Schenectady. When the living situation down there got a little tight, I was able to scrape together some pennies and move into an apartment on the first floor of an old Victorian in Queensbury. I haven't spoken to either one of them since that all went down. Tempers flare when you're in a confined space, I guess. My four rooms were enough for me. The big red couch was the only piece of furniture I had in the room and it swallowed the space whole; like a serpent's tongue slashing against the eggshell white walls.

I knew I needed to give this whole 'waking up' thing another try. When I got to my feet the world was on a tilt. I sidestepped my way out of my bedroom and over to a round end table that was on the side of my couch. It had a curved door that swung open to reveal a hidden liquor cabinet. I called it my 'Presidential Cabinet' because I believed that everything encased in there would never give me bad advice and always steer me right.

I don't remember what I drank that morning, but I know I killed the bottle. It went down harsh and burning, like drinking acid straight from a chemistry set. I remember feeling determined to get it all down my gullet, no matter how unpleasant that feeling was between my eyes. I breathed in steadily through my nose and let just the tiniest bit of the alcohol run out of the sides of my mouth. I remember feeling claustrophobic like the walls were slowly going to collapse on me. I felt warm and small beads of sweat began to slide down my cheek. I tried to smile but couldn't. I was too uncomfortable. I popped the buttons from my shirt and threw it down in a rage. I dropped the bottle on the floor, and amazingly it didn't shatter. The vignette ended with my knees caving, and me blacking out and collapsing onto the couch.

*   *   *

I was awoken from my alcoholic sleep by the warm vomit I felt sliding down my bare chest and collecting in my lap. My eyes were as wide as saucers, and it hurt to look at the windows. I stood up and screamed and inhaled that broken-down rotten stench of my throw-up. Once that smell had made its rounds in my nose, I made a beeline for the toilet, because round two was coming up shortly. And it did.

I stripped the rest of my clothes off after the last bit of vomit had completed its journey from bowel to bowl and I hobbled into the shower. I slithered into the bathtub like a snake, and the ice-cold porcelain shocked my skin into goose pimples. I turned the water on and it was like I'd jumped into a frozen pond. The frigid water shocked my skin and all my senses blinked like an out-of-service traffic light. My motor skills weren't fast enough to switch the water down to a warmer temperature, so I just sat there and shivered. I fell to the floor of my tub and fell asleep with ice-cold water freezing my naked body.

I recall looking at myself in the bathroom mirror after waking and shivering. There were tears, I remember that. So many things to cry about, not enough handkerchiefs. I needed to pack my duffel, which hadn't been used since I was discharged. I was supposed to meet Shep at the dock at 8 o'clock. The time on my watch said 11:15.

I drifted listlessly around my bedroom, with the dull ache in my temples preventing me from ever getting into any kind of groove. My concentration felt like someone had put a wet towel over my brain and poured cement over it. It was like throwing punches underwater. I began gingerly opening my dresser drawers and randomly, without looking, throwing things into the duffel. Underwear, tee shirts, dress shirts, and shorts all flung into the bag like a magician doing a handkerchief trick. When everything was finally in there, I began for the door. I had my keys in my hand, ready to go, when it hit me. I made an about-face and went to the Presidential Cabinet. I pulled a solitary bottle of Old Crow out and tucked it in the center of the duffel so the clothes would act as a cushion. I gave my apartment one last look.

I closed my door, ready to lock it, and noticed a note taped to it. I quickly attempted to take inventory of every bill I'd paid that month, and everything seemed to come back clear. Lights? Check. Water? Check. I pulled the note from the door and read it.

Moose's Walk.

He will know.

*   *   *

How do I deal with disappointment? I don't get disappointed anymore; I've been hurt and broken down so many times, I don't even react to it anymore. What's the point of crying? You're only going to cry again. I have lived by that credo for most of my adult life. I had to fake passion while working in the newspaper business- writers often have to go to *that* well plenty- but that was easy enough. I was a good enough bullshit artist that I could skate by without too much of an issue. I'd been disappointed by women too, and I tried not to let that bother me either, Sabrina notwithstanding. I thought I knew every in and out of disappointment there was. However, that morning, I was in for a shock. I realized I didn't know disappointment at all. Every ounce of disappointment in the entire universe was displayed in the face of Shep Gooley when I saw him sitting alone with his legs hanging over the pier, by himself.

I only knew it was him by his outline, as he was facing away from me as I approached. His shoulders were slouched, and his legs dangled off the end of the pier. His hat was off his head and placed next to him, letting the wild tangles of gray ride the subtle lake breeze. It was noon and I was four hours late. I stood behind him with my army green duffel at my feet, almost afraid to approach him. I didn't know what to say or how to say it. As luck had it, I didn't have to say anything.

He turned around to face me, with this weathered bearded face. "Fortune smiles on the patient one," he said. "I was a half tick from beating the road and sliding the chips." His mood brightened from there. "I'm a high C that you've made it."

"I'm so sorry Shep, I..."

"No, none of that," he said, wagging his index finger at me. "We don't the mins or secs for that brand. Come, come," he said. "Your car is tucked in a comfy hole?"

"I parked it on Ottawa in front of Florence Bateman's house. She's a friend of mine, she'll let it stay there."

"Kinderhook! Come, let's board the baby and underway!"

Shep's boat was moored to the side of the pier by a thin piece of rope. The ancient-looking craft bobbled in the water; a fifteen-foot bateau the likes of which had been used by Adirondack guides for generations. It was an amber-colored vessel with its hull ribs exposed. It looked like we were entering a giant fish that had been expertly gutted, but not deboned. There were two seats with old cushions on them to soften the experience. In the middle of the boat, Shep had placed his khaki knapsack next to the two weathered oars.

He jumped down into the boat as if he was walking down the street; calmly, with no hesitation, as if he had done it a thousand times before. He probably *had* done it at least that many times. Maybe more. I, on the other hand, tried to gingerly throw my duffel near his and watched it nearly skip off the seat and land into the drink. Luckily it hit the wall and didn't plunge into the abyss. I sat down on the edge of the dock and hung my legs off of it the same way Shep had earlier. I dangled my leg down, flicking my foot as it descended, trying to find some footing. Once I did, I slid down and the boat rocked feverishly. I grabbed the sides of the boat tight. "Is she gonna tip over," I asked, panicky.

Shep laughed. "She's truer than the bluest of skies. No need to gutwrench. Have a seat."

I stepped over the seat and placed my rear end on the red velvet cushion (which was older than dirt and didn't give as much support as I had anticipated). We waddled for a few more seconds before Shep undid the rope around the mooring and gave the dock a shove. We began to drift farther and farther away from the dock, gently rocking back and forth with the sturdiness and confidence of a newborn calf. He took his seat and looked about as excited as a military commander heading into battle. He threw me an oar, which I caught on the first try, surprisingly. He threw his off the portside bow and I did alternately on the starboard. As we paddled, the steel pier and the village of Caldwell left behind us. We were in open water.

As the world I knew slid back away from us, the water around us became increasingly calmer as we rowed. The water was a green-black color; just opaquely clear to a certain depth, but not clear enough to where you could see anything living in it. I was certain if you went down far enough to the depths fish would be flapping their tails and going about their business, but by the surface, nothing was going on. The water's color reminded me of the jar a painter would use when cleaning brushes; a conglomeration of many colors mixed to form a homogenized dead blackish green. I looked over the side to see if I could catch a reflection, but none showed. I didn't take the time to look fast enough. The lush green majesty of the northern woods surrounded us with nothing save a few shacks on the shoreline speckled the landscape.

When I was eight, I asked my parents to join the Boy Scouts. I begged and pleaded for what seemed to be days on end. Lost sleep on it. Got punished for it. Got scolded in front of the whole parish after Church one Sunday. After many scenes and many throes on their tender mercies, they finally gave in to my pleas and I was able to join. I attended precisely three meetings before I was pulled out because my parents couldn't afford the dues to keep me enrolled. I was never seen at a Boy Scout meeting after that ever again. I am sure that if I had by some miracle of God stayed in the club, I would have been much more prepared for this excursion with Shep. I paddled easily enough, trying not to break too much of a sweat as I rowed. It wasn't even one o'clock yet and I supposed things would get even hotter and more difficult as the afternoon wore on. I hadn't thought to fill a canteen with water, either.

"Hey Shep, " I asked. "Where exactly are you taking us?"

"Dunham's Bay," he said. "Further?"

"Do the words 'Moose's Walk' mean anything to you?"

He nodded yes. His nod was a knowing one. He didn't even need to speak the words. His nod told everything. "That's what gripped the fear lever. Knew it was coming all along. How'd you come across that name?"

I didn't know how to respond, so I told him the truth. "Oh, some-one just taped it to my door. Said that you'd understand."

He stopped rowing and turned around. He slammed down and walked over to me. "Open up the sound hole, partner," he said. "You better sweep out the miscues and notions of preconception. Someone is jagging you, son. They've got you riding the sleeping bull on some wacky troupe. If they are playin' a box game, then they know what's beyond on the eastern shore."

"Do you know how to get there," I asked, my patience waning.

"Yeah, that's the wave we're riding."

As it was just the two of us on that small boat, floating with not another living soul for miles, I thought I would try and get Shep engaged in a more modern, casual conversation. Perhaps I could break him of that speech pattern that he used. It wasn't bothering me per se, but I would have much preferred a normal conversation that didn't require so much thought.

"You a baseball fan, Shep?"

"Fan of baseball? Sure. Rounders modified."

I wasn't sure if he meant that baseball is a modified version of the game 'rounders' or if that was just another one of his malapropisms. "Who do you root for?"

"Grubs mostly. Sometimes worms if the stomach tells me to."

"No no no. What baseball team do you root for? I'm a Dodgers fan," I said. "Hate the Yankees." And still do.

Shep said nothing but continued to row. It was becoming quite apparent that my little experiment in conversational chit-chat had failed miserably. It was my fault. Why would an Adirondack guide know anything about baseball?

"Musial. I like Stan Musial," he said.

I nearly fell backward and into the drink.

*   *   *

After constantly rowing with the same motion for what seemed to be hours, my arms felt like they were just about to fall off. I stopped rowing. The army had done some work to get my tender rear end into shape, but I had been out of that stuff for almost two years. I hadn't had to climb any ladders or slog through a muddy river in a long time. I was hoping that both of those streaks would remain intact. We coasted on the water, with Shep doing most of the work. On occasion, he'd point out an animal or fish that would skirt by the boat. We'd seen a warbler fly over our heads in a crisscross pattern. We'd seen a rainbow trout flop up out of the water. But most of the time I didn't hear anything or see anything of any importance. We simply listened to the soft sloshing sound of the water against the hull of the bateau.

"Point yer eye up aways," he said. "Over'n the spot. See it?"

I looked past his hand to a small island that was not too far from the eastern shore of the lake. From where we were rowing it looked like a floating shrub; a densely forested dome riding the current of the lake. I told him I could see it. It had a foreboding look about it; I'm not going to lie. It looked like something out of Swiss Family Robinson or Robinson Crusoe or one of those Robinsons. It was still a ways off– no more than a dot on the horizon, and I wondered how long it would take for us to finally get there and make a camp.

"That's where we're takin' it down for the twilight."

I deduced that the island was where we were going to camp for the night. "How long do you think it will take us to get there?"

"2 minus a quarter on top of the mountain," he said.

I muttered under my breath, "Whatever the hell that means."

I reached over to my duffel and pulled out my moleskin notebook and pencil...and my bottle of Old Crow. I was able to gently balance the notebook on one knee while I unscrewed the cap off the bottle with my hands. The sun was baking us in the Springtime afternoon.

I took three, long, swigs and wiped the excess off my lips with my forearm. It burned. It felt like I was being burned from the inside out. I took two more mouthfuls and capped the bottle. A quarter of the was bottle gone in under a minute. I was right proud of myself. I returned to rowing. Those long strokes with the oar seemed to get longer and harder now. The muscles in my arms tightened and my fingers felt strange. The world was fading away from me and shimmering in the sun.

My tongue was dry. My forehead felt like it had been blown open with a shotgun. I was cold and warm at the same time. "Hey, Shep," I asked, feeling queasy. The bobbing of the small boat and swaying made my stomach tighten like a drum. Every wave that hit the boat sounded like a cymbal crash in a marching band in my temples. "Hey, hey Shep."

Shep turned around and looked at me. "Polluted, "he said. "God damn polluted."

In addition to my sickness, I had to pee so badly that my back was starting to ache. "I gotta take a leak. What should I do?"

"Drop trow and run the faucet over the barge!"

I stood up and all the blood rushed to my head, making me dizzy. I grabbed hold of the side of the boat and steadied myself. Shep was good enough to halt his rowing for a minute while I answered nature's call. I undid my fly and let loose a strong stream into the water. The ease in my abdomen came quick and my face broke out into a drunk's relieved smile. I opened my eyes to the shore where I saw a bull moose taking a casual stroll. The thing was a large, brown hulking mass of animal, with antlers that looked like Michelangelo carved them. It placed its head down and began to graze on some of the grass that grew near the shore. I'm not one for making up silly animal parables, but I could swear to God he was smiling at me.

*   *   *

"I write for the newspaper; I don't know if Herlihy told you that."

"Yup. He relayed the deets on that end."

"My mom always said I had a big mouth, I guess that's why I'm good at it."

"A mother's word is a two-ton brick. Didn't meet the lady. In th'early hours of life, I got kicked away. Never had a oppy to make the acqua-tnse."

"She left you? Your mother left you?"

"Yep. Left on the palette in a lumberyard. The trees'er all I log. Trees'er truth."

"Why did she leave you? Did you know your father?"

"No no no. Dunno the first or the last. A burden, I musta been. That's the fact, jack. With the jacks, they gave the learn of the land. Parlayed the know-how an' the go-to to make it 'round here. S'all old Shep knows. Don't know much. In the end, when the fin is raised, I ask the sky and the water to bestow an arc on me."

"So, you know trees? You learned from the lumberjacks?"

"Trees'er truth. Best scrib it. Trees'er truth."

"My story isn't as tragic as yours, I'm afraid. I am sorry you had to grow up in such a cold environment."

"Not my word! Not my word! The jacks are warm! Use the trees to make shelter. Use the trees to burn warmth and glow. Jacks taught of true and mystic. Know both."

"Mystic? What do you mean mystic?"

"Trees'er true. Ground is a secret keeper. Water is a vault. That's the world, son. A world entire breathes that the eye can't peep. It's here. Habitat- the woods."

Not much of what Shep said to me was making any sense back then. I'm not even sure it makes sense now. I decided to stop talking altogether because it was giving me more of a headache than I needed at the moment. I was becoming increasingly dehydrated and kept nipping at the Old Crow just to get some moisture on my tongue.

We passed a few smaller islets, which Shep was happy to point out. "Tea Island," he said. "Long Island." The daylight was beginning to fade as we paddled and paddled. Along the eastern shore, some animals could be seen going about their daily routine. For once, it seemed that we were the intruders on their property. A family of deer were sitting down to dinner. Two fat porcupines were cruising around for chicks in between the grass. A woodchuck lapped us in the water; perhaps jealous of the large, delicious wooden vessel we were sitting in.

The scene that surrounded us was an impressionist's painting; large swaths of greens with dollops of light reds and yellows surrounded us, with the glory of a fading azure blue as our canopy. The song of the birds was our soundtrack, coupled with the slight sloshing of the water against our small boat.

This serenity was suddenly and inexplicably broken by a chilling scream from our right in the wilderness. It was the most awful, painful scream I think I'd ever heard, including the time I'd spent in the military. The initial screech was ear-piercing and made my stomach churn. It was followed by three other less potent screams. It was the same female voice, all three screams. No birds flew. No fish were swimming around the boat. It seemed that everything, every bit of life around us had stopped. Life had gotten heavy and everything was weighing on us. We had both stopped rowing and the boat was momentarily at the mercy of the current. Neither of us moved. I held my breath and watched Shep for a clue what to do.

Shep snapped his head around and faced the eastern woods. His face was intense; his gaze seemed to go on for miles.

"Shep, what the hell was that?"

"That be the goal," he said.

Chapter Five

The small island where we camped for the night was at the mouth of a tributary that wound its crooked path into the messy, tangled wilderness. That small offshoot would be our road to Moose's Walk. The way the meandering water gently flowed out of the lake and into the wood, like the fine fading finishing streaks of an artist's brush, brought me to the depressing realization that the water would be navigable only part of the way. I made my peace with that right then and there but didn't have the guts to ask Shep about it.

I was correct in my first assumption; the island was thickly vegetated and most of the trees were of the tall variety, so tall you couldn't see the tops from the ground. They seemed to reach and grow from the earth and not stop until they hit the sky above. When we came ashore, we tugged our modest vessel up and onto the mucky brown silt, which was thick and chocolate-colored. I busied myself writing in my notebook about what had happened earlier in the day while Shep began to gather kindling for a fire. I waxed poetically on 'the American family's necessity to get back in touch with nature', 'how time had weathered old Shep to perfection like an old Hickory walking stick', and 'how anyone could do something as simple as pilot an Adirondack guide boat and be better for the experience'.

'Anyone who has ever craved to be among nature in its purest form deserves at least a week in the Adirondacks. It combines the thrill and excitement of a faraway adventure with the comfort of being here in your own country. I recommend the trip to any of you fathers out there who want to show your family a good time and get some exercise in the process.'

I conveniently omitted the part about the blood-chilling scream we had heard from within the deep bowels of the forest. After hearing it, I didn't mention it again, and neither did Shep.

As the remainder of the day waned, we found ourselves bathed in the glow of a campfire; trapped in the bubble of its light as the rest of the world fell into darkness. Shep opened his knapsack and pulled out unlabeled cans of sardines, bacon, and what looked like beef jerky. He placed everything neatly in front of him and then pulled out a battered blue coffee pot.

"Under this dark, the meal comes from tin," he said. "Tomorree, it springs from there," he completed his sentence by pointing outward towards the mainland, using a knife as a pointer quite forebodingly.

We ate our rations by the fire, which roared and illuminated the small area between the trees. The tastes didn't mix well, and I remember the briny nature of the sardines tasting strange with the smoky bacon. I picked at some pieces of fish that were lodged between my teeth and was able to experience the same juxtaposition of flavors all over again. Dinner at the Ritz, it wasn't. It was high time for a cocktail.

I leaned over to my duffel and brought out the bottle of Old Crow that I'd been nipping at the entire day. I remember feeling momentarily uncomfortable when I realized that I probably should've brought two bottles instead of one. I wasn't above the shame of asking Shep if he had anything in his knapsack that would be equivalent. I'd drank alone, and I'd drank with people. It was all the same time to me. But that was for another time. Right then, I had my bottle, and that was good enough.

I swigged at it and I saw Shep's face turn down in disappointment. "Yer in the manner of a babe," he said. "Suckin' from the teat! Forever at the nip!"

At his words, something deep within the recesses of my brain snapped. I swear to god I felt a tick in the back of my skull. My vision blurred and my fists became balled. "Now you listen. I don't comment on how you live your life, do I? Living like a damn vagrant in the woods." My words were chosen carefully and specifically. I wanted him to feel as badly as he had made me feel. "I go to work. I earn my damn living. What else is there?"

Shep shrugged his shoulders down. "Won't comment a foot on that. Book is closed."

There was an awkward silence and I continued to drink from the bottle. It was good to get that salty briny taste of sardines out of my mouth. I could feel the effect taking place. The heat from the fire was dehydrating me and the alcohol was ratcheting up at a breakneck pace. *'Who the hell was this bumpkin to tell me what to do? I earned my pay every week. I went to work like any other- maybe a little late here and there- but that's no offense. Besides, no one who ever really cared said anything to me about anything.'*

A rustle in the bushes behind us clutched our attention. It was quiet out there, beyond the orb of light thrown off by the fire. I sat up and Shep sat up too. Neither of us said anything, but we both attentively listened and tried to hear whatever it was again. A second rustle came, this time a little lower- a little farther away. I stood up and Shep shooed me to sit back down again. For me, that was strike two. In my logic, *'first, you tell me to put down the bottle, then you tell me to sit down?'*

Indignant, I stood up and yelled into the darkness. "I want you to come over here now." My voice echoed in the black. "Do you hear me? I want you to come and show yourself, God damn it! You think I'm afr..." Shep's wrinkled hand covered my mouth from behind. I was tempted to bite the sonofabitch's thumb right off. I shook myself loose from him and collected myself.

I turned around, and faced Shep... and...

*   *   *

The next thing I remember, and frankly I'm surprised I've remembered this much, I was lying flat on my back with my head propped under a bunched-up overcoat. The fire was roaring hot as ever, and my jaw was throbbing in pain and swollen. Across the fire and through the flames, I saw Shep watching me.

"It's about time you woke up," he said. "I thought you were going to sleep straight through the night."

I slid up against a fallen log. My mouth was filled with congealed blood. It felt like I had a mouth full of salty strawberry preserves. I spat it all over my shirt and both the liquid and clumps dripped into my lap. It looked like I had just thrown up raspberry jam all over myself. My jaw felt like it was dislodged.

"I've been watching you sleep for the past three hours. Your jaw is out of place; we'll need to get that back to where it's supposed to be before it sets the wrong way. Then you'll really be in trouble."

He walked over to me and opened my eyes wide with his thumbs. "You home," he said, lightly knocking on my forehead. "Sorry I had to hit you like that, but if we are going to continue on our mission, you're going to have to know your role. You were getting a little out of hand before. Now, if you'll allow me, I'm going to have to set your jaw back into place, so it doesn't heal crooked." He placed his two dirt-caked thumbs in my mouth, one on either side of my jaw, and applied pressure. I heard a pop deep within the recesses of my head, followed by a sharp, excruciating pain that I felt down into my groin, and more blood rushed down.

I did a trial run of an up-and-down motion of my jaw. It was still swollen as all hell, but at least it was in place now. "What...what was it?" My words were slow and choppy.

"What was what," he asked, calmly sitting down near the fire.

"That thing that we heard rustling in the brush. You know damn well what I was talking about."

He smiled. He cocked his head and spread his arms out as if he was mimicking a bird. "The trees are true. I told you that. But what can hide in the trees, isn't so true. The trees are a mask."

"What the hell are you even talking about?"

"There are things that run through these woods that you've never seen. There are things that hide in the dark, undercover. These are the things that can take a man and capture his very soul."

My head was doing figure eights and I just wanted to lie back down. Some twigs crunched under my legs as I got myself comfortable. My jaw was still in a lot of pain and I wanted a swig of my Old Crow to numb it. Not exactly Novocain, but it always did the trick. I reached over and tried to wrap my lips around the mouth of the bottle. I ended up spilling a little bit on my shirt because my lips couldn't close around it that much because of the swelling. In a moment that I was not particularly proud of, I opened my mouth as wide as I could and poured the whiskey down from three inches away. Once I had a nice mouthful, I closed and swallowed. Burning. That sweet burn that made me feel so right.

"I'm going to tell you what I know," Shep said. "I'm going to tell you about what goes on around here and what we're up against in finding your girlfriend."

"She's not my girlfriend," I interjected. "She's just a girl. I'm not even sure what her name is."

"That's neither here nor there, friend. If my theory is right, then she's out to do more harm than good. And you don't want her to be anywhere near you anyway."

"If you're going to spew some lonely hearts stuff about how women are the devil, you can just can it, alright? I've heard enough about that."

Shep smiled widely. "Your view is so small. It's like you're looking at the world through a thimble. It puzzles me how someone who can paint such broad strokes with words can have a worldview that is so miniscule." He snickered. "At least you *purport* that you paint broad strokes with your words."

I took another swig of whiskey and got myself comfortable. From that preface, I could tell this was going to take a while.

"Before we got here and took this place as our own, there were tribes of Huron's and Lenape's that made their life here. They hunted, fished, trapped, they're a deeply spiritual people. I'm one-quarter Lenape myself; that's how I got to know these tales. That's why I feel so at home in the woods. You called me a vagrant earlier, but I'm no vagrant, I promise. I'm in the house of a higher being when I'm out here. Can you hear it? Can't you see it? It's everywhere. There's beauty everywhere you look. When it gets light out tomorrow morning, make sure you take a good look around here at the higher man's handy work. My eye has been trained to look at these things and appreciate them. There's goodness around us. The trees are true, as the old folks like to say. Now, the place we're going to, the place they call 'Moose's Walk' is the exception out here. Legend has it that a moose was rooting around out there hundreds of years ago and somehow got possessed by this spirit. The people of the woods call it *The Wendigo*. A Huron hunter was out looking for a kill and came across this possessed moose. The hunter killed the moose and the spirit jumped bodies and inhabited the hunter. When the hunter returned to his family, he did not bring the slain moose. No. He was now instilled with a taste that no person should ever, ever have."

I remember being sick to my stomach listening to this.

"He killed his whole family. Slaughtered them." And then after a breathy pause: "Ate them." He stood up just then and began to pace the fire as he spoke. He looked like he had grown to be ten feet tall above me. "As time went on, other people got infected with this thing. The Wendigo. It jumped from body to body and person to person. Then, it had accrued so much strength that it began to take up multiple bodies at once. They craved the taste of flesh. Eventually, those who were Wendigo migrated out here to the woods where they could do their dirty deeds and not be seen by anyone. They were possessed, but not stupid. They've been out here...probably two hundred years now. There's a town too! Right there in the middle of the damn forest. It's overrun with growth and trees and brush and who knows what else, but it's there. I came across them as a boy and what I saw..." He broke down. His shoulders shrugged violently as tears overcame him. I stood up with the hopes of giving the man some consoling, but I lost my footing. I was on my back once again, looking at the stars through the trees. I had a pain in my tailbone to match my still-throbbing jaw.

"Me and a few friends had decided to emulate the 'jacks and took a camping trip up into the Eastern Woods. You know, like some kids put on their Sunday suits and pretend they're their dads going to the office. We had to be no more than twelve at the time. Stefan Rousseau's dad gave us an old yellowing map and a compass and sent us out on our way. We didn't take food or anything. It was supposed to be us getting to know the lay of the land. Kind of a crash course in survival, if you will. Anyways, on the third day, we came across this huge rock in the middle of the woods. This thing had to be nearly twenty feet high and ten feet wide. Behind it, we heard screaming and peeked our heads around. That's when we first saw them," he paused and swallowed loudly. "There were these horribly disfigured things walking in and around overgrown houses. They were snatching the screaming children like chickens. They plucked them from the ground and twisted their legs right off their tiny bodies. They were eating them. They were eating...they were eating the children." He wiped his nose. "Their clothes were just covered in blood." Shep broke and wiped some wetness from the corners of his eyes.

The alcohol-doused part of my brain tried to make connections to Sabrina. Guys are funny like that. If there's a woman involved, all roads of thought would inevitably lead back to the same place. And with Sabrina, there was a whole other interstate being built. Was she being hunted by Wendigo? Was she a Wendigo herself? Was she hunting me? Nothing made sense. All I had was a bevy of loose-fitting ideas that refused to meld together into a cohesive story. I was also drunk, so stringing anything together would have been a chore. I turned myself over on my stomach to try and save myself from choking on my own vomit should I have upchucked one more time.

"That's why my eyebrows raised extra high when you mentioned going in there. But you said this girl is in trouble, so..."

"I don't know if she's in trouble. She may have lured me out here as a trap for all I know. Like a fly to a damn spider."

Shep sat down next to me. There was a comfort in his grime that gave me a piece of mind when he sat that close to me. Normally I would have been completely opposed to having someone that filthy come that close, but with Shep, it was all right. He placed a hand on my knee. "If you thought there was real trouble out here, would you have asked me to take you here? Or do you know deep down that this girl is in real trouble and needs your help?"

My mind reverted to the night on the Steel Pier. "A man was standing on the dock the night I met her. He wore a long black overcoat and sunglasses, even though it was nighttime. I didn't get a good look at his face, but he called for her. He didn't seem pleased with her at all. Like she wasn't supposed to be there."

"Jealous lover," he asked.

"I already mulled that over and I don't think that's the case."

"Do you know so?"

"No. No, I don't. I guess you can file that along with the gut feeling that she was in trouble." I turned and looked out across the water that separated us from the mainland. It was stark black, not illuminated in the slightest. A low, dull humming of crickets was the only noise out in the darkness. "What's out there, Shep? What are we getting ourselves into?"

"There's bad stuff where we're going. Just a lot of bad stuff everywhere. Out there in the world evil gets diluted sometimes because there's enough good to quell it down. There's goodness out here too, don't get me wrong. But in that place, that Moose's Walk area, it's brimming with distilled evil, Frank. Pure. Bad stuff."

The way he was speaking soured my mood. I needed to ask him as bluntly as I could, "Can it be beaten? Has anyone ever confronted it?"

"We let the trees do their thing, Frank. They cover it. It doesn't exist. The trees are true. As far as I know, no one has ever tried. We just don't pay any attention to it. If you want to know the truth, I hadn't thought of it in years before you brought it up."

It was baffling how an entire community could be on the same page without ever verbalizing anything. They completely shut the light on bringing this thing to an end, and did so collectively. I guess in the end the mob rules.

"How long is it going to take us to get there tomorrow? And do we need anything? Should we have brought weapons or something?"

He shook his head. "It's not like we're in the movies here. There are no silver bullets or anything like that nonsense. You can leave that stuff with the Clark Gables and the John Barrymore's of the world."

"And Lon Cheney," I added.

"And Lon Cheney too, yes. I hate to break it to you but I'm not really sure there is a way to overcome it. It's been around so long and affected so many people that we've all given up on the cure. You've got to remember, we're," and I remember him pointing to himself and me, "not a very in-depth group. We do what we can to cope and survive."

My drunkenness had begun to rock me gently off to sleep. I can't recall any other words from Shep that night, but the ones he had told me stuck with me.

My dad used to have an expression 'I'm too tired to dream'. He'd usually say that to us after we had told him about an amusing or frightening dream. It's a good phrase- it made us all laugh. After years and years, I had picked it up along the way and used it quite a few times. Even in my older years, my dreams had become harder and harder to remember. But I tell you, that night on that small island, I remember every detail of the dream I had.

It's a cornfield, but there are no ears of corn on the stalks. It's hot. Hotter than hell. The only other time I can remember this kind of heat was the day after we bombed Dresden and we had to do a sweep through to make sure we got everyone. But this sure as hell wasn't Dresden; it looked like Nebraska. I'm holding a military-issue helmet in my hands, and I'm trying to catch rainwater that is tinkling down from the gray sky above. There was no color to anything. It looked like everything around me was made of paper mache. I pushed through the brush, snapping the stalks of dead corn in half as I barged through this field. I hear voices in a clearing, but of course, I can't hear what they are saying. I'm following the sound of their voices. I get close enough to see that there is a clearing in the middle of the cornfield. Whoever is speaking is having some sort of chat in the clearing. I get close enough to peer through, without making myself visible. It is finally revealed to be a family of four, seated at a dinner table; father, mother, son, daughter. The father is wearing a suit, which looks to be gray, but I really can't tell because everything is devoid of color. The mother has a housedress on. The kids are swinging their legs off the seats. As I progress closer, I notice they are all wearing masks. Ornate, horrible masks. The masks are all appropriate for their ages and family roles. The father's had large eyes with a wide grin. The kids were wearing the comedy/tragedy masks that they used on the pamphlet of every school play this side of Albuquerque. The mother's face was facing away from me, so I couldn't see what her mask looked like. I crept a little closer to where I could see what was on their table. In the center of the table was a dead, cooked, child on a silver platter. It looked to be no more than three years old. It was laid on its back with the arms and legs hog-tied. Around it, halved potatoes and onions dressed it as if it were a turkey. I was horrified and curious at the same time. All at once, the barren corn stalks began to fall around me like toppling dominoes. And finally, I was exposed- no longer under the cover of the corn stalks. And there was a new kicker too, my clothes had disappeared, and I was completely naked. My testicles shrunk back into my body, and I covered my mid-section with cupped hands. There was nothing to protect or hide against. I was naked. I felt like Adam after the incident. The father stood up at the table and slowly turned to look at me. That horrible, disfigured mask he wore sent bubbling ripples of gooseflesh against my naked skin. In his hands, he held a bottle of some kind. I couldn't make out the label. He continued to creep towards me and I could not make myself move. I felt if I moved, I'd be further exposed. I tried like mad to somehow wake myself, but it was pointless. He walked up to me, with his horrible face, and placed his exaggerated nose against mine. He poured the contents of the bottle he held over my head and it felt like a freezing cold shower. I then turned and

snapped awake to find Shep standing over me pouring water on my forehead. My first instinct was to try and catch my breath, which was proving harder and harder to accomplish. I took large breaths of air to regulate things. Once I got my breathing to a place that didn't feel like a heart attack was imminent, I stood up. As I stood and became more awake I felt the crushing blow of a headache grip my temples.

"Good morning, scout," he said.

Chapter Six

We snapped off bite-sized hunks of venison jerky for breakfast that morning, which wasn't the best choice for someone recovering from a dislocated jaw. With each tug, after I bit into what felt like one of my father's old belts, small pains traveled back through my gums and into the back of my skull. It was a different way to fuel up for a long day, to be sure. Bacon and eggs, it was not. I chomped down on the leathery morsels and tugged them, thinking my molars were going to get ripped clean out of my head. With each grinding chew, I tasted the spices Shep had used. Salt. A smoky favoring. Peppercorns began to get lodged between my teeth and I had to use the side of my pinky nail to fish them out.

After we finished our petrified shards of deer flesh, Shep prepped the bateau for the launch that would take us up the tributary, deep into the forest, and finally over to see what was happening at Moose's Walk. I continued to work on my chronicle; bullshitting my way through endless flowery sentences of 'moonlit inlets' and 'noble creatures of the forest.' I decided not to tell him about the dream.

"Are you transcribing The Bible over there," Shep asked as my pencil rocked furiously over the beige pages. I could have been. I had the impression that the lines I wrote in that book would never see the light of day anyway. "We've got miles to make today, my friend. And they're not easy, either. I'm not entirely sure what we're going to come across in there."

His uncertainty made my stomach drop a few inches and my feet tingle. It was like seeing your father afraid. I walked over to the shore-line that faced the tributary where we were going to enter. The water between the two areas was as smooth as glass that morning with the tiniest few ripples conducting the orchestra of the lake. I could see into the woods on either side and nothing looked out of the ordinary. It was woods. It was beautiful just the same, but it was still only woods. The water that ran east into the tributary looked choppier than the calm serene waters of the lake. We were leaving safer waters behind us.

"Shep," I yelled. "Shep come here, I want to ask you something."

He looked up from fastening his bag to the underside of his seat and came to me. "What's up?"

"How far up is this river navigable? I guess I'm asking if we're going to have to lug this boat on land eventually?"

His face exploded in a grin. "Let's get one thing straight," he said. "Waterways don't work like Main Streets in towns. It's not like you can hop on a bus at the corner of Aviation and 9 and take it into Saratoga. It doesn't work that way, I'm sorry to say. So yeah, you're going to have to do your fair share of humping on this trip."

"Would it be bad to say 'that's what I was afraid of'?"

"It would be what I was expecting you to say, Frank."

*   *   *

We departed the small island and steered the wobbly guide boat into the densely vegetated forest that hugged the river. The burning orb above us, which had been omnipresent the previous day, was now hidden behind a dark green veil of leaves clustered in the treetops above. I dipped my oar into the water and began to paddle. It was tougher than the calm waters that we'd been paddling on the lake. This water was moving quickly, and we were fighting against it. A part of me thought it would be great. My muscles would look fantastic when this was over and done with. '*If only my father could see me now,*' I thought. '*You should have sprung the twenty-five bucks to have me keep it up with the Scouts. It would have been worth the effort.*'

The vegetation on both sides of the river was dense, making it impossible to see very far into the surrounding wilderness. It was like two great curtains had been drawn on either side of us, and we were alone: God's lone creations. I thought I had seen figures of shadows running through the brush, but that wasn't the case. At least I kept telling myself that.

"Hey look over there, Frank. Quick or you'll miss it."

I turned my attention to the right shore of the river. On the shore stood one of the largest birds I'd ever seen gnawing ceaselessly at the carcass of, what I presumed was at one time, an animal. The bird's head was so quick and frantic in its movements that it looked like the needle on a sewing machine. It bobbed up and down, occasionally taking a reprise to swallow what it had chewed. The bird's body was an ugly brown color that melded into the forest behind it. The only way we were able to see it was by looking at the thing's sickly pink head. It wasn't a vibrant red; it was pale and looked like an undercooked piece of steak.

"He sure looks like he's hungry over there," I said, half-horrified.

"That's your run-of-the-mill turkey vulture. There must be millions of them out here. They're good hunters. I wouldn't want to be on the other end of that beak if you know what I mean. That thing's mouth is like a hacksaw. Cuts through anything."

The bird tugged at the insides of the dead animal, pulling out strands of intestine one by one. It would stop now and then, seemingly to admire the kill, as an artist would do when taking stock in the progress of a painting. I had lived in Northern New York since birth, so I guess I shouldn't have been all that shocked by this. My mind wandered for a moment and the dead animal turned into a human head. The bird pecked at the eyes and pulled at the lifeless tongue. I got a sympathy pain on the tip of my tongue, and I turned my attention away from the bird.

"We're going to have to hunt this afternoon, Frank," Shep said, only adding to the unpleasantness. "I'm hoping your stomach has an iron constitution."

It most certainly did not. But I had a secret weapon that would dull my perception to make things a little more bearable. I leaned forward, pulled the Old Crow out, and took two long swigs. I had killed three-quarters of the bottle and that worried me. I slid the bottle back into my bag quietly.

"What are we going to hunt," I asked.

"I don't know yet; we have to see what we see first. This isn't the Howard Johnson's out here. We'll have to forage a little, follow clues, go down trails."

"And what if we don't find anything?"

"If you're hungry enough, you'll find something."

I was hungry.

*   *   *

We veered the bateau onto the riverbank, and let the mud bring us to a halt. I jerked forward and almost came clean off the seat. I had been sneaking sips of whiskey all day and had kept a good hazy buzz. The Old Crow had done the trick, but it was playing havoc with my equilibrium. I stood up and almost lost my balance. My movements became more deliberate, like a cat's paw falls on a sheet of ice. Ahead of me Shep was already out of the boat and shaking his head in disapproval.

"I thought you weren't going to drink that stuff anymore while we were out here."

The anger welled up in me again, like lava cresting inside a volcano, but I was able to tamp it back down. I was too hungry to have this guy get mad at me. He was going to be the patsy to get me food. The hunter. The gatherer. I ignored him. I was getting well adept at that.

Shep began to survey the area with his hands on his hips and his back bent forward. He looked at the ground and at some broken tree branches. He ran his fingers into the dirt where he stood and placed them to his nose for a whiff. He looked so strange when he moved. The movements he made were…unnatural. I'd never seen a person walk like that. He looked like a bird; a crane or a bird of prey. For a moment his face turned into that of the turkey vulture we'd seen earlier. There was a kindred spirit about those who forage, I guess. They all looked alike.

"It was by here not too long ago," he said. "These branches in between these brambles are still wet, which means they haven't been snapped for very long. Come over here and feel this," he beckoned to me.

I clumsily walked over the put my hand out. I felt the cool insides of the broken branches. It almost felt like wet skin. My mind could have immediately made that association. "What the hell does that mean?"

"It means the boar that was here a while ago is probably still close."

I wanted no part of this. I didn't want to see it killed. I just wanted it sliced on my plate over the fire. That's all. "Do you mind if I sit this one out, Shep? I'm not used to this kind of thing, you know."

"Jesus H. Christ, Frank will you knock it off? Please? If you're planning on seeing some stuff later on, well, you better nut up and knock off this sissy crap."

"Please stop yelling at me. I'm not your son."

"All right. All right. Do whatever the hell you want, Frank. But when you're face to face with the Devil himself and you don't know what to do, and you're shitting in your britches, don't come looking for me."

"Take me home, Shep. I don't want to be here anymore. I just want to go home."

"You know what? No, I'm not taking you home. What the hell is the matter with you, anyway? You've got no insides? All you've got is blubbering skin with nothing behind it. I don't even know how you can stand up straight, to be honest with you. Is this how you want to be remembered? Is that how you're going to live with yourself for the rest of your life? Sometimes you have to just dig deeper into the well and pull some stuff up. This is serious out here. This is a gut check for me too, Frank. I've been steering clear of all this stuff for years. And I'm still *still* not convinced that I'm doing the right thing here. So don't think I've come to any epiphanies or grand visions, because it's not true. To be honest, for the first time in a long time, I have no idea what the hell I'm doing." He paused. "What I do know is: I *know* I'm hungry."

I walked away from him and sat back in the boat with tears streaming down my cheeks. I hunched over and began to sob. I knotted my fingers as if in prayer and held them up to my mouth to mute my cries. I was in the middle of the woods, drunk, about to watch an animal get slaughtered and gutted and come face to face with an evil that even a seasoned veteran wasn't sure could be beaten. In a move of sheer desperation and pity, I reached into the bag and pulled the bottle out.

When I looked up I saw Shep was there next to me. He placed a hand on my shoulder. "It's going to be okay," he said. "Everything is going to be okay. We're in this together. Look, I'm sorry. It's a hell of a lot better than being at it alone."

I welled up again with more tears. I couldn't remember the last time I had cried that much or that hard for that matter. My body convulsed like I was having an epileptic fit. I had constructed a fortress around the more tender parts of my being, and the remaining pillars of the redoubt were held together with a constitution that was barely fortified with any character mortar. The walls crumbled and in a brilliant flash of memory, vivid shocks of broken steps lashed across my thoughts like a striking lightning bolt. I'd been tested time and time again on every avenue that a person could be challenged, in war, in family, in love. I'd become numb to such things or forced myself to become numb. While the self-anesthetizing was somewhat of a fun adventure, the wheels had begun to falter. Engaged in the primeval, I broke. There were no bombers out here. No deadlines. No sergeants calling me 'tubby fat ass'. No headlines. Nothing like that. Out here you only existed.

"If you want, I'll go find the boar. You just stay here and…I don't know what."

As he turned to leave, shame sprouted in me and blossomed like fiery red tulips. I hopped out of the boat, my head still spinning like a top. I placed my hand on his shoulder. "I'm coming with you," I said. "Let's get going before I snap back to my senses."

We then went off to find the wild boar.

*   *   *

Our footsteps were crunchy as we stalked through the forest in search of our target. I stood twenty feet away from Shep, but my eyes were locked on his every step. I even tried to mimic his movements to a degree. His arms were bent, and his back was arched forward. His head was on a constant swivel. He was so utterly confident in everything he did. Every row of his oar, every footfall, every movement was done as if rehearsed and he was performing. I was beginning to lose my buzz and the slight headache I was so often used to returned in full force.

I was getting dehydrated and would have sold my arms for a drink of water.

"Shep. Can I take a swig of your canteen?"

"It's plain water," he said. "I hope you're okay with that."

I closed the distance between us and snatched the canteen from him. The cool, refreshing water soaked me from my tongue practically to my soul. I looked skyward, through the veil of tree leaves and I felt momentarily refreshed. As I brought my head down, I happened to catch something in my peripheral that stole my attention. Among the deep earthy tones of brown, green, and orange that composed the color palette of the forest a swath of beige stuck out in a heap a few yards from where we stood.

Initially it appeared that someone had thrown the discarded pieces of a broken mannequin among the fallen logs and rotting leaves. I ran over to Shep, slapped his arm, and motioned for him to look over to the left.

Rhythmic thuds began to bang in my chest as if a demon was beckoning release. Then the smell hit my nose and I got nauseous. There's no way to properly describe a decomposing body unless you've smelled one before. It was a rotting smell; a sweetly bitter rotting smell. We crept towards it, our hands instinctively over our mouths, as if that would make any sort of difference. I stopped, unable to make my feet inch any closer. I tried to get a glimpse from where I stood, but I wasn't close enough to get a look. There was a part of me that wanted to see it. I wanted to look at it.

I gingerly placed one foot in front of the other and walked with thoughtful steps over to Shep who was looking down on it. He then covered his eyes, with his mouth remaining agape. He had lost the composure battle, and it didn't matter. When I looked down, I understood why.

It was a woman. Well, at one time it was. Her head was intact, but everything else was torn open like a broken mason jar of raspberry jam. The area from her clavicles to her groin was just...missing. Parts of her thighs were gone too. Most of her organs were still there, but in some spots, you could see clear back to her spinal cord. Her face. God, her face. She looked like she was asleep. She looked like she was asleep in the most comfortable bed ever made. To pile on the weighted emotional albatross, something else hit me. Her face. I knew who she was. I *knew who she was*!

"Shep! This...this is Becky Geering. This is BECKY FUCKING GEERING! I went to high school with her. She works at the Royal Pines Lodge as a housekeeper. She...she went missing a week ago, but we..."

Becky still lived with her folks, so visions of her parents huddled around a telephone with petrified tones in their voices speaking to the local police immediately came to mind. I could see the black phone receiver shaking in their hands as they gave a shaky-voiced description to the police. They would lie awake for many nights in the hope that there would be a rap at the door and a warm hug not too far behind. She wouldn't show up for her shift at the Royal Pines and her manager would throw a tantrum about her not showing up on time. Her well-being wouldn't be a priority. But then the sobering news of her disappearance would wash over everyone in her life and they'd be faced with the grim task of reassigning her jobs and going through her personal belongings. They didn't 'belong' to anyone anymore. The whole ordeal only further depressed me and made my skin crawl. Every person when they die means something to someone.

Both Shep and I seemed to be captivated by the serenity of her face. When they say 'at peace' they mean it. And then it all became clear. It was like looking through a fog to finally see the shadowy truth on the other side of the room. Years and years blew by my mind in an instant. Other people like me refer to a thing like this as a 'moment of clarity.' But it was more than clear. It was borderline surreal. Shep had said everyone in the area had turned their heads when someone went missing and ignored it. Sometimes you don't realize you're part of a crowd until someone takes a wider picture.

"This is the route they take when disposing bodies into the lake," Shep explained. "They load them up on trucks or wagons, take them down the river here, to the lake, where they dump them in the water."

We tell our secrets to the mountain and wash our sins in the water. Once it's in the water, it's washed and buried.

"Wouldn't the bodies start to pile up after a while? You said they've been doing this for years?"

"That spot where we began, near the mouth of the river, is the deepest part of the lake. Three miles down to the bottom. Now you tell me, you know how many eaten corpses it would take to reach the surface? The lake holds its secrets. That's for sure."

"What should we do," I asked.

"What do you want to do? Sounds like you've got something in mind."

"We should bury her. It's a sin to leave her out here like this. She, she didn't deserve this. Nobody deserves this. She, she needs to be put in the ground. We can't leave her."

"If that's what you want," he said. "I'll run and get a trowel."

And so he did. With a modest trowel, we were able to dutifully work in scratching out a modest, if not shallow, grave for poor Becky. The ground was soft, thank God. A more experienced woodsman would've known that the ground was ripe to be moved because it had just thawed. I just thought we were lucky. And I still think we were. As we worked, I ached for a drink of Old Crow. But the thirst I had for that sweet burn didn't stop my resolve. I continued to move the dirt in hopes of giving this girl a final resting place out of the elements. After we completed the job, I promised myself I would go and indulge myself. We dug close to her, right next to her as a matter of fact, so we wouldn't have to move her far. She was far away from where she took her last breath, and it wouldn't be right to move her any further. When the hole was deep enough, we gently pushed her sideways into the hole and she fell in like a stiff piece of wood. Face down. Unclothed. I knelt to try and turn her over, but Shep grabbed my shoulder and shook his head. It didn't matter.

We covered her up. I crossed myself.

*   *   *

I remember going back to the bateau fleet of foot, hopping over fallen logs, and nearly breaking my rear a few times. In the forest, one misstep and you've got a broken ankle in two seconds flat. I hopped into the boat like a pro and scrambled for the bottle. I opened it and oh boy did it send me over the moon. Three big gulps later I was wiping my mouth. I always made sure to keep a keen eye on how much was left. This was going to have to last me a while, I supposed.

I had time to think, which has always been a problem for me. It would be a while before Shep would return with something to put in our stomachs and I had to busy myself in the meantime. I tried laying myself out flat and possibly catching a nap, but that didn't work. It crossed my mind to maybe strip nude and wash myself in the water, but I didn't want to take the risk of being wholly exposed. I stood. I sat. I walked a bit. I sat a bit. I tried to write, but I didn't feel like doing that either. I sat on a small fallen tree and scanned the landscape left and right. Everything was so quiet and solemn. The scene was funereal like I was sitting at a wake. I guess in a way I was.

The front of my forehead began to numb, and I knew the Old Crow was doing its job. Alcohol was always good for kicking up the dust on forgotten ideas and fears. Sitting in the midst of the forest I remembered how my brother-in-law Bruce had always said he wanted to take me hunting. This was before everything went down in Schenectady. Bruce was a big man. He worked at a paper mill down in Troy as one of the foremen. His chest must've been four feet wide at the shoulders. He took good care of Jane and that's all that mattered. His temper was hot, but then again, most guys I knew were known to blow their lids now and then. He'd wake up at 3:45 in the morning on days he was hunting. I'd be asleep on the couch as he was getting the car loaded up. When he opened the front door, I could feel the chill from outside. And I was thankful to be warm under blankets. I said he must've been goddamned crazy to go out that early in that kind of cold weather. But before things went sour between us, he'd always ask. He'd always give me the option to tag along. Sometimes I wish I would have gone with him on those trips. It might've made things turn out differently. Then again, things might've ended up just the same. The point is, he always made a point to *ask* and that's what made me feel good. He knew as well as anyone that I was going to say no to it. But that didn't deter him. I always got asked. And at that moment, on that log, I felt the most shame that I'd felt in my whole life. I shed some quiet tears, the sort of tears you shed while in quiet contemplation on a memory trip when alone.

I saw some movement to the left and I tried to focus on whatever it was that was coming towards me. Didn't take long before Shep's unmistakable mug came slowly into focus. I shivered in relief. He appeared to be dragging something behind him. It was an animal of some kind- right then I couldn't tell what it was. Shep's face was neither exuberant nor angry or triumphant nor defeated. His face was blank.

He came closer and saw me. "I got a small deer for us," he said.

Our lunch that afternoon was venison.

"Tough little guy. Took two shots from the .38 to take him down. Should be tender, though." He had reached me. "To dress this is going to take me a while. It may be getting dark by the time we're done. If that's the case, we're going to have to just stay here for the night and get going first thing in the morning. It's not the way I had planned it, but we don't have much choice at this point. I didn't plan on burying anyone on this trip."

I knew I was going to need some time to sober up as well. "Let's stay here regardless," I said. No point in rushing through our late lunch/dinner. Besides, I want to hear more of your stories, Shep. They fascinate me."

"Oh they do, do they?" He dropped the deer. "Why don't you go sleep and sober up? I'll call you when dinner's ready."

I did.

Chapter Seven

"That was the best venison I've ever had. My stomach is just about to burst wide open. How did you get it to taste like that? I mean, I've tried it before- like I said earlier my brother-in-law used to go hunting up on Tupper Lake. But that was the first time I ever enjoyed a deer like that."

I felt pregnant. I had woken to the intoxicating smell of grilling venison, and it seduced me over to the fire where Shep was standing watch over it. We then gorged on the most tender venison meat I'd ever had. The ones that Bruce would bring home were very gamey and a little tough, like trying to eat a piece of shoe leather or that jerky Shep had given us earlier. I can clearly remember my sister going to Forsythe's dairy in Schenectady to pick up three quarts of buttermilk to soak the venison steaks in. It was a rumor that doing such a thing would pull the gaminess out of it, but it never really worked but to ruin perfectly good buttermilk. But the steaks Shep grilled for us that day were some of the best cuts I'd ever had. Our modest knives slid right through the meat with very little hesitation. Shep looked full and satisfied too. To further enhance our evening, I pulled my bottle from its snug home, untwisted the cap, and downed four large, good mouthfuls. I winced a bit and put the lid back on. Shep rolled over and wasn't facing me anymore. His body was positioned with his back to the fire, and to me. It was becoming crystal clear that he didn't approve of my little coping mechanism. And who was he to judge me? 'May he who is without sin' as they used to say. I didn't care what he thought of me or what he thought of my life choices. If everything worked out in the end, I couldn't give a good goddamn. I already had a father once.

I was reclined against a log and watched the fire dance its lonely rumba before us as nighttime had come.

Shep turned himself around quickly, as if startled, and said, "What's it going to take, Frank?"

"What do you mean?"

"For you to give up the goddamn booze?"

"You don't get it, Shep. You just don't get it. I don't have a problem. I get up, I go to work, don't I?"

"You suck on that thing like it's your mama's teat. You don't even realize what you're doing, I bet."

"Listen, unless you plan on getting into a real dicey situation here, I suggest you let it go and be done with it."

"No, Frank, I'm not going to let it go. You need me to slug you in the face again? I'll do it. You're a young man, Frank..."

"I'm not that young, Shep. Don't even give me that. I'm 34- that's not exactly spring chicken material."

"Oh, so then it's fine to drink yourself into oblivion every night."

"I function."

"Oh, so it's only about functioning then? Well fine, you function. Barely. Herlihy told me about your nonsense of coming in late and carousing with seedy people until all hours of the night. What the hell kind of a legacy do you expect to leave?"

"Legacy? That's some bullshit Indian nonsense. Legacy? I've got no legacy, Shep. I'm an island in the stream, and I'm happy to be perched on it. Whenever I reach my hand out it gets bit."

"That's a horrible way to live, Frank. Horrible. And do you want to know something else? I think you're a liar, too."

"Now you're going to call me a liar? Great. Just great Shep."

"You are so wrapped up in your ball of misery that you forgot what the sun looks like. That's a shame."

"I don't need to sit here and listen to your nonsense Shep! I've had enough."

"You just sit there, and you listen to me! And..."

"HEY HEY HEY HEY." This shout from a disembodied voice; followed by the sound of rapid crunching leaves. I stood up and grabbed a tree branch that I was preparing to use as a walking stick. I braced for an attack and Shep did the same. He grabbed his .38 that was next to him and drew it toward the direction of the voice. Through the veil of the firelight, we could make out the silhouette of a figure walking towards us. It was a man.

"Please, I see your gun there. Don't shoot! I mean no harm, honest to God. Please. I'm desperate for help."

Shep and I exchanged glances and we put our weapons to our sides. As the man came closer his attributes became more and more in focus. He was a younger man, younger than I was at the time anyway. God, he was skinny. His body was built like a crane or a matchstick man. His very slender figure was dressed in a white suit- or what was white at one time. The suit was ripped in places (one of the pant legs was missing), and his hair was a disheveled mess of brown locks that looked to have been greased in place at one time. That was no longer the case. His suit jacket had large red splotches on the sleeves and the cuffs were jagged and ragged. I remember thinking he looked like a newborn chick that had hatched himself into a human's clothes.

"What's your story, stranger," Shep asked, suspiciously.

"I was kidnapped," he said, now standing before us and before the roaring fire. "I was kidnapped, and I escaped. Praise the Lord Jesus Christ I escaped!"

"Kidnapped? By who," I asked. "What happened?"

"I'll be glad to tell you, gentlemen," he said wiping his brow. "But I have to ask you something first. If you please have a canteen or jug of water I would sip. My mouth is dryer than a used-up well and I can hardly talk. I've been running through the darkness all night and I overheard your yelling and that's what brought me here. That and the Good Lord. Praise Jesus Christ."

Shep quickly ran to his satchel and provided our nameless stranger with some water. The man gingerly raised the canteen to his mouth and tried with all his power not to let his lips touch the spout. He hovered it above his face and let the cool water pool into his gaped mouth. He looked like a bass waiting to be snagged by a fisherman's hook.

After taking four or five good glugs the man wiped the sides of his mouth on his sleeve and sat down on the log. He placed his head in his hands and massaged his temples like a baker prepping dough. Thin streams of tears rolling down his face were shined and reflected in the campfire glow. He quietly sobbed for a moment or two and Shep and I said nothing. I shrugged at him, he shrugged at me. I leaned into the weeping man and placed my hand on his shoulder, which made him jump back, startled.

"What the hell happened to you," I asked. "Would you like some bourbon? I have a little to spare."

"I'm sorry," he said. "I don't imbibe that which is not the blood of Christ." He sniveled. "Thank you though."

I felt Shep's disapproving glance burning char marks in my cheeks. But my attention was fixed squarely on our newly found disheveled friend. "What's your name? Where do you come from?"

"My name is Reverend Clarence Hollenbeck. I'm not from here. I'm from downstate a bit. Southeast of Albany. I come from a town called Olive Hills."

"I know Olive Hills," I said. "That's east of Hillsdale, isn't it?"

"Yes, yes, it is."

"I had relatives in Schenectady, and we would sometimes go into Hudson for the poultry auction."

"Yes, well I am the sitting reverend at the First Methodist Church of Olive Hills. I came here on a mission to spread the word of our Lord and Savior Jesus Christ."

"That's nice. How did you end up in the middle of the woods," I asked.

"In due time," he said. "In due time. Please, you'll have to allow me just a little bit to catch my bearings. You have no idea what I've just seen and been through."

My insides were turning into an impatient aspic. I could sense pieces of the puzzle snapping together and the arrow they formed pointed right to Sabrina and that mystery man. I began to feel faint, so I sat down on the ground with my legs crossed. It wasn't the most comfortable way to sit, and I knew soon enough my legs would go numb, but I needed to sit down for this story. I wanted to be as close to this man, Clarence, as I possibly could. I didn't want to miss an inch of his story.

While he unraveled his yarn, Shep began to forage around the campsite for bits of broken branches and dried wood to stoke the fire. He was good at that and always seemed to return with an armful to keep the fire burning almost through until morning. It seemed that every move he made was done with extreme deliberation. He was always surveying- looking left and right, never marrying anything too quickly. To be an expert on the wilderness, you had to be able to keep your judgment in a state of constant flux.

He returned and plopped a large pile of wood next to his fire. "That should take us through until morning."

The shaken Reverend was no longer panting, and it appeared he had regained the composure he was hoping to lasso. "I'll tell you fellows it's a god-great miracle I ran into you like that. If I hadn't, I don't know where I'd be right now. With no sun I'd have no direction. With no water, I would surely die. God Bless the both of you for being here." He spoke with that reverential passion that only preachers can give. His cadence was calming, and his words measured to be perfectly humble, yet inspiring. I hadn't been in a house of God in many years, but his voice brought me back to the sermons and services of my youth.

"I came to Caldwell to be a guest speaker at the Methodist Church on Montcalm Street. I'm not sure if either of you two fellows knows Reverend Ballast over there, but he reached out to me and asked if I'd like to come up and give a series of talks on the Parables. The reverend and I have a few close associates; that's how he found me. After corresponding for a few months- a letter here, a phone call there- I agreed to put together a series of talks that he felt would interest his congregation. So, I showed up here about a week ago. I gave my first talk two days ago and it went swimmingly. The people were engaged, they had great questions, and Reverend Ballast was pleased. Every-thing was a rousing success. After the sermon, as the congregation passed me by, there was one person who remained near the entrance. It was a woman who stood there, staring at the ground. She looked very nervous, almost out of place, standing there by herself, so I decided to go over and introduce myself. She engaged me in a conversation finally."

I slid forward, and my stomach began to churn and ache.

"She said her child was very ill. Very ill. She asked if I would come to their house and possibly say a prayer for him. Beseech the goodwill of Our Lord and Savior Jesus Christ for him. Of course, I agreed. So, I got into her car and we were on our way. I remember her being very quiet on that car ride. I tried several times to strike up a conversation, but she wouldn't speak. She just kept her eyes on the road and didn't say a word. I've been around the grief-stricken before and I know their temperaments can be a bit odd. But there was something wrong. I knew it immediately. As we got farther and farther from the main road, through small trails and unpaved gravel roads, I began to get panicked. I politely asked, 'How much further the house was,' and she began to giggle. I came to the horrible realization that I was in trouble. If there was any remaining doubt left in my mind, it was put to rest. Something was going to happen to me, and only the Lord and Savior Jesus Christ would be able to save me. When you are in that sort of situation, the mind can run as wild as the wind."

I interrupted, "Excuse me, Reverend. Can you describe the young lady before you go any further?"

He seemed to think my mind was elsewhere. "I'm not sure I like the sound of your tone, but sure. About twenty-five years old. Curly brown hair. Slender figure. She was wearing a tan overcoat or raincoat."

"Did you catch her name by any chance," I said, with my heart perfectly lodged behind my tonsils.

"Well, that's just it. I'm not sure what her name is. She told me her name was Molly, but as the story goes on, you'll see why I'm not so sure about that."

"I'm sorry, go on."

"As I was saying, she veered off the main road and onto an unpaved dirt path that led up into the woods. It looked like the head of a trail that hunters would use. Anyway, she drove up this windy dirt road for what seemed to be ten or fifteen minutes. Not saying a word." When the Reverend spoke, he gestured with his hands to make his points seem more lucid. He had perfected this craft behind a pulpit, no doubt. "I had given up on trying to make conversation and thought about a way to make a possible escape. Nothing short of opening the car door and flinging myself out of it would do. She was going a decent speed for being off-road in the middle of the forest. But before I could take those thoughts any further, I noticed something ahead of us. It was a house. And across from it was another house. And as we gradually got a little closer it became clear that there were many houses. Eight or nine at least. All of them seemed to be overgrown with weeds and most of them were covered with leaves. They looked abandoned. It looked like someone took a regular suburban street and placed it in the middle of the forest. I was overcome with wonder at this. I'd seen abandoned buildings before, who hasn't? But this was an anomaly the likes of which I had never seen. The place looked like the set of a movie or something fantastic. I saw no one outside the decrepit homes as we rolled down the dirt road. However, and this is the queer part, I swear I saw figures rustling *inside* those abandoned houses. A figure moved across the window here, a shade flashed by a doorframe there. It was all very unsettling. At this point, the car had slowed to a gentle roll and I thought this would be my time to make a run for it. So, I slid my index finger under the handle and began to pull it out towards me. But I extended it as far as it would go, and it didn't unlatch. I was trapped, you see. Like an animal."

He stopped his story and crossed himself. He placed his hands together and began to mumble an inaudible prayer with his eyes shut and his mouth reciting.

"Excus...," I began to say, and Shep slapped my arm with the back of his hand.

Shep came in close and whispered in my ear, "Don't you know not to bother a holy man when he's in the middle of praying? Have a little respect, will you please?"

The Reverend dropped his hands and continued his story. "I'm sorry, what happened next was so awful, so godless, that I felt the need to beseech the help of Our Lord and Savior, Jesus Christ, to guide me through retelling it." A Pause. "The car finally stopped in the center of this arrangement of overgrown houses. They looked to be old homes. Most of them were wooden structures with peeling red paint and slouching roofs and some of them had front facades with ancient crumbling stonework. One of the homes was barely visible due to the number of green vines that had grown over it. It looked like it was being eaten by the vegetation. Most of the windows that could be seen were broken. The front steps were overrun with ivy and weeds. Molly got out of the car, walked around the front of it, around to my side, and let me out. I should've run right there. But with all those feelings of dread, all those feelings that something wasn't right, I still couldn't bring myself to run away from someone who potentially needed my help. It's just the duty. I was then violently seized from behind by someone I did not see, or hear. They had my head locked between their chest and forearm and dragged me away. I tried wedging my hands to push his bulbous arms back, but he was too strong. It was a man, I can tell you that much. He reeked of motor oil and sweat and pulled me backward and further backward. As I got dragged away I saw the girl I knew as Molly standing by the car, emotionless."

The man was a natural storyteller, Reverend or not. Although, to be successful in that line of work you needed to have a little panache when relaying information and the man did it perfectly. Shep and I sat there, riveted. For people who were cut of the same mold, he held us. We all told stories. We all appreciated good ones. This one had us both nearly grasping at one another.

"I was lifted off the ground and thrown through the entrance into one of the houses where a group of people were standing as if waiting for a surprise party to begin. The room was completely barren; there were no tables or chairs or anything like that. Just those people and their faces. Their horrible, horrible faces."

"What was wrong with their faces, Reverend," Shep asked, knowing full well what was wrong with their faces.

"They were awful. All of them had the same disfigured mouth that looked like it was full of shark teeth. They were pointed teeth, you know? Not human looking in the least. Their skin around the mouth was pulled back tight. So tight it looked like it would snap completely off the skull. And their eyes were white, with no pupils. And they all had that same crazed look, every one of them. Some were middle-aged, some were younger. I didn't get a good look at every single one of them, to tell you the truth. But when I hit that floor, they all tried to converge on me like a pack of wolves attacking a baby fawn. Or lamb." He crossed himself once again. "I'm not a man of violence, gentlemen. It's not hard to know that, given my choice of profession. But I kicked and snarled like a mule in that room. Don't ask me how I did it. I just thrashed around. I kicked my foot into their midsection. I couldn't even use any furniture to hide behind or defend myself because there was none. All I had were my wits, which were more than frazzled by that point. What made this all the worse was I didn't know what they were going to do to me. Were they simply going to kill me? Were they going to tie me up and hold me for ransom? All I knew was that they were coming at me relentlessly. Whenever I'd kick one back, another would come forward and I'd have to thwart another. I had no idea how many could've been hiding, either. Oh, it was awful. They made this sound, too. It sounded like insects buzzing around in swarms. One of them snuck around my side and attempted to bite my arm. I lunged towards him, threw my shoulder into his stomach, and sent him tumbling into four or five other ones that were standing behind him. That's when I ran out of the house to find Molly smoking a cigarette while leaning on the hood of her car.

At the far end of the neighborhood, or whatever you'd call a collection of houses in the middle of the woods, a normal-looking man stood, unaffected. He wore a long black coat, what looked like a black cowboy hat, and black sunglasses. He raised his hand at me and screamed, 'Sabrina! Get him!' But the girl didn't move. I was confused because she had said her name was Molly."

"Or Gertrude," I whispered.

"The girl did nothing. She continued to smoke her cigarette as I ran the other way. I looked to the other houses as I ran, knowing I was going to get no aid. I swear I saw a slovenly one. A big, overstuffed man—bald headed, wearing an A-framed tee shirt, which protruded against his bulbous gut, stood on the porch. In his hands, he held a human leg! And…and he was chomping on it like someone would eat a turkey leg! He took large bites from the thigh causing blood to rain down on his already filthy shirt. As he chomped down and bit through the flesh the insane smile never left his face. That's when the math added up in my mind. I repeated the Lord's Prayer and ran. I ran through the night. I ran with God. He protected me. I believe he sent me here to you gentlemen. Praise his ever-holy name. I haven't eaten in days. You don't suppose I could trouble you for a crust of bread or something I could put in my stomach?"

"We've got plenty of venison," I said, still tasting the charred amber flavor on my lips.

"Oh," the reverend said, disappointed. "I don't know if I should eat something that heavy. I feel as though I could throw up at any moment. I am so sorry to be so picky at a time like this, but my stomach just isn't right. Believe me, I'd love nothing more than a New York Strip right now with a baked potato and hot fudge sundae. But I'm afraid if I even attempted to eat any of that, its stay in my stomach would be a brief visit."

Shep immediately rose and began to rummage through his satchel. After moving around a bunch of clanking items, he produced a can of soup from the bag. "Tomato soup, Clarence? It's not the heartiest of meals, but it's something to keep on your stomach."

His eyes widened. "Oh, thank you, sir, and God Bless you."

Shep produced a perfectly sized copper pot and began to heat the Reverend's soup.

"So," he asked. "Are you gentlemen hunters?"

"Sort of," I said. It then occurred to me that I had no idea what we were going to do with him.

Chapter Eight

We offered the man asylum and a warm fire for the night, and he conked out soon after finishing his soup, splotches of tomato still staining his cheeks. His face looked peaceful as he slept, with his hands knotted at this midsection and the glow of the fire casting shadows across his filthy shirt. Truthfully, he looked dead. All that was missing was the casket.

"Okay. What do we do with him," I asked.

"I don't know, Frank. We can't take him back there with us, can we?"

"No. No, I guess we can't." I hadn't had much time to reflect on our own mission or if its necessity had gone past its expiration date. Sabrina's intent had been dragged through a muddy bog and that made me sick to my stomach. It pushed me towards the Old Crow and demanded I take a few swigs. Just a few. A mouthful at most. I couldn't do it while Shep was awake. I couldn't bear him to see me take a drink. His words. His eyes were too cutting.

"Do you still want to go," he asked. "We can turn around now and leave, and nothing will have changed. You'll have your article, and we can call it quits." Shep's face was that of a father, trying to explain to a child that there was no more ice cream, but sherbet was close enough and almost the same. "No harm, no foul."

He was correct. We could have quite easily slipped back into the boat and been back on the Steel Pier from whence we launched in no time at all. Well, maybe not in no time at all, exactly, but it would have been a lot easier than trekking through the forest and dealing with these things. Should we take the short route, we would have no scrapes to show for our wear; hearts beating, but hollow. It would be quick. My mind was split in two, and my heart was just about crushed. "I can't believe she's associated with those things."

"Associated," he said. "That's a weird choice of a word, Frank."

"Well, it's obvious she's one of them. After what happened to the Reverend, and me there's no doubt she's involved, right? But how? Am I wrong? What's her link? Is she one of them, you think?"

"I've never known a Wendigo to look normal in the face the way you both described she did. You would have known she was off by the look of her. The way he described them in his story was the exact same way they looked when I stumbled on them as a kid. Same faces."

"So, what's her link?"

"I don't know, Frank. Jeeze, but you're impatient sometimes."

I put the Reverend's story aside for the moment. "Okay. I meet her in The Lookout and she's sloppy drunk. It's not a tourist bar, but one that locals frequent. She was known by the bartender, so she probably frequented that place often. We talk outside, she gets whisked away by this same guy in the black coat and hat." I paused to try and collect all those thoughts. "If she was working with them, why didn't she offer to take me away someplace?"

"I don't follow."

"She's bait, Shep, don't you get it? They send her into town to lure people back to those woods for the others to feast on. She's a goddamn worm on a hook."

"That might be so, but then why did that guy interrupt her while your fishy rear-end was about to go hook, line, and sinker? She had you lined up pretty well if you don't mind me saying so. You would have been the next one to be driven out there."

He was right. I didn't want to fold and admit it, but he was. Shep's logic was born of trails and dirt, but it could be overlaid on anything. A kernel of jealousy still lives in me for that. "I don't know. What I do know is that we have a responsibility now to get this guy back to where he needs to be. Maybe something will click upstairs on the journey. For now, to be completely honest, I don't want anything to do with Moose's Walk or Wendigo's or any of that stuff. I just want to go home."

"I guess that's our only choice right now," he said, solemnly. "We'll get back to the village and go from there."

*   *   *

We didn't speak again that night.

We laid our heavy heads down on our makeshift pillows with plenty of thoughts to weigh them down. There's a point when a campfire burns down to smoldering embers that seem to chase themselves along the orange and crimson fire line and leave gray flecks of ash in their wake. The roaring crackle of flames that once engulfed the wood has long passed and only small flecks of orange pulse on the darkened logs. I fell asleep while watching these small bits follow each other around while my eyes grew heavier and heavier. I blew some breath onto it to make them plume up and brighten. But there was no use in it. The fire was dying out. And soon we'd be encased in nighttime's tomb.

That night I dreamt again. I hadn't dreamed so much in five years. *I saw Sabrina, but her face had changed. It was no longer the pretty young girl who chatted me up on the Steel Pier nights before. No. Her face had morphed into one of those monsters that Shep and the Reverend claimed to have seen. She was wearing that same beige raincoat she wore the night we met. Her eyes had no life in them; they seemed to stare right through me. Her mouth was wide open with the cheek skin tautly pulled back to reveal those sharp teeth, which dripped with a clear ooze of saliva. She stood in the middle of what I imagined that 'neighborhood-in-the-middle-of-the-woods' looked like. There were abandoned homes facing each other. The roofs were slouched and sunken in from the weight of decades of snow. Most of the windows were missing glass. She walked over to me, and I felt very uneasy. I don't know why I didn't run. Maybe I couldn't. They say you can't run in your dreams. She approached me and the smell of gear grease my father used to use when fixing the car came with her. It was a musty, slick smell. She moved her horrible, grinning, taut face close to mine. So close that I could swear I felt her breath on my lips. She panted heavily.*

"You'd give anything for a drink, I bet," she asked. In all the stories I'd heard, those infected with the Wendigo never spoke coherently, but in my dream she did. I didn't answer as I had nothing really of value to say. After all, this was only a dream. "There's where the bar used to be," she said, pointing to the end of the street. "But my father closed it town because he said there were too many masquerade parties going on until all hours of the night. You were at a few of them. I hope you're happy now."

She leaned in close to me, perhaps for a kiss, but this was no smooch. Her razor teeth bit into my cheek and took a hunk out of my face with a quick chomp; ripping the right side of my face off, sending sharp ripples of pain into the deepest recesses of my head. I felt her teeth scrape my teeth from the outside.

At that moment I snapped awake. I snapped my hand to my face, slapping my cheek, and felt the normal, stubbly, fleshy orb that was usually there. I could've used a shave, but who cared? It was just before dawn and the world was tinted blue as the rising sun was nothing more than a shimmering thumbnail at the horizon. I slowly and carefully walked to the boat, so as to not disturb the sleep of Shep or the Reverend. I grabbed my knapsack and found the Old Crow. I was well out of earshot so I undid the cap and poured four hearty gulps down my throat. I almost put the bottle down. I swear, I almost put it down. But I didn't. I raised it up high and guzzled the remainder of the bottle down as easily as if I were drinking straight tap water. Now the bottle was empty. I threw it into the river and watched the ripples take it away from me. It felt like I had thrown an arm or a leg away. I stumbled and that all-too-familiar frontal headache I was accustomed to came raging forward. The world became wobbly. I hadn't been eating very hearty meals and the alcohol went straight to my head. Faster than normal.

In the emerging dawn light, everything in the forest glistened from the slick layer of dew that covered everything. I walked up the side of the river taking long, deep breaths. The river wasn't very wide at this point. We probably wouldn't have made it much farther to Moose's Walk via the water anyway. I sat myself down on a large boulder that was on the riverbank. I remember the awful feeling of placing my rear end down in such a slimy puddle of dew on that rock. My face was wet too. Not completely from the dew, either. It was one of the few times that I realized I was crying after the fact.

My mind raced backward to days gone by and what the hell lead me to this moment: drunk and sitting on a god-forsaken wet rock in the middle of the goddamn woods. I was always introspective and from time to time I would just stop and revel in whatever misery I was in and try to figure out the missteps that had delivered me there. My life has and had been littered with those moments. They seem to weave in and out of my story like a stitch on a blanket. I remember sitting on that rock, looking out through the forest, and thinking 'How the hell did I end up here?' Sitting on a rock. Uncomfortable. Drunk.

I began to sob. My cries echoed through the trees, and I muffled them immediately. I didn't want to wake Shep or the Reverend. So, I bit down on my knuckle, with salty tears hitting my tongue.

My sister Jane moved down to Schenectady with Bruce in the middle of the War. She was a good girl. Four years younger than me, but a world ahead. During The War, she worked in a bandage factory in Saratoga that was once used to make dressings for horses. I'd get letters from her all the time, sent to ease the hell in every place I was sent. In every rotten stinking corner I was holed up in Europe I could always count on getting a postcard from Jane. She started each one the same way. 'Dear Bubba,' she'd write. When she was little she couldn't pronounce the word 'brother' so I became colloquially known as 'Bubba' to her. I remember getting one of her letters on a frigid Christmas night when I was stationed near Stuttgart. The mail call was out of control due to the holiday, and I stood in a crowd waiting for my name to be called. We were huddled in like sheep that night- body heat was the only saving grace. When my name was called, I pushed my way to the front to grab whatever was waiting for me. I got a slender box that was wrapped in a brown paper bag. I pushed myself out of the crowd, to an open spot, and began to open the package, sending shards of brown paper flying into the cold German wind. I opened the box, and a row of chocolate chip cookies were lined up like soldiers. Along with a note. Through my many years of problems, I've never forgotten the words that were written on that yellow piece of lined paper.

Dear Bubba,

When are you going to finally make it home so you can have these cookies when they come out of the oven? Mom and dad are worried sick. So am I. Christmas just isn't the same without you, Bubba. Hope things aren't too bad for you over there. Harry Sullivan won the race for mayor. So hopefully that's a good thing. We keep hearing reports that things are getting better over there. I hope so, Bubba. In the springtime, things are going to be different here. Bruce and I are planning to move down to Schenectady. If you ever need anything, we'll be here for you. We love you. Merry Christmas, Bubba.

I got back the following fall and everything around Queensbury felt different. The church bells that chimed from St. Mary's sounded out of key. The chops that I tried to eat just didn't taste right. I haunted the area in a floating hover for a few months, with my mouth in a perpetual pucker around the lip of a bottle. Those I did speak to, I kept it brief. I ate alone. I spent many hours in the cool, quiet shadows with goose pimples raised on my arms. While this period of isolation gave me ample time for contemplation, I soon realized that I couldn't afford to live on my own.

I took Jane up on her offer and moved in with them in Schenectady. I've already sung Bruce's praises enough, so I won't go on any more about that. I took a job as a junior reporter for the *Schenectady Gazette*. I began carousing with the other reporters, most of whom had been reporters abroad, and we all had a pretty jolly time of it. They were all big men; large in frame and in personality. They all had beards. They all hunted and fished. It was going to be my goal to emulate them and live up to the life they displayed. That's when things began to get farther and farther from me. Being drunk three nights a week turned into four. Then five. Getting home at midnight turned into 2, then 3 o'clock in the morning. One night, after a particularly long evening I returned home to Jane and Bruce's house. When I walked in the door Bruce was awake, sitting in the dark, with the cherry of his cigarette the only thing illuminating the room.

"Bruce," I asked. "What the hell are you doing up?"

"I might ask you the same thing," he said. "You realize it's 4 in the morning, right?"

I remember looking around the room for a clock, but they didn't have one in the living room. "So what?"

"My two-month-old daughter is in her bassinette in the other room, and you can't be making noise all the time, drunk, while she's in our house."

"So, take the kid upstairs with you and my sister."

"Why don't you knock off this drinking shit, Frank, and get your life together."

"HEY! YOU DON'T TALK TO ME LIKE THAT!"

The light at the top of the stairs flicked on and my niece Mariah began to wail bloody murder from her bedroom. In an instant, I knew I'd called down the thunder. Jane bolted down the stairs in her nightgown, skipping steps, and ran up to me.

"That's enough, Frank. Why don't you just go to bed?" Her face was rife with disappointment; the kind of disappointment only family members can truly know when one of their own had screwed up. She quickly turned around, clutched her robe at the neck, and went to tend to her daughter.

"You're really something, Frank. Really something," this from Bruce, who was massaging his bloodshot eyes. "We let you stay here for nothing, and you treat us with zero respect. It was one thing when it was just Jane and me, but we've got the kid now and things are going to have to be different. We can't have you stumbling in here drunk at all hours of the night."

"I'm a grown fucking man, Bruce and you're not going to tell me..."

Jane rushed down the stairs once again and once again marched into the room, this time with Mariah cradled in her arms. She lunged towards me and shrieked, "THAT'S E-NOUGH!"

The way she screamed, the way her voice shot through me like a bullet, set something off inside of me that festered and bubbled like a cauldron. My vision went blurry, fuzzier than it already was. My cheeks caught fire. I opened my right hand, reared back, and slapped her across the face as she held my infant niece. Her face turned orange like a jack o'lantern. Her eyes widened. All of this happened in the blink of an eye but in retelling it, everything has slowed to an agonizing crawl. She crouched over and caught herself on the arm of the couch and did well to hold onto her screaming child.

Bruce, well, he did a fair job on me that night. I landed in the hospital with two cracked ribs, a fractured skull, and a dislocated shoulder. They didn't call the ambulance for me. I left the house that night like blood from a wound; slowly, painfully. As the blood ran from my own body I limped next door and the old widower in the green cardigan made the call for me.

I had forfeited everything; slid all the chips to the middle of the table and put it all on black. After that incident, it was mandated that I was not to return to that house. I would have to gather up what little belongings I had while Jane and Bruce weren't home and I would have to find someplace else to rest my bones.

Regret has a permanent taste on the tip of my tongue and taints everything I place in my mouth.

*   *   *

When I returned to the camp Shep was already awake and collecting our things together to pack up. The Reverend still slept as cozy as a babe; with both of his hands folded under his head as a pillow. Even in his sleep, they were thoughtfully clasped in prayer.

"So, we're keeping to the plan, then," he asked. "We're going to get back to civilization and have that be that? No more thoughts about moving any further here?"

"Yeah," I said, unconvincingly. "Yeah, that'll be the plan. But I think it might be smart if we wait for him to wake up on his own before we get going. There's no sense in rushing."

That was true. With the way things broke, it was the only way.

"Hey, Shep."

"Yeah."

I froze. No words would come. "Nothing," I said. "Sorry for the bother."

Chapter Nine

When we did the trip in reverse, back to the Steel Pier, everything seemed to go faster. The rush and thrush of the water against the hull of the canoe seemed swifter. The wind tussled my hair with a vigor that sent chills down my arms. Perhaps being more familiar with the terrain played a part in it too. Maybe fear had been injected into our muscles and impacted the rowing. Perhaps we diluted our fatigue by adding another set of arms that could rotate turns caressing the glasslike shimmering water with the oars. Maybe we knew we were rowing away from something we shouldn't have been breaching in the first place. Or maybe deep down we knew we had to restart.

"Sure been a hunk o'sweetness to be in'th same circle," Shep said, stretching his hand out towards me. The Reverend stood silently away from us; with his hands clasped in prayer bathing him in the morning sun. It seemed that God was blessing him personally.

I shook Shep's hands, which felt like shaking hands with a weathered baseball mitt, leathered and calloused. "Maybe we'll get together another time," I asked. I sounded like an awkward teenager asking for a second date.

"If the writer wills it." He turned to the Reverend. "Man o'th cloth! Set foot here," he said, pointing next to him. The Reverend, startled, nearly jumped out of his loafers. He obediently walked to Shep's side and Shep threw an arm around him. "A query- an' no fibbin'! Do you walk straight with no deviation? Is the head a'facin' forward? Does the blood pump? Heart beat?"

The Reverend looked to me as if I had some answer. I did not. I shrugged my shoulders.

"Yes," the Reverend said, albeit cautiously.

Shep shook his head and let the Reverend go. He ran his fingers through this beard a few times and waved at us. He turned and walked away. He never said goodbye.

*   *   *

I offered to drive the Reverend to the Police Station where he could file a report on his kidnapping, but he surprisingly refused. "That'll be for another day," he said. "I'm still very tired, I feel that I could sleep for three days."

I knew that filing a police report would mean next to nothing anyway. The sheriff's deputy, most likely George Keifer, would take down a few notes on one of those long yellow forms, and then he'd fold it and tuck it away in an even longer tan filing cabinet where it would remain for only god knows how long. I would venture to guess there were at least eight or nine five-foot tall, steel, tan-colored file cabinets in the basement of the sheriff's station with yellowing police reports shoved into folders, collecting dust. None of them would ever see the light of day.

Rather than make that stop at the station, he took me up on my offer of a lift back to the church. He leaned his head out of my car window as I drove and let the breeze roll over his face with his eyes shut, like a dog riding shotgun. The drive was short, but he seemed to enjoy every moment of it.

The Methodist Church was a plain building; a typical Methodist structure with a few white pillars out front whitewashed in the brightest shade of purity anyone had ever seen. I put the car into park and turned to face the Reverend. He placed a hand on my cheek. "I bless your soul in the name of the holy Lord and Savior Jesus Christ. Who sits at the right hand of God. Look upon this man with a blessing and tiding."

No one had ever done that to me before. While I didn't go for all that religious mumbo jumbo, it made me feel better for some reason. It was genuine as fresh milk. It was as genuine as the trees. Trees'r true, as Shep had said.

"You take care of yourself," he said.

"You too."

*   *   *

I drove back towards Queensbury, drained, with muscle memory taking the turns on the wheel. I'm not sure how I made that ten-minute drive without smacking my car up, but I made it with no dents. My eyelids were like slabs of concrete that wanted nothing more than to give in and slam shut. At a red light or two, I caved and shut them for a little while. I was so tired. But I didn't want to go back to my apartment. Not yet. There was another urge that was tugging at my insides; I was famished. I hadn't eaten a real meal, or what would pass as a real meal, since that venison barbeque that Shep whipped up in the woods. I knew precisely where I would head first. I would fill my stomach to the brink of bursting, then I'd go home and sleep for about three days. The stomach pangs pulled me into Pete's in Glens Falls.

Peter's Diner was a Glens Falls staple, and although it was a bit south of my apartment, and thus out of my way, I frequented it a lot. Downtown Glens Falls was brimming with cars that morning. Large, pastel-colored vehicles barreled down Route 9 with fathers in their fedoras and mothers with kerchiefs and sunglasses. I was lucky enough to grab a spot out front and slowly stepped to the curb. There was a pack of nuns coming down the street and I let them pass in front of me. They were speaking Latin and seemed to move together as a flock of geese. They all looked the same with their wrinkled faces and ultra-white skin. I paused for a moment and thought of what a horrid life it was to be a nun.

When I walked into Pete's the first smell to slap my nostrils was grilled hamburger meat. Pete's had a long U-shaped Formica countertop with red round stools on the right. On the left side, there were four or five booths. I arrived at half past 11, so it was somewhere after breakfast but before the lunch rush. I had stumbled into this place quite a few times after being half in the bag and I wondered if anyone remembered me from those evenings.

Near the cash register, on the opposite side of the counter, a young blonde girl leaned up against the counter and cleared a plate setting. She slid the change that was left on the counter and placed it in a small pocket that was at the top of her apron. She was stunning; a vision in her white uniform. Her blonde hair had subtle brown highlights. From a distance, I couldn't get a good read of her age. I picked up a laminated one-page menu and started to peruse it.

I had reached the patty melts when from the other side of the menu I heard, "Well, if it isn't Queensbury's answer to a question about Hemingway that no one asked."

Jeff Hartley was Peter Hartley's son. He was around my age at the time. Brazen. Full of piss and vinegar, as they used to say. He fought in Italy and got his leg mangled up pretty good at Monte Cassino. When he got sent back he healed up and began flipping hamburgers and mixing milkshakes. Jeff wasn't an old man, but his face was worn and fractured. He had wrinkles on his forehead that he tried to cover with his cook's paper hat. His eyes were beaten. For all these drawbacks, he did everything he could to impose the opposite.

"Good to see you too, Jeff," I said smugly.

"You look like shit, Frank."

"Thanks. I appreciate that. How about a burger and a vanilla shake?" I threw the menu at him, not pleased with his insolent cockiness. He had picked the wrong day to push my buttons. At that moment I wasn't above slugging the son of a bitch across the face; even if he did have a Purple Heart.

He took the menu back in a violent snatch and scribbled my order down on his little notepad. I folded my hands and leaned my head against them. I knew where my next stop was going to be. Oh yes, it was clear as ice water. I needed a bed, stat.

"Excuse me, sir," a female voice whispered from the seat next to me.

I lifted my head slowly- as I had done many times at the pub and elsewhere. Seated next to me was a face I had seen before, but was strange to see it in these environs. Her being there felt oddly surreal; like an image I'd seen in a dream and then placed there in reality. I held out my hand to touch her shoulder, eyes wide, mind not thinking clearly, and said, "Sabrina!"

"Sshhhhh!" She cupped her hand over my mouth and left it there for a moment. She wore a light perfume that smelled like sweet peaches, and I was sure to take a few extra inhales while her hand was there. After all that had gone on, the trek through the woods, the reverend's horrible story, I was over the moon happy to see her face to face. How crazy was I?

She was dressed down that day, with a pair of beige slacks and a white blouse tucked in. Her mahogany hair, those lovely curls, looked as beautiful as ever. I wanted to throw my arms around her and tell her that I'd been waiting for her my whole life. I wanted to tell her that I could help with whatever trouble she was in. "I can't stay here," she whispered, looking around suspiciously. "I shouldn't even be talking to you, but…"

"SABRINA!" Lo and behold the door to the diner swung open, starling some of the patrons, and the man in the cowboy hat and long trench coat stood, stoic like a wax figure, and never moved a muscle. "Let's go, right now!"

The low hush of the patron's ambient conversations had instantly stopped, and everyone's attention momentarily turned toward the man in the black coat. After a second or two, the ten or twelve people resumed their lunches and returned to stuffing their faces with tuna melts and strawberry sundaes.

His second uninvited interruption had just about did it for me. I swung around and marched up to him. He was wearing the same round sunglasses he was wearing the night I saw him on the Steel Pier. I was hot in the face and my nerves jangled like loose chains. I grabbed the side of his jacket and whispered into his face. "If you don't get out of here immediately, I'm going to throttle you across this room, and you'll never walk again. Do we understand each other?"

He grabbed my hand and squeezed it with a tightness I thought only machines could muster. My fingers pressed together like apples in a cider press and my knees began to buckle. His grip never ceased, and it seemed all my gumption and resolve melted away under the crushing grip of his fingers. My body twisted and convulsed like a worm on a hook, and he ultimately let me go. I cowered back and sat down at the first booth, which had no one sitting in it. He extended his hand to Sabrina, and she ran to him as if magnetized, not even casting a half glance in my direction. I watched them walk past the diner through the large window that faced the sidewalk and in an instant, they were out of my vision once again.

"Hey, your burger is gonna get cold over here, tough guy," Jeff shouted from behind the counter.

I slid myself up, hand still in mid-throb, and went to the counter where I sat down and looked down at the most delicious hamburger platter I'd ever seen. Too bad I had a pain in the pit of my stomach that felt like a gorge. I knew if I put that in my stomach, it would be a very brief stay. Pity.

The young blonde waitress I had noticed earlier came over and began to clear the place setting where Sabrina was sitting. She picked up her glass, which had a pale brown residue left from a chocolate milkshake of some kind, a plate with a splotch of ketchup where fries were once dipped, and a few used utensils. As she cleared the remaining items I noticed something. There were words written on the paper placemat that had been underneath the place setting. The young girl went to take it away and I quickly snatched it. She gave me an odd look. I was embarrassed. I hated playing the fool in front of pretty girls. Lord knows I had great practice at it.

"Do you mind if I keep this," I asked awkwardly. "I collect placemats," I said, dumbly.

She said nothing in return. She would've been too young for me anyway.

Sure enough on the placemat, a note was written in pencil.

Frank- I need help. I'm not a monster. They watch me. All the time. Meet me at Au

'*They watch me. All the time.*' Did that mean they were watching me too? Did they know where I lived? What had I gotten myself into? She also wanted to meet me somewhere. Where was anyone's guess? I reverted to thinking that this was all an elaborate trap so my rear end could feed an entire colony of Wendigo.

I slammed my fist against the Formica countertop and my plate and glass bounced. My eyes wet. My insides felt like they were aspic and all the strength drained from my arms and legs. I felt like my body was being held together with thin pieces of string. I didn't know how much longer I could go on like this.

I slapped a dollar on the table and walked out, with my burger and milkshake untouched. I did, however, take the note.

Chapter Ten

I n the dawn's peachy sherbet glow the following morning, I found myself unable to take any comfort in its calming rays.

I felt like I was drowning. I couldn't catch my breath. I sat up and inhaled a deep, long breath, hoping that I would get over the hump and have a satisfied feeling of relaxation. Or at the very least the satisfaction of a full inhale of breath. But it wouldn't come. It felt like my lungs were constrained behind those thick ropes that they use to moor ships to port. My heart raced. I couldn't calm myself down. I rolled over in bed and looked at the time on the clock on my nightstand. 6:27 am. I had paced the floors like a soldier manning the parapet of a redoubt for a good portion of the night, checking in and giving a good hello to all the small hours. I'd counted all the animals. I'd done every bodily function.

My mind hopped and skipped to the answer. I knew what would help. It always did. Shep be damned. World be damned. I knew what the cure was, and I was going to go for it.

I jumped out of my bed and ran to the liquor cabinet where I rifled through a few wine bottles (they just wouldn't do for this situation) and found a bottle with no label on it. It was a clear jug, with a clear liquid on the inside. It could've been gin or vodka or water, but it was none of those things. This was authentic moonshine from the Ozarks that a friend of mine had sent me years ago. It really should've had one of those 'In Case of Emergency' signs across it. No time like the present.

The sweetness of it took me off-guard. It had a corn undertone that made it easy to take down, with a burn that was ten times worse than any of the stronger whiskeys or bourbons I'd ever tasted. I took down three large gullet-fulls, sending the liquid down my throat, and then took down another two. I wiped the sides of my mouth on my arm. I stood waiting for the effect. I walked into the kitchen and plopped the bottle down on the table. I paced the creaky floors of my apartment. My heart kept racing; my vision blurred. I felt a pop in my lower chest-near that grey space of my heart or upper stomach. Had I given myself a heart attack? Was I going to die right then and there?

Sweat slicked my cheeks. I tried to move around as much as I could; walking in and around my coffee table, to the window, passed the radio, and into the kitchen. I felt that if I stopped moving, my heart would stop and I'd collapse and die right there on the floor. Then the drunkenness hit me in full force.

I fell onto my bed, face down, with the room spinning around me like that tornado scene in 'The Wizard of Oz.' I grabbed onto my comforter for dear life, hoping that it would steady my brain and just make everything stop spinning. I just wanted the motion to stop. God, I would have given anything at that moment to just have the room stop spinning.

From the other room, I could hear my telephone ringing. It rang and rang and rang and with each ring, the knots in my stomach and forehead became more and more intense. The phone was in the living room, I was in the bedroom. I slid onto the floor on my hands and knees and crawled over to the black telephone that was still sending shockwaves of pain through my body. With every move I made, I slapped the hardwood floor open-palmed. I entertained the notion of ripping the wire out of the wall and putting an end to that.

I did no such thing. I raised the cold plastic receiver to my ear and mumbled a guttural, "Hello?"

"Mr. Phelps, we met earlier. While we do not wish you any permanent harm, we are asking nicely to cease any relation or contact with Ms. Potter. If we detect any movement towards that end, there will be more problems."

"Who are you?"

"Consider this a first and final warning."

The drone of the dial tone made me wince. I slammed the receiver onto the cradle and collapsed. I looked at the ceiling, which had a few dust bunnies and cobwebs lingering in the corners.

On my living room wall, adjacent to where I was laid out on the floor, hung a baby portrait my parents had taken of me when I was about six months old. The black and white starkness looked gray and dull. I was dressed like a girl- all the kids were back in those days. I was in a long dress that looked like a nightgown. In the portrait, my feet were enveloped by a tangle of crinoline and lace. My face was a mangled, scrunched puss of despair. I could've been crying at the time it was taken, but my memory doesn't go back that far. There were no toys around me in the shot. No props to enhance or make a cute pose. The picture itself was oval and hung there in a wooden frame that was painted yellow which subsequently had begun to chip. I stared at this picture from my drunken heap and I once again started to cry.

I remember a wave of nostalgia that pulled me down in its undertow. I remember it so crystal clear. All I could see in that baby's eyes was my hand slapping my sister. I saw the disappointment in her face, along with the fright. I had scared her, but compartmentalized was also the disappointment that was hidden behind her freight. All of my failures began to march to the forefront of my brain as if they'd been called for roll call outside the barracks; standing straight and true and laughing at me. I tried to shake my head as if the physical motion would shoo the bad thoughts away, but that did nothing save make me nauseous. I'd led a parade of disappointment beginning in my early years with my parents and bringing it current to my boss. It had been a long time since I'd been in any kind of committed relationship. I was a screw-up at work. My family had disowned me. Inside my brain, these sentiments churned like the back of a cement mixer. They rolled and tumbled and mixed and melded and I lay there crying and I got itchy and it was just the most awful moment of my existence. I writhed in turmoil for what seemed to be an eternity. I remember not finishing my paper route when I was 12 and getting yelled at by the director of Home Sales; another Herlihy-esque guy named Van Cook. He leaned down so that his spittle knocked into my cheeks as he reamed me out as punctuation to further drive home my humiliation. I had tried to wipe it away, but he slapped my hand back. I remembered letting our beagle mutt Brady run lose by accident and having him make a break for it. He tramped down the end of the dirt road that led to our house and eventually looked like a tiny splotch of tan paint until he was out of sight and out of our lives. I remembered Louie DeFalco's wide eyes, staring up at me as I held him in my arms in some wheat field in an outskirt of Dresden. He asked that I not let him die there, not then; to let me give him some more time so he could die in the hospital, like I had control over such things. I'd given all I had or thought I had. For all the tumult, all the constant barrage against the currents, it felt like I had come up empty; no better than the bums that sauntered around Glens Falls in the evening singing their horrible songs.

Amid this swirling mire of turbulence, a small burst of relief flickered briefly in my head. Relief. An answer. A small candle flame began to sway in the deep, cavernous, recesses of my soul. My faucet of tears ceased. I became somewhat robotic as if I had no control over what I was thinking or doing. It was like I was hypnotized but knew precisely what I was doing. I stood up and looked around my small abode; at all those erratically placed nothings that I had collected over the years. They were only ornaments to a mask. A mask with nothing behind it. I sprung up, still sick to my stomach, and ran into my bedroom.

I slid my closet door open and began to pick through suits that were neatly hung like soldiers. I took a grey, double-breasted sharp suit out and flung it on my unmade bed. I stripped my clothes off and threw them into a pile on the side of my bed. I grabbed a freshly starched white shirt off the rack and threw my arms into it. I buttoned the front without taking a moment to realize that I'd missed a few around my stomach. I slammed my legs into the pants and zipped the front. I picked a nice tie- one that had red and blue stripes running on an angle. I slung on the suit jacket and headed for the door.

I didn't stop to look in the mirror.

*   *   *

Route 9, the main artery that pumped the blood into our region and through its veins to the outer reaches, was quiet that morning. As I drove north, no one was on the street. The world seemed shut. Vacant. No motel doors were opened with the harsh smell of bleach bleeding out into the street. No old men standing at the edge of their pools with chlorine tablets in hand. No restaurant owners with crates of vegetables unloading them in the back of the kitchen. No wives running flags up the flagpole with the little yellow ribbon tied at the base. None of that. It was as if I was the only man left alive.

The trees were starting to come around and that was more noticeable the farther you went north away from the cluster of villages. I drove past my office at *The Mirror* and didn't give it a second look. It was hot in my Oldsmobile, and I cracked the window down so a slight spring breeze would graze my forehead and give me some relief. Trees had buds on them

Trees'r true

and some even had beautiful, vibrant green leaves gently swaying in the breeze. I wanted to pull over and maybe take it all in for a moment but decided against it. Stopping would probably only lead to more trouble.

So I shot through Bolton, Diamond Point, and Hague leaving only a trail of swirling leftover leaves in the wake. The two-lane highway was supposed to bring more people from every direction to the region, and it was doing its job in spades. Over the past few summers, people were beginning to show up from all over the state, and (more broadly) the east coast. I couldn't remember the last time I'd seen so many cars on the road. I guess that was good for the economy, for what it was worth.

With each passing mile, the houses got farther and farther apart and wide-open farmland with its gently furrowed rolling hills stretched in either direction. The romanticism of farming was never lost on me. I would have loved to farm a little parcel that I could call my own. Maybe I'd grow some beans or something. I passed a beef farm on my left and a sizable herd of Black Angus steer was in the fields, grazing the mid-morning away. Farming wasn't done up in these parts; too many rocks in the soil, but there were a few die-hards that hadn't given up. Cows always reminded me of my mother, because she grew up on a dairy farm. 'If you could only see me now,' I thought to myself. 'If you could only see me now, what would you say?'

She'd say, 'Franklin, cut the nonsense immediately.'

'Aw shucks, mom. You're going to yell at me now?'

'You're a fool, Franklin. You're a disgrace.'

'Jesus, mom. Really?'

I apparently couldn't seek refuge or comfort in imaginary conversations, as the results they yielded were just as cruel as the ones I was having in the real world. Imagine that. I looked to my passenger seat and half expected my mother to be sitting there with her arms folded and her face wrinkled in a scowl; a scowl with lines as hard as those furrowed fields I had passed a few miles back. I imagined her shaking her head, not pleading or bleating at all. She just shook her head at me and said nothing. A good tongue-lashing from her would have at least been something tangible. I wanted to get yelled at. I wanted someone other than Herlihy to yell at me in a fit of passion, even if it was because they were angry. But in my head, that plain vision of my sweet mother did nothing of the sort. She just shook her head at me and then turned away and looked out the window. I wanted to reach out and touch her arm to get her attention, but of course, I knew better. She wasn't going to be there in my passenger seat. She wasn't going to be waiting for me when I reached my destination. She wasn't going to let me bury my face in her shoulder and let loose some good, hard sobs. I began to cry again. I had done more crying over the past four days than I had in years. It was all coming out. The water was the cleansing. I pressed on the gas a little harder and the maroon '42 Olds picked up speed, whizzing by long stretches of open farmland and dense woods.

The last time I had traveled this far up Route 9 was when I visited Max Gunnarson right before I was deployed. He had opened up a construction business just outside Bass Bay and was raking it in pretty well. He married young and opened the place with his brother-in-law. He was missing a pinky on his right hand and had webbed toes. Those two maladies kept him out of the war, but the war influenced him in another way. That last time I visited he said, 'Frank, when this war shit is over, people are going to come back and want houses built! And guess who's going to build them?' Sure enough, he was correct. When everyone began to filter back into their small towns and villages in the Adirondacks, they wanted new homes to start their new lives. It was Gunnarson Construction Co. that would build them. To say he'd hit it big would have been a colossal understatement.

I'd driven 45 minutes up the lake's shore drive and even for someone who was born and raised here this was the absolute outer limits. There were no longer farms or homes at this point. It was strictly dense forest on either side of the tightly twisting two-lane. The forest wasn't menacing, however. I thought it might've been, but it wasn't. Perhaps that was attributed to that small flickering flame that was guiding me that morning. Eye on the prize, as they say. Eye on the prize.

I began to feel a tightness in my lower gut. I needed to take a piss and take one quick, lest I'd shower the Olds' upholstery in warm, yellow liquid. I gently pulled the car to the shoulder and hopped out. The tree cover blocked the sun, so even though it was hot in the car, it was pleasantly warm outside. I let loose a strong stream of piss against a rock and the relief was magical. As I was zipping my fly, a bundle of flowers strewn on the side of the road caught my eye.

I walked over to investigate, making sure I didn't plod into any of the large pools of chocolatey-looking mud that lined the road. As I got closer, I realized it was a bouquet. It was a bouquet, and it was placed there on purpose. There were bright red Peruvian lilies and white roses and lilacs. The colors looked fresh and vibrant, like a sunset caught suspended in time. Just behind the flowers stood a makeshift cross, with the word LEUKHEISER carved into the unfinished slats.

In between two of the flowers sat a note written on a card. I lifted the note and gave it a read. "Two years ago we lost you here. Rest in peace, Jeanie." The coolness of the tree shadow turned into a chill and my blood ran cold for a moment. I dropped the letter down and took a few steps back from the flowers, kind of feeling bad I had pissed not more than 10 feet from where someone was killed. I had an eerie feeling; the kind that makes your scalp go numb. Whoever Jeanie was, she was someplace better. Someplace where the pain wasn't so present. I hurried back to the car and got out of there before any other strange feelings overtook me.

My stomach was turning inside out as I hadn't eaten anything. The buzz from the moonshine had all but worn off. My guts ached for something to quiet them, but I didn't waver in my resolve. I had passed a few roadside stands with farmers selling produce, but I blew right by them. They'd have to save their dungaree and peaches hometown nonsense for someone else. I was on a mission. I fidgeted uncomfortably in my seat to try and get my mind off the hunger that was beginning to become impossible to ignore.

I saw a weather-beaten green and white sign that lifted my spirits. TICONDEROGA 5 MILES -->. I wasn't going to Ticonderoga, but it was close. I was rapidly approaching where I needed to be.

*   *   *

When I was about ten years old my dad took my sister and me to a place all local families visited. Just as the kids downstate would make pilgrimages to the Statue of Liberty and Radio City Music Hall, the kids who lived in the Warren County region of the Adirondacks all visited Ausable Chasm at one point or another. That was my terminus.

I pulled into the gray gravel parking lot and heard the crunch of the rocks under my wheels. It sounded like I was crunching over the bones of ancient people who had fallen dead there. I guess that sort of thing happened to be on my mind that morning. I tried like mad to remember what this place had looked like when I had been there last, but my memory just wouldn't go back that far. I tried like hell to conjure up where we parked, what my father had said, what my sister wore, but nothing would come. It was probably for the best. Sentimentality often poisons the well.

I ran out of the Olds all the while picking up my pants as I ran. In my haste, I had forgotten a belt. Throughout the parking lot, there were faded wooden signs nailed to the trees, giving directions. TICKETS. BATHROOMS. WATER FOUNTAIN. CHASM.

I approached the small, stained oak house that served as the ticketing station for the attraction. In the box office window, a sign in red paint read,

"CLOSED FOR THE SEASON. WILL RE-OPEN MAY OF '48."

It wasn't quite May yet, but it didn't matter. I ducked under the army green turnstile that was to the right of the ticket office and found myself in the middle courtyard that led to various parts of the chasm. Everything was abandoned and quiet. And so absolutely empty. Repurposed whiskey barrels that were used as garbage pails had no garbage in them. The examples of sandstone they had on display in the education section had no huddled children around them. The carts where vendors sold hot dogs and soda were covered in green tarps. The only sound I heard was my own breath, which was slowing down—but not by much.

One of those silly signs read: CHASM --->. I jogged towards it, and it led me to a dirt path. I began to walk down the crooked path, towards Ausable Chasm. The chasm itself had one of the largest sandstone deposits in the entire northeast. When visiting as a tourist that fact was drummed into your head, so you'd never forget it. A loon screamed in the distance, making my nerves jingle more than they had been all day. My hands were shaking so violently that my arms began to flap.

I approached what looked to be a clearing at the end of the thickly wooded trail.

It was a clearing all right. A clearing that led to the edge of Ausable Chasm. I approached it gingerly. I had developed a fear of heights after returning from Europe, so I sat down on the ground and scooted myself over to the rim. I hung my legs over the edge and looked down at the rushing water that ran through it. It was easily a 200-foot drop to the bottom. The sandstone wall before me looked like layers of puff pastry; flaky and layered. My stomach groaned. I was starving, but It didn't matter. I felt like I was sitting on top of Calvary. The tan, layered rock formations looked ancient and out of place among the green trees that had begun to bloom around them. The rocks didn't belong there. I opened my arms as if to catch the light breeze.

My thoughts bounced all over the place like a thousand rubber balls let loose inside a gymnasium. I thought of my sister recoiling back from my slap. I thought of Herlihy wagging his fat, hairy index finger in my face. I heard bombs exploding in the distance. I heard the last beleaguered moan of a soldier I'd never met; in a place I didn't know. I thought of my niece, who would probably be brought up without a mention of me. I thought of my mother wringing her hands when she found out I'd enlisted. That image did it. My mother. I stopped for a moment and could almost smell a turkey cooking. I had an image of Thanksgiving. It was Thanksgiving morning. She was at the stove, and she was looking at me while she stirred the gravy on the stovetop. She was wearing her blue housedress with the white frill across the chest and back. Her hair was brown and curly, and a few stray hairs were stuck to her sweaty brow. Her face was soft and welcoming; with her round cheeks and small mouth; a mouth that had planted many kisses on my cheeks and forehead. She looked at me and her face dropped from happiness to disappointment. She shook her head. It was then I knew all I needed to know. And felt all I needed to feel.

The light; that small candle flame that calmed my worries of all my trials was still barely burning. I lifted my rear end off the ground with the palms of my hands. The dirt shifted under me, and I felt the gravity begin to shift me forward. I inhaled deep and held it; my lungs were as full as blimps. I exhaled and took in the scenery once again. I pushed a little harder forward. I was about to fall forward when my progress was impeded by a voice that shouted from behind me.

"FRANK, DON'T!"

I turned quickly, eased the pressure, and threw my weight backward to counteract the gravity that was about to take me to my death. It was Sabrina.

"What the hell are you doing," she asked, running over to me before grabbing a hold of my shoulders and pulling me back fully onto the ground. "What the hell are you doing," she asked again. It was the most emotion I'd ever seen her display to that point.

I didn't say anything. I stood up and brushed off some of the dirt from the seat of my pants before losing what composure I'd feigned. It felt like my insides were seeping out of my skin. I doubled over, wailing like a madman, with Sabrina standing a safe three feet away. I began to hyperventilate. I couldn't catch my breath. I felt like no matter what I did, the breaths were not getting my brain the oxygen I needed. I fell and sat with my legs crossed. Sabrina continued to stand there and did not attempt to help. It was very strange.

When I composed myself, I asked, "What are you doing here?"

"Well, when I wrote you that note on the placemat I was beginning to write 'meet me at Ausable Chasm on this day, at this time,' but I figured you wouldn't understand it because I didn't write out the whole word or anything."

"And it just figures as much. I came here to solve my problems and run into you," I said.

"Solve your problems, huh," she said. "Kind of a cowardly way to solve problems, don't you think?"

"I'm no coward!" I was incensed. "I fought for this country on three God damn continents! I'm not a fucking coward!" Through the chasm walls, I could hear 'oward oward oward' echoing into infinity. "You're the coward! Baiting people to their deaths!"

"You don't know the whole story, Frank."

"Who's that guy that follows you around? Is he going to show up out of nowhere and whisk you away like he has the last two times?"

She didn't say anything. She looked like a girl was ashamed of a family member's antics. She was wearing her usual beige raincoat and her lovely mahogany hair was pulled back in a ponytail. She looked beautiful.

"Look, stand up and come closer to me," she said, with her hand held out. "I promise no one is going to whisk me away."

I stood up slowly, with my head swimming and my muscles crying, and walked over to her suspiciously, with my head on a constant swivel. I looked in every crevasse, every dark corner, and every tree. I stood beside her. I began to cry again. "I was so close," I said. "I was so close. Why did you have to come here?"

"Why don't we go somewhere where we can talk, okay? I'm good for at least three hours."

My stomach grumbled. "Can we go somewhere to eat?"

Chapter Eleven

We ate at a small diner in Keenesville. I took my car, and she took hers. When we first took off, I tailed her closely, with a million and one scenarios all vying for my brain's attention like obnoxious children waving their arms. These were supplemented by the fear of her taking an unexpected left and ditching me once again. Images of death and horrible grins pounced through my thoughts like rabid dogs. I then began to ease up and kept a bit of distance. Something was telling me not to get too close. 'This is the way Shep would have done it,' I thought. 'He'd be proud.' For all I knew I was going to die anyway. I shook my head in disgust. At least if I had gone through with it and pushed myself off that cliff, it would've been on my terms.

We ate our meals like animals that hadn't seen a morsel of food in days. I ordered two entrees; the chicken dinner, and a cheeseburger on the side, which prompted a side-eyed glance from our waitress, Ernesta. We made a friendly wager with her on whether I'd finish everything. I wish I were a betting man because, by the end of the meal, all that was left was a garnish of lettuce and a puddle of unused gravy.

Sabrina and I didn't exactly chat it up during the meal but rather sat across from one another in chess-like anticipation while the other diners went about their business around us. We shared a meaningless word here and there, but nothing in-depth. The diner was one of those Silk City diners that cropped up here and there along freeways. It was bullet-shaped, almost like a train car, and had brushed chrome adorning nearly every surface. It was getting close to afternoon time now, and people filed in and took their seats in booths and some even plopped at the countertop stools. Kids ate their ice cream and parents ordered Rumanian steaks, fried cod, and turkey dinners. This went on around us and I felt we were in a bubble; there, but not there. It was hard to breathe again. That could have been a result of my fear, or I could have possibly eaten too quickly.

"What's your name," I asked.

She looked embarrassed. "Sabrina," she said.

"Why did you tell me it was Gertrude?"

"Because that's what I do. It's how I operate."

"You're going to tell me everything. Right now." I felt like she was going to spill her guts anyway, but I needed, for my own sake, to verbally make the demand. Sometimes you must listen when your ego calls. It made me feel better. "You're going to tell me where you're from. What you're doing here. Who the hell is that man in the long black coat? And finally, you're going to tell me what's going on in those Eastern Woods."

She looked overwhelmed. "That's a lot of information to give," she said. "That could take all night." She sipped her soda. "Things aren't always quick sentences, Frank. Sometimes there's a lot of gray."

"Just tell me everything," I said. "I've got time."

"I don't," she said, looking over to the clock that hung behind the soda fountain. "I told you that. I have a very small window here or else there's going to be trouble. We're not dealing with normal things there, Frank. We're just not."

"Well tell me as much as you can before you have to leave."

"You asked me my name," she said. "My name is Sabrina Potter. I'm from Sharon, Connecticut. I'm twenty-seven years old. My father, Samuel Potter, owned a Hotel in Bolton for years. 'The Bolton House' it was called. We made our off-season residence in Connecticut and lived out of the lower quarters in the hotel during the summer season. It wasn't one of those grand hotels, but it was nice, you know. Eight fully furnished rooms. It was originally a mansion and my father converted it. We put a lot of work into it. It was beautiful. About ten years ago my father went missing in the middle of the summer. First week of July. We searched high and low, up and down, left and right, and we never found him. My mother and I had no choice but to run the day-to-day operations with heavy hearts for the remainder of the summer. That fall, we decided to get rid of the hotel and sold it. We sold it for a song. It seemed that everywhere we looked, he was there. From the flowers he planted to the wood chopped out back. It...it was just too much for us. We would've probably given the place away if we had to. And neither of us was strong enough to keep something like that going."

"So, wait," I interrupted. "He woke up one morning and just vanished?"

"You're not letting me finish, Frank. Patience. Please. He had gone over to the village to stop by the hardware store. The last anyone saw of him was him leaving Berger's Hardware. Then he was gone."

"Okay. Something tells me you know more about this."

She ignored my comment and kept speaking. "That winter we got word that a human skull was found by a hunter near the base of a mountain at the foot of the Eastern Woods. They did their tests on his teeth or whatever and it turned out that it was my father. It brought us an uneasy closure that only acted as a mask. I mean, yes, we knew he was dead. But there was so much more behind it." She spoke as if she was trying to convince herself. "There was so much more to find out. I ignored all the impulses for as long as I could. I tossed away many nights in bed. I broke it off with a guy I was seeing. It started to just take things over in my life. One by one. So, I finally decided to act on this. I came up here by myself. After the thaw."

"You came up here by yourself to do what exactly?"

"I don't know," she said, regretfully. "I wish I had a better answer for you, but I just don't. I guess I wanted to see if I could find anything on my own. I knew deep down that even if I didn't find anything, I could rest easy because I knew I'd done all I could. You know when you ask someone to help you find something, and you know for a fact they're not looking as hard as you are? It felt like that."

"When you came back, where did you go?"

"Well, I went to the spot where they found his skull, the foot of that mountain just south of the Eastern Woods. I didn't know the precise spot, but I took a road that ran through the middle of the forest. It's the only paved road on that side. It goes straight through. I parked my car and just wandered into the woods. That's when I disappeared too."

I hung on her every word. She did well to keep me captivated. Never once did a drink enter my mind as she spoke. That was a rarity among rarities during that stage of my life. Not even Shep's stories riveted me to that extent. There was a genuineness to her demeanor. It helped thaw the apprehension. I needed to know more. I needed to know what happened next.

"What the hell does that mean," I asked.

"I was kidnapped," she said. "I was kidnapped and never seen again."

The lump in my throat grew. I felt like I could throw up everything I'd just eaten. But I choked it back. "You...you were never seen again?"

"Correct," she said. "As I walked through the forest, trying to put the pieces of my father's disappearance together I was approached by a figure in a long black raincoat. He had a black Stetson cowboy hat and dark sunglasses. He was just standing there in the middle of the woods watching me. I got the feeling that if I tried to run, he'd catch me. The car seemed like it was a million miles away. It was that feeling of being caught. I did nothing. He didn't do anything either. I was afraid to move. I devised a plan to just run. That's all I wanted to do. Run."

She had my full attention. If this was a trap to get me, she was doing one hell of a job selling the contrary. "What did you do," I asked, dryly.

"I turned and ran."

"You ran?"

"Yes."

"Just like that? You just turned away from him and bolted out of there?"

"Uh-huh."

"And what happened?"

"Just as I suspected he took off after me. I ran as hard as I could, with my shoes kicking up leaves behind me in my wake. I ducked around trees, hopped over fallen logs, and sprinted over small bogs that had collected. I ran and ran, without once looking over my shoulder. I had no idea where I was going. I was in the middle of the forest. My shoes were soaking wet. In my panic, I saw the road but didn't see my car. I had found my way back, but not where my car was parked. I finally got to the road and began to run once again. This time, I glanced over my shoulder and the man was still very much in pursuit. His coat flew behind him like Batman's cape. You know who Batman is, right?"

I nodded in the affirmative that I'd indeed heard of the Caped Crusader.

"I huffed so intensely that I began to get lightheaded. My eyes went back and forth across the terrain in front of me left and right. It was a tangled mess of orange and brown leaves. This was right after the thaw- maybe the end of March- and all the fallen leaves that were hidden under the snow were revealed. And then amid all those earthy colors came a relief. I saw my car! I started to sprint like a deer jumping as I ran. I ran and ran and ran and..."

She stopped her story. I wasn't sure if it was for dramatic effect, or if she had just choked herself up.

"And what," I asked.

"And he was standing next to my car."

"Who was standing next to your car?"

"The man who'd been chasing me."

"That's impossible. You just said he was behind you."

"No, no it's possible," she said regrettably. "He was behind me *and* in front of me." She paused, looked at the ground, and raised her tear-filled eyes to me and said, "They're twins."

My blood went ice cold. "Twins?"

"Twin brothers, Frank. Identical in speech and look. They dress the same, they act the same. The only distinguishing mark they have is Jonas has no right ear."

"Who are they," I asked. "What are they?"

"Their names are Jonas and Ebenezer Van Slyke. They're the guardians of the group. They ensure a healthy line of food is made available to the infected."

"The infected?"

"Wendigo," she said. "Those who get possessed with the Wendigo crave flesh. The twins make sure there's a copious flow of humans."

"Why don't the Wendigo eat them? Aren't they human?"

"They're not human. They are a subspecies somewhere between human and Wendigo. They're not quite one or the other. How they got that way, I have no idea. This is just my theory."

"So how come they didn't bring you to the slaughter?"

"I told you this story is long. Just be patient. When they cornered me near my car I screamed as loud as I could for help. My vocal cords felt like chopped meat. They grabbed me under my armpits and lifted me off the ground. I kicked my legs like hell, mimicking the motion of riding a bicycle. But the two of them overpowered me, and my muscles began to give up the fight. I was being kidnapped, and no one would ever hear from me ever again."

My heart ached in my chest. I had all to do to choke back my tears. She spoke with such empathy, such detail. I felt her pain in a way I hadn't felt since the war. It was hauntingly familiar.

"They brought me to the Eastern Woods where the Wendigo were. I was dragged down the middle of what looked like an abandoned town. Eight or nine houses were facing one another. The houses were all run down, and some of the roofs were caved in. Most of the windows were smashed in."

I stopped her there. "I got this description from a friend," I said. "No need to go into that much detail. I got the point."

"Who told you? The old guide?"

"Partly. Someone else too. A preacher."

"He survived? The preacher survived?" Her mood brightened at the fact that the Reverend had escaped his ordeal.

I reassured her that the young reverend had found his way out of the hell, and right into our arms.

She shook her head viciously as if to refocus on the story at hand. "Where was I? Oh yes. I noticed moving shapes and figures in the windows of the abandoned houses. They moved through the cracked glass in silhouette, and my imagination began to run wild. The creatures, those Wendigo, began to exit their homes. When I finally got a good look at them, it was far worse than anything I could've ever thought up in my imagination. They walked strangely. Their faces had taut skin with razor-sharp teeth. I was held before them, between the two brothers, as an offering. One of the larger Wendigo crept close. He was the pig-man of them all. He wore a splotched filthy tee shirt and blue corduroy pants. He slowly walked to me and a clear liquid dripped from his smiling mouth and streaked down onto his tee-shirt-clad gut. I wrestled back and forth, but the brothers had iron grips on my shoulders. I pleaded with them not to kill me. 'Please don't kill me,' I screamed. 'Please. Please.' I yelled for my life. What little strength I had left was rapidly diminishing. At this point, other Wendigos were crawling out of the broken shacks. They had blood all over their shirts and their faces were red with maniacal grins. At the far end of the cluster of homes, I saw something roasting over a spit. It looked like a deer at first, but then it came quickly that it was a human being. Run through. Being turned over a fire like a lamb. The skin looked like roasted chicken and the hair at the top singed back and was burned into the scalp. I didn't have any idea what they were going to do to me before that. But when I saw that man on that spit, with that rod shoved up his ass and coming out the top of his head I knew. I was going to fall victim to not one sin, but two. I had to think fast because the fattest of them all was slobbering over me. I don't know what possessed me, but I yelled, 'I CAN HELP YOU.' I wailed. 'I CAN BRING YOU MORE!' After I screamed, they turned and looked at one another."

I had been correct in my deduction. There was no satisfaction, however. There was nothing to be celebrated from this. I felt hollow; like I was correct in assuming a runaway dog had been hit by a train. "So, they used you as bait, then," I said.

She nodded her head.

"Why didn't you just run away? You could've told them that you were going into town to drum up some bodies and then ran away. You...you could've been back with your mother! And safe!"

"I thought of that. I did; it's the most logical thing. But it was impossible, Frank. The brothers shadowed my every move. They were always a step in front of me and a step behind me. When I'd go fishing, they'd be close by. I had no choice."

Her face began to shed years and all of a sudden, she looked a lot younger than she had before. It may've been a trick of the fluorescent bulb that was above us or the waning hours of the afternoon. Whatever it was, I saw and felt her true age beam through. She looked naïve. She looked abandoned. Let down.

"You have no remorse for those who died at your hands," I asked. "You lead people to their deaths, Sabrina."

"I don't know if there's a right answer to that, Frank. I did it to try and preserve my own life."

"But by preserving your own life, people have been killed! Don't you think that's a little selfish?"

Her face frowned. Tears fell. She placed her head in her hands. "You are one to talk about being selfish, Frank. I know all about you. Your boss gave me a decent dossier when I dropped that note at your desk. Not all of us are Jesus Christ." She stopped briefly to wipe the congealed snot from the rim of her nose. "And if I was selfish...well maybe I want to make up for it now," she said. "Maybe I've had enough and saw my chance to finally end this nightmare."

"With me?"

"You're part of it."

"Why me?"

"Let me start from the moment when I decided that I couldn't keep doing this. The day I caught the Reverend I was standing outside the church where he was giving his lecture. Up to that point, I would go to a certain place- usually somewhere in town like a pub or a square dance- and reel someone in. And I did it so much, it became like second nature. We worked the hardest in the summer because all the tourists would descend on the area and were sitting ducks. It became like...like a job. So, there I stood outside the Methodist Church on Montcalm Street and I happened to look down upon a rock that had a plaque embedded in it. The plaque said, 'Given to the memory of so-and-so in remembrance of their life's light by their family.' The words *life's light* wouldn't leave my head. I repeated them over and over again. I got naturally distraught. I'm guessing my tears are what brought the Reverend over to me. His concern. Well, I used that to my advantage and caught him. But I felt terrible about it."

I recalled the Reverend's story and realized how perfectly everything fell together. It was as if I was standing before a giant puzzle that just had a corner completed.

"When I took him to the slaughter, I was disgusted with myself. When he tried to run away, I didn't run after him. I got chided badly for that. I'm surprised they didn't kill me right then and there."

She looked at me with her tears beginning to clear up. "Then I met you on the Steel Pier," she said. "I had gotten myself good and liquored up that night so I wouldn't be able to catch anyone. I figured if I was drunk, I could just tell the twins I had too much and that would be that. You were so...genuine that night. It was as if you were carrying a little light. A light of something greater. Your life light. I felt it."

That small life light was almost my death light. It was amazing how things got masked sometimes.

"How did you know where to find me," I asked.

"You told me you worked for the paper. I snuck into the office and used some context clues of my own. I asked some people. They don't think very highly of you over there, you know."

I nodded my head yes. *They?*

"I told the twins you were my next target, so I got to tail you around. It was no accident that I sat next to you at that café. I never thought you'd go to the Chasm. I didn't even finish the word I was trying to write. But you did. You were there."

"And I was thirty seconds from leaping off it. You happened to come along at the right time, I guess." In the middle of this confessional, I felt the need to regurgitate something that had been on the tip of my tongue. "I hit my sister. Can you believe that? Slapped her right across the face as she was holding her baby."

"I know you feel bad," she said. "But sometimes you get a second crack at things. Do you seriously want to just throw everything away like that?"

"I'm rotten, Sabrina. I'm no good. I'm a no-good screw-up."

"But don't you see you have a chance now to do something to bring you back up? People wish they had opportunities like this."

"I failed in The War and I'll fail now. You don't know me very well, Sabrina. And how do we beat these things anyway? You would have thought by now someone would have found a way to stop them. I'm guessing it's going to take more than guns."

"People pay them no mind, Frank. Everyone knows what they do, but they keep it a secret. The old guide knows how to rid them, but he's afraid. I'm sure knows, trust me. If we are about to embark on this, we'll need his help too."

"Shep has to come with us?" I sounded like a child was told a friend could sleep over.

"He's an experienced woodsman. We're going to need him. And like I said, he'll know what to do."

I played with the thoughts for a moment. It was getting later and things would be very different moving forward. I thought for a moment about going back to Ausable and finishing what I'd started. At least this time I'd die on a full stomach. It might've made for a more spectacular SPLASH when my lifeless body hit the water. There was one thing that I was having a hard time computing. "Where did you tell the twins you were going? You said they followed you everywhere. How did you manage to block out this time to be here?"

"I took care of them," she said, with a coy smile.

I gulped.

"Let's say, they can have the *illusion* that they run everything. They're resting comfortably at the moment, but they'll be stirring soon."

I gulped again.

"Here's what you're going to do. You are going to speak to the old guide, and you are going to spell out what we have discussed today. You are going to come to Moose's Walk with him and the three of us will take care of everything. Simple as that."

"Shep seemed a little iffy on heading back that way."

"He needs to be with us. We need him. No other alternative. You need to convince him." A pause. "We need you too, Frank. So, I'm going to trust that you're not going to do anything stupid. Do you understand me?"

I nodded, although I didn't particularly care for her overbearing tone.

"You're not going back to Ausable Chasm, right?"

I nodded again.

"All right then. From here forward I'm going to have to communicate with you using those notes. They won't be long ones- maybe a word or two. Three at the most. It's going to be hard, but I think we can get to a rendezvous point in the hills. I have to go now. But expect the first note sometime in the next day or so. But you need to talk to Shep immediately. Tonight, or at the very least early tomorrow."

She stood up and put her coat on. She leaned in and kissed my cheek. Close to my mouth, but not quite.

"How can I contact you," I yelled after her.

"You won't. I'll be in touch."

I placed a finger against my cheek where her lips had been.

Chapter Twelve

My sleep was mercifully dreamless, and boy did I need that.

There were no visions, no metaphors, no hidden meanings, and no masks. It was a restful state with my brain completely turned off. Plain black sleep. As I fell deep into sleep's cauldron, and the world began to slip away from me, I could feel the tense muscles in my arms and calves begin to release, as the shutting down of a large piece of machinery. Nothing would act as an impediment, no thought, no impulse, no desire.

When I began to shake out of it, I had to pull myself out. It felt the same as walking out of the ocean and onto the beach. It was a slow, heavy process. I felt that my two realms of consciousness had flipped; awake, the world was hazy and opaque with no lines of delineation or handles to grip. Asleep, everything was sharply lucid in a horribly defined reality. It was more akin to the reality that I had become accustomed to.

I had no idea where to find Shep. He was the first thing to pop into my mind. Followed immediately with, 'I gotta piss.' And those two events clashed and as I urinated. I would have to go to Herlihy first and ask him where he dug Shep up and where I could find him. I'd concoct some bullshit excuse that I needed to follow up with him after our adventure to tie up some loose ends. Put a ribbon on it. Get one more good quote as a wrap-up. Typical writer nonsense.

I went back to bed to lie down for a few more minutes. Herlihy wasn't expecting me back until the following day, so if I showed up late that morning, he would have no ammunition. Besides, the paper was the least of my concerns.

In my younger years, in my previous life, I'd always been a man of a man of reflection. Before and after everything, every decision, every mistake, I'd make sure to twist and turn my thoughts into pretzels inside my own head. I found this path to be the truth in all facets of my life, save one; the one that dominated my early manhood and placed scars on my soul, which I've realized, never healed properly. In the army, we were given orders and trained to obey them by blocking out all sense of reflection. As we were all taught in boot camp, 'over-thinking will get a Nazi bullet shoved up your ass.' None of us ever thought about how grand it was to be serving our country. We never thought 'God damn it, I'm going to be on the cover of '*Look*' when I get home. We didn't do any of that. We were handed our shovels and commanded to dig. And dig we did. We never asked why. We never asked to stop. We just acted.

I brought some of that back with me, I guess. But motivation still bothered me. I had volcanic eruptions of questions, and the continued elusiveness of answers was breaking my insides down like a slow acid. Sabrina filled in some of the gaps, but there were things she didn't know either. Like what, or who, the hell were these twins that fol-lowed her around? She had said they were a type of Wendigo, but not full-fledged. I didn't know what to make of that. I supposed I could trod on down to the library and start poking my head in books, but I wasn't sure that would bear any fruit. I knew who I needed to reach out to, and I knew he'd be apprehensive. I needed Shep to have a little of that 'don't think, just do' attitude that I'd inherited from my days overseas.

I remember my bed being particularly comfortable that morning. I had the covers pulled high, and the coolness of the sheets felt good against my feet. I swirled them around and effectively burrowed myself into a nest of comfort the way some animals do in the winter. But this wasn't the winter. It was springtime and everything was supposed to be coming back to life.

Everything around Caldwell kind of stopped dead cold after Labor Day. The whole town went to sleep like a giant hibernating bear. Snowpacks would fill the streets. School would be canceled for sometimes weeks at a time. This is going back to when I was a wee one. But everything, in its dormancy, always vowed to return when the calendar struck April. And we were in April. And like always, the slow crawl out of the winter was taking place.

My mind skipped like a 78 that had been overplayed. Did we all not notice what was going on? Was the entire community that blind? People went missing all the time in the North Woods and no one thought that it was a bit suspicious. I could only imagine that years before in a Town Hall meeting filled with derby hats, chinstrap beards, and brown suits the powers that be decided that *henceforth no one would ever speak of what was going on in the hills of the Eastern Woods.* The room would've been smoke-laden with a thick nimbus cloud of cigar emission. And the person presiding would slam a balled fist against the podium. These, I surmised, would have been Shep's ancestors. Of course, I had no idea. I only had a writer's intuition and an overactive imagination.

First things first, I had to go to work.

*   *   *

I walked in with a sense of purpose, which I'm sure took the rank and file by surprise. My typical entrance was more akin to a kitten being dragged in by the scruff of the neck by its mother. I was greeted by Lindsay Woll; the bubbly over-the-top secretary whose sole purpose on this green earth, I believe, was to please men. Any man. She reminded me of Ethel Merman if old Ethel couldn't make it in the pictures anymore. She came on strong, the way the smell of a potent perfume hits you when you entered a department store. She had her red hair tied up in a bouffant clip and wore blood-red lipstick to match. Nothing about Lindsay was subdued. "HIYA FRANKIE," she said, coming out from behind her desk. I placed my hand out in a *'you don't have to come around the desk to greet me'* motion, but she swung around the desk regardless. She planted an ink-blot-like smooch on my cheek and threw her arms around my neck. I tried to always keep a five-inch distance from Lindsay, even in the middle of a hug. I attempted to keep this practice standard because she was the type who would take a slightly overly enthusiastic hug as a marriage proposal.

I was able to peel myself away from her that morning with little or no resistance. Most of the desks were empty that day for some reason. It was strange because deadline was rapidly approaching, and things needed to be submitted at least 45 minutes before. Some of the account folks were huddled around Danielle Cerci's desk, chatting like chickens in a coop. I let them. I didn't want to say hello.

When I got to my desk, I was expecting to find another one of Sabrina's notes, but there was nothing there save the usual clutter that I'd left. I swear, Herlihy must've had a magnet attached to his forehead because before I could even settle myself in, he barreled through the lines of unmanned desks and came right over to me. He was smirking.

He was going to eat this up like a fat kid would lap up gravy with a piece of bread.

"Hi Frank," he said, his breath reeking of stale coffee. "How are we after our little excursion in the woods? Feeling okay?"

"I'm swell, Marty. Real swell." I was not giving him the slightest inkling of satisfaction. If I had to burst out into jumping jacks while singing the Star-Spangled Banner I would do it. I would do it just to see that horrible smirk get wiped off his stupid face.

"Yeah, you look good. Surprisingly. How was your guide?"

"Oh, Marty, let me tell you; we hit it off like peas and carrots! I think we've started a long-lasting friendship."

His face fell instantly flat, which he then caught and cobbled into a quick smirk. He did a superb job trying to hide his disappointment, but there was no hiding the annoyance behind his grin. "No kidding."

"No, no, no not at all," I said. The faux smile I was stretching was making the corners of my mouth hurt. Two of us were having a shit-eating grin contest, and I was winning. "As a matter of fact, we had such a good time, I want to follow up with him again! But, jeez, we had so much fun; we parted ways without ever exchanging contact information. You don't happen to still have a phone number for him...or maybe his address?"

The disappointment on his face was priceless. His jowly cheeks sunk low, and his arms dropped to his sides. "I want that first draft of this story no later than tomorrow afternoon. Clear?"

I nodded yes and he made a quick about-face and scurried off into his office, slamming the door behind him, sending the blinds that hung on the inside of the door into a full pendulum swing. He looked like an oversized child; a bully who had gotten bested by a punier wimp.

'*This has been the story of your life,*' I thought. '*Fight fight, fight all the time.*' Before I could gather my thoughts, the door to his office flung open again and he stampeded out like an angry elephant. He slammed an index card on my desk and walked back again. The chickens around Danielle's desk continued to cluck away at the situation. God only knew what they were saying.

On the index card, written in pencil, was the following information:

SHEP GOOLEY- ADIRONDACK GUIDE
15 Mountain Pass Road
Warrensburg

I folded the card up and placed it in my shirt pocket. In those days it seemed everyone wore a collared shirt to work. I wore mine because it made me feel important.

I knew Warrensburg. It was made up of one strip of shops with a shining white bandstand in the middle of town that they liked to deck out on certain holidays. On the 4th they would drape bunting off the sides of it and recite the Declaration of Independence. At Christmas, the Episcopal church's choir sang carols. I had attended the Declaration reading a few years prior.

Warrensburg wasn't exactly Rome or Manhattan, but then again, nothing around that way was. I knew that near the edge of town, there was a huge, abandoned hotel that hadn't been used in forty or fifty years. I had been told many a story about what the Lexington Hotel was like in its heyday and the types of characters of who stayed there. I had started to write a piece on it when I first joined the staff at *The Mirror*, but Herlihy had shot that down too. I thought at the very least it would maybe attract more people to come and check it out, but he would have no part of it. When I did the initial fieldwork, I was astounded that such a large, imposing building could be just laid to waste. It was whitewashed at one time, but that had eroded over the years. Chips in the paint and broken windows were the least of the problems. Above the porch, in front of the main entrance, the word LEXINGTON was written in black paint now faded gray. It was amazing that the anchor building of the town was now a large and abandoned eyesore. I wasn't sure where Mountain Pass Road was in proximity to the hotel, so I was sure I'd have to do some exploring.

I was able to slip out of the office without anyone catching me in the act. I'm not sure why I felt the need to slither out the way I did; after all, I wasn't on their clock. I guess I didn't want to add any more fuel to the fire over at Danielle's desk of cluckers. Most of all, I was glad that my path didn't cross one over-anxious secretary who would've asked me a million and one questions.

The day was getting hot, hotter than normal for the Spring, to be sure. It was that kind of heat that steams the mountains during the summertime. I rolled the window down as soon as I got to my car and a little relief hit me. Winters in the mountains can be trying, but don't let them fool you; the summers could be just as brutal in the opposite direction. The Almanac said that the summer of '48 was going to be a hot one. It was already too hot for me.

I drove to Warrensburg with the taste of anticipation on my lips. The springtime air was heavy but surprisingly invigorating. I felt like I was running on fresh batteries. I rode one of the newer roads, County Road 35, on the way to town. They had just begun to pave some of the secondary roads between towns and that was a savior. It was a slick two-lane blacktop road that had forest on either side of it. No other cars were traveling on it that day, so I had the opportunity to take my time and enjoy the birth that was happening all around me.

Crows crisscrossed in the air above me. Tall weeds grew on the side of the road, nowhere near their ultimate height. They were disturbed momentarily by the breeze from my car, but they conformed back straight once I'd passed. I blew by a dead deer on the side of the road; its tan and white stomach was dead and bloated. It was a buck and a big one.

Besides the abandoned colossus known as the Lexington, Warrensburg had one of the nicer movie houses in the area. It was on the square, wedged between Shirley's Lunch and the Law Offices of Debrunt & DeMarco. As I drove through the square, around the large gazebo bandstand in the center of it, I read

THE SEARCH
STARRING
MONTGOMERY CLIFT

sprawled across the theater's marquee in red letters. I hadn't been to a movie in forever. I thought I might treat myself to one after all of this was over.

There were four or five gardeners with their faces down in the dirt around the grassy area that surrounded the gazebo. They were planting shrubs and multicolored bushes. They looked like pink, white, and red bouquets arranged around the ornate structure of the bandstand. The columns and frieze looked like they had been freshly painted an eggshell white. The reflection was nearly blinding.

A group of kids crossed the street as I was stopped at a light. There were six of them, four boys, and two girls. They tramped across the street in their dungarees and long skirts in a pack, as if they were on a mission as well. One of the boys, the one with the ginger red hair, tugged on the ponytail of one of the girls and her face shrieked back in anger. She turned quickly and with a balled fist socked him one in the arm. The pleasure on the boy's face was priceless, although he was rubbing his bicep vigorously. They walked in front of me, laughing. My attention was so fixed on them that I hadn't realized the light had changed and I was being serenaded by a chorus of car horns behind me.

As I pulled through the intersection, I heard one of the girls singing, "Row row row your boat, gently down the stream. Merrily merrily merrily merrily life is but a dream."

*   *   *

I passed through Warrensburg completely and was greeted by a sign welcoming me to Chestertown. I had missed the road. I slammed my palms against my steering wheel and had all to do to keep from ripping it off the column. I pulled the car over to the side of the road and turned the engine off. God, was it hot that day. I knew once I got rolling again the wind from the motion would give me some relief, but for that moment I just needed to be still. I just needed to not be in motion for five minutes. I threw my head back and felt the congealed sweat on the nape of my neck. God damn it was hot. A day like that meant one thing; you could bet your ass it was going to be a long, hot summer.

The leaves on the trees hissed in the breeze like a serpent. They were just starting to get some leaves on them, and the ones that were up there rattled and rustled. I flipped a U-turn and drove back down Route 9, back into Warrensburg, and crept through, rolling like a predator.

Big Bill's Wrecking Yard was a mechanic eyesore on the otherwise quaint main street. The perimeter of the place was lined with jalopies and burned cars from another time. The street that ran perpendicular to it wasn't paved, and it disappeared into a wooded area behind it. I wondered.

I pulled my car next to a Model T that had been badly burned. The seats had large holes in them, and the windshield was cracked in a few places making spider web designs. I could only imagine what could've happened to this car to have it deserve such a fate. I jumped out and began to snoop around. The damn thing looked like Bonnie and Clyde's car after the fact.

I walked over placed my hands on the frame and propped my head inside the broken driver's side window. There were ragged shards of glass on the top and bottom of the window frame. The inside smelled like mildew; like a dank basement that had flooded and was never properly cleaned. There were other cars in the automobile graveyard as well; all of them in various states of decay. A few Buicks. A few Chevrolets. It occurred to me that I was walking through a graveyard. This was where cars came to die. And die they did. And rot.

The ground was uneven in places, due to cars being parked in the same spot for months at a time. They looked like a giant's footprints. I began to walk over to the garage area where I guessed 'Big Bill' conducted his business. If I could come across Big Bill, I'd ask if the road that ran past his station and into the woods was indeed Mountain Pass Road. Or, at the very least if it wasn't, if he would be nice enough to point me in the right direction. I wondered if somewhere around these rusted, antiquated buckets of bolts a Doberman or rottweiler was quietly stalking me. Places like this always had scrappy, mean dogs that meant business.

As I strolled through the broken fields of autos, I was taken back to Dresden the day after. Amazingly my mind was no longer in a Warrensburg chop shop. I was walking through the Innere Neustadt with my trusty 1903 Springfield clutched against my chest. The heat helped to complete the scene. And for the first time in days, I felt like I needed a drink. I wanted that sweet burn and that sweet head-numbing feeling that I had loved so dearly. I remember walking through deserted, burned-out buildings with families burned to a char.

A tap on my shoulder sent me spiraling through the space-time continuum and I snapped back to the present. I turned and was greeted by what can be only described as an absolute ogre of a man. He was a full foot taller than I was. He wore overalls with no shirt underneath. His skin was wart-infested, and patches of brown hair cropped up on the landscape of his scarred chest. He was round and tall and thickly built. His head was bald, and a stubbly unkempt beard strapped his face. He grabbed me by my shoulders and lifted me off the ground like a confused gorilla. I went into a complete panic and began to yell for my mother.

"Maaaaaaaaa," I yelled. "Maaaaaaaaaa."

I kicked my legs back and forth like an ant that was plucked from the ground. I tried to wiggle my way out of his grip, but his hands were like bear paws. I looked out to the street where it seemed everyone had gone away.

"DEBORAH!" The ogre bellowed. "DEBORAH!" I felt his breath on the front of my neck. "THAT DOESN'T MAKE SENSE!" He reared up again, "DEBORAH! DEBORAH. THAT DOESN'T MAKE SENSE!"

From the corner of my peripheral vision, I saw the small white door to the office swing open and a man come running out towards us. He ran while holding onto his pork pie hat, like a cartoon, and bee-lined right for us. "Stop, John!" he yelled. "You put him down right now!" The man was completely flustered. "JOHN!"

The lummox dropped me to the ground, and I fell backward awkwardly on my tailbone, which sent rivets of pain up my spine. The man that had beseeched my release was a foot shorter than I was, making him two feet shorter than the ogre. The ogre's face was lifeless and blank as if someone had turned a switch off the aggressor mode he was in prior. "Deborah," he said once again, this time quieter. "Deborah," again. "That doesn't make sense."

The shorter man had a thick mustache under a pug nose. He was also dressed in overalls but had a workman's flannel shirt underneath. He looked to be covered in automotive grime; the telltale sign he spent his life under hoods. "I'm so sorry," he said. "He gets a little testy when strangers appear on the lot."

He offered me his hand and I took it. His hands felt like worn-in baseball gloves, gruff and peeling. I pulled myself up off the ground and shook off some of the grass that had stuck to my pants. "Well, I guess no harm no foul on that front," I said. "I only got the shit scared out of me, that's all."

"Get out of here, John," he said, shooing the ogre away. The thing lumbered away towards the office like an elephant that had been scolded by its trainer. It seemed the only thing he was missing was a swinging trunk or an ornate headpiece.

"Are you Deborah," I asked the man playfully.

"No, no I'm not Deborah. Deborah's my wife. I'm Big Bill," he said.

I snickered and he laughed back at me. "And that's your son," I asked.

"Stepson. He's not right, damn retard." He glanced over his shoulder at the thing. "I tried to convince my wife to send him someplace, but she won't listen." He paused. "They never listen."

"Is he a loony," I asked.

"You could say that," Big Bill replied. "I mean, he wasn't right from the get-go when he was born. Then, when he was just starting to talk, his old man and mother had a pretty huge brawl outside their house. In the course of the fight, his pops must've yelled 'Deborah'- that's his mother's name. And someone else must've yelled, 'That doesn't make sense.' Now that's all he says. That's all he knows."

There was a pathetic sadness to the whole situation. I couldn't imagine what it would be like to have to take care of someone like that. Someone so helpless in the world. Someone who would never know enjoyment. Someone who would never know love. I felt bad for the whole damn situation and was sorry I had even thought to stop here and ask for directions.

"Well I am sorry for all the trouble," I said. And that was the truth. I didn't intend on screwing up this poor guy's afternoon. "But I do have a favor. I'm looking for Mountain Pass Road. Is that somewhere around here?"

He nodded. "You're looking for Shep Gooley, aren't you?"

"As a matter of fact, I am. How'd you know?"

"He's the only one that lives up there," he said, pointing to the road that led out of the woods and past his automotive graveyard. "Whenever some city-type is looking for a tour of the woods they come poking around..."

"Hey, hey! Wait. I'm not a city-type, I live in Queensbury. I work for The Mirror."

"All right, all right take it easy. Didn't mean to insult you there. That's his mailbox over there." He pointed to a rusted tin box that was nailed to the top of a two-by-four, which was knocked into the ground. "He gets a lot of mail. You'd be surprised."

Nothing surprised me anymore.

"How far up the road is his place?"

Big Bill put his hands over his brow to cover the sun and looked up the road and into the woods. "I'd say about two hundred yards past the tree line over there. He's pretty well remote."

"So you've been up there before?"

"Yeah, tons of times. The old man makes a mean jerky. He had Deborah, John, and I for supper not too long ago."

"Well, I'm going to pay him a visit. Thanks for all your help and sorry about the mix-up earlier."

"You have a good one," he said. He turned around and slunk back to whatever hole he was working in before I disrupted his life. "If your car ever decides to crap out, keep me in mind, will ya?"

I raised my hand to him in affirmation. I turned and began to walk to the road to the abode of Shep Gooley.

Chapter Thirteen

The road that led into the woods was surprisingly intact for something that was comprised primarily of gravel. Rain and snow often do a number on gravel paths over the years, but this one looked to be in pretty good shape as if it was recently redone. I would dare say a car could've made it up there with no problem. It was covered in gray gravel from the tree line up and into the woods and it crunched under my shoes. The forest wasn't very dense down around this part of the mountain, so I could keep my head on a swivel and see if anything out of the ordinary was luring about. I felt safe, though. I guess that was the feeling Shep gave to most people. He'd seen it. He'd done it. Follow his lead and you will be all right. I was hoping for the same reception when I called on him to help me return to the Eastern Woods once more to finally put an end to the Wendigo reign of terror.

As I approached his den, or lair if you will, small objects began to appear on the sides of the road. A few dreamcatchers swung by in the Spring breeze; a rocking chair that was missing its back; an antique birdcage that was rusted and open. It was a strange amalgamation of trash that led the way to Shep's abode. I could only imagine what wonders lay at the end of the path.

Slowly, almost without notice, I felt my steps become more difficult. My legs began to stiffen, and my breaths began to chug like a struggling locomotive. The road began to incline. I trudged upwards like an ox bearing a wagonload behind it. I needed a drink. Just one drop of whiskey would put me right. It tugged at me like a fisherman reeling in a catch. But I inhaled and fought it. More determined than ever I started to march a brisk gallop up the graveled road. Since I ended my days with Uncle Sam, I hadn't had too much physical exertion. If the version of me that was trudging up that road would have been in Dresden, I'd be nothing more than a pile of hamburger. The marching motion and crunch under my feet were reminiscent. I took deep breaths to keep chugging along.

In the distance, I could see the vague outline of a shanty. The structure was set in the middle of the forest. I couldn't make out many specifics at that point, but Shep's house wasn't too far off. My gallop became a sprint, and my shaky view became clearer and clearer.

'Get up that hill you pieces of shit!'

My thoughts began to drift and spiral. More and more. The body is powerful but the brain is even stronger.

'Brown. Down. Jacobs. Down. MacDuffy Down. Run you bunch of faggots'!

My vision began to get sparkly as if I was looking at the world through a kaleidoscope or an illuminated stained glass window. I hunched over and almost fell to my knees. I inhaled as deeply as I could and exhaled in a stream of breath. I dreaded when this kind of thing happened. I could almost hear the damn bombs going off in the distance.

I began to tremble, and my ears started to ring. This was how it started- every goddamn time. I lurched forward and threw myself on the ground and tried to keep my hands still. In some strange rationale, I thought that if I could just keep my hands from trembling the episode would be over, or at least come to a quick conclusion. But the harder I fought it the easier the world slipped in that gray-tinted vision of battle. I was no longer at the top of Mountain Pass; I was somewhere outside Dresen with the whole of my company about to get slaughtered. I heard bombs, I swear I did. I heard children crying and mothers shouting in languages I didn't understand. My trembling spread from my hands up to my arms and the convulsions didn't stop. I tried to swallow but couldn't. I closed my eyes and tried to block out that horrific ringing and the stench of rotting burned corpses returned to my nostrils. I balled myself up on the ground, placed my chin against my chest, and pressed hard. 'I just want to go home,' I thought. 'Please Jesus, just let me get home.' I breathed. Before you left the army, they gave you a two-hour course on how to deal with these kinds of episodes. They said that breathing was the most important thing so the brain could get as much oxygen as possible. That's what they said. And I had no other alternatives lined up. I breathed as hard as I could and slowly, color returned to the world around me. The war slipped away from me again, and the real world in all its splendor made itself known in the low rustle of tree leaves and the cool spring breeze against my forehead.

When I looked up a friendly face was there to smile through his tangle of beard. "Frank!" he said. "What the hell are you doing down there." He extended his hand and I grabbed onto it. I pulled myself forward and stood up straight. "What the hell are you doing all the way up here?" As he spoke he brushed the dirt from the side of my legs.

I didn't know how to begin. Usually, when I was working on a pitch, I would have time to collect a pile of crumbled-up yellow sheets of paper alongside my desk before I struck gold. But today, I had to think on my feet. And of all days to have to collect thoughts, this was not the most opportune one. My head was spinning like a top and the beginnings of a migraine were beginning to form around my temples. I knew I had to fight through this (I always had to fight) and get my plea across to Shep on the first try. There wasn't going to be any rewrite. There wasn't going to be any do-overs. If I blew this, there would be no going forward.

"To tell you the truth, Shep, I had some things I wanted to go over with you before I took our story to print. Some questions and comments for you, if you please."

His face cut through my bullshit like a hot knife through butter. "We'll talk," he said. "But you're going to have to come up to the house for coffee. I don't talk business without a spot of Joe."

"You don't happen to have anything a little more cheerful than that do you," I asked, with a conniving 10–year-old's smile.

"Number one: no. Number two: I thought you were going to give that stuff up once and for all."

I waved my hand at him. "Yeah yeah yeah," I said. "Let's get to talking and if we come to it, we'll come to it."

*   *   *

The structure and surrounding area that Shep Gooley called home was only called a 'home' for the fact that he received his mail there, and in the evening slept in the building. I guess it could be fair to say that four walls do not a home make. The exterior of the structure was made of multicolored corrugated tin and clapboard slats of wood, roughly patched together with no particular order or reason. The roof was steep on one side and shingled using what looked like hemlock bark. He had cut holes in a few spots and slid some windows in them. When I stepped into the place everything seemed to shake, and I felt my footfalls would cause the whole structure to collapse. I had to duck my head to enter the living area.

"It's a little rickety, but take my word, it's not going anywhere." Shep led me into the foyer area where he had five or six pairs of work boots piled in the corner. The interior space was an open room, with no separating walls on the inside. The floor was made of pressed board—some of the cheapest wood anyone could find. There was little to no insulation, save a couple of old bedspreads that were hung to keep the chill out in the winter. I could only imagine how well that system worked. In the center of the room was a potbellied stove with a coffee pot and sauté pan on the burners. Bare essentials, I guessed. There was an old couch that faced a large window that looked out the back of the shanty. If you didn't know any better, you'd thought you'd walked into a time warp. I swear. I felt like I had time-traveled. When I peeked over the couch, I saw a couple of issues of LOOK magazine and they reminded me what century I was in.

There was a stuffed straw mattress in the corner that looked like it was hand-sewn. It became more and more apparent that this was more of a glorified lean-to, less a house. Shep was the real deal McNeil when it came to this stuff. He didn't just talk the talk, he walked it. And from the way he showed me around the place, he walked it with pride.

"How long have you been here at this spot, Shep," I asked while taking a seat on his battered sofa.

"Oh- it must be close to thirty years now. The land belongs to my family. All I had to do was build the walls."

"I guess there's no plumbing in here."

"No. The closest thing I've got is a small brook that runs out back. And when I have to clean my clothes, well, that's a bit of a chore."

"How do you do that?"

"Launderette in Diamond Point," he said, smiling. "Why don't we sit out back, Frank? I get a little claustrophobic in here myself." He stood in the doorway and beckoned me by rigorously circling his hand. "Comeoncomeoncomeon."

I walked out of the back of his shack and was struck by the items he had in what could be considered his 'backyard'. There was a chopping stump with an axe wedged in the center of it. Next to it, a pile of kindling wood was neatly stacked about three feet high. There was a pile of long, round sticks too. I guessed these were going to be walking sticks once they were properly seasoned. Two Adirondack chairs were facing a small bluff that led down to a brook that ran through Shep's property. There was an ever-present rush of water there, so delicate, so light that you could've fallen into a trance if you listened to it long enough. It was one of the most serene and calm places I had ever been. I needed that medicine.

"Have a seat, Frank. The chairs are sturdy; built them myself."

The chairs were unfinished and had natural wood tones to them. They hadn't been painted or shellacked or anything like that. They didn't need it. I slid my rear down into the cradle of the seat and my knees were propped up. It felt like the seat was hugging me. Shep sat down next to me and began to whittle a piece of oak that he produced from his pocket.

"So," said. "To what do I owe the honor of this visit? I know you didn't hump your ass all the way over here just to say a how-do-you-do. And don't give me any nonsense."

"She found me."

"Who found you?"

"Sabrina."

"Oh?" His face dropped in disappointment. My fears seemed to be confirmed at that moment.

"Yeah. She hunted me down and was able to finally make contact. It seems that we were right; she was bait. She cut a deal with them to not kill her if she lured people into the Eastern Woods." For a moment I thought of using fancy talk and pleading my case with verbiage. Then I realized sometimes you must let things out with no filter, no space, no mask. "She wants us to get rid of what's up there. And I know you know how."

"What makes you say that," he asked while twirling the whiskers of his beard.

"Because I just do. You're the most knowledgeable person on this kind of thing."

Shep shook his head and rubbed his eyes with his bony fingers. He looked at the ground as he spoke, not looking in my direction at all. "You know, the lake we're talking about here has kept this secret for years. Back before it even had an English name. The Lenape called it 'Andia-ta-roc-te.' It means 'where the mountains close in' or 'where the lake is closed in by mountains.' Even they knew that a place like this would be good for keeping secrets. The only things around here that are true, and I mean true from the dirt up, are the trees. They tell the truth. But they hide things. They veil things. In and of themselves they are good and true. But behind them, wow. You never know what you're going to find."

I sat and listened intently like a child listening to his father. I never had a close enough relationship with my old man to sit and listen to sage advice, so this was new territory for me. But I took his words in and absorbed them. I also knew that my job might be easier than I thought. His words were nostalgic and knowledgeable. I wouldn't jump in yet though. I'd let him lead himself down the path to action. It was always easier that way.

"You asked me if I knew how to stop those things in the woods. Well, I've never done it myself. It's hard to act against something you've been taught all your life to ignore. I guess a small part of me feels bad about that. Inaction is the worst sometimes, isn't it? When you stand on the edge, on the brink of something, and look it in the face. And then what? You slink in reverse like a snail. I'm a believer in the earth, Frank. And I think the earth knows what it's doing. It's got to, right? It has been doing it for billions. Maybe it's asking for our help to pull the mask back. To end the secrets."

The crack was forming. All I had to do was play my cards right and the old man would be aboard.

"Do I know how to kill them? Sure. What's the one element that destroys? I mean, completely obliterates. You can sink things under the water and blow them away in the wind. You can bury things under the earth." He paused and his face lit up. "But fire," he said. "Fire obliterates. Fire evens the score, you know? But even with that, it's not a guaranteed extermination."

"Why?"

"The spirit needs a host. Once you burn the body, it'll just jump to another host. That's how this whole damn thing started. Remember the story I told you about the Moose? Well, we can burn everything over there, but it will jump from host to host. It could even jump into you or me."

"So, can't we trap it in something? Have it jump into a host that's…something that is…I don't know…incapacitated? Maybe have it inhabit a statue or something?"

Shep snickered. "I don't know, Frank. You and I are on the same level here. I've never tried this kind of thing. And I haven't fully said yes, by the way. I still have a lot of reservations about getting involved with something like this. These things are not simple, unfortunately."

Nothing was ever simple. This wasn't going to be any simpler than anything I'd done. "What's it going to take," I said, speaking like a bargaining business-type. "What's it going to take to have you come on board with me? I need you, Shep. I'm not going to pull any punches or dress it up in flowery bullshit. I need you on my team and I need you to play."

Shep leaned back in his chair and put his head against it. He looked upward, into the trees that surrounded us, upward towards a throng of branches and limbs that had sunlight pouring through them. "Why do you want this so bad," he asked me. "Who are you fighting for?"

His challenge cold-cocked me. "What do you care?"

"Because I'm not sticking my neck out for someone whose priorities aren't in the right place. I'm not having it, Frank- that's a promise." He paused and I saw his eyes begin to moisten. "I'm not risking my own life for stupidity. If...if we're going to do this it's going to be for the right reasons. You don't realize how dangerous this is."

The temperature had cooled substantially. A cooling spring breeze dried the small beads of sweat around my eyes. It calmed me a bit. Though it was a strange calm; like that moment you feel your foot slip out of the airplane when parachuting over a field of hedgerows. "You're wrong, Shep. I do realize how dangerous this is." I could've been sarcastic and recounted our little foray in the Eastern Woods. "The reasons are right, Shep. I wouldn't do it any other way."

"Well?"

"I need to do this. I just need to. It's as if I've been infected with something. Something like a fever. I've missed a bunch of steps, Shep. And I'm about ready to set a course to try and make it right. It's my only chance."

A small field mouse ran across our feet, darting by in a blur of tan and gray. 'Run away little guy,' I thought. 'No business of yours being here anyway.'

"I've lived a long time, Frank. And I plan to live a lot longer. Now, if you want to call that being selfish or what have you, you can go right ahead. But I'm out to preserve my own existence because my work on this planet isn't done yet. I'm going forward with this…"

My heart leaped.

"…because there's a part of me that thinks we can beat whatever is out there. I've tried to turn a deaf ear to it, but it's no use. If this is what is calling me, then I have to answer it. We'll go up there and take care of those sorry bastards once and for all. "

"How are we going to do it," I asked, feeling confident enough to ask such a forward-moving question.

"Burn," he said. "We're going to burn them motherfuckers right out of existence."

Chapter Fourteen

The house I rented in Queensbury was an older Victorian mansion that some loaded tycoon had built for his family near the turn of the century. 1896 sounds about right. It had these neatly planned turrets on either side with bay windows and a long wraparound porch. After the wealthy family sold it (I always say one day I'll get down to the library and look up what family historically owned it), Mr. and Mrs. Varney snapped it and divvied up the floors into multiple apartments. The house sat on the corner of Ridge Road and Sunnyside Road and the Varneys kept it immaculately clean. The wraparound porch was painted a battleship gray and was furnished with rocking chairs, complete with cushions and throw blankets, and Adirondack chairs that hugged you as you sat back in them. The porch overlooked Ridge Road, which had little to no traffic on it. For me, it always felt like a welcoming place. After everything that had happened in Schenectady, it was nice to have a place I could call my own, for 50 dollars a month. Welcoming feelings weren't exactly the norm.

I wasn't the only tenant, though. There were two other apartments in the house that were rented. I had the ground floor. A woman named Nancy Lawry had the second floor and a quiet younger guy named Curtis Boothe had the basement studio apartment. I never saw much of either of them, but when our paths crossed, I tried my best to be cordial.

Nancy was unmarried and in her mid-30s. She worked in Hudson Falls at a paper mill as one of the machine operators; a job she had taken during The War and had stuck with it ever since. She was not unattractive, but her face was far too angular for many men's tastes. She had a sharp jaw, like one of those Dick Tracy cartoon strips. She always wore pants, which was another turnoff for a lot of the guys, and she wore them high, to just under her bust line. Her hair was ratty and tangled most of the time and she kept it in a loose bun. You could tell that she tried to make the bun tight but did it half-assed. She was never in a particular hurry to get anywhere. She'd lazily throw an arm up at you as you made your way across the porch. She wouldn't exactly wave, but she'd throw that arm up in the air like a kid waving a pennant at a ballgame. She'd shyly smile sometimes if I held the front door open for her if I saw she was coming with shopping bags. She slid me a Christmas card under my door once or twice. She was an amicable enough lady.

The other renter, the young 20-something named Curtis was another story. I would hear him storm inside the hallway at all hours of the night. He liked to play his music loud at odd times. 5 in the morning on a Thursday. Midnight. He would play his records at blaring volume. One, in particular, was a country western artist named 'Chadwick Justice'. Now Chadwick had a bunch of hits on the Country Music Charts and even won a few awards because of it. But those weren't the ones Curtis would play. No. He'd play Chadwick Justice's Evangelical Christian recordings, which were released and recorded under the name '*John the Revelator.*' Those Revelator albums would blare up through the basement and shock me out of my sleep. I never took Curtis to be a bad person per se, but there was something wrong with him. He didn't receive much correspondence. No packages. No Christmas Cards. Nothing like that. Once or twice I caught him with his .22 peeking out of the basement window. When I questioned him about it he said he was hunting squirrels. Right. Hunting squirrels.

When I got home from Shep's, Nancy was sitting on the porch in one of the rocking chairs, clutching one of the seat pillow cushions against her stomach. She looked like her normal disheveled self, only her eyes gave away that she had been crying. Her face was swollen red, and her eyes were puffy and squinted. I thought if I simply angled my head down and passed by quietly without acknowledging her, I could've simply whistle-walked my way past her and into the foyer. I could've done that. But I didn't.

"Nancy," I called to her. "Are you all right?"

Part of my apprehension was quelled when I realized she was crying in broad daylight, where anyone could've passed by and seen her. If she didn't want help, she would've silently cried in her apartment. That's what I would have done.

She shook her head no. "Mom passed away this morning," she said. "She...she's gone." She began to sob. She looked up to me, for comfort. "How could she do that to me?"

I didn't know the woman was ill. I didn't know Nancy even had a mother. Some fellow tenant I was. "I'm sorry to hear that," I said. "Condolences." I awkwardly stuck my hand out to shake hers and then pulled it back. I put my hands on her shoulders and patted them. They were drenched from her sweating all day. "Was this...expected," I asked.

She nodded yes. "She's been sick for months. I told her to go see the doctor! I told her to get herself checked out! But she didn't listen to me. No one ever listens to me. No ONE! She's all I have. She's gone now."

"How old?"

"83. I should have just forced her. I should have just marched over there and taken her to the doctor." She digressed. "But she said she was fine! She said she was a-okay! Now all I can do is yell at her in my dreams."

"Okay," I said. "Well listen, if you need anythi…"

"And the best part is, I'm on none of her bank accounts and they won't allow me to access her funds. How am I supposed to pay for her funeral with no money?"

"Jeeze, I don't know. Maybe if you spoke to a lawy…"

"They just expect me to dig a hole in the backyard and throw her in it? I can't do that. I don't even…"

That's when I stopped listening, threw up my hands, and slithered like a slug into the foyer. I felt bad, I did. But she was hysterical, and I wasn't about to waste my time dealing with someone whose rational thinking had taken a permanent leave of absence. I didn't have the time or emotional investment to do such a thing. I still feel bad about that.

The foyer and hallway smelled musty all the time. The smells and sighs of the ancient walls and floors were just two of the prices you paid to live in an older house. The pipes rattled. The floorboards occasionally creaked under your feet. It took a minute or two for the hot water to come from the faucet. And you were always greeted by that musty aroma. It would get worse when they had the carpets vacuumed. It was an oddly comforting smell.

As I was turning my key, Curtis came through the front door (obviously he had done what I had planned to do and bypassed poor Nancy on the porch), wearing his typical uniform of a black tee shirt tucked into his jeans. His hair was a Marine buzz cut, which looked like blonde peach fuzz around the side of his head. His face seemed to be in a perpetual state of apathy. He never smiled, never frowned. He had a poster of some kind rolled under his arm and fumbled for his keys nervously. He peeked over at me quickly and then returned to trying to get the door open. In his struggle to keep everything together, the poster slipped out from under his arm and rolled down the hallway to where I was standing. It knocked into my shoe.

I reached down and picked the poster up and he sprinted towards me and snatched it out of my hand. He took the poster and tucked it back under his arm where it was before.

"Thanks," he said, never making eye contact.

He returned to his door that led to the basement and slammed it behind him like a rat burrowing down into a cave.

What Curtis didn't realize was that my army training sharpened my ability to access a situation, no matter how brief it was, and use it how I saw fit. And so what if I was being nosy? I was able to sneak a nosy peek at the corner of the paper when I reached down to pick it up. I had been wrong in my initial appraisal. The rolled-up poster wasn't a poster at all. They were floor plans for *The Ichabod Crane School* in Bolton as drafted by the architect.

'Funny,' I thought. 'Why would he need floor plans for a school?'

*   *   *

Below my bed, I heard a man talking loudly over a rambling guitar riff that seemed like it could go on forever and ever.

Now, we've all got evil in our lives. Evil is everywhere and it's our job to fight the good fight and rid this world of such things. The power of the Holy Spirit abounds me and makes me a warrior and God's Champion. You see I've been all over this great and wondrous nation from Lake Superior to Baja and back again twice. And you know what I see? Sin! I see sin on every street corner, every pub, every magazine stand. It's all sin! Why, the biggest sinners are the ones you never knew! And if everyone would band together and plant the seed of goodness in your neighbor's heart, we'd all get together swell. Like a daaaaaaaaaay slipped into niiiiiiiiight and the waves upon the beeeeeeacccch I sing to you, my lord and God and your good favor I beseaaaaach. I'll tell you folks the dirt and the filth is running our country into the ground. There are people at work who breed with the sole purpose of making our world a worse place to live. They must be stopped! And their spawn are everywhere! Running around like little mice through a kitchen. And I'll tell you what? Me and my traveling band, the one that makes our home in the Holy City of Nashville want each and every one of you to do your part to stop this infraction against the Lord. From prairies to bays and rivers and streams you mustn't let the work go undone as sure...

I remember lying awake with the covers thrown off my bed listening to this stuff boom up from the basement apartment. I pulled my watch close to my eyes (it was only just dawn) and I was able to make a guess at what time it was. That drivel he was blasting was driving me batty like waterboarding. Little things, inconveniences if you will, had a habit of piling up and piling up until the foundation couldn't hold anymore. Everyone makes concessions. 'Oh, it's never perfect,' is what the perfect people say. They tell you that to shut you up. But it's small inconveniences like loud, awful music that can drive a man to the brink of doing something harsh.

I had made several complaints to the Varneys about Curtis' music, but nothing was ever done to stop the problem. 'The kid's an odd duck,' was the most I was getting out of it. As I tossed and fussed in my unkempt bed sheets the image of those rolled-up blueprints hitting my shoe kept bothering me. What the hell was he doing with a plan for an elementary school? Suppressing those thoughts was like putting one of those gag snakes back in the tin can. I did my best though. I turned my attention to the other thing that had dominated my thoughts.

Sabrina; the person who changed my life in one minor drunken encounter on the Steel Pier. I began to formulate what Washington Irving once described as, 'sugar-coated thoughts' about the fair Sabrina. I saw Sabrina in my mind's eye. I replayed that night on the Steel Pier over and over again, each time saying a word or two differently and evoking a different response or outcome. In these dreams, I was able to express myself clearly. I was able to turn her feelings. I was able to just run off with her with no threat of Wendigo or any other problem. It would just take a few key phrases. Occasionally I'd start the scenario and restart it because I didn't like the choice of words I used.

The music underneath me was relentless and still going on as the predawn hours quickly moved to daylight's first rays without regard for my body's exhaustion. I rolled over and face-planted into my pillow. I could've used a drink right about then. It wasn't the first thought I had, so I supposed I might've been making some progress in the eternal struggle of the will versus the bottle. The Presidential Cabinet had some good stuff in it, just waiting to be called on. But I resisted. I tried to disjoint my legs from my mind and make them not work. This was an old trick I had learned where you render your legs immobile by convincing yourself they couldn't move. It was how many boys kept from running away from enemy gunfire in the heat of battle. I fought then, and I'd fight now.

I stood up in the pale blue light of early morning and walked across my creaky floor, while *John the Revelator* sang another song about how 'loose women dig graves for the righteous man.' I was going to knock on his door and ask politely if he would turn the music down just for the next hour so I could at least get a little bit of shut-eye before heading out into the world.

Before I could even get out into the hallway, I halted myself. 'He's just a kid,' I thought to myself. 'Just let it go, you don't want to get into an altercation with someone you're going to have to live with for the foreseeable future. Just let it go, go back in your bedroom, stuff some cotton in your ears, and call it a day.' I didn't want to add to the mounting throng of troubles I had and confronting this little shit about his music being too loud would have been pissing turpentine on a brush fire.

Curtis's parents had been by to visit only once in the entire duration I lived in that house. They were an elderly couple; much too old to be his parents, so I initially guessed they were his grandparents. However, when I spoke to the Varneys about having him stop playing his music, it was told to me that the elderly couple were indeed his parents and that he was one of those 'change of life' babies. I'm no doctor, but I was willing to bet that's why he was such an odd character. They wore older brown and beige clothes, the both of them did. Their dispositions were old. They looked old. They lived old. When they visited, they sat on the large porch with a pitcher of lemonade between them. I gave a quick wave as I walked by; I wasn't introduced or anything like that. When I got into my apartment, I ran into my kitchen and peered out the window over my sink that looked out onto the porch to get a closer look.

Their son didn't make eye contact with either of them. He sat while they talked at him, with his head slunk down low, almost between his knees. He looked like he would have rather been anywhere else on the planet rather than sit there at that moment. His face was blank, but it was more than that. When kids aren't paying attention to the scolding of a parent there's a bit of life in their eyes that tells you they are receiving the information, but they don't like it. Curtis's face was more like someone who was deaf and mute- stone cold and glaring past everyone and everything. That look on his face chilled me then, and as I thought about it again that morning, it chilled me once again. I couldn't get the idea of those plans out of my head.

As far as I knew the kid worked a job as an assistant porter in one of the motels in Caldwell. Which one he worked at escaped me, but it was one of the smaller ones that butted against the shoreline of the lake. In addition to the many nights of blaring Gospel music, we would occasionally have evenings when his telephone would ring at all hours because of a busted pipe or faulty electrical work at the motel. Those nights he would wake and slither out of the house, to his beat-up hunk of junk, and glide up to fix whatever was wrong. That was all I knew about him up to that point.

I tossed and turned for a few more moments and the music below came to an abrupt halt. I could hear that interference noise record players made when you lifted the needle from the vinyl. I leaned over to my watch- which I could see perfectly now, as dawn had broken the day wide open- and it said 6:27. I flung my legs off the bed and crept like a cat over to my window that looked out onto the porch. I saw Curtis's leather jacket-clad back walking away from me to his car. He was going to work.

So was I.

*   *   *

There are things you learn in the army, survival skills if you will, that they don't teach you in basic training or the classroom. They don't give you a wrap-up and there's no review or test. These are the things you would learn as Kraut sons of bitches and Japs hurled bullets past your head. Survival. Being Johnny-on-the-spot. Some people were good at explosives, others could load their gear in under a minute. Everyone had their specialty. Well, one of the things I got particularly good at was picking locks. We were looking for shelter in Bavaria during one of the shitstorms and there was a church near the edge of town.

We crept up close to it and the door was locked. Our commander, Field Marshall Grenier, got that thing opened quicker than a whore's legs. I never forgot what he showed me. I became very good at it.

I used that knowledge as I stood in the musty-smelling hallway with a thin piece of steel wire poked into Curtis's lock. I kept my head on a swivel, which probably made the process take longer than needed. As I manipulated the wire my breaths became increasingly short, and I began to sweat. I halted for a minute and drew in a long, deep breath to try and reset my body. I could feel the mechanism inside the lock, and I continued to poke and prod my way around inside. In and out in and out I went, but there was no satisfactory click. I thought about just aborting it for a moment, but I refastened my resolve and dug in deeper. There had never been a lock that couldn't be broken, and I was determined to get this thing opened. Suddenly, a waft of freshly brewed coffee descended on me from out of the upstairs air duct and my heart filled with panic. Finally, after what seemed to be ten or fifteen minutes of work, that familiar 'click' sound happened and all the muscles in my body relaxed.

The door opened and creaked like a whining bullfrog; I was expecting that. In the history of breaking and entering no one has ever opened a door without it emitting a whiney creaking sound. I slipped inside, and gently closed the door behind me. I pulled the light switch that dangled in front of me and the space around me was illuminated in a sickly jaundiced yellow glow. I stood on a landing that had a darkened stairway in front of it that led down into darkness. The landing and stairway were wooden and painted a sterile gray color; the same gray that was used to paint the porch, I assumed. I stepped forward down the stairs and descended into Curtis's basement apartment. The light from the landing only lit half of the steps and the rest of the way down they were shrouded in darkness. I carefully stepped down the stairs and felt the wood give a little under my footfalls. I hopped down the last three steps and found myself in virtual darkness.

There were two or three windows that had been covered up using what looked like cardboard and tape, so only a tiny bit of daylight shone through slivered spots that weren't taped completely. There was enough light to illuminate the room so I wouldn't trip over anything or walk into furniture. It reminded me of the barracks we had in Basic Training. It was a studio apartment down there, so everything was placed in its specific corner. To the right, a military issue cot was neatly made. It was one of the tightest beds I'd ever seen. To complete the image, he had the most flat, uncomfortable-looking pillow at the head of it. If it wasn't a direct military issue, then it was a damn close copy. His walls were bare, save for a few pictures stapled to the walls near his bed. I carefully walked over and began to look at them.

Among the pictures he had stapled to the wooden paneling was a picture of Satan tempting Jesus (Satan appeared as the hooved goat/man and held a chalice out towards a rather pious-looking Jesus), a newspaper clipping about the murder trial of Chester Gillette (also known as the man who murdered a young factory girl in cold blood because he knocked her up and didn't want the baby), and finally there was a poem written by a man named Castleton Brigsby, a name I would never forget. It looked like it had been copied out of a book and transcribed using a tabletop typewriter. I don't remember the words verbatim, but I remember it was something about the righteous doing their part to make sure that blood would be spilled, and the infidels would be taught lessons. It sent a shiver from my feet to the top of my head.

That's when the door at the top of the stairs opened and my heart nearly stopped beating. Left to right I scanned, looking for a place I could throw myself simultaneously thought of a good alibi in case he caught me. The bed was too short to hide under, and there were no other large pieces of furniture. Look. Look. Scan. Scan. But ah! Yes- the bathroom. There was a small bathroom on the other side of the room. Before I could even think about another option I skipped across the basement in three large bounds and slid into the tiny washroom, leaving the door somewhat ajar. I could hear the sighing wooden steps as he made his way down. The descent was slow and plodding, though, and that took me as being particularly odd. My breaths sounded in- ternally like a five-piece marching band, and I did all I could to tune them out. 'It's only loud to you,' I thought. 'They don't hear it as loud as you do.' I composed myself and watched the figure float down the stairs and into view. It wasn't Curtis. It was Nancy.

She wore, what my mother called, a duster or a housedress. The one she wore was powder blue and had lilies printed in an all-over pattern. I watched her move around the room curiously as if she had something in mind that she was hoping to discover. Had she been down here before?

She went to his small kitchen table, which had two chairs. She rifled through some papers, lifting envelopes and holding things up to the minimal light. On the table was a rolled-up document. She unfurled it, looked at it for a moment, and dropped it. When it hit the table, it snapped back and rolled back up into a perfect cylinder. She turned quickly, as if spooked, and quickly ran back up the stairs, two by two, much quicker than she descended.

I slowly opened the door with my breath held and tried to keep even the slightest movement perfectly silent. As I exited the bathroom, I felt naked; there was no cover or anything I could throw myself behind in case of enemy penetration. If someone were to come down the stairs at that very moment, I'd be exposed and trapped at the same time. There wouldn't be any way of talking myself out of this one. No matter how much my creative mind tried to convince myself otherwise. I got another chill.

There were more questions now. Why was Nancy snooping around down here? Had she been in my apartment too? What was she looking at on the table? It all made my stomach hurt and I tried to stop thinking about it. I had to begin to talk myself down from the ledge. 'The worst that can happen to you now is a slightly uncomfortable situation,' I reminded myself. 'There is no one hiding with a submachine gun or grenades.' I reminded myself to breathe. My lungs felt awkward.

When I reached the table I saw the mess of papers that Nancy was looking through. It was odd to have such a mess in the middle of a space that was so meticulously bare and well-kempt. The paper she had uncoiled was indeed the floor plans for the Ichabod Crane School. There were also pamphlets for hunting courses and a stack of papers jammed in a manila envelope with the word INFIDELS written across the front in red ink. There was also a yellow legal pad with the word: CRUSADE scratched in blue ink at the very top. Under it, the word SCHOOL. In the upper right-hand corner, 4/28 was scribbled. That was the following day. Under that was 7:45 am START.

I stepped away from the table with my heart beating so fast I thought I'd faint. "Oh my god," I said aloud. "Oh my god."

My attention was grabbed by a quick, glistening sheen that came from the foot of his bed. The sparkle bounced from the polished walnut butt of a rifle that poked out from under his sheet. I turned in a flourish and ran up the stairs, taking the steps two by two, and got to the landing to notice that Nancy had turned the light off. I grabbed for the knob, knowing deep down it wouldn't open. I gripped it hard and turned it and miraculously it turned to the right and the door swung open. I was so full of relief that my knees almost gave way. I went back into the hallway with the presence of mind to re-lock the door from the inside and eased it closed.

I stepped out onto the porch and the light breeze swirled around me. I must've looked like shit. It was a good thing no one was around to see me. I sat in one of the Adirondack chairs- the very same ones Curtis and his family sat in when they visited. I immediately got up and moved seats as it made me uncomfortable to even sit in a seat that had that association.

I moved to the other side of the porch, the side that didn't face the street, and tried to calm myself down. The weather was strange that morning with a milky white sky and thick humidity. It looked like we were going to have one of our infamous Adirondack rainstorms at any moment. The fact that I was outside made breathing easier at that moment. I put my head back against the chair. I could've fallen asleep. My muscles ached so badly. But not as badly as my soul ached.

The call to action, which was compelling me to move forward, started as a light drum roll. It was low and steady like the sound of hickory drumsticks bouncing off a snare head. That small light I had always thought of was beginning to get brighter. Then it happened.

Madmen sometimes claim that thoughts in their minds fester and bubble like a pot of boiling water. Perhaps I was mad that morning. But my thoughts began to move and churn and bubble rapidly. It all made horrible sense. And with that, a peace came over me. A peace of goodness, of righteousness.

I needed to get in touch with Shep. And if possible, Sabrina.

Chapter Fifteen

I went into Caldwell later that afternoon. I decided to take a stroll along the Steel Pier and return to the scene where all my life's new interesting twists had started. Part of me wished Sabrina would just show up and we could talk. I would turn my head she'd be there. Presto! She'd listen to what I had to say. That was how much of my life had been up to that point; wish for something to happen, wish for someone to appear, hope for a formation of a feeling, and be left with a wholly unsatisfying void. That space, which reflected the hole inside me was further magnified by the horrors of what was going on in the Eastern Woods, and how badly I needed to play a part in stopping it.

The steamboats were getting their yearly freshening that afternoon. I could smell the bleach wafting over the breeze from the decks of the ship to the pier. The deckhands scoured the ships with mops and buckets, each of them hunched over with their bristles scrubbing down every inch of them. I had seen similar. Close, but different. All that work that I saw was for survival. I guess what they were doing had to do with survival too. Everyone had to eat, right?

Speaking of eating, I was getting hungry myself. I didn't want to go back to Queensbury, so I stayed local and walked over to a small shack on the corner of Steel Pier and Canada Street called 'The Weiner Hut'. It was the kind of place that brimmed with Greenies during the summer months, closed like a clam after Labor Day, only to return to form when the Spring buds bloomed. It wasn't anything fancy, but I wasn't looking for a steak and potatoes meal. Sometimes all you wanted was a hot dog and a Coke.

On the sidewalk, a sandwich board stood pontificating an interesting zinger: 'LOCALS- COME IN AND TRY THE NEW SPECIALS BEFORE THE GREENIES COME'. I laughed a bit. 'Greenies' was a colloquial term for the tourists that would descend upon us every year.

I walked up to the bar and the smell of grilling hotdogs and slightly bitter sauerkraut made my stomach warble. There were a few locals I knew eating in corners, but I wasn't in the mood to chat. I slung my legs over and waited for the short brunette waitress to come over and take my order. Two dogs and cola would set me right. I folded my hands like a kid in church and patiently waited for my order. The quiet of the afternoon and the cool breeze blowing from outside were rather nice. I closed my eyes for a moment to take it in. The tranquility didn't have but a moment to make itself at home.

Behind me, I heard the low rumblings of an argument erupting. Voices that had started low, like light taps on a tympani drum, had begun to rise, with their intentions cutting and biting. All of that comfort that had been there a moment ago vanished. The yelling made me uncomfortable, and my stomach began to churn. I suddenly wasn't hungry anymore. I wanted to disappear.

"AFTER ALL THAT HAPPENED," the man asked. "YOU STILL DON'T LEARN!" His voice was burly baritone but cracked upward as he finished his yell. I could hear the frustration in his voice. It was oddly familiar. I didn't want to be nosy, so I just ignored it and returned my attention to the laminated placemat that also served as a menu. I thought that perhaps if I perused some of the other food items, I could rekindle my appetite, which had skipped away.

"I SAID DON'T GO OVER THERE," the man boomed once again.

Behind the counter, against the back wall, was an advertisement for *Jack & Jill Ice Cream* that was painted on a mirror. I was far too bashful to turn around and make it obvious that I was being nosy, but I wasn't beyond looking in the mirror to get a look at what was going on in the corner behind me.

The woman was in her mid to late twenties and her hair was cut short, yet curly. She stood at the table with her hands still on it; as if she was playing a game of tag and the table was acting as 'home base.' She wore a peach sundress and had large sunglasses propped on the top of her head. A small child, a little girl, sat in the chair next to her red flannel shirt-wearing (I guessed) father. From where I sat, in the imperfection of the looking glass, I couldn't make out the features of anyone. Then it all became focused.

"JUST LET ME BE, BRUCE," she yelled back at him.

My stomach instantly curdled like rancid milk. This time I did turn around on my stool and looked over to the corner where my sister, Jane, her husband, Bruce, and daughter Mariah were sitting and (up to that point) enjoying a leisurely afternoon lunch. I put my arm up to wave and I only made it about halfway in an awkward flap.

I saw the way Bruce was looking at her. I saw the way she was looking at me. There was no way on planet Earth that she would be able to come over and say hello to me. Her own flesh and blood. She obediently sat back down, like a trained spaniel, and didn't wave back. She didn't so much as even look in my direction. I'd go so far as to say she positioned her body away from me so that there was no mistaking a gaze in my direction. I briefly entertained the notion of walking over there to give a closer 'hello' but thought better of it. The shadow and specter of what I had done knocked me over and rendered my legs useless. Plus, I didn't want to get my sister into any more trouble than she was already in.

'You deserve every moment of this,' I thought to myself. 'You're the one who did what you did. And this is what you get.' I just wanted them to leave, to get out of my line of vision, and get out of my life. I just wanted them gone. 'He could've been quiet about it,' I thought. 'He could have grabbed her forearm and just told her NO don't go over there.' But he didn't. He wanted me to feel every shingle of pain that my inner conscience could dish up. And he was right. I felt like a gutted deer.

They paid their check and hurried out the door. This is where in the movies the sister would stretch an arm back or give a slight wave to let the brother know that she still loves him and things- although in a bad state- could never come between family. That didn't happen. They melted away from me, all three of them, out into the street. I sat there for a moment or two, catching my tears with thin paper napkins. The smell of hotdogs was no longer pleasant. All I could smell now was the salty oily smell of the fryer. I slid my chair away from the counter and walked out.

I made sure to go in the opposite direction.

*　　　　　*　　　　　*

I drove to Shep's. It was the only place I felt safe. There was a burning need inside of me to tell him about Curtis.

*　　　　　*　　　　　*

"And you are one hundred percent sure," Shep asked. "You realize if you're wrong, something terrible could happen."

I outlined my idea to Shep after speeding away from the hotdog place with the foul taste of regret burping up inside of me. "I am sure.

All the pieces fit together. And like I told you, it all will fall together. Almost too perfectly."

I'd begun to conjure images of what Curtis was planning and the whole thing made my guts bubble. Man-to-man combat was something I'd seen before, and was even comfortable with, to a point. But his plan. Oh god. It fired up a rage inside of me that turned my vision red. When I got my hands on the son of a bitch, all bets were going to be off. His cowardly smug disposition would be broken if I had to kill myself doing it.

"And you're going to bring him here," Shep asked.

"Yes. To do what I to do will take privacy, but it also needs to be a place with tools. You have plenty up here."

"You're becoming barbaric, Frank. And I don't like it," he said, with his hand stroking his beard.

"Barbaric? What that kid plans on doing is barbaric. What I'm going to do is righteous and good! Don't you see? This can all end in one fell swoop. And then, god almighty help me, I can rest."

Shep stood up in his chair and looked out into the wilderness. "I hope you're right, Frank," he said, peering through the endless maze of orange and brown that was beginning to turn green. "You know what they say, Frank, *be careful when hunting monsters that you don't become one yourself.*"

For the first time since I had met him, Shep looked his age. I don't know why. When I had been with him out in the wilderness, he had a spry sensibility about him that seemed to shed his years like a chameleon skin. He had hunted, tracked, climbed rocks, and ran. In everything he did, he had an internal light that seemed to be burning brighter than any person I had ever known. But it was a letdown for me, and I recall feeling that a part of me couldn't break free and fully succeed without his wholehearted blessing and participation. I had no choice but to take him as he was and push forward with what had to be done.

"While I thank you for your input, I think I'll be fine." I walked over to him and placed my hand on his shoulder. "Meet me at my house, tomorrow morning at 6 am sharp. We'll track him, then attack him."

"Okay, Frank. Okay, whatever you say."

I hadn't realized I was doing it intentionally, but the phrase 'track and attack' was something we used to say in the Army. My head swirled and each thought I had seemed to bleed into the next one. Everything was looking like a Monet painting, but I was feeling the best I'd felt in months. And I knew when all was said and done Shep would be proud of me, and I could finally sleep a sound slumber.

*   *   *

I knew it was going to be there.

I just knew it.

As I drove back home from Shep's house, with my heart afloat and my disposition sunny, I knew it was going to be waiting for me when I got to my door. Call it intuition, call it luck, call it stupidity. Call it whatever you want, but I knew that when I got home, I would find something either taped to my door or slid under it.

As I opened my door, I noticed a lonely piece of paper folded in half sitting out of place in the center of the hallway between my living room and kitchen. I felt like a kid on Christmas morning who had woken up to a brand-new shiny toy under the tree. I snatched it up quickly and closed the door as if I was trying to keep this a secret. I bolted into the kitchen and turned my light on. I opened the letter and began to read what was scribbled on it.

IF you ever break into my fucking apartment again I'll gut you like a motherfucking fish you son of a bitch

This was not the message I was anticipating. I nervously looked over my shoulder and around my apartment. Perhaps I should've drawn my curtains like they did in those espionage moves. I walked out of my kitchen slowly and into the living room. Everything was in its place. Nothing was moved; there were no signs of someone forcing their way in. The door looked normal. All my windows were intact. I still stalked my rooms carefully. I moved from one room to another slowly scanning each crevasse and hiding place I could think of. I opened my closet doors, looked in the bathtub, under the bed, and behind my bookshelf. There was no one else there. I was alone. Alone with my thoughts.

How?

Did I drop something? I must have. But how did he link it to me? I've never had business cards. I didn't have any other identification, save a driver's license. Did he realize that his papers had been moved? I stood in my apartment stuck halfway between being completely petrified and utterly baffled. The note stoked my ever-increasing paranoia and made me jittery as if I'd downed five or six cups of coffee. Then I remembered Nancy had been down there too. That must've been it. She saw me hiding in the bathroom and went back and immediately reported it to the little bastard. It was the only thing that made sense. But she was down there so briefly. How did she see me?

My paranoia caught fire and suddenly I was enraged. He had called me a 'motherfucking son of a bitch.' I huffed like an agitated bull and a crooked smile began to form on my face. I began laughing. 'He had the balls to call me those names, that little prick bastard,' I thought. Well then. 'So much for being a Soldier in God's Army.' I wondered what 'John the Revolutionary' or whatever that asshole's name was that blared till all hours of the night would think of using such verbiage. That stood to reason though; some of the most foul-mouthed degenerates I knew were also the ones taking sips from the chalice each Sunday.

Things were moving. And they were moving quickly. It felt like I had jumped onto a merry-go-round and full speed and I hadn't quite got my bearings yet. Sometimes a toe in the current is all it takes to pull you down into the undertow.

*   *   *

I was exhausted.

I had spent most of the evening staring out my window, up at the star-filled heaven above the house. I was lucky enough to have a window close to my bed, so I could stargaze and daydream as I pleased from the comfortable position of lying down. On some nights I would fall asleep while talking to the blackened sky above. It offered no insight. It offered no words. But on certain occasions it made me feel better after having these conversations.

'I hope Mariah is going to be all right,' I thought- sending my prayer out into the dark, black abyss above me. 'I hope that whatever I did didn't scar the girl too much. Although she was probably too young to even remember anything that had happened.' My heart felt as if it was being tugged out of my chest. I would've been a good uncle. I might have gone to toy stores and taught her how to fly a kite. I would have done all those things. I would have been a perfect fit; a handyman, always good for a joke. I'd even write her a poem if I was so inclined. I take it back. I take it all back. I swear to you, heavenly father. I take it all back. I'm repentant. I'll do my tithe, I promise you.

Little Mariah. Little girl. Little children. My mind slipped into a fantasy vision. It was so vivid. *I could see Curtis with his smug, blank look. He has a long-range rifle in one hand and he's marching down a hallway. As he walks down the hall he passes by large oak tag posters with bright pictures, drawn in crayon, of dinosaurs and religions of the world.*

The drinking fountains are low to the ground; lower than normal ones. From down the hallway, there's a chorus of kids singing 'Row Row Row Your Boat'. A teacher is scolding a young man for not sitting upright enough. It smells like pencil shavings, here- that musty wooden smell of my youth. There's a splotch of sawdust in the corner of the hallway as a reminder that a kid had heaved their lunch in the not-too-distant past. There are doorways with numbers and letters on them. K-1. K-2. Curtis peers his dead gaze into one of the rooms, through one of the glass panes in the door, and scouts the room out. There's little Mariah in the corner, dressed in her blue gingham dress like Dorothy from the Wizard of Oz, playing with oversized building blocks. She looks like my sister, I think. That's a good thing because Bruce isn't much to look at. Curtis's face is emotionless; like he's already dead. He raises the rifle into the room and

I snapped out of the vision. I wasn't asleep. But I wasn't fully awake, either. My head hurt. My chest hurt. Everything seemed to throb in a dull nagging pain that went everywhere. I felt hungover. I knew that feeling well. But I hadn't put a drop to my lips in what seemed to be an eternity. I hadn't had a cigarette, either. Not that I had been a chimney beforehand. But it had been quite a while.

I heard something rustling beneath the floorboards. I heard things being moved. I heard the sliding of furniture. I heard things being dropped into tin cans. He was awake. It was three thirty in the morning. And he was awake. I knew it was coming. The music came as it always did. Loud and evangelical. Although it wasn't as loud as other mornings. I remember that. I couldn't quite make out what 'John the Revelator' was talking about, but I'm sure it was something about fighting the evils of the world and making good on God's eternal crusade for righteousness. I rolled over to the edge of my bed to try and listen closely to what was being preached, but I still couldn't make it out.

Time wore on and the hours slowly crept towards daybreak. At first light, things began to come into focus in the darkness. I must've looked at the clock every five minutes and saw that minute hand mock me by going so slow. I decided that I'd had enough lying down and I sprung up and began to hastily dress. It's amazing how tough buttons are to do when you're in a rush to get your shirt on.

My stomach rumbled. I made myself some buttered toast and a cup of tea. I wished I could make coffee but couldn't risk the aroma wafting all over the house. It was now 5:45 and time was growing very short. I crunched on my toast and it was delicious. Perfectly hit the spot. I didn't usually drink tea, but when I did- it was English style (another inheritance from Europe). Milk and sugar. I was going to dress this tea up as much as I could to have it taste like coffee.

The world was still waking up when I looked out my kitchen window and saw a figure walking up the path that led from the street to the house. My neighborhood was still very much asleep at that hour. One or two of the houses had the dull flicker of nightlights in their kitchens illuminating the windows. If I didn't know any better, I would have thought that the figure was a homeless person. But I knew better. It was a straggly outline, with waves of hair flying in the wind behind them. It was Shep. He was here. Lucky for me, the music was still blaring from downstairs.

I placed my tea- which I had decided was a poor excuse for coffee- on the countertop and briskly walked to the door. I slowly and carefully threw the bolt open and the door surprisingly didn't whine or creak. Maybe the Gods were working in my favor after all. Shep entered the hallway, and I beckoned him over to my apartment.

He didn't look surprised to see me.

I collected him and closed the door. He was dressed in his usual attire; flannel shirt and corduroy pants, with workingman's brown boots that were caked in mud. His large beard covered most of his torso and his flowing hair whirled behind him. Today he wore a prospector's hat, which was somewhere between a Cowboy hat and a porkpie. When he stepped into the apartment, I threw my arms around him and gave him a large embrace. He waited for just one moment before reciprocating the same with me. I slapped his back with a couple of hearty open-palmed bangs before letting him go. He had a salty smell about him- always. It mingled with the smell of dirt, but he was never 'dirty.' He was of the earth, through and through.

"Good to see you, Shep," I said.

"The day it says a'howdy," he said.

"Would you like some tea," I asked.

CHAPTER SIXTEEN

We must've looked ridiculous, the two of us, sipping tea and talking quietly in my kitchen at sunrise. My kitchen hadn't had much use since I'd moved in, so the tea set needed a good rinse before I poured the hot water into the cups. I could swear I still tasted the musty smell of the cabinet when I brought the cup to my mouth, but then again it might've just been the Earle Gray I tasted. Shep sat with one leg crossed over the other and lazily rocked his leg back and forth like he was keeping time. He leaned against the wall with his head looking up at my ceiling and offered a response here and there. His arms were folded, and he'd occasionally scratch one of his elbows through the shirt.

"Where be the hands when the feet get a goin'," he asked.

"His note said 7:45. Around 7:15 we should peek out the window and wait for him to go. Then we can trail him over there."

"Aha. And we throw the net when?"

"Outside the school."

"HA! The proximity is a hairline," he asked. "The mind don't work overtime for a plus?"

"Overtime for a plus," I asked.

"Tackle early! Reap later!"

"I don't think that's a good idea, Shep. We need to get him during the act, not a minute before or a minute after. It will be so much sweeter if we do it that way, don't you agree?" It was like waiting for the last moment to release during sex; getting this bastard right before the moment he was about to pounce was the only way I was going to feel completely fulfilled.

Shep nodded his head slowly but didn't look directly at me.

Looking at Shep, and watching him process what had gone on, I was inspired to seek an interview with him after everything was over. A book on him, on his life and adventures might be a possibility as well. I was certain that he'd craft words and phrases that would envelop the reader and be a smash with the publishing powers that be downstate at Charles Scribners or Doubleday and Company. To hear the yarns and tales of an authentic Adirondack guide, in his own words, complete with the pops of a campfire and the smoky flavor of cured meats interspersed woven into his words, would, in my opinion, be a lucrative project. I'd help the course along, of course. Perhaps add some commentary here and there. But the stage would be Shep's. It would be his time to finally shine. I thought it a fantastic idea. I also thought that it might help him financially down the road. I couldn't see him living in that shack through the harsh winters as he progressed into his later years. At the very least, I'd ask if he wanted to bunk on my couch when the weather turned. The idea seemed promising. Though I wouldn't mention anything until after everything had settled. As of that moment, I wasn't sure either of us would live past mid-morning.

Shep sat and munched on some toast, buttered Wonder bread with a smear of raspberry preserves. It was a simple breakfast for a person who only knew simplicity. But conversely, in that simplicity, he might've been the most complex person I'd ever met.

We didn't talk too much at the table that morning. After Shep had eaten his toast, he remained in his position; leg up, arms crossed, head back against the wall. His eyes were shut, too. If I didn't know any better I would have thought he was in some sort of prayer stance that Hindus used. I just sat and watched him while my horrible tea lingered in front of me. I'd take sips of its bitter coldness and then place the cup back on the table.

While we sat there the muffled voice of *John the Revelator* spoke under us. The kitchen was the worst place to be if you were trying to hear what was being spewed from the speakers below. But we still heard it.

Sleep and all its empty promises was trying to take me at that moment, but I fought it off. I squirmed in my seat, itched imaginary itches, and even widened my eyes as far as they would go. There was no way I was going to let sleep take me. I stood up to stretch and the voice below us stopped. I heard that familiar interference sound of the record needle being pulled from the vinyl. Then, below us, we heard nothing. I instantly wasn't tired anymore. I felt as if I was injected with caffeine.

I leaned over and began to stir Shep. "Shep," I said, tapping his arm. "Shep, come on, I think he's leaving."

Shep snapped out of his trance and stood next to me. We looked out of the kitchen window through my pierced blinds, and out towards the street. We waited.

Mothers passed by pushing large bassinets. Old folks were out for their morning constitutions. A couple of jays whizzed by riding on the spring breeze. It was all confirmation that springtime had officially arrived in the Adirondacks. We heard the front door slam open and immediately Curtis walked out, carrying something wrapped in burlap sacks in his right hand. The force of the door slam caused us both to jump a little.

He disappeared behind the neighbor's high pine hedges and was on his way.

It was time for us to go too.

*   *   *

There were three ways to get to the Ichabod Crane School. I was sure that Curtis would take the most logical one; which would be to take Route 9, up through Caldwell, and then bear right onto 9N and then finally a left onto Trout Lake Road where the school was. By doing that, he would hit a bevy of traffic lights and most likely run into some morning traffic. The shortcut I had in mind would take us through a few suspect unpaved country roads, but it would get us there quicker than he would. The roads would be unpaved and gravel in some places but getting us there ahead of him was the only thing I cared about.

"You're iron with the drive-sense," Shep asked as we pulled away from the house.

"I know where I'm going if that's what you're asking."

We turned off the main road in Queensbury, and onto a recently paved street that didn't even have a name yet. It was a steep hill that had large wheat stalks on either side of it. A farmer named George Bumford had donated this small section of his field to the county for them to begin the paving job. I knew this information from personal experience; I had written a story on it over the winter.

"Bumford's fields of grain a'flowin," Shep said, pointing on either side of the road.

"That's right, Shep. How did you know?"

"Bumford's a heartstrung amigo from the wee hours."

"Right."

My car windows were down we both had our arms stuck out, letting them play on the breeze. Shep's beard was being pulled out of the window. After getting a bit frustrated at this, he finally held it in place, against his chest with his left hand, while the right still rode the breeze.

I happened to catch a quick look at my face in my sideview mirror and my mouth was open in a crazed smile. Shep looked relaxed. If he had any touch of nerves, his body language didn't give anything away. He looked like he could fall fast asleep at any moment. It was too quiet in the car, so I flipped the radio on to break up the silence.

Bing Crosby serenaded us as we traveled past pasture after pasture. It was stunning how much this desolate stretch of road reminded me of the fields in Belgium. I shook my head a few times. *Not now*, I thought. My pulse began to race. *Not now.*

Something in the road ahead of us caught my attention. "What is that," I asked, pointing out the windshield to the horizon straight ahead.

Shep leaned forward and placed his hand above his eyebrows. "As if the face of mad destiny shone like the shining sun!"

"What is it," I asked again, curter this time.

"A tangle in the fishin' line! A cloud!"

As we approached it, it became clear what it was: there was a dead cow in the middle of the road with two people standing over it. The two of them were identically dressed, wearing worn pale blue dungaree overalls and white undershirts that could've used a few rounds in some bleach. One of the figures was taller and old, the other one was young, maybe no more than thirteen I guessed at a moving distance. I tapped the brake and we halted just before we reached them. I could feel my blood pressure rising in my face.

"What the hell is going on here," I yelled, nearly hanging outside my driver's side window. "This is a road for vehicles!"

The older one had his arm around the younger. They both looked grief-struck. The father's face held back tears and the younger one had wet cheeks. The older one looked up at us and said, "Clover's dead." The cow's hulking wrinkled black and white body was strewn across the pavement with its stomach side facing us. Behind its hindquarters, the smoke of a pile of steaming hot manure wafted into the spring morning breeze. Must've been the last thing it did before keeling over.

"Friend, while I appreciate that you just lost your cow, we have to be somewhere very important very soon. Now you need to get this thing out of the road so we can pass." I had no time for sympathy for dead livestock.

'C'mon son," the father said. "Let's get a rope."

They walked off the shoulder of the road, and beyond the trees. Soon enough, they were out of our field of vision.

I anxiously paced back and forth in front of my car four or five times. My eyes never left the area of trees where the father and son had disappeared. Shep leaned against the side of my car with his butt propped against the fender flare. He stood with his arms folded as if he was simply waiting for a bus. My internal clock was ticking away and the seconds it was running off made me crazed.

My face was flushed hot, and I pounded my fist against the roof of my car. I could almost see that squirrelly bastard driving up 9, with his smug face and emotionless demeanor. "Get in the car, Shep."

"Repeat," he said.

"Get back in the car. Let's go."

He obeyed and we got in the car quickly. I slammed my door so hard I thought I had broken it off the hinge. I turned the key and slammed the shifter into reverse. Shep's face was puzzled. I went backwards for about twenty or thirty feet, and then shifted into drive and pounced on the gas pedal. Our heads jerked backward from the thrust. Neither of us had time to yell before the front bumper of my car nailed the dead cow, Clover, if you will, right in the stomach and pushed her bloating corpse to the side a bit. After the impact, there was now a little bit of room to maneuver through. I didn't bother to look at Shep.

I backed up once more and turned my wheel slightly, thinking that I had enough clearance to make it around. As we drove my front passenger side wheel ran over Clover's nose, splattering blood all over the pavement, and subsequently all over my wheel and tire well. I looked in my rearview mirror and saw the carnage that I'd left behind me. Part of me was sad and I looked in my rearview mirror briefly. Part of me just wanted to press on forward. Just like usual.

Time was now running against us, and I remember feeling dizzy from being on edge for so long. I didn't know if Shep could drive, and I wasn't about to ask him now, but we might've been better off. I just tried to take long, dragging breaths and hoped that would do the trick to get me to a place where I could function. The time on my watch said 7:23. If I didn't burn rubber, we would never make it on time.

As we drove up and down hills, around corners, and through thickly vegetated roads, homes began to appear more frequently. Every time we went over a hill, we were thrown upwards out of our seats. I didn't think to look at the speedometer, but we must've been going close to 90 miles an hour. We hit something, a rock or piece of blacktop, and the both of us jumped in our seats. I cautiously hung my head out of the window, hoping against hope that I didn't hear any wheezing sound or knocking near the tires. No strange sounds. I composed myself and gripped the steering wheel a little tighter.

Houses in clusters usually meant you were getting closer to a main road. Up ahead I saw the blue sign with orange writing that said WARREN 42. We were getting close to Trout Lake Road. I gunned the gas; the pedal was pressed as far down as it could go and in the back of my head, I worried that the damn thing might just combust under the hood.

When we reached Trout Lake Road, I cut a left quickly and we almost tipped. I don't know how close we came to going over, but it felt like I could've stuck my hand out of the window and slapped the ground. I began to ease off the gas and parked the car across the street from the school.

The school was set back at the top of a long clear, grass-covered hill. A circular driveway twisted its way from the street, up the hill, to the parking lot where faculty and staff left their cars. The building itself had been recently renovated after a six- month-long haggling session with the town board. It was a single-level school, with brand-new bricks on the façade and freshly painted orange lines in the parking lot.

I turned the car off. Shep and I sat in silence. The sun was out in all its glory. It made that green grass look lush and somehow delicious and fresh. Someone must have cut it earlier because it smelled like watermelon. It could've been a baseball park if it was any more manicured. But the morning was getting on and it was getting hot. I didn't know which way Curtis planned to enter, so I tried to keep my head on a swivel. Shep didn't need to be told to do the same. In the moment of reflection, thinking of how beautiful the grass was, a brown thing darted into view. It came from across the street.

"Let's go. SHEP! Let's go!"

We threw our doors open and left them that way, awkwardly agape. Shep jumped onto the hood of my car and slid across it. We almost got creamed by a milk truck that was thundering at full speed, but it passed us by; the second time a thing of dairy threatened to impede our progress. The street was quiet that morning; no one was around on the street or in cars. The two of us quickly looked both ways and began to skip across the street. We reached the incline, on the grass, and I put every inch of my soul into every step up that hill. I had run up hills before. This was nothing new. Shep was fifteen feet or so to my right. God bless him, he matched me step for step. It gave me confidence. It gave me pleasure. We ran, but we were both silent in our sprints. We didn't make any noise at all; no rebel yells, no war cries, although I admit, I had to use restraint to keep it inside. For the moment I was no longer chasing Curtis, I was chasing a piece of shit Nazi with one of those stupid helmets. My heart leapt. Curtis was fast, but we were going to be faster. Curtis ran with his rife at his side in his right hand. His form was incorrect. A soldier always carried his weapon in both hands when taking a hill and pressed against the chest. He, on the other hand, ran like a coward. I could feel us gaining ground as we closed in on him.

I gave a hand signal to Shep to start to move closer and we began to close our distance. Curtis stopped a few paces before hitting the parking lot and that's when both Shep and I knocked him to the ground. His rifle harmlessly fell a few feet from us and Shep was good enough to collect it. He kicked and squirmed on the ground like a wounded insect. "NOOOOOOOOOO," he screamed, his voice cracking like a child. "NOOOO YOU MOTHER FUCKERS!!!" He kicked my thigh with one of his flailing legs but was unable to stand up. I balled my fist and planted a fistful of knuckles on the side of his face. My knuckle hit his nose with one hard, yet perfectly placed, blow and it stung like hell. But after the hit, he was no longer kicking and screaming. He was unconscious.

Reality kicked in at that moment and I scanned the area for witnesses. There wasn't a soul on the street. His screams hadn't so much as disturbed a butterfly. There was just green grass and a quiet street below. The windows in the school had been shut and no one heard his loud cussing. "Come over here, and let's get him into the car."

As we grabbed him up, my attention caught someone standing at the bottom of the hill on the sidewalk. I had no time to question anything, so I grabbed Curtis under his armpits and Shep grabbed his legs. Shep had been suspiciously quiet during the execution of this whole ordeal and that made me nervous. We hurried the limp body of the would-be killer down the hill, to the sidewalk, and the figure on the sidewalk came more and more into focus. It was Nancy, wearing a peach sundress and hiding something in her right hand.

We took our last few steps off the grass, and it was confirmed. It was Nancy, all right.

She looked brokenhearted as if she'd been fired from a job or lost a boyfriend in battle. Her face was pouting, and her eyes were blood-shot. Either she was crying or recently had been crying. She shook her head in complete exasperation. "I heard him talking about this," she said, her voice gravelly like a cement mixer. "I was going to stop him, but..." She trailed off. "Glad someone got to it." She shrugged her shoulders and turned away from us. Her shoulders dropped and she looked exactly the way she did when I saw her on the porch a few afternoons earlier. When she turned the object in her hand was revealed to be a cleaver. She was going to butcher him right there.

That in and of itself was disturbing. I can't imagine how children would deal with someone getting gutted right outside their classroom. He'd shriek and squeal and oh the blood! Nancy would probably have been arrested too. Someone would have seen her. Someone would have watched her butcher this little piece of human garbage. She looked quite disappointed that she didn't get the opportunity to do so.

I know I would've felt the same way.

She meekly turned away from us and began to walk down towards the intersection. "Nancy," I called out. She paid no mind to my beck-on. She simply turned her back and walked away from us.

"NANCY!"

Chapter Seventeen

Curtis remained unconscious for nearly an hour and a half.

I was tempted to take him to the Wendigo in the unconscious state he was in and hope for the best. But there were a few things that tugged at me that would not permit me to do such a thing. First, he had to know that he was being held accountable for what he intended to do. For proper justice to be served the accused must have their crimes read aloud and be made aware. Second, we needed to be sure he was put in a vegetative state so there was no possible way for the spirit to escape. I wanted the Wendigo spirit to enter him while he was incapacitated.

We chained him, Shep and I did, to one of the large trees that was on the back side of Shep's property. We set it so his arms were bent backward around the base of the large oak. We faced him towards the forest. When he screamed, and I fully intended on making him scream, only the forest would hear it. It would be our secret.

*   *   *

"I'm not going to be any part of this," Shep said. "The nuts and bolts of this are all you. When the time is right, you can give me a yell." His face didn't look right. His words were throaty. If I didn't know any better, I thought he was going to break down. He turned away from me and walked to his shack, where he closed the door behind him.

I would have much preferred him to stand by my side in performing this, but I didn't give him any grief. This was only the means to an end anyway. I didn't go about pushing thoughts on people. My only concern was justice.

I hadn't heard from Sabrina. I hadn't seen her. Since all of this went down with Curtis, I hadn't received any notes. I hadn't had any contact. She wasn't even part of my consciousness at that moment. I should've been a better person.

I set up a bucket of water I'd collected from Shep's well. I grabbed the cold wooden handle and threw the water in Curtis' face, sending streams of water down his cheeks and dousing his clothes. He snapped awake- and when he fully came to, he was pissed off.

"Untie me you cocksucker!" He pulled at the chains. "UNTIE ME!"

I naturally stepped back from him. He thrashed back and forth like a captive animal. And that's just what he was; an animal.

"What were you going to do to those children, you bastard?" I spoke to him calmly. "What...what were you going to do to them?" I began to cry. "ANSWER ME!"

He stopped his thrashing. He lowered his head towards me so that his eyes were tucked back behind his brows. He then said calmly, "I was going to kill and fuck every last one of them. And it was going to be sweet. It was going to be so sweet. Seeing their little heads blown apart. Blood everywhere. All in the name of..."

I slapped his face with an open palm, and it reddened instantly. "Tell me more," I said. I pulled out a switchblade that I'd hidden in my pocket. I gripped the handle and popped the blade.

"You think this is going to stop with me," he said, defiantly. "There are thousands of us..."

I dug the blade into his side, and he howled like a dog that had been struck. His shriek made my earwax jiggle. It felt like I was cutting a chicken and blood began to pour from the wound. His body became tight, and I could see his hands were instinctively trying to move towards the wound. But they were bound. My hand turned red, bathed in the blood that was rushing from his side. "They are just children, you fucking animal!"

"They are the work of SATAN," he screamed. "HELP!" He began to convulse and scream. I guess his primal instinct was to call for help.

I removed the blade from his flesh and threw it off to the side. It made the sound of a knife cutting watermelon as it exited. I took my stainless-steel Zippo cigarette lighter out of my shirt pocket and flipped it open. "You know what this is, pal," I asked.

"Fuck you," he spat back at me.

"This is fire, my friend. Fire answers to no one." I pulled the striker and a fat flame danced on the wick. I held it to his face. I brought the flame close to his apathetic face and let the fire burn his cheek. He rocked his head back and forth violently to try and escape the flame. "Don't move, sonny," I said and held his head in place with my hand. I held the flame to his cheek for a moment and he screamed wildly again. He struggled with all his strength to try and break the chains. He tried to lurch, wiggle, and pull. But the chains were no match for him. He wasn't going anywhere. His flesh began to burn, and his mouth was constantly agape, screaming.

I pulled the lighter away and flicked it closed. The metal was warm in my hand. I reached for the axe that was leaning up against a small birch tree. "Look at me," he said. "LOOK AT ME," he demanded again, his chest rising a falling like a child playing with a balloon. I thought it might burst wide open. I did as he instructed and looked at him, at his arrogant young face, now scarred with a black hole on his right cheek. He did the unthinkable. He began to laugh at me. His eyes widened and he cackled at me, in my face. His laughter echoed through the trees and went through my head.

I reared the axe back and went to work. After four or five hacks his foot finally came off at the ankle.

*   *   *

When it was over, I didn't feel well. I felt nauseous. I didn't want to go inside Shep's shack, so I walked down to the small creek that ran through the back of the property to wash the blood off. I gave a glancing final look at Curtis' body, hung lifelessly like an oil rag suspended from pieces of tree bark. He wasn't dead. But he might've just as well been. I leaned down to the water and cupped my hands. I let the cool ripples run over my calloused fingers and I splashed my face. I once again looked back at the body. I found a flat, dry rock in the riverbed and I sat on it.

I didn't feel the expected feeling of vanquishment. I didn't feel like a hero. I just felt like what I was; a madman who had tortured and mutilated another human being almost to death. I felt a feeling of dissatisfaction; hollow and alone. "Shep," I called up to the house. "Shep!" I wanted Shep to be there at that moment. I wanted his presence, if not to talk to, then to just physically be there as another human being. That's all I wanted. Company. Of all the emotions that had run their way through me during that time, this feeling of internal blackness and void was the strongest. I was not expecting this.

The pages of my mind flipped slowly that afternoon. They turned from one page to the next in deliberate movements, none of which got any closer to the end of the story. It just went on and on with no relief, like a nagging headache that didn't stop. I had pinned a lot of hope that this endeavor would help me. I shifted my weight a bit, as the rock under me wasn't the most comfortable of places. I sat and

I thought. And I thought. And I can't really tell the details of what I sat and thought about. I know most of it had to do with what got me to that point. I thought of my mom and dad. I thought of Jane, Bruce, and Mariah. I thought of my dog Ripley who died when I was 12. I thought of Chief Marshall Arthur Harris. I even thought of Herlihy. And the lake. And how much nicer things were from behind the trees. The trees around me knew some secrets, didn't they? But the trees were true, as Shep liked to say. What hid behind the trees is what you needed to watch out for. I had been among the forests for some time. I had planted my seeds among the great birch and oak. I had made myself comfortable there. And I suppose many people have done the same. The Wendigo did too. And so did the person who had vanished. Sabrina. Everything could have been traced back to that fateful evening on the Steel Pier. If I hadn't stepped out of the bar to get air, maybe I wouldn't be in the middle of the forest, covered in a dying man's blood. Or maybe I would have? I felt like I had nothing to hold on to. Maybe I would have been better off going over the edge of the chasm. Maybe. But I didn't. I could once again thank Sabrina for that. I was in search of a winch. All I got was a rock tied to my waist.

There was no milk and honey here. All that remained was a bitter film of anger that shrouded me. My mother, whose name I had called often in battle, would be embarrassed. My father, whose name I hadn't uttered in years, would be embarrassed. Not that they could hear me, anyway. What was left? I found myself with nothing else to hide behind. There was no place to take cover. Now what? I needed to do something with the catatonic person I had tortured and beaten almost to death. For a quick second, I considered maybe nursing him back to health. However, that flicker of flame was extinguished pretty quickly. The light, the flame that had been beckoning me for my entire life was muddled and I could no longer see its glow. My desperate search had once again led me to a dead end. I tried to stop thinking for a moment. I cleared my head by imagining a large white movie screen in my mind; the kind that they had at the Ritz Theater in Glens Falls. It was stark white and quiet. Just plain and white and hanging there. But then the writer's side of my mind began to take over and other things began to pervade my mind. *I could smell popcorn. For effect, I even imagined the velvet curtains pulled to each side. I could feel the uncomfortable seat under me. The movie screen turned black, and a countdown appeared on it. 5...4...3...2...Boop! There was no sound. Just the outside rustle of a sweet breeze through the trees. The opening titles came on, written in an Arabian font: Sabrina in Trouble was the name of the film. It was not in Technicolor, so there were some black-and-white pops and skips in the film. The film co-starred Bert Lahr and Jack Benny. Still no soundtrack, though. Sabrina came on the screen, looking as beautiful as ever. Her hair was a little different, but she looked just as I remembered her. Almost to the T. She was wearing a long sequin gown that had small flecks of light flare off of it. Behind her was a long ribbon that was being held in place between two poles. It looked like something you'd see at a race. A race. 'Do it,' she said to the camera. 'Do it.' She placed two fingers over her lips and blew a kiss to the screen. The screen faded black and there was an inscription screen that came up. This film is for you.*

"What the hell are you doing down here," Shep asked, tugging on my shoulder. "If you don't hurry up, he's going to bite it up there and then your entire plot is going to go to hell. Not that it's far from it already."

"I feel like I want to throw up," I said.

"Well, whatever you're going to do, I suggest you do it fast. I don't know how much longer I can take this. If we're going to do this, then we ought to get a move on. Moose's Walk isn't easy to get to when coming from the other direction."

"Other direction? What do you mean other direction?"

"Well, we're not going to drag that mutilated kid through the streets of Caldwell. That is unless you want to attract a whole heap of attention. I don't think you want that. At least, that kind of attention. The plan is to come down from the north and go at it that way."

"When we get there what are we going to do?"

Shep removed his hat and placed it in his hands. "Like I said, Frank, the only way to beat these things is to burn them. We get there, we burn everything. Every last building. Every last person. And like you said, once it jumps into his body, we carry it to the water and throw him in."

I was expecting him to say, 'And that will be that' but he said no such thing. His face of solemn duty told me everything I needed to know. He was a man of the land, who was brought up among nature. And here we were, about to embark on a journey to perhaps rid the earth of these fiendish beings. The gravity of the situation made my chest heavy, and it became hard to breathe. I knew he was uncomfortable with what I had done to Curtis, but there was no changing that now.

"We need to get going," I said, wiping some perspiration from my brow. "When do we leave?"

"Midnight," he said. "We cross the lake at night, and head into the tributary under the cover of darkness."

I gulped. "We're going to be on the water at night," I asked.

He shook his head, yes, and a knot grew in my stomach.

There was something about being in a small boat, on a lake, in the middle of the night that just bothered me.

*   *   *

We walked together, almost in lockstep, back to where Curtis was chained to the tree. He was slouched forward with his head cocked down and his shoulders dropped. I placed two fingers under his nose and felt very faint breezes of breath. "He's still alive," I said.

His face was still frozen in that defiant puss. Just looking at him made that internal combustive anger boil up in my stomach. "Let's go, Shep. Let's get things ready."

"I hope you don't think this is going to be easy," he said.

"I hope it's not," I said. "Wouldn't seem right." I extended my hand towards his face and waved it a few times. I ran my index finger down his bloodied nose and his mouth snapped at my finger like a snapping turtle, and nearly took a bite out of it. In a quick snap, I punched him in the face, causing a stream of crimson-brown blood to shoot from his mouth, and he went back to his comatose state. I wondered how many of those he had in him.

We freed him from the chains and his semi-lifeless body collapsed like a folding chair when he hit the ground. The both of us backed up away from him like freighted cats. Shep nearly tripped over a severed foot that I had tossed to the side. He looked at me, disappointed, and shook his head. I looked down at that heap of a monster and delivered another firm kick to his dying midsection. His worn leather jacket was almost completely soaked in blood. It looked like something out of a horror film. Lon Cheney. Those types. But this wasn't a movie in my head. It wasn't playing at a matinee down at The Ritz. No, this was very real and very close. He still had that smug look on his mouth. It just wouldn't go away. "Son of a bitch," I said. "Who's afraid now," I asked. "YOU DON'T KNOW PAIN!" I screamed and I couldn't breathe. I was hyperventilating. "Who's fucking afraid now? WHO'S AFRAID NOW?"

"I am," Shep quietly replied from behind me.

Chapter Eighteen

Neither Shep nor I had much to say to one another for the remainder of the afternoon and into the evening twilight. All the closeness and goodwill that we had worked to cultivate had suddenly been winnowed away; blown away on my seething breath. We hardly made eye contact. When we walked around one another, we awkwardly danced as we passed by. He began to get dinner prepared; a sauté of lake trout, onions, and beets cooked in a skillet. It smelled good enough, but I wasn't convinced that it would have the taste part of the equation. While he busied himself cooking, I wandered around his vast property, all the while nervously wringing my hands. I wanted it to be nighttime so terribly. I wished to see the sun go down and the sky turn that purple-orange color that quiets even the most tempestuous of lives. It was on that coming of nighttime and our overnight endeavor that I hung the hope of feeling normal again. Something as simple as seeing an Adirondack sunset would have done wonders. But there was no sunset to see. The sky had clouded up to a milky gray in anticipation of a rainstorm. There would be no calming sunset; only tumult and rain.

Periodically I'd go over to our victim...my victim...and place my fingers under his nostrils. He began to look more and more like a child as the afternoon went on. Layer upon layer of age stripped away from him like peeling back the skin of a fruit. He was going to murder god knows how many children. He was going to violate their bodies and do horrific things to them. And I had stopped it. I had put an end to everything. Including his life.

I had grown accustomed to seeing evil face-to-face during my stay in Europe. Don't let anyone fool you; I saw it on both sides of the trench. Anyone who says they didn't see horrific shit coming from their own side was either blind or dumb. Evil is a coat that people put on. I still say that underneath layers people were good. Are good. And what I saw strip away from that dying boy was a layer of evil as thick as a fresh leather duster. He wore it long, he wore it well, and eventually, it became a part of him. I pitied him. He'd meet his creator and then what? Then what?

I felt the weight of a judge on my shoulders as the twilight gently skidded on toward the blackness of night. My court was good and final. I was consistent, if anything. I still didn't feel like I'd accomplished anything. I would walk over to Curtis' body and begin cursing under my breath. I'd curse at it and ask it what it planned to do with those poor innocent schoolchildren. I wasn't asking to know. I already knew. Each time I felt a little bit of remorse for what I had done and what I had planned to do, I would just look at his smug face (which never changed at all, by the way) and my rage would rise once again. It was the only way I knew I could go through with the plan. It was the only way I knew how to deal with anything.

I began to run scenarios about how we would finally put this monster away. For good. I wasn't looking forward to a moonlit bateau ride with a grizzled Adirondack guide, but I supposed these were the sacrifices one had to make. That was another thing: I resolved that I would be done with him too, after all of this was over. I thought Shep would have been more on board with this mission and it gnawed at me that he wasn't more enthusiastic. I couldn't understand how his logic worked. Then again, he was raised very differently than I was. I know that now. I knew it then too, but there was something shrouding my ability to fully see it and understand it.

In a long line of people who didn't stick by me, he was just the latest and the greatest to fly the coop when things got tough. I stupidly thought that I understood him, and he understood me. So much for that. Well, I planned on being the leach that used him for the rest of our time together and then that would be the end of it. I'd probably never see him or hear from him again. His type got by without a care in the world.

That's when it hit me that I hadn't checked in with my job in days. God only knew what kind of crap I was going to get from Herlihy when I eventually made my triumphant return. I hadn't written anything, either. I didn't even carry my Moleskin with me. This was coming from someone who documented every single day he was in the Army. I'd slouch down in some hell pit in Europe, with bombs exploding thirty or forty feet away from me. Sometimes dirt and rocks that were blown up by the bombs would hit my boots. I would sit there and think, 'My god, when is it going to just come and hit me? When is it going to stop teasing and go full bore and do it?' So funny how things can change and reveal themselves. So, so funny. And as the days had progressed from that awful night on the Steel Pier when everything went haywire I had become more and more distant from who I thought I was. I wasn't drinking. I still don't know how that happened. I guess I just found better things to do. Not that I was a heavy smoker, but I hadn't done too much of that either. I could really go for a cigarette now, though.

If I could ever go back and talk to myself, I would have grabbed myself by the scruff and said, 'Knock it off and move away.' That's the truth. I would have just dropped everything where it was and gone somewhere else. I had always heard that Western New York was a land full of opportunity. I could've moved to Rochester, changed my name, and no one would have ever heard from me ever again. I'd lived alone before. I could open a can of tuna when I was hungry and I knew how to wash sheets. I could pick up a job at a paper out there, no trouble. Maybe even meet a girl. Honeymoon over at Niagara Falls. But I didn't do any of those things. I stayed put.

'Sabrina is going to be there when all hell breaks loose,' I thought. 'She'll be there when we come in with our torches burning.' I knew that once the cavalry arrived she would be there, with her coy smile. Then, after everything went down, we would get out of there. Maybe we'd move away someplace. Maybe Rochester.

Evening came and with the darkness came a soft mist. The air was heavy with moisture, and everything seemed to smell like sweet dew. There was so much hope and promise that rode in with that smell. A new beginning, perhaps. An ending, maybe. Before we sat down for an undoubtedly awkward meal, I decided to take a little stroll. I walked down Shep's road to the street, where Big Bill's auto graveyard sat lonely, yet wholly full.

I stood among Fords and Chevrolets of days gone by. There was a small light in the office window burning lowly and I could make out the distinct outlines of two figures hunkering over a table. I slowly walked over, through the rows of cars, completely petrified at the fact that I knew places like this usually kept guard dogs on the prowl in the evening. I managed to ignore the thought and crept closer to the grimy window. I looked inside.

Big Bill and John were leaning over a roughly fashioned tin table that looked like one solid sheet of metal that was bent down on four sides. Big Bill (whose ironic name didn't hit me till just then) held an engine part in his greasy paws. "This is the outside of the gearbox, John. See, look." The smaller man held the part up to the lumbering man-child that stood by his side like an obedient dog. "You've seen one of these before."

"DEBORAH!" He yelled, almost in a convulsion. "That doesn't make sense."

"And we need to find better seals on this so that it'll fit right," Big Bill said, ignoring John's outburst. "I think we should probably get going for the night. I think your mom said we were having meatloaf tonight. And I hate when meatloaf gets cold."

The man-child proclaimed his usual outburst. "Deborah. Deborah! That doesn't make sense."

Big Bill grabbed a hold of John's hand and led him over to the light switch. I ran and hid behind a tan coupe that had its windshield removed and interior shredded and, watched their every move. Every move that Big Bill made, he kept John's hand in his. They walked out of the office and shut the door behind them, making the red CLOSED sign pendulum back and forth. "I think we should go and listen to the Yankee game on the radio when we get home. What do you say about that?"

Once again, John beckoned his mother and pointed out once again that something didn't make sense. I watched the two of them walk out, through the barrage of twisted auto wrecks, and disappear onto the street. They never let go of one another's hands. It impressed me almost to tears. It made me feel like a fool.

I collected myself the best I could and walked out onto the sidewalk. I kicked a discarded soup can down the street. It was so quiet that the clanging of the can rang out in the darkness. Warrensburg had only a few streetlights in those days and Big Bill's didn't have one. As I walked up the main street, past the silent shops, I came to be illuminated by the glow of a streetlight. I leaned against it and placed my head in my hands.

I rubbed my eyes until they went temporarily blind and yawned a few times. When my vision came back into focus, I saw a man standing at the end of the block. He was looking at me. He was dressed in a black trench coat, black hat, and black round sunglasses. It was one of those things that trailed Sabrina. She had told me their names, but at that point, it just wouldn't come to me. 'Van Steuben,' I thought. 'Van Buren?' It was something Dutch-sounding. I remembered that one of them had an ear missing.

"What do you want," I asked the figure. "What do you want with me?" To be truthful, I didn't exactly yell this at him, so he may have not heard me. He said nothing but continued to stare at me. He was standing at the foot of Shep's road, on the corner near Big Bill's.

I turned around and looked in the other direction. I hoped against hope that I would only see a darkened street, but that wasn't the case. In the shadows, I could see another man standing in the darkness. It was the other brother, for sure. They had me in a pincher's formation.

"WHAT DO YOU WANT?" I screamed this time, hoping to possibly stir some folks awake who were blissfully away in their homes.

"WHERE'S SABRINA?"

Nothing.

"WHERE IS SHE?"

My mood was shifting from fear to anger, and it was moving rather quickly. I took off towards the one that was standing near Big Bill's place and walked at a brisk pace. I was tired of fearing them, tired of not knowing. To my utter shock, the man didn't move a muscle. I walked to him and grabbed his collar on the jacket.

"ANSWER ME YOU SON OF A BITCH!"

He didn't speak. His face was as smug and unreachable as Curtis's had been. It was as if I did not affect on him whatsoever. That frustrated me to the point of tears, once again. I looked over my shoulder and saw the other brother standing behind me. He had moved at least twenty feet without making so much as a scuff on the sidewalk.

I shoved the one that was standing in front of me, and he staggered sideways a few steps. The one behind me grabbed my arms and put me in a full nelson. I jumped up and down trying to break his grip. I flailed my feet, trying to kick back into his stomach. Whatever this thing was, it had me, and it was dragging me backward. I didn't end my resolve. I shouted and cursed and kicked and tugged as the heels of my feet scraped against the ground.

Then, during all this thrashing and flailing I was dropped to the ground. I felt the back of my head plop into a square of grass that was near the edge of the sidewalk. My beck wrenched and a pain shot from my lower back to my shoulder. I turned my head down to see John, Big Bill's son, standing over me. He had the two brothers by the scruff of their overcoats and lifted them off the ground. They dangled above the ground like tabby cats that were misbehaving. "DEBORAH," he bellowed. "DEBORAH!" He shook the two of them like rag dolls, knocking their hats and sunglasses off their faces. I leaned back against my palms without getting off the ground. John was a hulking mass of humanity and made the two brothers look like vermin. He parted his arms with the brothers still in his grips and proceeded to slam their heads together. "DEBORAH!" He repeated as he smashed their skulls together once again. "DEBORAH! That doesn't make sense!" He didn't stop in his intensity or his speed. Over and over and over again their skulls crashed together. Their mouths began to gush blood like leaking faucets and their eyes looked like they were asleep. All the fear and fight that they had emitted had been beaten out of them.

Under the pressure of John's thunderous blows, the skulls began to sink inward and crack. The skin around the skull began to wear and eventually ripped wide open. John never once stopped. As he slammed and slammed small pieces of brain matter began to fall to the ground and plop like gelatin. Their eyeballs eventually shook loose from the sockets and knocked around like pieces of a perpetual motion game. I curled my legs back to avoid getting hit. Their bodies were covered in blood, and so was John. He didn't stop, until a voice called out of the darkness behind him.

"John!" The voice yelled, "JOHN! NO!"

A figure was running towards us. I knew instantly that it was Big Bill. John threw the bodies to the ground, almost in disgust, and they lay one on top of the other. I stood up and grabbed at my aching back which was barking something fierce. That fall to the ground was a little more intense than I had initially felt.

The father's face looked horrified. "What did you do???" He asked John. "What did you do??" He slapped the ogre across the face in one hard wallop. "Oh my god!" His face blew open wide in astonished horror at the scene his son had created.

"No," I said, stumbling to my feet. "Bill, no. He helped me. They were roughing me up and he came over and helped." I got to my feet and the world looked strange. I don't know if I'd sustained a concussion or what, but I knew my perception of what was going on around me wasn't very sharp.

Bill came over and looked into my eyes. "Turn your eyes toward the streetlight. Come here." He pulled the skin under my eyes down and pressed it against my cheek. He examined me as I'm sure he'd examine a '38 Chevy. "You have a concussion," he said. "Did they hit you in the head?"

"No, when I fell my head banged against the ground over there," I said pointing to the small patch of grass. I didn't realize how close I'd come to mashing the back of my head into a pile of dog shit that was possibly four inches from where my head made contact. That would have been the icing on the proverbial cake.

"You hit it on the dirt or the sidewalk?"

"On the dirt. That little patch before the curb."

"Makes sense," he said. "If your head hit that concrete, you'd probably not be able to talk to me right now. Fuckers," he said, turning to look at the brothers. "What a damn mess." His cavalier attitude led me to assume that this was not the first time he'd dealt with something like this. "Who are they?"

"I don't know really. I was up at Shep's, decided to take a walk down here and they pinched me and tried to drag me away."

"That's strange," he said. "They look a little familiar, but I can't place where I would have seen them." I stopped and thought for a moment. "I mean, people drop their cars off all the time, and I can't keep track of every face that comes in with a busted radiator hose. But there is something about them that's triggering off the old brain piston if you know what I mean."

I didn't, but it didn't matter. "Look, we've got two dead bodies here. We need to do something with them and do something fast." I didn't want this responsibility. I had my own things to tend to for the evening and the last thing I wanted were two dead brothers lying in the middle of the sidewalk.

I crouched down close and opened one of the jackets to see if I could find anything interesting. They wore a heavy-scented cologne that smelled like pine needles. I reached into the inside pocket of the one with the slightly bigger nose. I felt a handkerchief and nothing else. No gun. No knife. Nothing. Just a goddamn snot rag.

"I don't know if it's such a good idea to be doing this in the middle of the street," Big Bill interjected while scratching his meagerly-haired scalp with the brim of his cap. "Maybe we should…"

I put a hand up to shush Big Bill and he obliged. I rifled through their every pocket and found not so much as a ball of lint. Whoever or whatever these things were, they traveled light.

"Let's take them up to Shep's," I suggested. "At least we can get them out of view." I didn't stop to think how Shep would feel about two dead bodies being trudged up to his property, but at this point in the game, it was our only option. We couldn't risk someone walking their dog and stumbling on them. 'He's already pissed off at me,' I thought. 'I couldn't do much more damage, right?'

Big Bill instructed his stepson to pick the men up and he did so; throwing one over each shoulder as if he was carrying sacks of flour. The sidewalk was covered in blood. It looked like someone had butchered a pig right there on the pavement.

"I'm going to run inside and get a bucket of water to get some of this blood off the sidewalk," said Big Bill thinking out loud. The to his son, "You wait for me at Shep's and I'll be up there in a little while, okay?"

I told him that was fine, and John began to follow me.

*   *   *

Shep was outside when he saw us tramping up the road to his house. He had a small fire going and was lying down next to it. When we began making noise, he sat up and looked similar to Rip Van Winkle after he had awakened from his doze. He had looked content and peaceful for that brief moment. He stood up as if he was spring-loaded. "What the hell is *this*," he said, walking briskly towards us.

"The leftovers of a problem," I said.

"Frank, what the hell are you talking about? What the hell is this?"

John dropped the two dead brothers to the ground. He was now completely covered in blood. It splotched his face and cheeks and his hands looked like he was wearing red latex gloves. He had been quiet for most of our walk up the road. But he did belt out one, "Deborah," as the brother with both ears intact continued to bleed out all over his shoes.

"What the hell is John doing here? Where's his father? He's probably worr…"

"No, no Shep. It's fine. His old man will be here shortly. He helped me out," I said. "How's our boy," I asked. It had occurred to me that we hadn't checked on Curtis in a while. Before I walked down to the street, I had been looking him over in fifteen-minute intervals.

"How's our boy? How's our BOY? You've got two dead people here, Frank. Jesus but you're dense. To answer your question, I don't know, Frank," Shep said. "I don't know how our 'boy' is or was or whatever."

I explained to Shep what had happened in as quick a language as I could. The evening was wearing on and soon we'd have to leave. As I spoke, I watched his demeanor thaw. When I had started to speak his face was pickled in a frown and he wouldn't face me. He stood there with his arms knotted and face staring into the fire. As I told him the details of what happened he placed his arms at his sides and turned to face me. After I brought him up to speed, he eventually placed a hand on my shoulder and began to massage my tense muscles. He lightly slapped my cheek twice for good measure.

We walked to the back of the shack where we'd left Curtis' comatose body.

The woods were unrelentingly black at that hour. Shep had a kerosene lantern that looked like it belonged in 18th-century London. He looked like that tarot card of the hermit; with his long beard and outstretched arm with the lantern. Everything around us looked like it was sneaking behind shadows. Every wind-blown leaf and every creature that scurried would appear ever so briefly, then dart out of sight. It didn't help that he swung the damn thing back and forth as we walked.

As we turned the corner two small, but distinctive, orbs of yellow were illuminated by the lantern's light. We froze. The dots seemed to be mystical and not attached to anything. They hovered together, side-by-side, like fireflies. But these were no fireflies; they were the crazed, shimmering eyeballs of a wolf, and a big one at that. Its features, which were once blackened out by the darkness of the forest came into our light as the animal approached us cautiously. The fur around its mouth was stained red and it sent its tongue around the perimeter of its mouth in lightning-quick circles. I didn't realize it, because fear had all but incapacitated me, but this wolf had been dining on what was left of Curtis Boothe and we had interrupted his dinner. We were far enough away to only see the wolf illuminated by our glow. He was a large gray bastard; the kind that you'd hope to see behind glass in a Natural History Museum. What a specimen he was. His snoot was buried in Curtis's neck, which was now a gaping hole of mangled flesh and tendons.

"Shep," I whispered. "What are we going to do?"

"Nothing. He wants nothing with us." He paused. "He has his food."

"So?"

The wolf finished chewing a part of Curtis's rib meat and stared back at us with its mechanical, heartless gaze. There was no passion in its work, no relish in its eating. For something that had ruined so much of our plans, torn our plot asunder with each bloodied chomp, it proceeded with little notice. My stomach hurt.

And then, the final insult; the wolf put its head down and began to step backward. It looked indignant with its mangey head raised high and stepped into the dense thicket with slow paces. The dark forest swallowed it. We were alone then.

When we deemed the moment clear, we walked over to where the mutilated body of Curtis Boothe lay in a heap of mangled flesh and bone. I followed close behind him. The body wasn't dead before the wolf attacked it. All the work and preparation I'd sunk into this was ruined; blown out like a candle flame when a spring wind blows by. My mouth hung open for a moment and Shep had his hands on his hips. "I guess things take care of themselves, sometimes," he said.

I sobbed. "It's not fair! I did all the work. For nothing! God damn it!" We inched closer to inspect the remains and Shep lit the body with the lantern. His chest cavity was completely ripped open, exposing his insides nearly back to his spine. Some of the organs in his upper intestine were still intact and filled with fluid. His chest and neck were eaten too. Shep then brought the light to his face; a face permanently frozen in fear. He must've tried to scream, because his mouth was open, and his brow was furrowed. He looked petrified. He looked as if he had been beaten.

Rearing back my foot I kicked the corpse. "You piece of shit, you!" I got two or three more kicks in before Shep thought I'd had enough.

"Frank, Frank, stop it!" Shep commanded. He grabbed my arm. "He's gone. It's over," said. I threw my arms around him and cried into his shoulder, my body quaking in a wreck of nerves and tears. He returned the hug and began to pat me on the back. "It's over, Frank. You're okay."

But that was just it; I wasn't. Far from it, actually. I let everything I had kept inside of me spill out of my eyes. My tears were caught by a ragged flannel shirt and a tangle of beard hair. I balled my fists and lightly tapped Shep's lean shoulders. "I want to go home," I said. "I just want to go home."

"We're getting close, Frank. You can't stop now. When everything is all done, you can go home."

To this day, I don't understand why his winds had changed suddenly. Maybe he felt sorry for me. Maybe his heart was turned after mulling things over during the afternoon we spent in silence. This and everything else have replayed in my mind repeatedly. We were emotional piles of mud.

And it had finally started to rain.

*   *   *

We were still left with three...well...more like two and a half dead bodies; bodies that would begin to rot, decompose, and smell sooner than later. Shep and I went back around to the front of his shack where Big Bill had finally arrived.

"Shep," he called. "Christ on the cross, Shep- we have a problem here. I've never known the boy to be that violent!"

Shep stroked his beard a bit and examined the two dead brothers. I can remember their brains lurching out of the inner crevasses of their mashed skulls and looking somewhat like ketchup-soaked macaroni and cheese. He walked around them like a stalking animal, ready to pounce.

I leaned in close to Shep's ear and got a whiff of his scent of sawdust and sweat. I quietly said, "Sabrina had told me once that they were a breed of Wendigo."

Shep kneeled and pulled open one of their coats away from the body. "Hate to break it to you, Frank- but much like everything else that idiot told you- that was a lie too. These two are as human as you or I."

"Maybe she just didn't know," I shot back. "Maybe she was scared and confused and had no idea what they were. No one knows everything, Shep. Not even you."

I watched as Shep took a long deep breath and let it out slowly. "That's right," he said. "That's right."

Big Bill and John had made themselves comfortable, sitting on a large fallen tree that Shep had turned into a bench. Big Bill stormed over, obviously not impressed by our chatting. "Hey! We've got two dead guys here. We need to do something with them and do it quickly. So, the two of you should shut your pie holes and get with it!"

"DEBORAH! DEABORAH! That doesn't make sense!"

"Can you please shut him up," I burst.

"FRANK!" Shep said, sounding like a frustrated father.

"Don't talk about my son that way. I'll shut you up, you loser," Big Bill said.

I could have hit him. I really could have. But that would have made the situation all the worse. Something clicked inside my feeble brain; something that released a new kind of endorphin that I'd never felt before. I realized that I had won a small victory in myself. In the past, in my days of liquor and temper, I would have, without thought, reared my arm back and clocked that bastard right in his jaw for talking to me like that. To be fair, that was also a part of the residual training that I'd taken from the Army. But I didn't do it. I didn't feel the urge to knock him down or punch his lights out or any other overused cliché for decking someone. For the first time in a long time, I felt like I could control things. I could control my temper. I could control my actions. It was one of the most liberating feelings I've ever had. Ironically, the control I felt and the ability to keep things in check had freed me.

"Bill," I said. "Let's not do this. I don't want to do this right now. We don't have the time."

He stared at me for a moment. His attitude lifted a bit, and his face wasn't so hard anymore. He probably thought I was afraid of him. Bully for him.

"John," Big Bill said. "Come on, let's get the hell out of here. They'll figure it out." He gathered himself, fixed his shirt collar, and wiped his hands on his pants. "You're welcome," he said in my direction.

Once again, the two grabbed hands and proceeded to walk down the road in the blackened night.

"What do we do with them," I asked, motioning towards the dead brothers.

"We're going to the lake," he said. "The lake has secrets." Gooseflesh sprang up my forearms and tingled up to my neck. "What's a few more?"

Chapter Nineteen

That horrible silence returned like a tide calmly flowing to the shore after a thunderous ebb while we rode through the darkened streets and back up toward Diamond Point. I turned my windshield wipers off, the click-clack sound halted, and there were no pleasantries. There was no music in the car that evening and no conversation. The storm had left a heaviness in the atmosphere that hung over the mountains like a wet bed sheet draped upon the majestic, rolling trees. It was stifling.

We rode with the dead bodies, all three of them, in the trunk of my car and the smell was beginning to become overbearing. I drove with one hand in front of my face to try and mask the unpleasant stench of rotting flesh and the other on the wheel. When we parked the car, I had intentions of leaving the doors open to try and air the stench out. I pulled a forgotten stiff handkerchief from my glove box and placed it under my nose as I drove to try and further diffuse the stench. I could waste time trying to explain the sharpness and pungency of the aroma, but it would do no good. Suffice it to say it was one of the most horrible smells I've ever encountered.

"So where are we going," I asked. It had been so quiet my own words gave me a headache.

"Got a skiff to the N. 'bove Diamond Point. She's wedded to a dock. She's a veccky one, but true. Loaded brimside with provvies. Things needed for the run. We'll touch the water and push off from there."

"Do you have supplies? I don't want to get there and have to rely on fists."

"Skip the needle! Just paylayed I got the provvies! We'll gaze on the this 'n that whence we step off. "

My mind was a little more at ease knowing that we weren't walking into a meat factory with blindfolds on. I wished he had told me these things earlier. I tried to understand why he didn't. Everyone had reasons.

"Can you believe we're doing this," I asked. "Does it seem real? Do you think so?"

He scoffed at me. He began to stroke his beard as he always did when he got a good meat and potatoes topic to wax on. "Real," he said. "We do the top of the chop, but nary a molly be real."

"So everything is fake? Everything is false? What kind of world do you think we live in, Shep?"

He shook his head in a fatherly manner. "You're not movin' the beans. What's real," he asked me. "What's the flesh n blood 'real'? Is this mechaney real? Road real? You can't keep callin' on the reality stick. Reckon why? Real is a million-eyed stranger. No 'reals' are ever going to kiss the same babe. So, what's a-doin'? We trek a-through wooded glens to go on a hunt for the dark. It's real, all right. As real as a mother baking bread for her fam or a lillywhite getting raped at edgepoint or bombing a city in Krautsberg." He stopped and cleared his throat. "If we make it out I beg and plea on the honor of the grand cloud-sitter."

I clenched my body. I was petrified of what he was going to ask of me. "Yes," I said, cautiously.

"Don't hide behind tombstones!"

*   *   *

"Tilt the eye to the kiln-brick warehouse. Peep? Veer a right when we come upon. But be 'lert! It's a quickie."

We came upon the building, and it was hard to see in the darkness. What we were able to see was slightly illuminated by the headlights of my car. It looked like a spotlight trailing a jailbreak.

The warehouse had almost every single one of its windows busted. Some of them looked like monster's mouths, agape with sharp teeth. In its prior life, it must've been one of those Dickensian workhouses for preparing whale blubber. I deduced this from a faded silhouette of a black whale with oil droplets coming out of its spout that was drawn on the side of the building. It looked like it had been abandoned for quite some time. The broken windows were undoubtedly the work of children and angry passers-by. I had driven by the place a million times but never turned down the road to get a better look. In its current state, it spoke of young packs of kids walking streets together. One of them picks up a good-sized rock and chucks it at a window, and that satisfying crash sound makes him smile. I could also see behind the veil of time where many serious-looking hearty souls unloaded cargo in those large wooden crates with block letters stamped on the side of them. In my head, they looked like an Army of Bluto from the Popeye comic. The warehouse sat on the edge of the lake, and the bottom floor had a loading dock that jetted out onto the water.

We got out of the car, and I left my headlights on. Shep took the lead and began to walk into the darkness and walked up a few stairs where the loading dock was located. Half of the dock was covered by the second floor of the building and the other half was exposed outside to the elements. Ships would bring the cargo, leave it on the portion of the dock that was open air, and then whatever was dropped off was brought to the inside area of the wharf. I followed him, with my eyes opened wide; trying to make out any shapes that might've made their residence in a place like this. The dock was missing a large piece of it on the right side. The wood was corroded and snapped upward in jagged pieces. It looked like a giant had ripped those sections of the wharf to shreds. I recalled what had caused it; a bad winter storm two years earlier. It snowed fifteen inches in one day. The weight of the snow caused the corroded wood to buckle, and finally collapse. It made me ultra-cautious of my footsteps and I hoped I didn't fall right through to the water underneath us. I began to veer my footsteps to the left, trying to keep as far away from the damage as possible.

"Shep," I called out in the darkness. "Is this safe?"

His disembodied voice chuckled. "HA! Safer'n a noontime summer sup!"

That sounded like it was a good thing. However, I wasn't convinced and continued to walk cautiously. I could swear I felt the floorboards bending under my feet. There was a creaking sound; one which I wasn't sure was the wood sighing under my weight or my breaths wheezing with each step. Each sound made my heart jump a little, as I was now in complete darkness. The rain had started up again, and I could hear the drops pounding against the tin shutters that were bolted against the outside of the building.

It was quiet, yet loud at the same time. Scattered around the covered part of the wharf were ancient oil drums and large spools of rope that looked like they were taken from a giant's sewing kit. I laughed a nervous chuckle when I thought of how this place could snap back to life rather quickly if someone was willing to sink a few bucks into it to revamp the building. There were cobwebs in every corner, some of them rather beautiful.

"FRANK! A HAND FRANK."

I got that familiar pang in the pit of my stomach, and I took off running towards Shep's voice. "SHEP! WHAT? SHEP!"

I left my fear of the floor collapsing behind me and began to run to the part of the dock that was outside. I scanned in the darkness and was being pelted by large, hard drops of rain. He yelled my name once more and once more I followed the echoing reverberations of his voice. I had to wipe the rain out of my eyes a few times.

He was standing near the edge of the wharf, frightfully close to the edge. And there was someone else next to him. It was a woman wearing a raincoat, facing the water. Without thinking I instantly shouted, "SABRINA!" I called out. "SABRINA!" My heart began to float in my chest. For all the mystery and heartache, she had finally come back to me! And it was at the perfect time as well! Just in time to ride into battle with me! I never thought such a serendipitous event could ever befall me. I got to her, grabbed her shoulders, and turned her around, poised to give the biggest, deepest kiss I could muster. All was in order except for one small detail: Nancy Lawry, my upstairs neighbor, greeted me. My face fell back in complete shock.

"I've seen that look a time or two before," she said.

"Nancy! Nancy? What...what are you doing here?" I spoke trying to mask my disappointment.

Shep walked away from us, hopped into what I assumed was his skiff, and began poking around.

Her face looked worn and tired as more raindrops glazed her mannish face. Her bemused grin told a million stories of a million hardships. Her coat seemed to pull down on her shoulders as if there was something heavy attached to it. Of all the people who had danced in and out of my life, Nancy won the prize twice for popping into circumstances where I would have never guessed she would appear.

"What am I doing here," she repeated. "That's a good question, Frank." She trailed off and stared across the black lake, with the sound of water hitting water the only soundtrack. She never looked me in the eye but seemed to be fixed on speaking to my shoes. "I'm here because I don't want to be anywhere else," she said. "I'm tired of fighting everything. I don't want to be anywhere anymore."

She looked like a soaked scarecrow that was filled with extra stuffing. Her words broke my heart. I had to say something. I couldn't let the silence go on for any longer. "Come on, Nancy. You don't mean that."

"And who are you to tell me what I do and don't mean." Her voice whined like a child throwing a tantrum. "You're the one that pushed me over the edge anyway, Frank."

"Me? Me? What the hell did I do?"

"I was supposed to stop Curtis. ME! I was supposed to be the one to get him. I spent months listening to him through the vent in the house! Only to have you come in and swoop in and take all the credit. Do you know what that's like? To see a project of yours go completely belly-up like that and get snatched away from you? Mom left me, you ruined me. I don't want this anymore."

"I'm sorry, Nancy. I...I didn't know."

"Oh hell, Frank it's not your fault. It's just the way it is. It's some-one's fault, though." She reached into her pockets and pulled out two large rocks; so large she couldn't hold them, and they slammed against the wooden dock. "I came here to make it stop, Frank."

"Look, I'm probably not the person you need to talk to right now," I said. "I'm sure we can get you somewhere, someplace. But it's not me, Nancy. I don't know if I can help you."

She turned away from me and looked once again over the expansive darkened body of water. "No one can help me," she said. "There's something else that can't be helped either and it's been slowly eating away at me since I can remember. We all have these preconceived notions of what's what and how things are supposed to go. And when our insides are pulling us in the complete opposite direction, there's trouble. And I've been in this trouble for so long, I feel like I forgot what it's like to be normal."

From the side of the dock, I saw Shep's figure in the boat standing with his arms crossed, waiting for me. I turned my attention quickly from Shep to Nancy, who was still looking down at my shoes. "If I ask you to come with me and my friend, and help us, would you come?"

She looked at me, made eye contact for the very first time, and shook her head. "I don't think so. I can't do anything else and I don't want to do anything else." Her face looked as if she'd dipped it in water. Tears and rain pooled on her jowls and dripped onto her coat.

My shirt was practically glued to my back and my pants were heavy from the water. "Come on, Nancy. Please. We'll fill you in along the way." I thought for a moment. "It may be a shot at redemption for you. One chance to make things right."

"WE'D BETTER PUT THE GAS DOWN," Shep yelled, while pointing at his wrist, then up at the sky.

She didn't say anything. It was another uncomfortable few moments of quiet. While I would have enjoyed giving her the opportunity, I was not going to stand there and waste any more precious seconds. I knew it would be sun up soon, and that's when the real moments were going to shine. I slunk my shoulders and tapped my hands against my sides. "Suit yourself, Nancy. I don't have time to play this game with you on this dock." I walked passed her and over to where Shep was. He had gotten out of the boat. "We need to get those bodies loaded now. I'm not going to wait for her to make up her mind all night."

I stomped back to the car to begin hauling the bodies. The rain had let up again, so there was only a fine mist in the air. The beams from my headlights looked like two pillars shooting out of the front of my car. I stomped and tramped. Strange to be on the other end of the lights. As I got closer to the car, I noticed something was wrong. The trunk was opened. We hadn't opened it yet.

My stomp quickly turned to a sprint and my arms flew back and forth as I ran. When I made the turn around the corner of the back of the car, towards the trunk, my fears were realized. There was nothing in the truck except my spare tire and a crumpled-up edition of STAG magazine. It had been opened for some time, as that foul smell had all but gone. I slammed the trunk shut with all my power and nearly broke it. I looked down and examined the area of the trunk near the lock and there was a large portion that was bent upwards. Crowbar break-in. Before I walked away, I noticed there was a message written in blood on my rear window.

YOR DED

My knees buckled a bit, but I was able to maintain myself and not hit the ground. I went around the car and found the passenger door was open. I poked my head inside and gave a quick look around to see if anything else had been left, defaced, or stolen. I looked under the seats, in between the cushions, with my hands feeling around every dark crevasse for something that might have been left behind. When it had become apparent that nothing else was touched, I slammed the car door shut and began to slowly meander around the car. There was no hurry or sense of urgency in my steps or actions. My blood was boiling once again. I kicked the gravel and small rocks cascaded all over the place.

From down the hill, I saw Shep illuminated in the headlights. He was trudging back up the hill towards me. Oh boy, was he going to be in for a surprise when he got up here. He waved his hand in a beckoning shake. "What's the stop," he asked. "Time's a losing battle!"

"The bodies are gone, Shep. Someone stole them. All three of them, GONE!," My words were matter-of-fact and calm- like I had just told a kid the store was out of ice cream. I was just too beaten to have any other kind of –umph in my cadence.

"Gone? Up and walked?" His voice began to get quivery. I had always admired Shep for how 'in control' he always appeared. He was the perpetual answer man; the one who knew how to work out every issue and every problem. But for the first time in my knowing him, he looked spooked and confused. "So what? Deal?"

I didn't have an answer for him. It then dawned on me that Nancy was left alone down on the wharf. "Shep, where's Nancy?" There were just too many things going on for my tiny mind to take in. It felt like someone was building a house on top of a thin layer of logs. There would be only so much I could take.

"Left by the waves a-crashin' near the skiff."

A single gunshot blast was followed by a scream and the two sounds tag-team echoed in the night. It came from down by the water. On the wharf.

Shep and I looked at each other and then tore ass down the hill kicking up wet gravel behind us as we sprinted. A million thoughts whirled around my mind, none of which made any sense. I was becoming faint again. I felt like if I didn't labor to breathe, I would stop breathing altogether and keel over right there on the dock. I became very aware of my breaths and the world seemed to fade. It was hard to see down by the wharf; the car's headlights only did so much to illuminate the area. But there was enough to have a little bit of an idea of what was around.

Shep and I got there in time to watch Nancy tumble off the wharf and splash down into the lake. As her body hit the water a fair amount of it splashed backwards and onto the wooden wharf sending waves of tide backwards. By the time we reached the edge, she was floating away and sinking. In the darkness, we would never find her. I noticed something else; the rocks that she'd removed from her coat were missing.

Seeing her tumble off that wharf, and into the black abyss, impressed me and my shoulders shuddered. "What the hell is going on," I yelled into the darkness. "I know you can hear me! Why won't you answer me!?"

Shep came closer and threw his arms around me and let me cry into them for a while. It was a comforting feeling, although his long strands of beard felt strange against my cheeks. He patted my back reassuringly. "She didn't have to die, Shep," I said. "There was no reason for her to die." I felt Shep begin to shudder too. It appeared I wasn't the only person getting emotional.

Nancy had never directly affected my life until that day in front of the school. Maybe that whole scene *was* supposed to play out differently. Maybe the pages that we'd written were incorrect. Neither Shep nor I moved. We allowed the rain to fall on us and made to attempt to seek shelter. The rain was not light, but a pouring outburst from the sky.

It was hard to know where the rain stopped and the tears began. She was gone now; stepped out of our lives like an actor roaming the stage and gone right into the darkness. It took a few moments of deep breathing before my composure had completely returned.

On top of Nancy's death, the bodies were gone. I brushed the hair back off my face and began to hyperventilate once again. I tried slow, deep breaths. Slow deep ones. The breaths give air and air gives life. I made sure to try and keep things in front of me.

"Do you think whoever killed her took the bodies," I asked Shep.

He shook his head and shrugged at me. "Our guesses are duel horize-parallels."

"Whatever it is, or whoever it is, it's trying to stop us. And whoever it is has been following us too. I don't like it." I looked back up to the car and remembered the misspelled message that was written on my car's window. "We're being chased," I said.

"Peers a thing or two is a tryin' to red-sign us."

"It does look that way."

"So, what's the manual?"

I began to walk towards the boat. "We're getting in that boat and we're going to Moose's Walk," I said. "It'll be harder to track us on the water."

Chapter Twenty

I knew full well that piloting a skiff in the middle of the night across a darkened lake was going to be difficult. I made no false illusions or hopes about that. What I didn't know was that it would be one of the most physically demanding things I had ever done.

When launched away from the dock, after I had shut my headlights off and parked my car on the main road, the weather seemed like it was turning a bit as the rain had finished its tantrum and more moonlight was shining through some fast-moving clouds. The canoe we paddled was smaller than the boat we'd rode on during our initial trip. That first trip seemed like ages ago. The canoe was most likely only intended for one person to pilot, so we were already pushing things by having us both in it, not to mention a bevy of canned foods and pickled vegetables that Shep had loaded up. I was glad to see it as I had developed a craving for that venison jerky he had made us last time. As we paddled, I silently wondered how we would have carried three extra human beings on this thing. If the bodies hadn't been filched, we would have had to stack them up like cordwood.

The current was strong and naggingly persistent that night and kept pushing us southward. We oared like mad, trying to keep our course steady across the lake. The oars were slick from being left out in the rain and it was hard to get any kind of tight grip. I held with both hands and stroked the water with every muscle in my arms. I would periodically take breaks to give my arms a rest. When I stopped rowing, my muscles burned. I knew that later I would pay the price and have massive waves of pain radiating from my neck to my fingertips. Shep never got tired. He never waned, never faded. I don't think I would ever tire of watching him work. When he was put on a task, especially a task that made use of the land or his hands, he would knock it down like a bowling ball slamming into pins. His work ethic was dangerous. Often you would get mesmerized by what he was doing, and then slack off yourself. I tried not to fall into that trap.

There was a small sliver of moonlight shining through the remnants of cotton ball clouds as we took off. But Mother Nature's nightlight didn't last too long. Soon we found ourselves in complete and utter darkness. The boat bobbed left and right in a drunken sway as we rowed, and we began to operate completely by feel. There was a time or two when my elbow scraped the water because we were that close to tipping. When I was in the war and I would get afraid, I would simply close my eyes for a moment, reset, and then proceed. That didn't work when your eyes were wide open and all around you was an abyss.

There were a few instances where I swear I felt something knocking on the bottom of the boat. It felt like someone's knuckles banging on the hull. God, was it dark.

"You feel that, Shep," I asked, continuing to row. "You hear that?"

All I received was an earful of water slapping against the side of the skiff. A couple of minutes later the knocking started up again. My body tensed even more than it had been. I gripped the cold, wet oar and continued to paddle. I couldn't see anything around me. I couldn't see Shep in front of me. He could have fallen overboard for all I knew.

"Shep," I asked the darkness. "You feel that?"

"Prolly a beaver," he said. That was all. He was right. Probably just a beaver. Beaver or not it scared me deep into my bones. A little light would have done us good. Just a small flickering flame would have done us wonders in that vast dark lake. But it was not to be. The darkness ate us that night.

The Army preached a survival technique called 'Mind Displacement'. It was a technique that soldiers would use if they were in a precarious situation such as being tortured or being stuck in an area of extreme hot or cold. It was meant to focus your mind elsewhere and let the elements do what they will to your physical body. I had to use it a few times while I was in the service but never dipped into the well when I returned to the world. As we fought a hard current, with our slippery oars, I set my mind in flight elsewhere. I didn't even have to close my eyes.

I could almost taste the cool lemonade in the sweating glass pitcher on the table on the porch. The porch wraps around the house; the kind of home that harkens to the pre-Civil War South. What a beauty of a house. And it's a good thing I'm on a shaded porch; it looks like it's a scorcher out there.

There's a vague burning smell too. But not a sour burning smell. No, it's not the kind of burning you want to turn away from. It's burning charcoal. Someone has a barbeque lit. I walk off the porch, down the stone walk, and follow the small path that leads to the street. It looks like Queensbury, but it's not. I know Queensbury better than any city on the earth. There are birds and blue skies.

As I hit the sidewalk, I noticed a man in front of the house next door whitewashing a fence. He's crouched down and his face is covered. He's wearing a Zorro mask- the kind that will cover the nose and the area around the eyes. He's stroking the slats up and down with the brush but never looks away from me. He's kind of giving me a crooked eye, but I don't pay him much attention. After all, it's summertime. No need to get into any spats with a neighbor during this time of year. Besides, if he looks at me that way one more time, I'll pop him one in the mouth and that will be that.

From behind me, a young toddler comes bopping down the walk. The child is not of a speaking age yet, but I can hear them coo like a dove. I turned around and there before me stood the most gorgeous baby boy I'd ever seen. His blonde curls looked like curly q's and were perfectly complimented by his rosy complexion. He wore a small white sailor's suit, with blue piping around the chest. I crouch down and extend my arms and I meet the child in an embrace. The baby smells like talc and I swear I could feel some powder on his arm. I kiss his soft cheek and run my fingers through his tangle of toe. I stand up and cradle the child in my arms.

Something keeps drawing me back to that neighbor in the Zorro mask who watched me. I walked back a few steps, with my baby still in my arms, hoping that the man had gone. But to the contrary, he's made some progress and is getting closer to me. He still paints with his deliberate strokes, all the while watching me like a hawk. His mouth is bent in a smile, but he shows no teeth. It looks phony. It looks spiteful; just like Curtis' had looked. I cradle the baby's head in my hand and walk back up the path and to the house.

Our house felt like a home. I stepped into the house, which found me in my living room. 'Reena,' I called. 'Reena, where are you?' Our coffee table had a glass top and an oversized marble ashtray on one end, and a folded newspaper on the other. Above our sofa, which was a red-colored Queen Anne style, hung a Vermeer painting- The Music Lesson. 'Reena,' I called again.

I walked into the kitchen where our brand new, almost blindingly white, oven was ajar. The icebox matched it too. On the butcher block countertop sat a bowl with flour and eggs in it. I peeked my head over to see what other ingredients were lined up on the counter. A bag of sugar. A small bottle of vanilla. If I didn't know any better, I'd think someone was about to bake a cake or cookies. 'Reena?'

Through the kitchen, a door let out to the backyard. Still holding the baby, I pushed the door open and stepped out onto a concrete slab that butted against the back of the house. There was a table set with plates, forks, knives, and glasses. It looks like a birthday party. Or a celebration. It's warm enough to be a July 4th gathering. The backyard is in the shade at the moment, because the sun is beating on the front of my house. Beyond the concrete slab, a rolling hill of grass sweeps downward where it is met by the edge of the forest. Something tells me I'd better not go down there. At least not now with my child in my arms.

'Where is everybody,' I yell to the universe. 'Reena?' I try to remain calm. I walk back into the house and walk past the cake ingredients. The living room looks untouched as it had looked before when I walked in the door. Then the baby begins to get restless in my arms. He kicks and flails his arms I remember finding it hard to keep still. I walk back onto the front porch where the pitcher of lemonade still sat on the small table. I placed the baby down on one of the cushioned seats that flanked the lemonade table.

'Who are you looking for,' a voice behind me called.

I spun around and was face-to-face with the masked man. He still had that damn sly grin. 'I'm looking for my wife,' I said. 'What have you done with her?'

'Who said I did anything to anyone? I'm just standing here, partner. No need to sling accusations.'

I wanted to slug him right in the face. I knew that if I did, he wouldn't tell me where my wife was. I knew he knew. And I knew he probably had a hand in making her disappear. 'Where is she?'

'I don't know what you're talking about,' he said. 'But I do know you slapped a baby across the face.' He paused. 'Everyone knows. And everyone is talking about it. Herlihy might even let you go because of it.'

'How do you know so much about me? Who are you?'

'Oh stop acting like you don't know. I know you know. You have to know. You can't possibly be that dumb.'

He reached into his back pocket and produced a photograph. It was a picture of Sabrina. She was bent over laughing with a finger pointed at the camera. She was wearing her raincoat, her tan one I would think. She looked like she was having a pretty hearty laugh. The masked man put the photo back in his pocket and walked away.

'See you soon,' he said. He stepped down my walk, onto the sidewalk, turned, and went back towards the fence he was painting earlier. I turned to the chair and my baby was gone. I ran to the seat and all I saw was one of the cushions dripping with the reddest blood I had ever seen. I screamed

and realized I was moaning in the boat. The sloshing sound was back. The darkness had returned. I was in the middle of the great lake- the one the natives called 'Andia-ta-roc-te.'

"It can't be all that bad," Shep said, still churning his oar mechanically off the side. "Do you need to whimper like that over there? You sound like a cat that's getting its tail pulled. Some Army guy you are."

I was amazed at how quickly I had been able to successfully return my mind to its rightful place. I shrugged off Shep's zing and kept rowing. "How much further do we have to go?"

"You talking distance or time," he asked.

"Both."

"Probably another ten minutes of rowing. Another 2/3's of a mile. It's been a while since I crossed here. I used to take tours on this route all the time. Only we wouldn't go south when we hit- we'd go north and up near Mount Defiance. That's nice country back there."

"Shep?"

"Yeah."

"How do you feel about what we're doing?"

"You keep asking me that. I don't know," he said. "I don't even know anymore. You're talking to someone whose whole life has been in nature. Growing things. Hunting things. Making do with what the earth gives you. This situation here is a little out of the box for me, to tell you the truth. What does it matter what I think anyway? You're going to do what you want to do, right? Isn't that the plan?"

I shot back, "With all your spiritual teachings, you mean to tell me that the world is as plain as the dirt in the earth? That everything ends in the physical world? Come on, Shep- I might not know you for that long, but I know you're full of shit when you say things like that. I don't mean to call you a liar to your face, which is pretty impossible because I can't even see you, but I know better than that. I don't believe that for one second. I just don't."

He rowed on and ignored me for the moment. "I guess I was used to dealing with the better side of spirits. The good side of the coin, if you will. I kind of ignored the other side." He stopped. "We all did."

"Do you think we're going to make it," I asked again, realizing I had the impatience of a child.

He stopped rowing and placed the oars in the boat. He gingerly turned around, trying not to knock any of our supplies over into the black water that we floated on. "Again," he said. "I don't know."

"Who told you that fire destroys them?" I leaned in and tried to match eyes with him. "How do you know?"

Shep leaned back and stroked his beard. I didn't see this; after all, it was still some kind of oblivion all around us. But I sure heard it. I heard the wooden seat sigh as he adjusted himself, and I heard the dry stroking of his hands against his beard. "After I had stumbled on the camp when I was a child, I ran home and told one of the 'jacks what I'd seen. The one I ran to first was a man named Lionel Rainwater. When I found him, he was working with a few other 'jacks putting a fence together around our property to try and keep the deer from eating our vegetables. I was beyond frightened. I remember feeling like the world was shimmering like I was in a trance. Like I was hit by a thunderbolt or something. Well, Lionel was a big man. Tall. He looked like a tree if that makes any sense. His face looked like a carved piece of stained oak, tan, with hard lines. We weren't related in the least, but he had always a special feeling for me, I guess. He taught me most of what I know about things. I mean, the other 'jacks had their hand in how I was brought up too, but there was some kind of connection between Lionel and me. When he died in 1912, I must've cried for three months straight. He took care of me as if I was his own. Maybe it was because I was part Lenape myself? Who knows? That's something he took with him to the grave. Anyway, I ran up to him and threw my arms around his neck, and I was hysterically crying into his shirt. I remember getting dirt all over my face because he had so much of it caked on his shirt. He asked me what the matter was, and I told him. I told him the truth; some younger friends of mine had stolen a small boat, paddled up to the creek, and stumbled onto Moose's Walk. I remember this, Frank, I swear, so vividly, I feel like I'm watching it play out in front of me. He picked me up off the ground and my feet dangled back and forth. He cradled me in his arms and gave me comfort without even saying a word. He didn't have to say anything. He brushed the hair off my forehead and said, 'What you saw today was the face of evil. You mustn't look at it too long or it will get into you too.' He said, 'You must never go back there. We must leave those beings to their own devices.' Naturally, I asked Lionel if anyone had ever tried to beat these things or get rid of them. He said, 'Those things can only be beaten by the ultimate enveloper. The one inside each of us; that flame- that fire.' Lenape love fire. They're mystified by it. It can do so much yet destroy in the same instance. Fire is illumination. Fire is fuel. But fire can also be destruction. There's a fire in all of us; a fire that can vary in size, but never go completely out. Well, that is- until the end."

I thought about that flame that I always perceived I had inside me; the one I had nearly extinguished myself. I felt embarrassed to tell him about that, and how it wasn't the first time in my life that I'd tried something like that. They say that gene runs in the family, like big ears or webbed toes. My mother's brother, Uncle Pib, killed himself when he was 29 years old. I didn't know of any others off the top of my head, but the fact that he was so close on the family tree bothered me. Always did. That's why I wasn't completely shocked that I had driven myself to Ausable Chasm that day. When I thought of Sabrina, and how she'd saved me, I got hot in the face and embarrassed. I didn't dare say any of this to Shep.

"All this talk of fire," I said, trying to veer the subject to a better place. "I've got to ask. And you'll forgive me if..."

He tapped his fingers against my shin. "If you're going to ask about women, you're not going to get much from me."

There was something about us talking in the complete darkness that sprung my tongue. It felt like we weren't physically close to one another at all, although we were close enough for him to tap my knee. He couldn't see me and I couldn't see him. It was almost like we were writing letters to one another or speaking on the telephone. I bet it's the same feelings Catholics get in the confessional booth. There was an invisible barrier between us.

"Maybe I wasn't going to ask you about women. Why did you get so defensive?"

"Because I know your type, Frank. And I know you. Probably better than you think I do. And I don't talk about those things."

"Why?"

"Because I just don't."

"Not for nothing, Shep- but you're saying a lot by saying nothing. I can tell there's a stinger somewhere in your past. Something that makes you uncomfortable." When interviewing someone for a news story, I was always good at getting the person to open up about something they had previously kept secret. It was all in the framing of the question. I would walk the line between insulting and sobering. "Who was she?"

"No one," Frank. "She was no one because she didn't exist." He paused. "Now will you please knock off the questioning?"

"She was pretty, I bet," I said. "Blonde hair, red lips?"

"If you think that I would go for anyone who matched that description, then you're crazier than I originally thought."

I barreled though, not stopping my resolve. "You liked the way she tasted too, I bet. She had that smoky sweet smell about her. She would always glide when she walked. And you two shared some great nights together." Perhaps I was being a bit rude, or being a plain, dyed-in-the-wool asshole- but there was nothing else going on. We couldn't see each other, anyway. What did it matter?

"You're not going to stop until I let it all out, huh? Even if I have to make something up just to shut you up?"

"But you don't have to make it up, because it's true. I've never met a man anywhere who didn't have at least one girl rip his heart out of his chest and do a jitterbug on top of it." I paused. "Even lumberjacks have their stories, I bet."

He snickered. "Ha! Lumberjacks have but one love, Frank. It's a love that people outside the circle can't understand. They're face-to-face with work all the time. Morning, noon, and night. There's no time for any of that other stuff."

The fact that he was resisting me was only making me prod even harder. What I had said was true; there wasn't a man born on earth who didn't bear the brunt of a woman sometime. It was unnatural if that wasn't the case. I quietly rowed again, trying to peer out through the darkness.

As I was trying to conjure my next barb, something caught my eye in the far distance off the starboard side. It was a small flame in the darkness. I wasn't sure if it was an actual light or if my mind was just playing tricks. I stopped rowing and my muscles sighed. I tapped Shep on his shoulder (or where I thought his shoulder would be) and spoke. "Shep, look. Look to your right."

I can't verify whether he did or not, because I didn't see him do anything, but he did say, "There's someone else out here. There's someone else on the water." I felt him shimmy in his seat and his oar went silent. He placed it back inside the boat. "I would do the same, Frank. Just stop rowing for a minute." That was comical; I had already taken the liberty of halting my rowing.

My eyes were locked on that small flame in the darkness, that beacon of mystery in the middle of the great, dark lake. We bobbed in the boat and the waves lightly slapped the sides. "What do we do now," I asked.

"I don't know. But I don't know what that is out there."

The light seemed to be stationary itself, as it hadn't moved an inch since we'd stopped our progress. "Is it a flame or a light," I asked.

"Looks to be a light. Like a camping flashlight. See the beam that it's casting?"

I didn't.

"The light from a flame on a candle wouldn't shoot out like that. Whoever that is, or whatever it is, has a flashlight."

"Can it see us?"

"Probably not. Unless we get close enough to where we're illuminated by the shaft of light."

It was still. We were still. The wind had subsided to nearly nothing and the atmosphere hung hot above us. We floated for a while and didn't throw the oars back into the water. The current of the lake would push us south if we didn't begin rowing soon. Neither of us touched those oars.

"We can't just float here, Shep. We're going to be taken off course."

He said nothing. He then placed his oar in the water and began to gently ease it into the water, with not even the slightest splash. He began to row and we began to move forward again. His breaths were heavy. I took up doing the same. I mimicked him perfectly, dipping the oar into the water quietly and pulling ever so gently. Our eyes were both fixed on that illumination in the distance. I know mine were. I'm pretty sure Shep's were there too.

As we got closer to the light, I began to see the beam Shep had mentioned. It shot out of the source and looked like something out of a jailbreak scene from a prison movie. It began to move and scan the surface of the water. My heart almost stopped.

"Shep," I said. "Shep."

"I know," he said, his voice rough with exertion. He said no more.

We were blinded in an instant when the beam shot directly at our faces. The boat and everything in it was illuminated. I began to paddle harder and Shep didn't move. On the contrary, he had his hands in his lap and seemed to be calm about the whole situation. "Shep! Row! Row!"

He didn't. He simply placed one arm up, calmly. I stopped rowing and tried to regain my composure and my breath. My hands were beginning to get chaffed from the rowing and I knew they'd be blistered before long.

"HELP! I KNOW YOU'RE OUT THERE I NEED HELP!" The voice was a man's and it reeked of desperation. It was followed by a companion female voice.

"Campers got lost," Shep said. "Happens all the time. Let's see what they want."

Oars in water, we paddled like mad towards the light. I scrunched my face and gripped the wood so hard I felt the splinters digging into my palm. We leaned forward and rowed hard, slamming waves of water behind us. The pain in my arms was no longer a problem, as I could no longer feel them anyway. We sloshed and rowed and paddled, cutting through the current as bravely and neatly as we could.

As we made our approach the outline of three sullen figures began to emerge in the paltry glow of the flashlight: two larger ones and a smaller one. We paddled against the current and the closer we got, the faster we rowed. Funny enough, neither of us said anything in return as we rowed closer.

I guess neither of us knew what was waiting for us in that small boat.

When we got close enough the situation revealed itself. On the small tin skiff stood a middle-aged man, glasses, hair askew, white collared short-sleeved shirt smeared with grime. Next to him, was a small female; short red hair, which was tightly bobby pinned up. She cowered behind the man. And finally, a young girl- no more than six or seven I would have guessed clung to the woman's leg.

"Thank god," the man said. "We've been out here for hours."

"What are you doing in the middle of the lake at this hour," I asked. 'Not to know your business or anything..."

Our small boats kissed, and it sent the older woman and younger girl scrambling for balance. They didn't fall, but they were close to it.

"Well, believe it or not, we're here on vacation," he said.

It made sense.

"We're not far from shore," Shep said. "Let's get there and then we'll get you some food. Do you have oars?"

The man looked down in embarrassment. "No. That's the problem. My daughter threw them overboard by accident."

Shep gave the stranded family (or what I perceived to be a family) the once over and shook his head disapprovingly. "I guess you are the prototypes for being up Shit's Creek then, aren't you?" He bent over and began to search through one of the many satchels that were snuggly packed into our small boat. After tossing two or three aside he presented us a rope.

"We're going to tow you in," he said.

"We're going to what," I asked. "I would have sworn you just said we were going to tow them in. But I know that can't be right."

Shep chuckled. "How do those arms feel, Frank?"

*　　　　　*　　　　　*

I do not believe I have ever cursed as much before, or since.

Chapter Twenty-One

I laid myself out against the foot of a large oak and the twisted fur-rowed bark dug deep into my back, leaving its imprint. My arms had gone nearly numb and dangled against the ground like useless empty hoses. I imagined that this was what those fellows who had their limbs blown off felt like. I'd seen one guy get his arm ripped from his body like an ant's leg. My chest would not calm its rapid rising and falling. My legs ached. My head ached. My palms had become blistered and were sliced open with pink raw tender skin exposed through streaking droplets of red blood. I faced my palms to the sky, to not have anything come in contact with them. A cool wind soothed the pain minimally, but it still hurt like a son of a bitch. I was pretty chapped at everything; Shep, these tourist assholes who had caused the trouble, and everything else that came along to place me at the foot of an oak tree, a few hours before dawn, with an exhausted body and soul.

Shep gathered some kindling wood and started a fire. The family did nothing except huddle in blankets and shiver. I couldn't move and didn't dare try. I sat there, casting my burning glare towards them. I tried to ball a fist to express manifestation of rage and when I did, blood poured down the side of my hand and down onto my pants. So much for expressing anger.

Dawn would be breaking soon and the perpetual darkness that had sheathed us began to burn away with the impending squint of first light. While the fire burned before us, we relished the stability. We needed to get off the water. We needed to be on dry land. Luckily, for their own sake, the family didn't say much. They thanked us quickly but saved their story. That was a good thing, as I was in no mood to hear any nonsense. They were all huddled together as if they were some strange three-headed monster, cloaked in a sheet Shep had dug out of the boat somewhere. Their eyes were shut, and their mouths hung open. They all had the same sedated, peaceful face. The father had a bit of a needle nose about him, which the little girl had inherited in spades. But the little girl had the mother's eyes. Christ, she could have cut them out with a knife and glued them to her face. I watched them sleep.

Shep was the last of us to sit down. After he finished his forage he plopped against the hard dirt, with no blanket or anything, placed his hands across his chest, and began to slip away into the temporary death of sleep. The way he was positioned he looked like a stiff. All he was missing was the satin liner and pillow. He always crossed his legs too, while he slept. He'd done the same thing each time we had to lie down for shut-eye.

In the distance a loon screamed and everyone around the camp was shaken awake. God, I hated those god-damned things. The little girl began to quietly shed some tears and buried her face in her mom's arm. She was petrified to be there. She might've been home in a bed somewhere, grabbing onto her dolly. She had light brown hair and round cheeks that came down to a somewhat pointed chin. She was covered up to her neck by the blanket, and her little digits grabbed onto the sheet. She looked like something out of a children's picture book. She looked like a cherub. She reminded me of Mariah. That's when my stomach turned over and I couldn't get myself comfortable no matter how hard I tried.

Each time I moved, something else prevented me from getting completely comfortable. I felt hard, jagged stones digging into the small of my back. My head began to feel like a million small insects were crawling along my scalp. I twitched and shook my hair out like a lunatic, trying to get that uncomfortable feeling to go away. I stood up at the base of the tree and got jealous of the peaceful repose that everyone else was enjoying. They were all so snuggled in their slumber and there I was, standing in exhaustion with no guarantee of sleep. I looked to the skiffs, which were pulled up onto the land, and wondered if it was a good idea for me to try and grab a few winks in one of them. A hard, tin boat bottom was a minor upgrade from jagged rocks poking me in the back. It wasn't much of an upgrade, but it was an upgrade, nonetheless.

I crept over, trying not to make a sound, and managed to break every last twig that found its way under my shoe. I got to the boats and was astonished to see how similar both of them were. They might've come from the same marina at one time. I never asked how Shep got his materials, I just knew they he had them. Shep never struck me as the stealing type, but you never knew.

I threw my foot over the side of the boat and got and eased myself into the tight quarters. I slowly let my back down against the grimy bottom of the boat and began to inhale the ammonia stench of ancient fish guts that had long since been ripped out caught and discarded. That rotten stench that singed my nasal passages. That briny smell made me uneasy, and I did all I could to ignore it. A bottle of something cheerful would have no doubt helped. But there was none around here. Not for miles and miles. I finally closed my eyes.

My mind wandered like a small child lost in a big city. I imagined this family, whose names or stories I had yet to hear, where they came from, and how they ended up in the middle of the lake. Imagine that, we were so tired that we didn't even ask them any questions. No, questions would be for later. Now, we slept. Only I couldn't. I could lie down with my eyes closed, but there was no sleep.

My thoughts strolled over to Syracuse; the town I assumed was home to them. The father, whom I decided I was going to call 'Ralph' worked at the Ondondaga Brass Factory, a large brick building that sat in the lowlands of the town. 'Ralph' had pulled a few of his buddies aside on his lunch break and said, '*Hey, I'm gonna live like Davy Crockett for the next few days.*' He had a small, bent brochure that he'd snagged from the Union Office. 'Ralph' and his buddies were eating their lunches out of tin lunch pails and sucking on Camels that poked from the corners of their stubbled mouths. '*That's sure swell,*' one of the cronies says. '*Boy I'd like to get up there one day,*' another says. They were people everyone knew. 'Ralph' worked hard for his wages, the factory wasn't the safest of places, but if you had half a brain in your head, you'd be fine. When the work was done and the whistle blew, it was time for 'Ralph' to head home; to a modest little ranch that was painted a lovely shade of powder blue. The little girl, who I decided was named 'Nancy' might be skipping rope in the driveway. From the small porch 'Gwendolyn' or 'Wendy' as she liked to be called, stood with her arms folded. '*Hard day, Ralphie,*' she asked. '*The roast is almost done. Why don't you come inside and have a snifter to unwind.*'

I relaxed a bit, lost in the haze of fantasy. '*Man, oh man, that would be the life,*' I thought. '*When everything gets in order, that's how my life is going to be. When all the chips fall everything is going to be cool as a cucumber.*'

But as was the case in almost every facet of my life, my rest was quickly stirred. I didn't physically feel anything. I had that feeling that I was being watched. I snapped my eyes open and hovering above me was a figure. It was the woman from the boat. 'Wendy,' if you will. She had left her three-headed monster of a blanket and walked over to me. Her face was a pale white, further brought out by the blue tinge of early morning. She had taken her hair down out of its tight beehive.

"Sorry Mister," she said. "I didn't mean to startle you, I...I was just taking a walk is all."

"Is that so," I asked, rubbing my tired eyes. "Well, I'm awake now. It'll be dawn soon and I'm going to guess everyone will be awake."

She looked prettier with her hair down. In the morning light, I could see that her face was like a doll's, somewhat long and narrow with high cheekbones and a small button nose. Her build was slight, and her light blue gingham dress was smeared with dirt and grime. "I guess you're right," she said. "Do you mind if I sit next to you," she said.

I sat upright and tapped the other seat in the boat. "Please, be my guest."

She sat next to me, close to me, and the ever-so-faint remnants of her perfume wafted over to me. She was probably the best-smelling lost person in the history of the world. There was a layer of dirt on her arms and cheeks that seemed to be glazed to her skin with sweat. "Where are you folks from," I asked.

She let out a guffaw. "Where are we from?"

I didn't like the way she repeated me. It all seemed too familiar for me, and it immediately put me on edge. "Brattleboro, Vermont."

"Vermont, huh?" I leaned closer. "And what does your husband do in Brattleboro, Vermont?"

"I'm not married," she said. "That's not my husband." She paused and inhaled a deep breath. "He's my brother."

"And the little one," I asked, feeling as puzzled as ever.

"That's a long story," she said.

God, she reminded me of Sabrina. The way she spoke in teasing terms, the way she would give just enough information to tell you something by telling you nothing at all. She could have been her twin. They didn't look physically similar, well, maybe a little. I thought to myself, 'Whoever this dame is, she chopped Sabrina's disposition right off of her.' I began to rub the top of my thighs nervously. "Well, what's the scoop? We've got time."

She began to wring her hands violently. It looked like she was washing her hands with invisible soap. "We're in trouble," she said. "We're in so much trouble I can hardly even think about it." Her eyes wet. I didn't know what to do, so I did nothing. I looked down at the bottom of the boat and knotted my hands. I planned to let her cry her tears and eventually, she'd compose herself and we could move on. But she didn't stop. She began to vocally sob, and I tried to hush her. Morning had broken and the blue light of dawn had given way to gorgeous ethereal daylight. The last thing I wanted was a chapped brother coming over and seeing me sitting with his sister in hysterics.

Between her sobs, the musical interlude of forest birds played around us like a juxtaposed soundtrack. I looked back towards the campsite, and everyone appeared to be planted where they had been when I left. I was stunned that Shep wasn't up yet and foraging for kindling or berries. We had gone through a long night and I supposed the exhaustion had finally caught up with the old guide.

"What's your name," I asked. "I realize we were never formally introduced when we ran into you."

She wiped her eyes. "Gertrude," she said. My blood ran ice cold. "People call me Trudy."

I stepped away from her and felt my right foot sink into a cold puddle of loose shoreline sediment. Gertrude, or Trudy as her friends called her, put her arm out towards me in a vain attempt to steady me as I wobbled in the muck. Her face looked confused.

"What are you," I asked. I realized I'd asked a zany question, so I followed it up with another one that was slightly more normal. "Where did you come from?"

Her face became cross. She snapped back at me, annoyed, "I told you, mister. Brattleboro, Vermont. Don't you listen?"

It bothered the hell out of me that she didn't answer the 'what are you' part of my question.

I asked, "Spell Brattleboro."

Her mood instantly lightened, as if I'd told a joke. Gertrude, or 'Trudy' began to chuckle. "Excuse me," she said.

"You heard me. Spell the name of the town where you come from."

"B-R-A-T-T-L-E-B-O-R-O. There, are you happy?" She sat down on the edge of the skiff and folded her arms. "Anything else tickle your fancy? Want to know who our mayor is or what my mother puts in her three-bean casserole?"

"I'm sorry," I said. "I'm really sorry. I haven't been myself this week."

"Well, we've established that we're in a heap of trouble. What's got *you* down, cowboy," she asked, standing up.

We were standing in the light of the new day and the low rush of the lake's waters began to creep their way into the riverbed. "I don't really know," I said. "I met a woman and since then everything has been haywire."

"Sounds like you're smitten in love," she said. "That's not necessarily a bad thing."

I hadn't boiled my situation down that much since meeting Sabrina. Was it really that simple? 'I met a girl and things went fubar?' Maybe it was that simple, after all. It still didn't explain everything. I felt like I was trying to jam an entire worm-laden chocolate cake in my mouth.

"Hmm, that's an interesting one, cowboy." She reeked of confidence, and it made me uneasy. I wasn't used to that type. Call me strange- whatever. It wasn't what I knew. She tugged on my shirtsleeve and said, "Why don't we go for a walk along the water?"

I looked over my shoulder, through the overgrowth that shielded the sleeping members of our troop. I thought, 'If this guy wakes up and sees me fraternizing with his sister, he's libel to think something was up. Something...wrong.' Perhaps against my better judgment- what little I had left- I stepped over towards her, measuring my steps. I looked back once more and couldn't quite see the slumbering folks anymore.

We took a few steps along the shoreline of the lake. The morning sun shone off the small waves and created a blanket of burning diamonds on the surface of the water. It was a beautiful morning. One of the more beautiful ones I could remember. I kept a small distance just in case someone had stumbled on us.

"So, what's your trouble," I asked. "You said you were in trouble."

She stopped walking, turned around, and looked at me. "It's...involved. It's not as easy as playing a record back. There are a lot of things. A lot of moving parts."

"Nothing's easy," I responded. "I guarantee you the story we have to tell is much more involved than anything you have."

"Like I said, we're here from Vermont. The little girl is sick. She's dying."

"What's the problem?"

"Well, firstly let me tell you that she belongs to a man who lives below us in our house. We kidnapped her." Once the dam was breached, her words flowed out to me, and I received every morsel of them. "The man doesn't take care of her. He works as a janitor or something at North End High School."

"No mother," I asked.

"No, cowboy. The old lady skipped town a while ago. My family owns the whole house where we live. We sublet the basement to this man and his daughter. We stood by for long enough and let things go until we finally couldn't take it anymore."

"What made you so suspicious?"

She looked back over to the group of sleeping bodies. "She's not right." She turned back and looked at me earnestly. "One morning I was in the backyard of our house with a basket of laundry. I was going to put a few things on the line because it was such a nice day, you know? I came across the little girl with a half-eaten squirrel sticking out of her mouth. The thing's gray legs were still kicking out of her mouth like a broken toy as she chomped down on it. There were blotches of blood around the corners of her mouth and her dress looked like it was stained red."

That whole scene made me sick to my stomach.

"I ran up to her and slapped the thing out of her mouth. But she ran after it and attacked it again like a wild dog or something."

Her story made the sides of my head throb. I could feel my heartbeat thud in my temples. I got down on one knee and caught my breath.

"I told you our story would shock you. Anyway, her eyes were full of blood, like she'd been out drinking all night. I picked her up and she kicked like a mule in my arms. I carried her inside the house and upstairs to our apartment. She was kicking and screaming and ranting the whole way up. The neighbors must've thought I was murdering her. So, I brought her upstairs and that's when my brother saw what was going on. He comes over to us and says, '*Trudy, have you lost your mind? What's going on over here?*' That's when I told him what had gone on outside. The girl had gone into some kind of sleep or hibernation because she had stopped screaming and her eyes were shut. We laid her down on the chaise lounge in our parlor and propped her head up. She slept soundly and without movement. She did, however, have this low hum coming from deep inside her chest. It sounded like gears churning along. We got her to open her eyes and they had returned to normal. Whatever it was had run its course and she seemed to be back to her normal self again."

The whole thing was strange. It just reeked of effort and unbelievable circumstances. "So why did you bring her here," I asked. "Why didn't you tell her father?"

"That's just it, cowboy. When she woke up, we went downstairs to let the little girl into the apartment, and the door was ajar. We walked in and...well, there we found Papa."

"Dead?"

"As a doornail," she completed. "He was pretty mangled up, too. Looked like an animal had gotten to him. That's when we put two and two together."

"Why the hell did you bring her here," I asked, as the pieces of the story began to slowly come together.

"Well, to be quite honest, we came here to get rid of her. It's been hard, though. She doesn't seem to have any recollection of anything."

"And she hasn't flared up and attacked anyone or anything since you've been here? How about in the car ride on the way over here?"

Trudy looked back at the sleeping girl as if to reaffirm what she was going to say. "No, not at all. She's been a cherub the entire time." She paused and sulked a bit. "But we can't have something like that running around loose. What happens if she flares up again and hurts someone?"

A curiosity lurked from behind my weathered psyche. It wriggled its way out in the open and out of my mouth. "How did you plan to do it?"

She looked beside herself as if she couldn't form another word. "We were going to just toss her overboard."

The lake has secrets.

"What stopped you," I asked.

"We ran into two people in the middle of the lake."

I slunk back. Did the little girl deserve to be tossed overboard and drowned like a plague rat in the middle of a darkened lake? Possibly. As Trudy said, they couldn't have a monster like her roaming around. And what does one do when a monster is afoot? One destroys it, if it has the means. It doesn't matter if said monster happens to look cherubic.

We had taken them off course the same way they'd taken us off course. Even Steven. The universe has an interesting balancing act going on sometimes. During our talk, a high, *shrill scream* echoed from the campsite. It cut through trees and our skulls alike and sent a flock of resting loons shooting up into the sky above us.

Trudy took off ahead of me and dashed through the underbrush and over logs. The way she sprinted made me wonder if her story wasn't just another crock of shit. It seemed to hold water, but there were clues in the way she ran, and the look of panic on her face, that made me think otherwise. It could've been my imagination. I shook it off and ran.

When we got back to camp Trudy's brother, who I had mistaken as her husband, had the girl lifted off the ground with her legs kicking like a pissed-off bull. He bit his lower lip in determined tension while keeping her as under control as he could. His glasses shook on his nose with each turn and gyration of the girl. She had smears of fresh blood around her mouth that looked like she'd gone headfirst into a bowl of raspberry jam. Her eyes had gone blood red, just as Trudy had described them in her story, and the skin around her face was tightly contorted, revealing more of her teeth.

Shep was propped haggardly against a tree and held his left arm against his body the way injured birds clasp broken wings to their breasts. The hand that clenched his forearm gushed blood. His face, the little of it that wasn't covered with hair, had turned stark white. He hunched himself over and nearly fell to the ground. It made my heart skip a beat.

"Shep!" I called to him and ran to catch him. "Shep!"

He leaned over and panted heavy breaths and eventually fell into my arms. "She got me, Frank. I slapped her away from me, but she got me." He held his arm up and showed the perforations where the girl's jagged teeth had sunk into his shirt, skin, and practically down into his bone. When he released the grip on his arm for a moment, I saw a fleck of white in the wreckage of mangled skin and fat. She had bitten him through to the bone.

"What can I do, Shep? What do you need from me?"

I looked into his gray iron eyes and swept some of the tangles of hair out of his face. He winced in pain and a lifetime's worth of wrinkles appeared on his weathered face. He wiggled around for a bit and then became completely still. I cradled him in my arms like the child I never had.

On the other side of the camp, the little girl wrestled in the arms of her captors with an unrelenting thrashing that was somewhat machine-like. Trudy tried to calm the girl while keeping her terror fairly in check. "It's okay," she said. "It's okay, just calm down sweetheart."

The monster heaved one last good thrust and burst out of the man's arms and left him standing stupidly with his arms wide open as if conducting a prayer service. I held Shep tight and close against my chest, as the monster ran off away from us, into the thick woods that surrounded us. Trudy took two steps towards running after her but stopped. She smacked two balled fists against her outer thighs and then came back to the man in the glasses and threw her arms around his neck. She whispered something into his ear and the man nodded slowly.

"I'm bleeding too fast, Frank," Shep said in between gasps.

"Don't be silly, Shep," I said- lying to the man's face. "We're going to wrap this and get you to a hospital."

"Frank," he said. "Just stop it. For once in your life can you just look at something in the eye for what it is?"

He was right, as he had so often been. The nearest hospital was in Glens Falls and it would take hours to get there. I let him down onto the ground slowly and his body lay flat like an opened cot. His breaths began to get shallow, and his eyes closed.

Trudy and her brother came to where we were and knelt beside us. They were both in tears, red-faced, shoulders shrugging in unstoppable shutters. The man placed a hand on my shoulder. "I'm sorry," he said. "I'm just so sorry this had to happen." His words were barely understandable. Tears poured from his eyes like buckets of rain streaming down from above. He embraced Trudy and they wrapped arms.

I looked back down at Shep who looked oddly comfortable. He opened his eyes and looked up at me. "The falcon comes out only twice a day," he said. "See the falcon, be the falcon, in the light of the morning. Fly high. Fly high. Don't end up among the trees. Tree'er true. But that's it. Be the tree. Be the tree. Be true..." His head cocked ever so slightly to the right and faced the water. It was there that Shep Gooley left this earth.

"I'm sorry," the man said again.

"You're sorry? You're sorry? Do you even know what you've done by bringing that monster here? Do you even know?" My blood boiled and I began to pace around the campsite. I looked over at a heap of Shep's belongings, which belonged to no one anymore. Thirty seconds prior they'd had an owner. "You see these things? They don't have an owner anymore! Do you get it? He's gone. He's gone. He's fucking gone!"

The couple came to me and embraced me. Our grime made one rather large ball of disgusting closeness.

The man spoke. "I know you lost your friend," he said. "But we've lost our daughter."

Chapter Twenty-Two

The three of us spoke for nearly six hours.

The day waned behind us, and our steady conversation kept us locked in a hypnotic trance that set our mouths moving in rapid motion while the world went on about its business around us. I sat and patiently recounted my story, beginning with Sabrina and that night on the Steel Pier. It took me a long time to verbalize what I had felt towards her and why, as it had gone through several edits machinations, and revisions. I must've spoken about her for at least two and a half hours. As I recounted each agonizing step of my story, every glimmering detail that I remembered seemed to offer me a sorry kind of solace. Recounting a tragedy can help get over an emotional hump. However, when you repeatedly return to the same well to drink, you'll find trouble. I weaved my story and Trudy and her husband, whose name was revealed to be Kevin, listened intently to what I had to say. I retold what I had done to Curtis and what I'd dragged Shep into. I even delved far back enough to dredge up the horrible stuff that had happened in Schenectady. I laid everything out on the table for these two strangers. They didn't know me from Adam. But I found their ears comforting. I just talked and talked and talked.

When it was Kevin and Trudy's turn to speak, they went on at length about what had happened to them and what had brought them to the middle of the lake under the cover of darkness. Most of what Trudy had told me was true, with a few small fibs lining her story. They *were* from Brattleboro, and they *did* live in a house that was owned by Trudy's family. But that's where the truth took an unexpected left turn off the cliff. They lived in the upstairs apartment of the house and a man named Roy Ebersol lived on the ground apartment. They had been married for six years- Kevin got a 4-F when the war started because of his vision- and their little girl, Kayla, was four, going on 5. The girl had been playing in the backyard and Trudy *did* find her with the squirrel carcass hanging out of her mouth. When she scooped the crazed girl up and ran her inside it was Roy she had found dead and bleeding on his living room floor. The girl had bitten into his neck and blood still squirted from his severed veins like a punctured garden hose. In telling her story she got more and more upset. She said Roy died with one of his arms outstretched as if he were waiting for someone to grab his hand and help him. Kevin seldom interspersed during that conversation. He looked listless and would periodically take his glasses off wipe his brow and massage his temples.

They told another compendium story of how Kayla had bitten the hand of one of her schoolmates as they played in the sandbox. She attacked a neighbor's wife. She killed a deer that had wandered into their backyard. They weren't sure what was wrong with the kid, but she developed these intermittent fits of insanity that would drive her to acts of violence that centered on her biting something or someone. After some time, the attacks would quell and she'd return to normal. But the damage had been done. One person was dead. Multiple animals had been mutilated. It was only a matter of time before the police got involved and that was the last thing Kevin and Trudy needed. Traditional medicine offered no help; the girl was as physically healthy as other little girls. After the third attack, they called a Roman Catholic priest in to see if the girl was possessed. After saying a few prayers over the sleeping child, nothing happened. The thing that was inside her- the being- knew how to hide within her to avoid detection. Trudy told me of many sleepless nights that were spent watching the clock and watching their daughter. They had reached for answers in every conceivable direction but had come up empty each time. The only remaining decision to be made was how to get rid of this demon. Unfortunately, this also meant getting rid of Kayla.

"We looked at each other," she said. "We looked at each other and then reflected inwards. We knew she couldn't go on like that. We knew that she was destructive, but when was it going to stop, you know?"

Kevin brushed his hair with his fingers and said, "We didn't decide in two seconds flat, is what she's trying to say. When you come face to face with something like that it...it's just not something you jump into." He spoke in a matter-of-fact tone the same way accountants did when tallying up your year-end finances. His matter-of-factness didn't exactly meld well with Trudy's blunt, laid-back style. But then again, opposites had been known to attract.

"So...," she said.

"So...," he said.

Trudy took a breath and closed her eyes. She searched for her words, wrinkling her lips as she thought. She tilted her head towards the leaf-covered sky and brought her head back down. Her eyes had wet again. "That's when we decided that there was no other choice. Our baby..." She broke down dond my initial instinct was to catch her, but Kevin beat me to it. I raised my hands palm side up and took a few steps backward. I would have to show my compassion in another way.

"Do you have any idea about when she could've gotten infected," I asked. Perhaps I was being tacky, but in my estimation, we'd left formalities a while back.

Trudy wiped her nose on her shirt. "She had wandered away from us one afternoon while we had her in the park. We were just talking on a bench and before we knew it an hour had passed, and she wasn't on the swings anymore. All we saw was this one lone swing rocking back and forth with no one in it. We called for her for a few minutes, then got up and started looking." She took a breath before beginning again. "In the middle of the park, there's this bridge that has a small creek underneath it. That's where we found her. She looked fine, though. Fine enough, really."

It was becoming clearer that Trudy and Kevin were not in the running for parents of the year. I was going to ask if they had immediately taken her to see a doctor, but I just saved my breath.

"Well, these things, the *Wendigo* are much like your daughter. From the stories Shep shared to the story the reverend told- everything matches up. And I'm sorry to say, your daughter seems like she's caught the same thing. I thought it was only something confined to the backwoods of the mountains, but I guess it spread to Brattleboro too."

I didn't know how or why or the connection between Moose's Walk and Brattleboro. Maybe there was no connection. Or maybe these things lived throughout society, and we were just too pigeon shit blind to realize it. There was enough death and turmoil in the world to nearly destroy the whole human race. What's a little demonic cannibalism added to the fire? "I plan to try and end whatever it is that's going on out here. I'm just blindly swinging for the fences; I'll be honest with you about that. I don't have a clear-cut plan, but I'm driven. I need to come face to face with whatever's out there and stop it. I don't know how I can continue to breathe if I don't. I've done plenty of real shit things in my life. I feel...I feel I owe it to Shep to at least try." I stopped talking and let my dry tongue get slick with saliva.

"This ends now. Too many people have been senselessly killed. This stops. If I die trying, then so be it."

I waited for them to say they'd join me, to enlist in the army of the good, to wave the battle flag of the republic, but they never did.

*   *   *

Shep's body had begun to bloat and the skin on his hands and cheeks turned to a purple-blue color. His eyes had recessed into his skull and his hands were at his sides, fat and open towards the sky as if waiting for rain. His stomach was protruding out and making the buttons of his flannel shirt hang on for dear life. I hadn't yet decided on what to do with him. A proper burial with the fanfare or mourners wasn't going to happen, so I began to jar loose other creative possibilities. I could've tried to dig a trench and buried him where he fell. I could've walked him to the river's edge and thrown him into the drink. Either way, it wouldn't be fitting. Not for the life he lived.

"I'm wondering what to do with my friend," I asked, nodding my head towards Shep's body.

Kevin wiped his tears. "Whatever you need to do, we'll help. We have some supplies in our boat. It's the least we can do." While he didn't strike me as the type to plant a garden in his backyard, or even own a shovel, my heart warmed at Kevin's offering.

After a moment or two of quiet reflection and thought I came to the only conclusion I would be comfortable with. "I want to bury him," I said. "I want him to be where he loved the most."

Poor Shep. He didn't deserve to die like that. He should've had a mess more years ahead of him. Sure, his age had withered some of the pleasantness from his demeanor- but the man was pure good. And he deserved final respect.

*   *   *

I didn't expect Trudy to help us, but she did. Kevin and I began to scratch out a grave, and Trudy got to work as well. She picked up one of the smaller trowels that had been stored away in their boat and attempted to make the walls of our trench straight. I swung the pickaxe hard; each blow knocking more and more dirt loose for Kevin to scoop and pile. It was with each swing the reality sunk deeper inside me. I was committing a body to the ground and all the hefty responsibility that came with that was on my shoulders. We didn't speak much while we busied ourselves with the work. I guessed that we talked ourselves into oblivion and had nothing more to say to one another.

The dirt was rich and brown- full of worms, beetles, and grubs slithering and crawling around in it. It smelled sweet; the kind of earth that would be good to plant a crop. For such a desolate area, in the middle of the uncharted mountains, there was much life. And subsequently, much death. We piled the dirt around the trench in small hills of earth that would easily be put back once Shep's body was placed in it. I made sure to keep the swings coming, as we couldn't afford to have a shallow grave. If a shallow grave was the result, we could've counted on an animal digging him up and going to town.

"Do you think this is good enough," Kevin asked with his brow now caked in mud.

"No," I said. "Deeper." The sound the axe made when hitting the dirt was a 'chuck-chuck'- sound. "We need to go deeper."

The man didn't say a word. He gave me not one ounce of grief and continued to slide the shovel in and remove the loose dirt. As he did that, Trudy did her work as well, making sure the sides of the grave would hold and not cave in.

"This is one hell of a hole, cowboy," she said. "We're going to hit Chop Suey by nightfall if we keep this up."

"Just a little more," I said. "We're not quite where we need to be, but we'll be there soon."

My arms were aching, and the swings of the pickaxe didn't have quite the fervor they did when we had begun digging. Trudy had stopped sculpting the walls and Kevin took longer stops between heaving the dirt. The hole was nearly four feet down; a more than respectable depth for a grave. I held my arm up with the little strength I had and said, "That's good. That's enough."

Kevin and I walked to Shep's decaying corpse and he grabbed his ankles and I grabbed him under his armpit. We lifted him off of the ground (which felt like we were lifting him out of a hole). He was heavy and completely rigid. It felt like we were lifting a cord of lumber. We walked him over to the grave as if we were moving a bookcase and dropped him down perhaps a little too violently than I would have liked. We had little strength to do anything with any sort of delicacy.

I looked down at my friend. I didn't say anything but had a small internal conversation.

'Shep. I'm sorry this is the way it's ending. You deserve better and I deserve better, but that's neither here nor there now. I hope wherever you are it's nice. I hope it looks like Santa Anita or Bora Bora. That's what you deserve, my friend. You were the closest thing to a best friend I've had since before The War. And although our time together was short, we sure packed a lot into it, didn't we? I'm going to get to the bottom of this and stop the madness. I promise you that. I'm going to have my moment out front and center, don't you worry about that. Everything is going to be fine.'

I started throwing dirt around his feet and worked my way up towards his torso. I wanted his face to be the last thing to be covered. Kevin and Trudy stood back and let me work, with my warm tears making mud on my cheeks. As I continued to bury him I saw less and less of his body. He was hidden from my view and returned to the earth where he belonged. When he was no longer visible, Kevin and Trudy helped knock in the remaining dirt.

The forest floor now had a large, brown bump in the middle of it. It looked like a giant mosquito bite in the middle of the fallen leaves. We had worked our way through most of the day and my stomach sounded like one of those B-52 fighters. God, I wanted a hamburger just then. With double cheese dripping out of the sides. I would have given just about anything for one of those.

"Did you guys bring provisions," I asked.

Kevin shook his head yes. "Mostly salted meats, though. Nothing that would fill you."

"Honestly, I'd eat tree bark," I said. "Do you have enough to spare?"

Kevin looked in the direction his daughter had run and said, "We do now."

*   *   *

We ate Shep's funeral dinner as the sun set down over us, shrouding the forest under the blanket of nighttime. The smoked meats were going to make us thirsty in the end, but they had some canteens back in their boat and we (I) had a few in our (my) boat. After we ate, I built a fire and we all sat around and watched the flames dance. For the first time in days, I felt like I wanted a drink. And maybe a smoke. I had neither. I guess it was good that I *wanted* one and didn't feel like I *needed* one.

"I'm not going to try and tiptoe around this," I said. "In an hour I'm going to Moose's Walk and I'm going to see for myself what's going on there. And if something or someone is looking out for me from above, I'm going to stop it." I paused and remembered how reluctant and then enthusiastic Shep had been about the whole thing.

"I'm not going to force you two to do anything you don't want to do but know that's what I'm planning."

Trudy leaned back against her husband with a drowsy look in her eye. "You've sure got a way with words there, cowboy." She nuzzled closer to Kevin and he threw an arm around her shoulder. "This is kind of nice out here, isn't it? Almost like we're actually on vacation."

Her dismissive tone, and her carefree- almost lackadaisical- body language reminded me of...There had to be a connection between the two. I had convinced myself. "Are you sure you've never heard of Sabrina Potter? Even in passing?"

She once again shook her head no.

"How about the last name? Does the name sound familiar?"

Both Kevin and Trudy smirked.

I should've just asked them if they knew any 'John Smiths' while I was at it.

"So, your sister and brother-in-law just ignored you that day, huh," Kevin asked, obviously recalling the yarn I'd spun earlier. I thought it was an odd time to bring such a thing up, but I was game. "I don't understand that."

"Well, you'll remember the whole slapping incident. Those things don't go over lightly, I'm afraid."

"You should just show up to their house one day," Trudy recommended in her sleepy daze. "You should just walk right up to the house and slam on the door and say, 'judge not, lest ye be judged' or some fiddle-faddle like that."

"How about I turn this conversation back to where I started it and ask again; are you with me or not?"

They looked at one another and then they looked at me. Trudy leaned forward and the flames illuminated her face. "I thought that was decided."

"I'm afraid the two of you didn't do a real good job making your-selves clear one way or the other. I'm sorry if I wasn't perceptive to your ramblings."

Kevin spoke, "No need to get defensive, Frank. Do you know where you're going?"

"We need to go south. Moose's Walk is south of here. How far south? I don't know. But if we keep moving, we should find it."

The sounds of the forest at night sang a humming lullaby to ensure there was little to no silence. Occasionally one of those damned loons would start screaming and we'd all jump out of our shoes.

"And what's the scoop once we get there, cowboy? I mean, we don't have any guns or anything. Can guns even hurt these things?"

"No," I said, flatly. "No guns, no bows and arrows, no spears, no cannons. Shep told me that there was only one thing that could stop these things, and that's fire."

Kevin stood up quickly, nearly knocking his wife over. He walked over to their small collection of camping equipment and produced the largest box of matches I'd ever seen. It had the familiar *Diamond Birds Eye* logo on the side of it.

"Okay," I said. "You've got kerosene?"

They nodded.

"All right then. As soon as the fire burns itself out, we'll get mov-ing."

I don't know if we were tired of speaking or petrified, but I can't recall any of us saying another word until we left.

Chapter Twenty-Three

Daybreak mercifully cracked through the night's thick black crust. The world around us caught up to our consciousness and we tramped through some thickets and weaved around broken logs.

It was nice to be able to walk without the threat of slamming into an unseen tree or getting attacked by a stalking animal. But we didn't care. Morning came as it always did and the three of us could barely stand straight (even those of us who didn't have major gashes on our calves). We sat for a while with our legs crossed and just drifted into naps. It seemed that the world had cut us a break and gave us a small reprieve of non-action. Even the humming sounds that haunted us in the nighttime had stopped and everything was peaceful. But, as I'd learned years before and miles away, peace is almost certainly a prelude to unrest.

The three of us positioned our backs against the large stump of a fallen oak, which acted as some support for our necks. Our eyes were closed, and my mind occasionally fell into sleep, like a kid playing on a teeter-totter. I made sure I snapped back awake, though. You can't sleep when the hunter is somewhere out there.

I began to hear voices, which scared me at first. A sign of shell shock was hearing voices that weren't there. That's what had happened to

Benny Convington. But the sounds began to get louder and louder and seemed to bellow up from behind us. They were coming from the other side of the log where we were propped. They were human voices.

"Please Jimmy, I swear I didn't know. Honest. Please, you gotta believe me!"

The racket woke the three of us up, almost simultaneously. It sounded like something (or someone) was being dragged through the forest with their heels scraping through the fallen leaves. We peered over the log and watched the scene play out before us. There were four men in long, black trench coats and fedoras. Their attire was eerily similar. You might've mistaken them for wearing a designated uniform of sorts. The one that was being dragged (I had been correct in my prior blind assumption) was wearing a Sharkskin gray tweed number with brown shoes. He was shorter than the rest. His face was round like a perfectly formed ball of flesh-colored clay, with pipe cleaner eyebrows and a furrowed brow that poked out from under the brim of his hat. The hat matched the suit, by the way.

The two men that were dragging him were large brutes, almost as big as Big Bill's son John. But these guys were more 'put-together'. They each had 5 o'clock shadows and stern, rigid faces. Their arms locked behind the shorter one's back and were keeping him from moving. It was odd to see such a scene play out in the middle of the wilderness.

We tell our secrets to the mountain and wash our sins in the water. Once it's in the water, it's washed and buried.

The third member of this quartet, the one whose name I deduced was 'Jimmy' from the pleading man, was also draped in a long trench coat. He stood away from the three and paced like a hungry lion; looking as if he wasn't quite sure what to do with his prey.

"You say you didn't know," the lion asked, reaching to his side to present a pistol stuck in his waistline. "I think you're full of shit, Mac," he said.

Quietly I tried to keep all the principals straight. The aggressor was someone named 'Jimmy' and the prey was 'Mac'. Kevin had his hand over Trudy's mouth in a preemptive mute of a scream.

"I swear to God, Jimmy. I swear I didn't know nothing. I told you Rothstein was the one who was running the whole thing down there. I'm a nobody, Jimmie."

Jimmy didn't answer back right away but mulled over things like an Emperor. "How did you get involved with Piping Rock, anyway?"

Piping Rock was a Casino in Saratoga Springs that attracted every walk of life from degenerate gamblers from Albany to high-rolling businessmen from Boston. It was a den of vice, nestled in the foothills of the Adirondacks. I knew a few guys who had gotten mixed up in some bad situations down there. I didn't know who 'Rothstein' was, but I imagined he had some clout. The only *big wigs* I remembered were Martin O'Flaherty and Nico Capobianco. They had ignored prohibition, engaged in prostitution, the whole nine yards. It was the kind of place a lonely guy might've sought some approval from the opposite sex. For a price.

"My brother Andy said it was a quick way to make a few clams," the frightened man, "Mac", said. "I wasn't trying to get in deep here, I swear, Jimmy."

I was the only one watching. Kevin and Trudy both had their heads turned away and their eyes closed. It looked like they were praying.

"Let him go," the lion (Jimmy) said. The two captors removed their arms from his and stepped away. The hum, which had been omnipresent since I had placed one toe in the wilderness, had completely come to a halt. There were no screaming loons. The rush of water cascading over and through rocks had ceased. There was nothing. It was as if time had frozen. "Turn around and get on your knees," the lion instructed, coldly.

The man began to sob. He wiped his brow with a handkerchief as liquid regret poured from his eyes. The front of his pants began to darken, and a large, circular stain appeared. He crouched down and turned around as he was told.

"Take your hat off," the lion said.

The quivering man did it and placed his hat in his hands.

Lion took the gun from his hip. It was a glistening .38. The morning sun shone off the barrel and threw droplets of light around the trees. "I want the last thing you think about on this earth to be what you did and my voice..."

"MAMA!! MOMMY!! HELP!! MOMMY"

The crashing boom shot through the trees and echoed outward like a single hit on a snare drum. As the echo died it sounded like thunder rumbling in the distance. From where I was looking, it appeared that he had spit out a large wad of pink and red chewing gum. The man, 'Mac' I guessed, slunk down and collapsed forward, with the entrance wound still smoking in the back of his head. Kevin's face was stoic, and his hand formed a tight seal around Trudy's mouth. Her eyes were wide open like saucers and her nostrils were flared open. I thought she might bite right through his fingers.

I continued to look at the three remaining trench coats and watch their actions. They stood in place for a moment or two, with 'Jimmy' still holding his .38 at the dead man. It looked as if he was afraid he would get up and start at him. But alas, that was a killing shot. 'Mac' wouldn't be getting up any time soon.

"What do we do with him," one of the non-shooting trench coats asked.

"Let him rot," the lion said.

*　　　　*　　　　*

The three of us didn't move for a while after that.

I was frozen because I didn't want to get shot. There was still way too much to do, and I'd come too far to throw it all way on a couple of hoods. Who knew if they had seen up us, and were waiting for us to stand up and pop us each in the head? We didn't move an inch. I had an itch on the end of my nose that warranted a good firm scratch, but I had to let it go. I couldn't risk making any movements. Trudy seemed to fall asleep in her husband's embrace. His eyes were closed too. We didn't audibly say anything to one another, but we knew we'd better stay put for the time being.

Trudy's dress had bunched up pretty high and her thighs were almost completely exposed. Her legs were slightly ajar and I casually and carefully readjusted my position to get a better look at what was between them. She wore white satin underwear that conformed to the shape of what was behind it.

I began to have notions of peeling back the layers of her clothing, revealing her skin slowly. I thought about how nice it must feel to have someone that close to your body. I wished she was that close to mine. Better yet, I yearned for the time when Sabrina and I would be in the same position as Kevin and Trudy. When she saw what I'd gone through and fought and battled, there would be little doubt that we would end up together forever. I fought my impulses to reach my hand out and simply caress her exposed skin. Instead, I sunk my down into my trousers. She looked so beautiful in her peaceful sleep. So precious. So pure. Her hands held her husband's forearms as if he were a life raft keeping her afloat. I couldn't wait for Sabrina to mimic that position and fall asleep holding onto my arms.

I began to think on the various fires that I'd set during my lifetime and how I would go about extinguishing every single one of them. Preachers would call it 'making amends' but I wouldn't even go and slap such a fancy title on it. I knew deep down I was a good man. I was a fighter, in both spirit and physical exertion. If they saw me coming back with an atoned heart and clear mind, they would *welcome me back and herald my arrival. I knew this was going to be the case. I just knew it. I'd go and kiss my sister on the cheek and I'd shake Bruce's hand. He'd offer me a cold beer from the Frigidaire and I'd politely say no. I promised myself I wouldn't drink anymore. So I'll take a soda pop instead. Then we'll eat dinner and I'll tell them all about Sabrina. How she'd won my heart and how our wedding plans were getting underway. Imagine that! Franklin Phelps about to be a married man! And they said it couldn't be done. Well, it could. Old Frank showed them, didn't he? Then we'd wed. Our reception would be somewhere nice, like Niagara Falls. The small flicker of hope that I'd followed would eventually illuminate the darkness of the shroud I had been behind. The cover would be lifted and the grand revelation of that wondrous light would be able to light up my entire existence. Then, I could finally achieve everything and everything would work itself out. It is man's greatest struggle. And I will win. And I will show that grinning bastard who was boss. Hell, I would even extend a hearty hand to Herlihy and apologize for all the trouble that I'd caused him. After all, he had a hand in landing me here. I'll win because I fight. And all I know is fight.*

On that day as I completed my fantasies, I knew for sure that there would be one last fight before moving to the next round. I was ready for it.

Chapter Twenty-Four

I took it upon myself to do my best Shep impression and attempt to scrounge for something to put in our stomachs. Kevin and Trudy were quite useless when it came to that sort of thing, so I delegated firewood gathering responsibility to them. It was a rite of passage you could say and it made me feel strangely important. Some fruits of the forest were only edible when cooked, so they had to be diligent in their kindling gathering. It had been so long since I'd sat down to a good meal that my insides felt like a wet towel getting wrung out. I figured I had lost around ten pounds, easily.

I hunched over and examined leaves and shrubs. Part of my ability to do this came from the Army; the other half was all Shep Gooley. I cradled some blackberries and mushrooms in my arms while trying not to spill them out and all over the ground.

When I arrived back at the fallen timber Kevin and Trudy were rifling through the dead man's pockets like he held the answer to some lost riddle. They had flung his trench coat wide open and his pants pockets were turned inside out. They worked like maniacal, yet untethered, pickpockets, combing every crevasse of the man's bloated corpse. I nearly dropped what I had foraged in horror at what I was seeing. "What the hell are you two doing," I asked.

"We were just curious," Kevin said, meekly; perhaps a bit embarrassed at the frantic rate they were pillaging. "We wanted to know who he was and where he came from."

"What for," I asked.

"To tell his family, cowboy. Let them know what happened out here."

I was shocked. "And won't they ask why we didn't intervene?"

"They had guns, we didn't," Kevin said. His smug, matter-of-factness had decided to make a return.

"Say, how's your leg," I asked.

"No better, no worse."

"It's still there," I asked. "That's what I was asking. Leave the dead guy alone."

Trudy held up a folded brown wallet with a few crumpled bills poking out of the top. "His name is Bernard," she said.

I told her in the sternest voice I could muster, "Shut up."

"Two kids, he had some pictures in here too. You sho..."

"I SAID SHUT UP!"

Kevin took a step towards me. "Hey," he said. "Take it easy and I don't appreciate you yelling at my wife like that."

Trudy looked at the body, then back at me. "We can't just leave him here to rot, Frank. We need to bury him or something."

It hadn't occurred to me to do any such thing. I assumed that we'd walk away from the dead man and let nature take its course. If he turned out to be the supper for a group of buzzards or coyotes, then so be it. He was of no consequence to me. As far as I was concerned it was just another hood getting his just deserts for messing with the wrong people. The bastard probably brought it on himself. Plus, I was through scratching out graves for people in the middle of the woods.

His face was frozen in mid-scream. His eyes were closed and red bloody jelly oozed out of him. I crouched down to get a closer look at him. You could still smell the cologne he had splashed on earlier that day and his tears were still wet on his flabby cheeks. I closed his gaping mouth and stood up in disgust.

"If you two want to waste time kicking dirt on the bastard, then you go right ahead. I have a date to keep."

Trudy snickered at me, and it made me furious. "A date with who," she asked. Her face almost transformed into Sabrina's. "Who's waiting for you, Frank? Huh? A bunch of possessed cannibals. They're waiting for you. Who else? You think that broad is going to be on the other side of the rainbow? Boy, do you have another thing coming, cowboy! You're lucky if you even make it out of here. You don't think we're upset? Our child is missing and possessed and probably scared. God knows where she could be. So, if we're taking the time to show some fucking respect for a dead man, then so be it. But if you want to continue to tramp on full speed without thinking, then go ahead. You can either help us or don't, Frank."

I wanted nothing more than to wrap my hands around her neck and squeeze. And squeeze. No female had ever talked to me like that, and I hated it. It made my hate boil up like lava and I wasn't entirely sure I would be able to control myself. But somehow, some way deep inside my consciousness- a consciousness that had traded in gin for patience- a small cameo picture of Shep appeared. *Don't get mad, Frank. Come on, now. You're better than that. I know you are. Don't do anything stupid. Need I remind you of the last time you flew off the handle when a woman raised her voice? Do you remember waking up in the hospital with all those tubes sticking out of your nose? Remember? Don't do it. Keep your temper, Frank. It's not worth it.*

Much like the steam escaping from the brakes on a locomotive at the station, my anger was released. I had never believed in ghosts, but if that image of Shep wanted to visit and haunt me, I'd be most appreciative. It was good to see him, even if it was brief. His words were to the point, but caring. I felt like he gave a shit about me. That was a hook I'd been looking to hang my hat on for as long as I could remember.

"Fine, but what will we use to dig," I asked.

She raised her hands and wiggled her fingers at me.

*   *   *

We had created yet another blemish on the forest floor.

This time it was harder. I had opened my water-logged satchel and rifled around for a trowel or some kind of digging tool, but there was none to be found. Sediment had coated everything in the bag, and everything looked like it had survived Pompeii; brown and crusted. There were no digging supplies. We had no breaks or fresh water. We had our hands, the craftsman's tools of ancient civilization. There was so much dirt lodged under my fingernails that I thought they would pop up like a car's engine hood. We stood over Bernard's final resting place and looked at the brown disturbed earth and surrounding brown and orange leaves. We were the last people to ever see Bernard alive, and the last ones to see him dead. It was an experience that seemed to sear emotion into my soul like a branding iron.

After our funereal duties were complete, the three of us collapsed like folding chairs and let the air stream out of us. I had placed a good amount of grub in a pile near the foot of a dogwood and supposed I should get around to cooking it soon. I was so hungry. Hunger ran through my midsection like acid. My stomach warbled; my head hurt. I had to dig deep to get the motivation to start a fire and use Shep's cast iron skillet to cook the forest's bounty.

My shoes were still uncomfortably soggy as I walked over to the tree to collect our food. Both Trudy and Kevin were dozing now, with their mouths agape like toads and their breaths gently rising and falling. For a moment I thought of deserting them again. It seemed that kernel of possibility refused to leave my thoughts. *'Should I just go,'* I thought. *'I could just leave them here in their slumber and they'll be no wiser.'* But the other side of my brain, the side that I had tried to quiet for some time would always show up and tell me otherwise. *'Be a good guy, Frank, and cook these people something to eat. They lost their daughter and they're willing to help you. You can't turn your back on help at this stage of the game. It's too late. You probably need them to help you.'* I didn't want to believe that to be true, but I had a hard time shushing those thoughts. It reminded me of a stray cat that kept coming around looking for charity. I'd feed the cat.

I crouched over the meager pile of wood they had collected and placed the kindling in a teepee formation. I dug through Shep's bag, looking for a piece of glass or a (in the best-case scenario) a magnifying glass. As I rifled through the bag it seemed that Shep had everything BUT a piece of glass. There were ropes and pieces of wood and plastic and rubber and fishing hooks. There was even a beaten-up copy of *For Whom the Bell Tolls* that looked like it was missing the last 100 pages. 'Typical Shep, never threw anything out,' I thought.

My fruitless search for glass left me unfulfilled and frustrated. I happened to look over to the two resting Brattleborians and my frustration quickly lifted. I crept over to Kevin and slowly removed his glasses from his face. This would do.

I once again hunched over the pile of wood and positioned the glass lens above it. I turned the glass slowly, hoping to capture and concentrate one of the shafts of light that were streaming through the trees. At that time of day, they looked like beams of pure heaven. I caught one after a moment or two and the leaves began to smoke and smolder. I held my breath. The other leaves began to catch, and I gently blew a stream of breath onto the flames and stoked them. It began to intensify in a small line of bright orange and then in a burst the smolder transformed into a flame. I had created fire.

I went back to Kevin and placed his glasses back on his sleeping head.

I rustled placed the food into the cast iron skillet and held it over the fire.

A large, seasoned piece of wood crackled and popped, and Trudy and Kevin both woke from their nap. "Hungry," I asked.

*   *   *

After we finished our meager meal, and the earthy taste of cooked mushrooms had coated our tongues, we began to walk south.

We casually sauntered through slashed white dogwoods and a few cedars. Two or three cedars had been split, either by lightning or old age and the sweet/spicy smell they gave off was wonderful. It smelled like the inside of a chest my parents kept at the foot of their bed. It was their linen storage space and whenever I got cold, my mother would grab a blanket out of the cedar chest, and I would wrap it around me like a papoose. The smell of the cedar box had gotten into the knitted material and that distinct smell would waft up my nose. Smelling it then in the middle of the wilderness brought me a much-needed calm. But that, as everything else, faded away as we marched farther and farther towards our destination.

Through a thicket of trees and overgrown hummocks, I saw what looked like the form of a structure. I didn't say anything at first, as I thought for a moment that my brain was starting to wear down and I was seeing things. But the closer we got, the clearer the outline became.

It was a stone building of large cobblestones mortared together with cement or some other gluing agent. Ivy ran up the side that was visible to me (us). From where I was standing it looked like the forest was trying to eat the damn place. When we had reached a close enough proximity, I nudged Trudy. "Look," I said. "Do you see that?"

She nodded yes and then in turn nudged Kevin, who felt the need to blow on his filthy glasses to clean them to see the house clearer. "It's a house," he said. "We're saved!"

"Not quite," I said and pointed to a tree ten feet from us.

Nailed to it was a weather-beaten, wooden sign with painted words that were hardly legible. The wood was split in places from extreme heat and cold and splintered off in a few places. What had once probably been a vibrant tan color had faded to a sickly gray. It faintly read: MOOSE'S WALK. We had arrived.

My heart skipped beats and I felt faint. I gave the immediate area a quick survey and saw a large boulder to our left. It was a colossus of granite and stood probably twenty feet high and ten feet around at the base. "Come on," I said. "Let's get behind that rock and figure this out."

The three of us carefully stepped towards the enormous rock and tried to make as little noise as possible. This was easier said than done because with each footfall we made a quiet crunch. It didn't help matters that Kevin was practically dragging his leg behind him. I secretly wondered how much longer that leg was destined to remain attached to his body. We were about halfway there when out of the corner of my eye I saw something moving outside the house. It could've been a deer. It could've been anything. But it ran quickly, and I couldn't make out what it was.

Once we nestled ourselves behind the rock I began to think of plans of attack. I had visited this moment often over the past weeks and in each scenario, I had Shep by my side to finish the problem off. In my vision of how this played out, we had torches and weapons and fought the good battle side by side. We would ultimately be victorious, because of his expertise and my drive to win. Of course, Sabrina would be waiting for me on the other side of the battle. It would be glorious. Unfortunately, with the motley crew I had assembled before me, this was not the case. I was forced to improvise, and I needed to thank the Army for teaching me the necessary skills to deal with such a dilemma. I had to feign democracy and ask Kevin and Trudy what thoughts they might have. If you wanted people to eventually follow your orders, you needed to give them the illusion that their opinions mattered.

"Any ideas," I said.

"You're the expert, cowboy," Trudy said.

"I think we should maybe try to…I don't know…maybe circumvent them. Maybe head a little farther east and then loop around them." Kevin's words trembled out of his mouth the way chocolates do when coming out of the end of a large assembly machine. He was trying to maintain somewhat of an Alpha status, but it was merely thinly veiled pure fear.

"We need to start a fire," I said. "We need to start a large fire- a big one. Shep said the only thing that can stop these things is fire."

Trudy tugged on my arm annoyingly. "But wait- once we burn them, the bodies die, but the Wendigo Spirit leaves the body after death and looks for another host, right? Do I have that right?"

"Yeah, that's right. I hadn't thought that far ahead." It's true, I hadn't. Way back when it had been my idea to leave Curtis to be the host body, incapacitated. We didn't have a body now and that was troublesome. "I guess once all the host bodies are gone, the spirit will just dissipate and go away," I said, not believing a word of it myself.

"Maybe it'll just fly up into the atmosphere or something. I've never killed one of these things, so I'm not real sure what to do."

A light clicked off in Trudy's eyes. Sheer terror swept her face, and she slapped her hand over her agape mouth. It was a horrible realization. I had thought about it myself. It seems that she had come to the same grim thought that I had. "There's no way to save her, is there?" She didn't weep out loud, but tears just pooled around the sides of her eyes and streamed down.

"I don't know, Trudy. I wish I did. But I just don't."

Kevin's lower lip began to quiver as well, but I saw him do everything possible to contain it. He coyly wiped his small tears and asked, "How many are there?"

"That's another good one," I said. "I haven't the foggiest." I tried to remember what Shep had told me about his encounter with them. I was drunk when he told me, so trying to filter through memories was a lot like trying to find your way home on a foggy night. "I remember him saying that they were eating children and that churned his guts." I rolodex-ed my mind as hard as I could, but I just couldn't remember if he'd thrown a number at me. That was my fault.

It then struck me who Kevin resembled in both action and word: Mr. Hayden, my high school Glee Club Director. We all thought Mr. Hayden was a little fruity, truth be told. He lived alone in Hudson Falls in a house that he shared with his mother. We once threw rotten apples at his house while having a good time. God, that had to be back in '36 or '37. We parked outside his house in the darkness, with our harvested rotten fruit that we'd collected from the windfall at Tinklepaugh Farms. We drove up and threw the apples in the darkness, hearing their squishy smacks against the windows and wooden siding. We saw lights go on in a few rooms and my buddy Chester hit the gas pretty fast as we sped away down the road. The other guys in the car were all howling like wolves and punching each other in the arm. I tried to get into the spirit by putting on a fake smile and popping a few in the shoulder, but deep down the regret that I felt was eating my insides like acid. I had nothing against Mr. Hayden, even if he was a light stepper. The guy had never wronged me personally. He would wake the following morning to clean up a yard full of rotten apple remnants. I had considered stealing my dad's car when we got back and running back there to clean up some of the mess. I never did. I didn't sleep well that night, but I never made it back to Mr. Hayden's house. I felt bad then, and looking at Kevin's face, that feeling of sympathy came back over me.

"I'll do what I can to save your little girl," I said. "Whatever I can."

He held his hand out to me and I grabbed it and gave it a good shake.

"Hold onto your hats, cowboys," Trudy said.

*   *   *

"How are we going to start a fire with no matches," Kevin asked. "There's nothing around us that could even be used for that. What's that thing people in the Stone Age used to do? Hit two rocks against one another? Damn it, I wish we had those matches."

You could see through the treetops that the sky was clear and blue with no signs of clouds anywhere. If we were anywhere else, it might've been a nice day. And that reminded me, 'What day was it anyway'? It also brought into focus a truth that I hadn't considered. I would most likely not have a job when all of this was over, since I'd been missing for so long. Even if I did my best to explain to Herlihy what had gone on, he'd probably just blow a gasket like usual and call me names and that would be the end of it. I'd have to start getting out there and talking to other local newspapers in the hopes of getting some writing gig somewhere. Maybe Saratoga? Who knew?

I saw something flash like a bolt of lightning across the ground. When I looked, it was gone. Then it returned. And then again it was gone. It was a white orb that seemed to be jumping from the trees to the ground- then disappearing completely- then returning once again. I was stupefied. "Hey, did you see that," I asked Trudy and Kevin.

"See what, cowboy?"

"There was a white orb or something. It jumped from the tree to the ground and then it disappeared. It looked like a light." I saw it again. "There it is! Look!"

And when we looked, it zipped off again. It was an annoying little episode, but one that flickered my flame of hope. "Kevin, move your head again."

He moved his head to the left and to the right quickly and the orb appeared again! "You see it? There it is!"

"What is it," Trudy asked.

"It's the sunlight concentrated off his glasses. Your glasses, Kevin! That's what I used to start the fire back at the campsite! All we need is a pile of leaves and we've got our fire!" I began to jump up and down like an idiot who had...well...discovered fire. Twice. I slapped my palms against the rock with such force that they went numb for a moment.

"We need to gather dry sticks and leaves. The older and dryer the better. If you come across something with even the slightest bit of wetness to it, throw it away. We can't use it. You guys did a good job last time, and I expect nothing less this time. Any fallen timber or dried grass will work as well. We will need to make the biggest bonfire possible. This is going to take a few hours at least. But we're going to do it. Also, if you find large, sturdy sticks, collect them. We are going to make spears out of them. The plan is this: we run them through with the spears, and then push them into the flames."

Kevin began to smile. "And the burning bodies will keep the fire going."

"Exactly. Now, we need to get ourselves moving and collect whatever we can. We can work side by side or by ourselves. I'll be swell either way."

We split up. I broke off alone and Kevin and Trudy worked together. I extended my shirt and made a sling where I could collect twigs and branches. I hunched over and searched out the perfectly seasoned pieces that we'd use for kindling.

After being hunched over and bobbing up and down, my back began to bark at my tailbone. I stood up straight and stayed that way for a moment to relish in the sweet relief. I was lightheaded too. I was determined not let my mind or my body betray me at that late hour.

Chapter Twenty-Five

In my search for the perfect bits of kindling, I lost track of time because the next thing I knew the sun was lower in the sky but shining bright as ever. It had to remain brightly lit. It was going to be our salvation.

Time was fleeting, but that was of no consequence to us. If they were going to kill again, it would only be one more to add to the pile. When the fight began, I hoped it would go quicker rather than slower. But right then, we weren't racing against any clock. As I foraged, I rehearsed the plan of attack in my head, playing out the beautiful retribution and destruction. I thought about how I would fight them. What I would say. I'd run so many of them through that the lake might just overflow. And then, when all was done, I'd finally mend the fences that I'd broken down. And Sabrina would be waiting for me.

I returned to the rock with my arms full of dried wood. My fingers were now pricked with a multitude of splinters and some of the wood had splotches of my dried blood on them. It was a good thing that the *'trees'r true'* as Shep had so often said. These trees needed to be true or else there would be a lot more trouble. It felt good that some of my blood would be used to burn these bastards.

Trudy and Kevin had made a decent-sized heap of wood themselves. Somewhere around two or three feet of it. Kevin was rubbing the end of a long, straight branch against the rock and forming a point on the end of it. *Maybe Mr. Certified Public Accountant had some man in him after all*. I dumped my wood on their pile as quietly as I could. The sound got their attention and Trudy walked and Kevin hobbled over to me. I was still waiting for that leg to give up and fall right off.

"We're ready, cowboy," she said and pointed to three, four-foot spears that they had fashioned out of sticks.

"I didn't know you two had it in you," I said, only half joking.

"Brattleboro isn't exactly Chicago or New York, Frank. We learn things there just as well as anyone from here."

I walked up to Kevin and gave him a sturdy once-over. He would be going into battle with me. I looked into his eyes and saw a hundred digits flying at top speed. His brain was too fast for his body to react. He was smart. He was stealthy. He would fight alongside his wife and myself. While I would have initially preferred having Shep Gooley at my side for this fight, Kevin would suffice, and then some.

"Your glasses," I said, and held my hand out, palm up.

He brought them from his face, collapsed the arms, and placed them in my hand. They were wire framed; the kind that people who couldn't afford the plastic ones would wear. They looked and felt flimsy. Well, flimsy or not, they had a job to complete. I turned around and surveyed the mound of dried and splintered wood. I walked towards it, leaving Kevin and Trudy frozen in place.

I crouched down and tried to find which side the sun was the most powerful. When the back of my neck began to sweat, I knew I'd found the right side. Kevin and Trudy watched me like an audience in a surgery gallery. I moved the glass ever so slightly to the left and right. It took a minute or two of finagling, but a weak dot of light appeared on one of the dried timbers. I tilted the glass ever so slightly and the small dot of light got a little more intense. And then it got slightly brighter.

And then a little more. And still more. Small ringlets of smoke began to waft upwards, and a shiny bright cherry of flame formed on the side of the wood. It was only a smolder at that moment, but there was no mistaking it; we'd created fire.

Emboldened by the smoke that was beginning to ride the light breeze, Trudy and Kevin came closer and their eyes widened when they saw the small flame. Kevin's eyes had tears in them. My smile was beginning to hurt the sides of my cheeks.

"Blow on it," I commanded. "Gently blow on the small flame and it'll catch quicker. The two of you, come now!"

As I had commanded, they leaned over, squatted down, and began to lightly blow their breath on the meager flame. I had moved the concentrated sunlight to another piece of timber that was laid on top of it to try and get another flame started. With a few tinkering motions that log eventually caught as well.

Two flames, about the size of a clenched fist each, burned with an orange root and ate away at the wood. The three of us stood back and watched. The wind helped fan the meager flames and they grew and grew with each passing moment. Gray smoke now bellowed from the pile and sent swirling shapes into the air that danced like ghosts among the trees. Soon, whatever was on the other side of the rock would take notice of the smoke, and then all bets would be off.

*   *   *

A short time later we were watching a four-foot ball of flames.

We leaned against the rock with our spears in hand. I clenched mine so tightly that the indentation of the bark made my already chewed-up palms sting. None of us moved or made a sound. Occasionally the tight pop of a crackling piece of timber would give us a scare, but that was all. The forest was giving us a reprieve from its unending song.

Then, as if an unseen door was thrust open behind us, we began to hear a loud groaning sound. It was like a bear's roar, but it didn't have the same animal quality. Something about it had a human aspect to it. The three of us clenched our spears tighter. I had been in a similar situation a few years before, on another continent. I closed my eyes and beseeched the goodness of whatever being was looking over us. I saw a small flame in my mind's eye. I opened my eyes and looked out on the bonfire that was now fully thriving.

From our right, we saw a figure come around the rock, which our backs were firmly pressed against. It was a gruesome being, homely in the face with the taut skin around the mouth and eyes. The skin was purple-blue, and the thing's clothes looked human. Horrendously out of date, but human. The monster was human at one time, but there was nothing human about it now, save for vague bodily attributes. It walked erect, like a human, but its back was slightly curved, and its arms swung as it moved like a monkey. It moved to the fire and studied it. There as it moved streams of clear liquid dropped from its tight jowls. It let out a large roar once again, and what sounded like an army of responses called back from beyond the rock.

Two or three more came from our right. They looked much the same; same crooked back, same tight-skinned smile. Same black eyes. They looked to the flame as well, and even stuck their mangled excuses for hands out to feel the warmth.

Something inside me snapped and my fear broke away from me like a newborn chick escaping an egg. '*Do it for Sabrina*,' a voice repeated in my head. '*Do it for Sabrina*.' I inhaled the deepest breath I could muster and screamed so loudly that my throat became sore. This got the attention of the three Wendigoes that were near the fire, and they snapped to attention and immediately came at us.

I rammed the one who had appeared first with the sharpened end of my spear through the stomach, like a bayonet. That's how I had been taught. Oozing brown fluid poured out of the stomach and my spear was caught in the monster's guts. He pulled away from me, but the spear was still sticking out of his midsection. I grabbed the end of the spear and yanked it out, reclaiming it. The end of it was dripping with a brown gelatinous substance that looked like boiled pig's blood. The creature looked down at the hole in its stomach and it came right back after me. He stepped forward, flailing his arms about like a banshee. I used the butt of the spear to crack him one across the face and the monster winced. I thrust my spear forward once again, this time running him through the chest. The wound was deeper than the last one and all the tugging I did couldn't get the spear dislodged from the monster's chest. I could only direct it where to go. I figured now was as good a time to see if Shep's killing method was solid. I pushed the monster backward, into the heart of the bonfire and immediately its flesh caught and engulfed it. I used my foot to simultaneously push the monster further into the flames and free my spear from its chest. I looked left and Trudy and Kevin were fending off the other two creatures who had meandered into the picture. I was surprised at the ferocity with which the Vermontians fought. They both screamed and hollered as they ran the monsters through. I watched as the flames overtook the body of the Wendigo, whose body was now serving as kindling. It kicked in anger, attempting to fight back against the flames that were purging the body.

Amid the tangle of red and orange flames, a collection of what looked like bees began to form. The tiny black dots hovered for a moment and hummed. They moved in a synchronized hypnotic ballet. Then, the small dots collected themselves into a tight ball, creating one large mass. The congealed mass of black dots lingered over the tops of the flames for a few seconds and then flew straight up into the sky, among the tall trees, and dissipated like a firework. I happened to look into the flames at the burning monster's face and could have sworn it resembled a normal human being. This could have been caused by the distortion of the fire but I knew better. I knew better indeed. Shep had been right all along.

Kevin and Trudy had run their Wendigoes through as well and were having just as hard a time removing their spears as I did, if not harder. I ran to their aid and rammed my spear through the back of the one Kevin had caught. The scene reminded me of old paintings I'd seen of Indians fishing with spears. I remembered one where a particularly angry-looking brave held his spear high over his head, with a steel gray salmon impaled on it. "Let's put this bastard on the coals," I yelled.

We walked the impaled Wendigo, who was still giving us quite a fight for someone that was twice run-through, over to the fire. It kicked its legs like a lamb that was about to be slaughtered and tried to throw us off balance by grabbing our spears and twisting. I felt the extra strength that was built up in my arms get put to work. We brought him before the bonfire and with great relief we yanked our spears out. The injured creature stood for a moment, dazed. I lifted my leg and gave it a good hard kick to the chops and it collapsed into the bonfire where it immediately caught fire and began to incinerate. It writhed in the flames for a moment or two and the skin on its arms began to bubble and fester like melting cheese. As it burned the same swarm of bees rose out of the flames, collected itself into a ball, and flew up into the sky.

"Did you see that," I asked, pointing upwards.

Kevin nodded. "What the hell was that?"

"That's the spirit. That's what infected these people."

We heard this from the other side of the fire, "Uh, guys- little help here!" Trudy was in trouble.

We rushed around the fire to see that Trudy was struggling with a particularly bulbous Wendigo. His gut protruded over his brown work pants, and he wore a shirt that was splattered in dried blood that had turned brown. She had speared him through his fat stomach, and a particularly copious amount of that brown slime was shooting out of the wound like an open fire hydrant. He was pushing her backward when we finally got there. Like Shep's favorite player Stan Musial, I gripped my spear and took a hearty swing at the creature's head. The sound it made was like a ball hitting a leather baseball mitt. The monster lurched sideways and both Kevin and I plunged our spears into its sides. It wriggled around on the ground like a caught snapper, and I was able to pull my spear out fairly easily. I motioned to Kevin and pointed to our shoes. We walked up to the dying monster and kick-rolled it into the blaze the way dockworkers kicked kegs across wharves. When this particular Wendigo caught fire it set off an explosion within the flames as if it had been wrapped in gunpowder. It looked and sounded like someone had thrown a mortar in the middle of the flames. It bellowed and screamed as it burned and twisted in the flames. And then, after a few moments had passed, the kicking and bellowing stopped, and the same swarm rose above the flames and flew up into the treetops.

The three of us were out of breath, adrenaline-infused, and feeling overly confident that we were on our way to making a little history and finally putting an end to the horror and tyranny that had been running rampant in the Eastern Woods. "Well, we've killed our first three Wendigo," I said, trying to emulate Patton. "Let's hope the rest of them are just as easy."

In between sucking wind, Trudy asked, "Okay, cowboy. We need to go beyond that house over there in the distance, right?"

I nodded yes.

"We can't keep walking them over here to the flames. There'll be more of them, right?"

I nodded yes.

"So, what's to say they won't attack us from behind while we're walking the caught ones over here? It's too risky and I don't like it."

She had a point. It felt like someone had poured ice water on a flannel blanket. I stopped and thought for a moment as the pride and confidence seeped out of the bottoms of my shoes. For these things to be beaten, they had to be burned. The fire that we'd built was not close to the 'town among the trees' that Shep had described. We could have hoped for a strong gust of wind to blow the flames in the direction of the town, but that was a long shot. Plus, we needed a purer concentration of the flames. There was only one logical way to fix this; we needed to bring the fire to *them*.

I pulled my shirt over my head and took it off completely. I folded it under my arm and slid my legs out of my pants as well. Kevin and Trudy stared at me with a wide-eyed look of disbelief.

"This is hardly the time, cowboy," she said.

"Take your clothes off," I said.

"Excuse me," Trudy asked.

"The both of you. Strip naked. We're going make torches from our clothes."

I slid my boxers down and stood before them naked as if in Eden, save my socks and shoes. My body was covered in purple-domed welts from poor hygiene, and they speckled my torso in clusters of bumps of various sizes. A few of them had turned to boils and were puss-filled and ready to burst. My manhood was shriveled and drawn in like a scared turtle. There was no time for shame at this point.

Both Trudy and Kevin began to disrobe. While they undressed, I began to wrap my clothes around the end of my spear in a tight coil to make the fire burn slower. As I swirled my shirt my eyes happened to catch a glimpse of Trudy's naked body. Her body was covered in welts like mine, but I was able to see through that, past that, to her beautiful curves and patches of perfectly soft, white skin between the dots of imperfection. Her breasts were perky and jiggled quickly to and fro as she took the bottom pieces of her undergarments off. I needed to look away to avoid any trouble (it would be hard to mask at this point) but I couldn't. Something inside of me demanded that I keep watching her. Her careless motions gave me a comfort that I hadn't felt in a good long while. Kevin was now naked too, except for the scrap of his wife's dress that was wrapped around his calf. It was no longer tan or white but stained pink from collecting the blood.

After they had tied their clothes around the ends of their spears we walked to the bonfire where the stench of burning flesh filled our noses and charred flecks of ash rained down from the fire. We placed our torches into the flames, and they caught, all three of them.

"Well, let's get a move on," I said. "When we get to the village, we burn everything."

I walked in front and Trudy and Kevin walked behind me. My balls swung around like a pendulum on a clock, and it was hard to ignore. But I did my absolute best to keep my head on its usual constant swivel. I felt oddly free walking around in the nude. Part of me felt somewhat vulnerable, but there was a decent part of my mind that felt like I could conquer anything that stood before me. As we walked a beaten trail began to make itself visible under our feet. It was made of stones and gravel and had a mud mortar to keep it together. I was careful where I stepped because the rocks were a little slick with dew. We were getting closer to that first house which we saw from the rock.

As we got closer the house became clearer. It was a wooden cottage; the type you would have seen in a Hansel and Gretel vignette. The main observation that made me hopeful beyond words was the fact that it appeared to be made of *wood*. The windows were missing or bashed in. A few of the panes had jagged pieces of glass jutting up from the frames, which made them look like the teeth of a wide-open mouth. Two small sandstone front steps led to the front door, which was slightly ajar. The windows, one on either side of the opened door, had been destroyed. I began to walk to the house before Trudy called me.

"Um, cowboy," she said.

I turned to face her and saw what she was looking at. To our right, just around the bend was the village in the woods. There were eight houses sporadically paced around a center green and each one looked precisely like the others. I stepped down and away from the first house and began to walk towards the village.

Creatures of every size, shape, and build were roving in and out of the houses and across that open green. We couldn't tell what they were doing, but we saw them; all of them hunched over and disfigured. Some had female bodies; some of them had male features. Some were tall and some were short. It seemed that this disease knew no limit to who it would infect. They seemed to meander back and forth and in and out of the houses with no rhyme or reason. They looked like workmen poised to begin a project. I knew the closer we got, the more of a chance we'd have of being seen. I pulled Kevin and Trudy close and whispered, "We'll move around the perimeter and start the burning from the back sides."

We moved to the side of the path and walked among thorny weeds and thistle. It felt like hell against my bare legs and thighs. I heard oohs and aahs from behind me, which was enough to indicate that Kevin and Trudy were feeling it as well. However, our torches were still burning with all their orange goodness and that was enough to keep us pressing onward. As we walked the weeds and grass got higher and higher.

We nestled to the back of one of the houses and I held my flame to the corner of a dovetailed corner where two pieces of wood met. Kevin and Trudy did the same on the opposite side of the structure. I pressed the flame there, praying to something that the wood would catch.

Trees'r True

Finally, smoldering folds of fire began to catch onto the sides of the house. They crept and spread slowly at first. We lightly blew air onto them, and the flames intensified and raged. It seemed to take eons for the flames to finally move along the side of the cottage. But we stood there, patiently- not out of want, but out of force. Soon the side of the cottage was in flames and smoke began to choke us as we moved to the next house.

Once we got there, we did the same thing; the same ritualistic placement of our torches; the same slow smolder, which led to an eventual engulfing of flames. We worked quietly and kept our eyes constantly fixed between the houses and noted where the creatures were meandering. I didn't feel fear, though. Perhaps that was another side effect of serving, but I wasn't scared. I was naked, armed with only a torch and two underlings, but I was not afraid.

We then heard howling and balling coming from the center of the village. It sounded like the loon's call, but as the creatures lost wind, it turned to a guttural moan. It was apparent that our handy work had been noticed.

The first cottage we had lit was now completely in flames and the two next to them were well on their way. Flames began to spread through the wooden structures and cracks and pops rang out as the wood festered and burned. More of the creatures began to exit the cottages and howl as if wounded. We crouched together behind a cottage and leaned in close.

"Now what," Kevin asked.

"Now, we get in there and show these bastards what's what."

When I ran out from behind the house, time seemed to slow down. I didn't know what the sensation was, or what was causing it, but I'd never felt it before. I'd heard stories of guys who had gotten 'Shell Shock' say that it felt like the world was being sucked into a vacuum. It felt like the world was traveling through fresh molasses. During my stint overseas, nothing ever even came close to that. When I was overseas, time seemed to be running *faster* than normal. It was as if everyone was moving at a hyper-speed, and I couldn't understand a word anyone was saying. But this was the complete opposite. Things slowed down and I was able to see them looking at me. They were startled at first and a few of them recoiled backwards when I made my entrance. But once they realized that I wasn't one of them, that I was a living non-creature, they all descended on me and began to paw at my arms with their grimy fingers. I slammed a few of their heads with the butt end of my torch and brandished the flames at their overly smiling faces. My movements were made to be quick and precise, but it felt like I was fighting underwater.

They were everywhere. They were pouring out of the cottages like rats abandoning a sinking ship. The four or five houses that we'd lit were burning nicely with flames belching from the broken windows like dragon's tongues. Out of my peripheral, I saw one of the creatures blanketed in fire. It waved its horrible arms up towards the sky and then dropped to the ground as if it had been shot. The same collection of bees rose from the body, collected, and flew up among the trees. Kevin and Trudy had joined the fray and were waving their torches as the creatures. One of them tried to jump on Kevin from behind and Trudy put her flame to its back, and it immediately dropped. It looked like children playing with ants. One of them came perilously close to knocking my torch out of my hands by swatting at it with an open hand. But my resolve was firm, and I gripped the spear as hard as I could. I kicked the monster down, and I pulled a muscle in my groin while doing so. I guess having my balls flopping around with no support was going to catch up with me sooner rather than later. They continued to pour out of the cottages in droves, like clowns out of those small clown cars at the circus. But the three of us kept pushing back on them. I two-hand shoved a grinning monster into the burned-out window frame of a burning house and ran towards the center of town, near the square. More of them marched out. There must've been fifty of them if there was one. They all walked the same, had that same grinning face, and were all in different manners of dress. Some had knickers and breaches on. Some of them had corduroy slacks. Some of them looked to have silver pants and ripped zoot jackets. But their faces were all infected. My heart was thumping uncontrollably and sweat poured out of every pore on my body. Each time I turned I ran into the stinking hull of another monster; another creature possessed of a spirit. I shoved at them, and through them, with every ounce of energy that I had left inside of me. I felt like a football running back simply hitting bodies and trying to avoid their awful mouths.

I snapped my head back and faced skyward and when I did the world returned to full speed and there was utter chaos around me. Things began unraveling around me full throttle. One of the creatures held Trudy by the neck and had her raised off the ground at least a foot, with her legs flailing in a desperate attempt to shake loose. I ran to the monster and held my flame to the center of its back, leaving a round, burned mark in the center of its gray skin. It lurched forward in surprise and anguish and dropped Trudy to the ground. She fell but was able to somehow keep her balance while coughing and inhaling deeply. Kevin had been sparring with two larger creatures, thrusting his torch at their faces in half-jabs. Each of the monsters before him wore tattered gray, collared work shirts.

I ran to help him, balls still swinging between my naked legs, when something caught my eye near the end of the block. A figure had been standing next to the tree, but then ran and hid behind it as if shy or playing a game. Something was out of place. Something was not right. In the fleeting moment that I saw it, it looked human. But it looked uninfected. It wasn't a Wendigo. It had briefly made its presence known but then ducked back behind the base of the tree. Joy overtook me. Perhaps someone was here to help us. Maybe it was Sabrina!

With the careful steps of a cat, I crept to the tree, ducking and weaving. "Hello," I said. "Hello, if you're there, we need help. I know you can see what's going on. We're stuck here. I'm stuck here and we need assistance."

From behind the tree, a hulking mass of a man made his presence finally known. It was a man, with salt and pepper hair, dressed better and more modern than the rest of these creatures. My eyes widened and my jaw nearly made an indentation in the forest floor when I came face to face with the person standing behind the tree. Standing before me was none other than Martin Herlihy, the Editor-in-Chief of the Lake George Mirror. My boss.

"Herlihy," I asked, completely dumbfounded. "Herlihy?"

"You're not drunk for once, Frank. It's me, all right."

"What the hell are you doing here?" A knot began to form in the pit of my stomach, and I vomited yellow bile all over myself, my mid-section heaving like a bellows.

Trudy and Kevin had disappeared. I wanted to see them. I needed to see them, but they weren't there. I wondered if they had perished. Or maybe...

"What am *I* doing here," he sounded insulted. "I spent a lot of time out in these woods, Frank. I know them like the back of my hand. You forget I come from a long line of 'jacks. I know all about these things out here and what they do."

My brain at the time couldn't process all this information. "Where is Sabrina," I asked. "If you've hurt her, so help me god..."

He snickered back at me. "So help me god...what, Frank? What are you going to do? You're standing naked with all those things behind you just trolling around. No protection." He leaned in real close. He was so close I could smell his aftershave and shaving cream wafting up my nose. Those clean antiseptic smells made me feel somehow dirtier than I already was. "You don't remember what happened at the company Christmas party last year, do you? You fucking drunk."

"Christmas party," I repeated. I didn't know what he was talking about. I furiously flipped my memories, trying to remember what he could have been referencing. I quickly became frustrated, but I still tried to remember. Certain things were popping in and out of my thoughts, but that was it.

Herlily snickered once again. "You don't even remember you son of a bitch. Well, let me give you a little refresher. Where was our Christmas party last year?"

That part of it I remembered. "It was at The Sagamore. What the hell are you getting at?"

"That's right. Do you have any special recollections about that night?"

Memories flickered like a flint desperately trying to ignite. I recalled sitting at the bar. It was a long mahogany slab with a mirrored back. The bottles were backlit. It was some joint. I remembered flirting with a few of the secretaries. I remembered sinking my teeth into one of the best slices of prime rib I could remember. I remembered us singing along with a Bing Crosby record. "I don't know what you're talking about, Herlihy. I really don't."

"As the night went on and you got more and more intoxicated you began to flirt with someone. And that flirting led to you stealing away to a room in the upstairs."

"What?"

"YOU FUCKED MY WIFE, FRANK. YOU FUCKED MY WIFE!"

Through all my indiscretions, and my shame, and passed through the annals of missteps, I swear then and swear now that I didn't remember that. But his statement echoed over and over through the trees. The forest spoke back the truth. His accusation brought up a well of indignation in me and I spat it back at him as I had spit up that yellow bile a moment earlier. "I did not! You're lying!"

My first instinct was to call him a liar because I had no recollection of doing anything of the sort.

"Really? Well, maybe this will jog that bourbon-soaked sponge that sits above your eyes." At the foot of the tree, huddled in a heap was an olive-green jacket. It was a standard Army issue, and I'd seen a million of them a million times before. He tossed it at me in disgust. "This is what I found her snuggled up in the morning after." I caught it and examined it.

It smelled like cigarettes and had a small burn mark on the right sleeve near the cuff. I turned it over and looked at the front. Above the left breast pocket was a name, sewn in black letters- as clear as day.

P H E L P S

"And I swore I'd get you back, Frank. Let alone all the nonsense you put me through at work and everything else. You're a drunk, you're a failure, Franklin Phelps."

My rage boiled and festered inside me. I had nothing holding me back. "What about you? You're a goddamn accomplice to murder! You talk about me fucking your wife? You know about these things out here and don't do a goddamn thing about it! What the hell kind of a person does that make you? You're not exactly the barometer for morality."

"It ensures good newspaper sales, Frank. A little missing person here, a little vanished camper there- and we've got some great headlines and great sales." He paused and collected his thoughts. "We're dealing with an ancient power, Frank. That's why I got into the newspaper business in the first place. We can manipulate the news and control the narrative. As a writer, you should appreciate that."

"How did you even get here?" I asked.

"I told you, rummy. My father was a 'jack. His people know this power better than anyone. I've been doing this for 15 years now. I've even hired a few underlings to help make sure the population is fed. I saw what you did to the twins. Who's the real monster here, Frank?"

"You're a madman," I said.

"You're dead," he spat back at me. "And I don't speak to the dead." He placed two fingers in his mouth, gave a hearty, loud, ringing whistle, and then kicked me in the midsection with his loafer. The wind left my body, and I doubled over, seeing nothing but blackness in my vision. His kick caught me off guard and I rolled around clutching my stomach in absolute agony.

I could lie and tell you that everything that had brought me to that moment flooded my thoughts like the water through a burst dam. I could tell you that I reflected on what I'd done and what I'd failed to do. I could tell you that in that moment a light shone somewhere deep within the caverns of my mind. I could tell you that, but it wouldn't be true. I'm not a liar. I'm a lot of things, but a liar isn't one of them. Now I can look back at the deep, thick brushstrokes that brought me to that moment; naked and surrounded by possessed creatures at the helm of a scorned lover. I can tell you honestly that I don't remember the broad at all. If he had my coat, I guess I must've done something with her. But not then, nor now, do I have any recollection of anything like that happening. Then again, I was drinking a lot back then. I've racked my brain for a long time about that and it always comes up empty. Now I can firmly say that I ended up naked in the middle of the forest because I couldn't keep my dick in my pants. Some way to end up. One thing stood out above all this stuff; he never confirmed or denied where Sabrina was. Maybe she would be there soon. I'd have to fight to find out.

All hell began to break loose around me. They scurried out of the cottages, around the structures that were still burning, and began to moan those horrible loon-like calls that send shivers up and down my back. Something bit my ankle, hard, and I tensed in pain. The pain shot up my calf and into my thigh. I looked down to see what had caused it and I was looking into the possessed face of Kayla. She had the same stretched facial skin as the others did and her teeth had grown substantially since I had seen her last. Blood, my blood, was splotched around her lips and mouth. I reached down and grabbed her by the throat and lifted her up off the ground. I barreled my way through the throngs of Wendgo that were now crowding me the area and sending a putrid, suffocating stench into the air.

"Trudy!" I screamed as loudly as I could. "Kevin! I've got her!"

Other creatures had begun to claw at my shoulders, and I was bleeding in two places. I looked around through the throngs of monsters and finally I caught a glimpse of the Kevin. I hurried towards him, leaving other Wendigo in my wake, with the little girl still raised above my head with my fingers dug into her throat. Her legs kicked like a mule and a few times I almost caught one to the cheek. I delivered her to her parents, who were fending off other creatures in front of one of the burning buildings. Kevin took the girl under his arm the way a carpet salesman would carry samples.

We ran up the two steps of the burning building at slammed the door behind us, leaving a few Wendigos banging at it after we slammed it shut. There were a few tables and broken chairs scattered around the room, with walls that were engulfed in complete flames.

"Let's put her near the flames," I said. "We can burn it out of her."

There were creaky noises and popping sounds as the wood continually was eaten by the fire. We didn't have much time; the building was going to collapse soon. Our naked bodies were now slick with perspiration and the light of the fire glistened off every inch of us. The wrapping at the door had stopped, most likely because we were encased in a momentary fortress of flames.

"Bring her over here," I said.

They did as I instructed and brought the girl- kicking and bellowing- to a corner where the flames were at their most vicious and rolling. We carefully inched her face close to the flames. Her hair began to burn and that horrible, dank smell of burned hair began to waft around us. She kicked and floundered like a fish, but the three of us held her in place. It was like trying to hold mercury. Kevin and Trudy were in absolute hysterics; both shouting and cursing and commanding whatever was in their daughter to leave. The skin on her forehead finally caught and it began to blister and bleed. Her mouth opened as wide as I'd ever seen a human mouth open and she let loose a blood rippling scream. From out of her mouth flew the swarm of spirit. Her face muscles loosened, and we pulled her out of the fire. She was crying. She was badly burned. But she was alive.

The swarm of the spirit was up near the ceiling now, just floating there. The three of us quickly ran for the front door and Trudy and Kevin pushed through. I was behind them and as I went to exit, I felt a jolt run through my entire body. I had gotten electrocuted once when I was a young boy because I had stuck my hand in an electric socket. The feeling was similar. But this was different. This was followed by an immense pain around my jaw. I felt my muscles begin to contract.

It was in me.

*   *   *

I was suddenly starving. My insides felt like a dough mixer that was filled with acid. I would have eaten just about anything, as long as it had meat to it. Dead animals. Flesh. The need for that pulpy, juicy, salty, bloody taste began to take me over and I joined the throngs of Wendigo in the middle of the village. There was a part of me, in the back of my brain, that was aware of what was happening. I knew that this lust for flesh was not natural. I knew that somewhere inside of me was Franklin Phelps, writer for the *Lake George Mirror.* But I could do nothing about it. I honed in on Trudy who I happened to see near the path that led to the large rock. Her body looked delicious. I wanted to bite into her thighs and run my tongue along her delicious curves. I ran after her.

I didn't see Kevin, so I knew I'd be in the clear. We ran and ran and ran- over logs, through swampy muck, past grazing deer, through underbrush. My tongue wagged out of my mouth like a hound chasing a rabbit. My groin began to hurt because my balls had been slapping in between my thighs as I ran and jumped. But she was oh so close now. The bottoms of my feet were bloody and began to ooze that brown liquid. My blood had been infected too.

I could see a clearing in front of her, over her shoulders. It was the lake. It was the water called Andia-Ta-Roc-Te. Lake George. I lunged at her like a leopard chasing a jackal and sank my teeth into her shoulder, ripping off a nice, good chunk. She screamed, piercing my eardrums. We tumbled to the ground and began to tussle in the brush that lined this portion of the lake's shoreline. She had me at arms-length and my vicious ferocity didn't let up. I wanted to stop, wished I could stop, but I couldn't do it. There was no way that I was going to let her live. And then...

Blackness.

The blackness lasted for but a few seconds. I turned around, looked over my shoulder, and saw Kevin with Kayla in his arms and a large piece of timber in the other. Trudy was seated on the ground beside them grabbing at the open wound on her shoulder. Kevin placed Kayla down, geared up like Stan Musial, and hit me in the head once again with the jagged piece of tree. I spun around from the impact but didn't lose consciousness.

I turned myself over and hovered over the edge of the lake and looked down at my reflection in the water's ripples. The water was so clean, so pure, and so shining, that it served as a mirror. I looked at my deformed face, past my eyes, and deep into the pit of my soul. And I no longer saw that small flicker of light. Instead, I saw darkness; an abyss of unending night staring back at me. I relaxed every muscle in my body and let it lurch forward. I fell headfirst into the water.

All the air vacated my lungs and I floated downward further into the depths of the great lake. My air bubbles trailed me down like an umbilical cord to the world that was fading away from me beyond my feet. The water was cool that day, and it felt good to be immersed in such a pool of pristine clarity. I imagined that this must be what it feels like to be born. But as the air bubbles got smaller and smaller, the world slipped away as I floated down. I then felt something. The only way to adequately describe it was a *tearing* sensation. My body felt like a piece of masking tape that was being torn off a piece of wood. There was too much to do. Too many fences to mend. There was Sabrina. I had to crawl up back and out of the water and get back to land. This tearing sensation went on for a few moments and as it progressed, I felt lighter and lighter. It was freeing, in a sense. I felt light. I looked down and was able to break free of what was anchoring me.

I eventually found myself back on land.

Chapter Twenty-Six

When I got back on land, I was wearing clothes again. I was wearing my white collared short-sleeve shirt and my brown corduroy pants. I was completely dry. There were no signs of Trudy, Kevin, Kayla, or anyone else for that matter. It was only the lakeshore sand and me. There was a cool breeze that I felt from my scalp to my feet. I had my loafers on. The sky had turned overcast, and it looked like it was a moment away from opening up and bellowing a torrent of rain. It was chillier too. It didn't feel like April weather anymore. I was confused and scared. I began to walk back into the wilderness.

My head ached and I was a little dizzy. I stumbled around for a moment, trying to catch my bearings as to where I was. I didn't have a compass on me. The sun had gone behind the clouds, so I couldn't tell where east or west was. I felt completely disoriented, as if someone had blindfolded me, tied me up, and placed me in a foreign place. I had no idea what had happened or what was going on.

I needed to find Sabrina. I needed to find her. She was somewhere in those woods, and I needed to get to her so we could finally get away from everything. We'd hightail it out of these woods so fast it would make her head spin. I walked for what seemed like hours, through the thickly overgrown hummocks of the Eastern Woods, shouting her name as loud as I could.

"SABRINA-INA-INA-INA-INA," my voice echoed, and called her name back to me.

I was in the middle of yelling her name when through a thicket of dogwood trees, I saw the outline of a figure in the distance. I thought it was a deer or a small brown bear. But it was neither. This was a fully erect human being. "HEY!" I ran to it. "HEY!"

I ran with my anticipation brimming out of every pore in my soul. When I got closer, I got a better look at who it was. It was a man in his mid-sixties with, a neatly kempt white mustache and white hair. He wore a white collared shirt with a red vest over the top of it. Slight build, but not scrawny. His hands were in his pockets.

"Excuse me," I said. "I need your help."

"My friend, I'm sure I can't help you," he said. He looked as tired and lost as I felt. But there was no panic in him at all. The air about him was vaguely upper crust. His mustache was too well-kempt, and his hair was perfectly parted to be side. He reminded me of a librarian.

"Well, who can?"

"No one here," he said.

I broke down and asked, "I'm looking for a young girl. Her name is Sabrina."

His eyes widened. "Hey! That's my daughter's name," he said. He extended his hand to me. "Sam Potter. Nice to meet you."

*   *   *

I didn't chat with Mr. Potter for too long. He said he'd been out here in the wilderness for quite a long time and couldn't seem to find his way out. I asked if he remembered how long he'd been out here, and he couldn't remember that either. He said whenever he tried to leave, he would get distracted and end up staying put. He described it as a force of duty, a force from a promise. I don't know what that means, exactly. I'm not sure what anything means. I had a duty to my country, and I served. I had a duty to my family- which I screwed up- but I want to take steps to fix that. And of course, I have my duty to find Sabrina and get her out of whatever trouble she may be in. She told me to be here. She told me.

I ran into that idiot that I'd seen in my dream, too. The one with the Zorro mask that was painting his fence. He drifted out from behind a tree and winked at me and gave me a shot with his hand that was positioned like a gun. 'Gotcha,' he said.

There have been a few times when I've tried to leave too, but...I don't know. It seems that the days don't ever really end. I haven't seen the sunshine since I can remember. All I can remember is that sense of unfulfilled blankness that keeps repeating over and over inside of me. What I could have done, what I can do to fix things.

Sometimes I feel like I'm caught behind the haze of a dream, like I'm seeing things through the white foggy haze of a tulle veil. The world seems shapeless sometimes, with no defining characteristics. I sometimes feel that everything around me isn't real. The only thing I do know is the bitter sting of regret, which I feel almost constantly. That, and the longing for the loving touch of someone else. I wish I could see the sun again.

That light, that flame that burned for so long and acted as my compass has been out of my reach. I wonder sometimes if it was ever really there to begin with. Or was it, perhaps, a lure; a lie that people gravitate towards with no real ending? Maybe the truth lies behind the mask of the wilderness. I've looked internally, and it's no longer there. I've looked externally, and I can't find it there either.

Maybe you're never supposed to find it.

Maybe that's the point.

-Mamaroneck, NY
September 13, 2014
FINISHED:
-Eastchester, NY
January 10, 2024

www.ingramcontent.com/pod-product-compliance
Lightning Source LLC
Chambersburg PA
CBHW051214130726
47988CB00001B/89